THE
SEPTEMBER
HOUSE

THE
SEPTEMBER HOUSE

CARISSA ORLANDO

BERKLEY
NEW YORK

BERKLEY
An imprint of Penguin Random House LLC
penguinrandomhouse.com

Copyright © 2023 by Carissa Orlando
Penguin Random House supports copyright. Copyright fuels creativity, encourages diverse
voices, promotes free speech, and creates a vibrant culture. Thank you for buying an authorized
edition of this book and for complying with copyright laws by not reproducing, scanning,
or distributing any part of it in any form without permission. You are supporting writers
and allowing Penguin Random House to continue to publish books for every reader.

BERKLEY and the BERKLEY & B colophon are registered trademarks of
Penguin Random House LLC.

Library of Congress Cataloging-in-Publication Data

Names: Orlando, Carissa, author.
Title: The September house / Carissa Orlando.
Description: New York : Berkley, [2023]
Identifiers: LCCN 2022060591 (print) | LCCN 2022060592 (ebook) |
ISBN 9780593548615 (hardcover) | ISBN 9780593548639 (ebook)
Subjects: LCGFT: Horror fiction. | Novels.
Classification: LCC PS3615.R529 S47 2023 (print) |
LCC PS3615.R529 (ebook) | DDC 813/.6—dc23/eng/20230201
LC record available at https://lccn.loc.gov/2022060591
LC ebook record available at https://lccn.loc.gov/2022060592

Printed in the United States of America
1st Printing

Book design by Daniel Brount

This is a work of fiction. Names, characters, places, and incidents either are the product
of the author's imagination or are used fictitiously, and any resemblance to actual persons,
living or dead, business establishments, events, or locales is entirely coincidental.

This book is dedicated to the good folks in the psychology department at the University of South Carolina, who encouraged me to publish something but weren't specific as to what.

THE
SEPTEMBER
HOUSE

PROLOGUE

It was our dream house.

I knew it from the moment I stepped onto the property for the real estate tour. I knew it from the moment I saw the listing in the newspaper, if I'm being honest. The tour was a formality. I would have bought the place sight unseen.

The house, however, was truly something to see. It was a Victorian, with cobalt paint and neat white trim and an envy-inspiring porch that wrapped around the whole house. The driveway was long and the yard was sprawling and the place was blissfully isolated, hidden by trees on all sides. And there was a turret—an actual *turret*—that made the house look just a step behind in time, but purposefully so. My feet had barely even touched a pebble in the driveway before I knew that this place was my—*our*—home.

I had never really had a real home before, even as a child. My family had moved around quite a bit, bouncing from house to apartment back to a house and once even to a little trailer for a while—it all depended on how things were going and whether or not my father was taking his medication. The older I got, the more I found myself wishing for something permanent, a house with heavy bones, a place where I could sink my roots into the ground and become an immovable object. Leaving the chaos of my family seemed to be a step towards this dream, although in retrospect it might have been a touch naive to expect any level of stability in my twenties. I didn't exactly find my house and my roots, but I found a husband, which seemed to be close enough.

Hal understood the draw of a house, of a home. His family had also been transient to an extent, and from the time we were newlyweds, Hal and I shared fantasies of owning a gorgeous old house, preferably Victorian. We waxed poetic about him tapping away at novels in an office filled with rich wood, me creating masterpieces in a sun-drenched studio, our child playing delicately in a lush backyard. We would fill the home with antique furniture and throw lavish parties, casually reciting the history of each corner of the house to our admiring guests. We would maybe even be included in one of those magazines that featured historic homes, photographed as we posed in our luxurious sitting room, then again in the master bedroom, then again in the greenhouse (of course we would have a greenhouse), a centerfold for a different type of fantasy. More than that, we wanted a house—a home—that was nothing but ours. A place where we could live and grow old and die.

Of course, married life never quite proceeds in the direction you imagine. Hal had difficulty getting his writing published and had to cobble together employment through freelance-writing gigs, crafting little fluff articles for the local paper, and teaching a few classes at a community college. I balanced raising our daughter, Katherine, with odd jobs—retail, administrative assistant, substitute teacher. I painted when we could afford art supplies.

We were transient like our families before us, bouncing from house to apartment to house to different apartment as circumstances dictated—always renting, never owning.

But after some struggles (and what family doesn't have struggles?), it all started coming together as Katherine approached her late-teenage years. Hal sold a few of his books and received modest but steady royalties from them. I was painting with more frequency and had some pieces displayed in a local gallery. We found a little house to rent that was in a decent state of repair, with a landlord who didn't jack up the rate too terribly over the years. We settled in, decorated the place to our liking, and for a while it almost felt like ours. Almost. By the time Katherine left for college (full scholarship, my smart girl), we had found stability, but had put aside our dreams of getting a place of our own, old Victorian or not. It was no matter—we were one another's home, and that was more than enough at times. Harold, Margaret, and Katherine Hartman—a transient family of three.

We weren't really even looking to buy anymore. Who knows what compelled me to flip to the real estate section of a newspaper I rarely read, but there the house stood in all its beauty. Victorian, just like we had wanted. Impossibly old. Impossibly beautiful. And for a price so low that Hal triple-checked it with the real estate agent before we even scheduled a tour.

The house would need minor restorations; that was certain. Still, for a place that hadn't been occupied since the nineties, when its possession was unceremoniously turned over from the last owner back to the bank, it was in surprisingly good repair. The house was nearly a hundred fifty years old but had aged gracefully, appearing composed and wise instead of decaying and haggard. A paint touch-up here, some wood refinishing there, and the place would be as good as new.

As the real estate agent guided us through the house, Hal and I gawked like children, pointing out where furniture would be placed, claiming rooms for our own. Hal picked a grand room on the second floor as his office and decided where in the room his desk would sit before the real estate agent even made it up the stairs after us. I had claimed the sunroom as my studio from just a photo in the listing, and was already imagining myself painting away through sunny afternoons. And of course, we both agreed that our master bedroom would be at the top of the stairs, where we would wake and stare out the gorgeous picture window.

"I am legally obligated to disclose to you that there was a death in this house," the agent said, still catching her breath as she caught up to us on the third floor but not so out of sorts as to accidentally use the word "murder." "Well, two deaths. The lady of the house and a housekeeper. But it was over a hundred years ago."

We were barely listening, busy picturing ourselves sipping morning tea in bed, looking out that window.

"That was a long time ago," Hal said dreamily.

"Yes, it was," the agent said. "And the homeowner at the time, the man who . . . you know. Well, it seemed as if he had been suffering from some sort of psychosis. He later took his own life. A real one-off sort of situation."

"A house this old, you would almost expect something like that," I said, not even listening to my own words as I peered inside the closet. The *closet*!

"And the other deaths in the house," the agent said, her voice so quiet as to be barely a sound, "seemed to be natural in nature."

I didn't hear her because Hal had just called me into the bathroom, and I was nearly moved to tears by the claw-foot tub. The agent seemed relieved by our lack of follow-up questions and the tour continued.

I didn't care much for the basement—unfinished and window-less, with dirt floors and a dank smell. It had a bit of a *wrong* sense to it, and I felt goose bumps break out, but I figured that it was just the cold air and dim lighting. We commented to each other that we would have to finish it after we moved in, install flooring and do something about the light and the smell. There was a half-hearted tone to our plans for the basement even then, and I was relieved to notice that we wouldn't have much reason to go down there—the water heater and the boiler were in a utility closet to-wards the back of the house; the breaker box was in the kitchen. We didn't spend too much time down there and didn't notice that the agent remained at the top of the stairs, peering down at us from the well-lit hallway.

Then we got a look at the backyard and forgot about the base-ment entirely.

Maybe if the two of us had paid more attention to any of the horror movies we'd seen over the years, we would've been aware of how thick we were being, but we hadn't and we weren't. In-stead, we bought the house and celebrated with champagne (for me) and sparkling cider (for Hal). We finally had a house that was ours, just *ours*. To live and grow old and die in. Katherine was surprised but happy when we broke the news to her, and she promised she would visit once she could take time away from her new, high-paying job and her new, high-achieving girlfriend.

This is all to say, we were home. This is all to say, you would have had to pry us out of this house with a goddamn crowbar. Me, anyway. As it turned out, Hal could be dislodged a little more easily.

The first few weeks we lived in the house were blissful. But then, of course, it was only May.

ONE

The walls of the house were bleeding again.

This sort of thing could be expected; it was, after all, September.

The bleeding wouldn't have been so bad if it hadn't been accompanied by nightly moaning that escalated into screaming by the end of the month like clockwork. The moaning started around midnight and didn't let up until nearly six in the morning, which made it challenging to get a good night's sleep. Since it was early in the month, I could still sleep through the racket, but the sleep was disjointed and not particularly restful.

Before Hal absconded to wherever it was he went, he used to stretch and crack what sounded like the entirety of his skeleton. *Margaret*, he would say, *we're getting old*.

Speak for yourself, I would reply, but he was right. I was starting to feel a bit like the house itself sometimes—grand but withering, shifting in the wind and making questionable noises when the foundation settled. All the moaning-and-screaming business in September certainly didn't help me feel any younger.

That is to say, I was not looking forward to late September and the nightly screaming. It was going to be a long month. But that's just the way of things.

As for the bleeding, it always started at the top floor of the house—the master bedroom. If I wasn't mistaken, it started above our very bed itself. There was something disconcerting about opening your eyes first thing in the morning and seeing a thick trail of red oozing down your nice wallpaper, pointing straight at your head. It really set a mood for the remainder of the day. Then you walked out into the hallway and there was more of it dripping from in between the cracks in the wallpaper, leaking honey-slow to the floor. It was a lot to take in before breakfast.

As early as it was in September, the blood hadn't yet made it to the baseboards. Give it a week, however, and it would start pooling on the floor, cascading down the stairs in clotting red waterfalls. By the end of the month, deft footwork would be required to walk down the hallway or descend the stairs without leaving a trail of prints throughout the house. I had grown practiced in dodging blood over the past few years, but even I had slipped up on occasion, especially once the screaming was in full effect. Sleep deprivation really takes a toll on your motor functioning.

I used to worry over the walls, getting a bucket and soap and scrubbing until my arms were sore, only to see my work undone the very next day. By the end of the month, it got so bad that I could rub the sponge over a crack in the wallpaper and watch a fresh blob of red leak out of the open wound that was the wall over and over again. *The wallpaper is ruined*, I fretted, but it never was. It all went away in October. So now I just allowed the walls to bleed and waited patiently.

The first year we were in the house, Hal tried to convince me that the bleeding was just a leak. An oozing red leak. He carried on with that line of reasoning much longer than was logical. By the time the blood had poured down the stairs and Hal was almost ready to admit that maybe it wasn't a simple leak, October hit and the blood vanished. Hal considered it a problem solved. I suppose he thought it was an isolated event and never considered that these things might be cyclical. He seemed surprised when the blood returned that second September. *There's that leak again*, he mused, fooling nobody. Everything, of course, changed after the third September, and Hal's opinions about the bleeding during this fourth September could be best summed up by his abrupt absence. I supposed I ought to feel trepidatious about facing September alone. However, I was never quite alone in this house, now, was I?

I COULDN'T TELL YOU WHY THE WALLS BLED. I COULDN'T TELL YOU WHY THERE WAS screaming at night. I couldn't tell you why a lot of things happened in this house. Over the years, I had developed a few working theories about the goings-on and why September made everything so much more difficult, but each was half-formed at best. Eventually, one has to give up asking questions, just accept that things are the way they are, and act accordingly. So when I woke up to a wall dripping with blood and to a foggy head from not-quite sleeping through hours of moaning, I simply nodded and got on with my morning.

My only plan for the day was to try to get some painting done. I had learned from past experience that it became difficult to focus on painting or really much of anything as the month progressed, what with the sleep deprivation and the blood and the loud noises and the wounded children running everywhere. As such, I wanted to front-load my pleasures in the hopes that they could carry me through the remainder of the month. Planning is important. So I set myself up in my sunroom studio with a blank canvas, hoping for inspiration. However, I soon found myself staring at a canvas painted entirely in red, which seemed a bit derivative, given the circumstances.

I tapped my paintbrush against my lips and stared at the red canvas, plotting out what to paint. It might have been nice to do a nature scene—some peaceful flowers, waving trees—but all I saw in my mind's eye was a child's face, mutilated and screaming. Perhaps painting was not in the cards for today.

A dull headache poked its way behind my eyes—a foreshadowing of the near-incessant headache I would have by the end of the month—and I sighed, giving up. I plopped my paintbrush, dry and useless, down on my easel and stood. Tea. It was time for tea.

As I walked from my studio into the living room, I could hear Fredricka moving around upstairs, doing something or other in the second-floor bedrooms. I knew all the doors were closed along that hallway (*What will we ever do with a five-bedroom house, Margaret?* Hal had asked me when we reviewed the listing. *We'll have guests*, I had responded, a rare moment of prescience for me), but I could still hear noises from within, different from the usual disturbances that arose from behind those closed doors. Jostling and rustling, the changing of linens. The scraping of furniture across the floor in one room, then a light crash coming from another. Fredricka was lively today.

September had an effect on Fredricka. She became busier, more chaotic. She was nervous. She didn't like September, she told me once. She had seen more than a hundred Septembers, so she ought to know.

For her part, Fredricka expelled her September energy through cleaning, stacking things, and rearranging furniture in nonsensical ways. None of these chores were necessary, but I understood her intentions. One has to control something in the face of the great uncontrollable. I left her alone.

Fredricka usually made the tea, but it seemed like it would be my responsibility today. A frown crept onto my face, and I reminded myself a bit of a spoiled child. I chastised myself for my entitlement. Making tea, after all, wasn't particularly burdensome, and it was a bit of good fortune to have Fredricka around at all, considering we hadn't hired her. She had come with the house, in a manner of speaking. Still, one gets used to routines. As I rounded the corner out of the living room and into the foyer, I tried to remember where we kept the tea bags. Fredricka might have moved them. She liked to move things in September, and not because she wanted to be helpful. For all I knew, they had been shoved behind the toilet.

Lost in my thoughts, I was startled to hear a voice behind me.

"Tea, ma'am?" Fredricka asked. Apparently, she hadn't been too distracted to make it, after all.

Despite my surprise upon learning that Fredricka was a nonnegotiable fixture of the house, I had come to realize that I enjoyed her presence. She was reasonably benevolent, or at least as benevolent as anything in the house could be. Still, the sight of her was always a shock to the system. Fredricka was a tall woman, and grand, in a way, as the house itself, with so much of her walled off and expressionless, unwilling to open and allow a peek of what lay inside. And of course, there was that gash on her head, gaping open like a split pumpkin, where the axe had sunk in over a hundred years ago. The wound began at the top of her forehead and stretched down through her right eyebrow. Her eye was sunken in as a result, pupil drifting, not quite right anymore. That took a while to get used to looking at.

I smiled at her. "I can handle it if you're busy."

"No trouble at all, ma'am." Fredricka drifted down the hallway that ran parallel to the stairs and led into the kitchen, her long smock fluttering behind her. I followed.

The kitchen was the brightest room in the house, surrounded with windows displaying the greenery outside, which was just now yielding leaves tinged with yellows and reds. It had been one of the biggest draws of the house for me, with two large ovens, a glimmering white sink, and rows of ornate cabinetry (original wood, mind you). It turned out to be comparatively peaceful in here, and I usually ate my meals at the kitchen table instead of in the grand dining room just a few feet away. For some reason, the blood never made it into the kitchen, so this room would be a particular haven as September raged on. A true blessing, that was; seeing blood staining those pristine surfaces, however temporarily, would have broken my heart. I'd grown used to seeing carnage inches from my food (Fredricka prepared most of the meals, after all), but one must draw a line somewhere.

Fredricka busied herself with the kettle, filling it with water and placing it on the stove. Not wanting to stand like a statue waiting for Fredricka to serve me, I walked over to the basement door just off the kitchen to check the wooden boards nailed into the doorframe. I had replaced them recently, but I tugged on each beam all the same, testing the strength. Four of them were firm, but one wiggled a little. I inspected the nails—just as I thought, coming loose. In the year since the boards had gone up, I found that the nails did that from time to time. Checking the boards was essential. I made a mental note that the beam would need to be replaced soon. Not urgent, but best to act on these things sooner rather than later. I gripped the doorknob and gave it a tug. The door remained closed, held tight by the boards. I traced my finger over the small crack—a recent addition—that snaked down from the top of the door nearly midway to the doorknob, sharp but not large enough to threaten the integrity of the wood. Everything, for the most part, was as it should have been.

Turning back into the kitchen, I noticed that Elias had materialized next to the stove. I sighed. Elias could be a bit of a bother.

Elias was nine or ten. I could never remember. Whatever his age was, he was scrawny, with a smattering of unruly dark hair on his head. He always looked the same—gaunt and empty, his dirty white cotton shirt draping over dark shorts, and one sad knee sock dangling by his ankle. He stared at me with milky eyes and a sullen face. He didn't have any visible wounds like Fredricka, but could somehow be just as eerie, if not more. I couldn't interact with Elias the way I could with Fredricka, although God knows I'd tried: I tried asking him questions, telling him to tap his foot once for yes and twice for no; I tried asking him to move the planchette on a Ouija board; I even tried making outlandish statements about World War II just to get a rise out of him. Nothing. So I hate to say it, but I started treating him like a plant, narrating my life out loud to him with no expectation of him responding or even hearing. *It looks like rain today, Elias. Oh, Elias, seems like the mail is running late. Not that we're expecting anything but bills, anyway.* For his part, Elias just stared.

"Can I make you something to eat, ma'am?" Fredricka asked, busying herself around Elias as if he were not there. Elias and Fredricka had nothing to do with each other and I had never seen them interact. I had started to assume Fredricka didn't even see Elias until one day she referred to him as "that boy." No clues regarding Elias' perceptions of Fredricka were ever available, seeing as he never spoke, only howled periodically.

"Some toast, perhaps?" I responded. I moved to the pantry to retrieve the bread before Fredricka could get to it. We had an electric toaster, but Fredricka's ability to use technology popularized after her death was sporadic at best. I tried to teach her about the toaster and even had her successfully use it once, but her preference was to roast the bread on a toasting fork over a fire, like she used to do. It was muscle memory for her; she just did what she was always used to doing. I understood and even empathized (aren't we all creatures of habit in the end?) but the process took forever and I was hungry.

"I think we still have some strawberry jam." I motioned to the fridge. This would give Fredricka something to do. After months and months of trying to convince Fredricka that she had no obligation to be our housekeeper and was free to do whatever she wanted on this earth, I learned that all Fredricka seemed to be capable of doing was work, and all she wanted from me was to be given things to do. All right, then.

Elias watched me with those unblinking eyes as I retrieved the bread from the pantry and a plate from the cupboard. He was like the *Mona Lisa*, eyes following me about the room, expression unreadable. It had initially been unsettling, but one grows used to unsettling things.

Fredricka rummaged around in the fridge. "We do have strawberry jam, ma'am," Fredricka said. "Or, if ma'am prefers, we also have blackberry."

"Blackberry sounds good, actually." I turned with my bread and walked towards the toaster. Elias was standing directly in front of it, empty eyes leering into mine. This was going to be a problem.

"Excuse me, Elias," I said. Elias didn't reply or move, but I wasn't expecting him to. I reached past him towards the toaster. As my arm drew near, the white of Elias' face turned black, as if it had been on fire for a long, long time. His milky eyes boiled into embers and his mouth stretched into a gaping maw, fangs gleaming as he shrieked, diving for the flesh of my arm. Elias did *not* like his personal space invaded. However, I was practiced in this game, deftly dropping my bread in the toaster, pushing the lever, and retracting my arm in a matter of seconds, receiving only the lightest of grazes from Elias' fangs. Just a scratch, not even bleeding. No need to even apply hydrogen peroxide. This wasn't my first time trying to prepare a meal while dodging the fangs of a dead child who wished me bodily harm.

Upon being denied the chance to remove a section of my flesh with his teeth, Elias let out another shriek, which sounded like a dying jet engine. He vanished inside of himself, and the kitchen was again quiet, save for the sounds of Fredricka arranging jams on the counter behind me.

Most of the things in this house had left Hal alone, choosing to bother me instead of him for reasons I never quite understood or found fair. Elias had been the lone exception, taking his own version of a liking to Hal, which was a bit more violent than most people's version of a liking. I wasn't sure what the connection was, but Elias certainly enjoyed frequenting the room Hal had claimed as his office. I wondered if that room used to be Elias' playroom, or possibly the room in which he died. Regardless, Hal had not cared for Elias. I certainly understood his perspective, but I couldn't see the point of expending all that energy on hating something that, in the grand scheme of things, mostly just stared and occasionally tried to bite. Just stay out of range of his teeth— a fairly easy solution, all things considered.

Fredricka retrieved my toast from the toaster and spread the blackberry jam liberally. She handed me the plate and tended to the tea while I sat at the kitchen table, chewing pensively. When Hal and I had first moved here, the sight of Fredricka's wound was a bit challenging around mealtimes, and I found myself needing to look away from her while I ate. However, one gets used to horrible things, and today I could watch her with ease while I ate, licking jam off my fingers and thinking about the remainder of the day. Despite how little I had to do, I liked mentally arranging my schedule. The days had a habit of blurring together, especially now that Hal was gone. It was helpful to plan tasks, to accomplish things.

"I was hoping to go for a walk later today," I said to Fredricka in between bites of toast, "but it looks like it might rain. Disappointing. I don't want to sit like a lump in here all day."

"Needs must when the devil drives," said Fredricka.

"Indeed," I said. "Maybe I'll do some yoga." I was unlikely to do yoga, but saying it out loud made me feel productive, and Fredricka wasn't going to argue with me. "I don't think I'll get much painting done for the rest of the month. All I can think of is children's faces and the color red. I've done that a hundred times over." I was also thinking of Hal, but I didn't say so out loud. There didn't seem to be very much of a point to thinking about Hal with any sort of frequency.

Fredricka made no comment about my questionable inspiration. She set a cup of tea in front of me. "That sounds excellent, ma'am."

I thanked her and sipped at my tea, trying to think of other activities for the day. The days had been growing dull. Fuzzy.

Fredricka shifted, antsy. "If it is acceptable to ma'am, I would like to get back to my work upstairs. I have many beds to freshen."

"You know you don't have to change out those linens," I said, fully aware of the futility of my argument. Fredricka didn't *have* to change out the linens, but in some ways she *did*. She was driven to by a force I likely wouldn't understand until after I died myself. Muscle memory, and all that. "Nobody is using those beds."

"One must change out the bedclothes, lest they start smelling stale."

No use in arguing. I waved her away. "Go right ahead, then," I said. "Thank you for the tea."

"You're welcome, ma'am." Fredricka turned and began drifting out of the kitchen. On her way out, she paused as she passed my phone, which was charging quietly on the counter. She turned her head to look back at me. "I believe ma'am will find"—she nodded in the direction of the phone—"she has received a message from her daughter."

If Fredricka had difficulties using a toaster, you had better believe she had no concept of how to use a smartphone. She never touched the thing, even when rearranging everything in September. It was completely outside of her realm of technological mastery, and she spent most of the time acting as if it didn't exist, much like she did with Elias. Still, she possessed an understanding of the ways in which my phone connected me to the world, and she had an uncanny ability to sense when I missed a communication, clueing me in to messages and voicemails of which I was unaware.

Shit. "Thanks, Fredricka," I said, moving to the counter to get my phone. I glanced at the screen. One missed call, one voicemail, and a series of text messages, all from Katherine.

Call me back, she texted. Then, *As soon as you can.* Then, *I really need to talk to you about Dad.*

Shit shit *shit*. She was getting more and more insistent. She used to just text, which was so much easier to ignore. Then she started calling, which was harder to avoid. She was calling almost daily now, and the text message follow-up pointed only at an increase in urgency. *I'm not giving up*, it said. *I can outlast you.* I would have to call her back, appease her.

The phone chimed in my hand. Another text message from Katherine, whose ears must have been burning. *You're ignoring me.*

I sighed.

My finger was hovering over the screen, about to press CALL, when I looked up and caught sight of a small, slim figure hovering wordlessly near the basement door, not really there but not *not* there either. A little girl, sallow skin, chunks of dirty hair hanging over her face. She wore a dress that might've once been blue, with little white flowers dotting the fabric, but was now more of a slate, approaching black. At one point, something terrible had happened to her skull. One of her eyeballs, not quite solid anymore, drooped from its socket as she stared at me.

Everything in this house stared at me. Little pranksters playing a staring contest, seeing who would be the first to blink.

Angelica. This one was Angelica. She was the first of many who would arrive, a Paul Revere of sorts. *They are coming.* I didn't know all their names, but I knew Angelica.

"Hi, Angelica," I said, resting my phone back on the counter. It was September all right. The children arrived, one by one, in September.

Angelica didn't say anything. She never did. She lifted an arm, as thin and knotted as a tree branch, and pointed a grimy finger at the basement door.

Oh, I had fallen for that one before. That first September, when I thought all these apparitions were problems for me to solve, I had fancied myself a regular Nancy Drew and thrown myself into whatever wild-goose chase these pranksters wanted to send me on. I'd since learned better. Some mysteries don't need to be solved, only coped with. That was one of the reasons for the boards nailed over the basement door. One of the many reasons, that is.

"You know I'm not doing that, Angelica," I said.

Angelica, of course, said nothing. Her pointing finger never wavered.

"It's nice to see you again," I said, changing the subject. I didn't expect a response but wanted to be polite nonetheless.

Nothing. Pointing.

"Well"—I lifted my phone off the counter, making plans to call Katherine from my studio—"I had better get going. Things to do today."

I had turned and was nearly out of the kitchen when I heard a tiny voice behind me. "He's down there."

Well. That was new.

I pivoted and looked at Angelica. "Oh?" I asked.

"He's down there," she repeated, her voice like rusty wind chimes.

Angelica usually didn't speak—none of the pranksters did, aside from Fredricka. Sure, they made little sounds—like sobbing or wailing or howling or shrieking or that dying-jet-engine noise like Elias—but never words, never full sentences. I wondered what had brought this about. Very probably, this was due to me ignoring her pointing finger, walking away from the basement instead of down into it, like the travesty that had been last September. When Katherine was little and I told her she couldn't have a cookie before dinner, she would whine and cry and stomp her feet, knowing that sometimes, if I was tired, I would give in. She could outlast me even then. If this was Angelica's version of a temper tantrum, I would take it. She couldn't outlast me like Katherine. I had grown stronger, and the stakes were higher.

But of course, Angelica was right. He *was* down there, in the basement. He had been down there since Hal and I moved in. The basement, it seemed, was where he lived. Hence the boards.

I wondered if the others would also talk when they arrived. A part of me was interested in having someone else to talk to, but it was unlikely they would be good conversationalists.

"I know, Angelica," I said. "Thanks." I turned and walked towards my studio. Behind me, I heard a sound like gasping for air that grew into a high-pitched scream before an abrupt silence. Angelica was gone, at least for the moment.

KATHERINE ANSWERED THE PHONE ON THE FIRST RING.

"What the hell?" she said instead of *Hello*. "I've been trying to call you for *weeks*."

"Hello," I said. "How have you been, dear?"

"Fucking *worried*," she spat. "Mom, I can't get ahold of Dad."

"Language," I said. *Shit*.

I lowered myself into an old chair in the far corner of my studio. Aside from the kitchen, this was my favorite part of the house, and I figured it was a decent place for what was likely to be an unpleasant conversation. I had painted these walls yellow, a happy color that shone when the sunlight hit it. However, today the sky was a wall of gray and the yellow seemed out of place, mocking me with its cheer when everything else was dark. Insult to injury, really.

"Mom, I'm serious," Katherine said. "I've been calling him for weeks now and his phone just goes to voicemail. And now I can't even record a message because his voicemail is full. I know he doesn't like talking on the phone, but this seems wrong. What's going on?"

I had been putting this conversation off as long as I could. I had hoped, fruitlessly, that I could put it off until October, but I knew that was a long shot. It was difficult. Prior to Hal's being gone, Katherine called at least weekly, and even though it was typically only she and I who conversed, she usually asked to say a quick hello to her father. Katherine and Hal had never been particularly close, but Katherine maintained a begrudging obligation to attempt at least a superficial relationship with her father. Hellos when she called, vague assurances that her career was going well, general inquiries about Hal's opinions of the weather. Enough conversation to last at least three minutes and preferably no longer. It had a checklist sort of feel to it: *spoke to my father, chuckled at his jokes, didn't mention any lingering grudges.* Minimum due diligence as a daughter. The trouble was, now I couldn't give her even those three minutes with Hal, and it seemed unlikely that Hal would reach out on his own.

"Mom." Her voice was insistent. "You need to tell me what's going on."

Maintaining the facade these past few weeks had grown increasingly difficult. For the first couple of weeks after Hal vanished, I had been able to dodge her requests to speak to her father by claiming he wasn't at home or was busy working on his new novel and couldn't be disturbed. Once I even pretended to go get him for her and *walked up to his office*, phone in hand.

"Hal," I had chirped at no one, "Katherine wants to say hi." I clutched the phone to my stomach, hoping it would muffle my voice enough for Katherine not to expect to hear Hal's reply.

I had stood in silence, staring into his empty office, estimating how long his response—were there one—would have taken, before putting the phone back to my ear. "Oh, I'm sorry, dear. He can't talk right now. But he says hello and that he loves you."

After Katherine and I had said our goodbyes that day, I lingered in Hal's office, as if he had been there the whole time. I saw a thin film of dust on his desk. Fredricka usually avoided this room—she preferred to stay out of Hal's sight, as did most of the pranksters—but I could tell her that she could tend to it now if she wished. I turned to leave and there was Elias, standing directly in front of me and staring with those milky eyes, his face starting to blacken with my nearness.

"Don't judge me," I'd said.

He gnashed his teeth in reply.

There was only so much dodging I could do before Katherine became concerned. During our last phone call, she had commented that she hadn't spoken to Hal in a little while. "I know he's busy," she had said, "but maybe you could put him on for a second just to say hello?"

"He's away," I said quickly. "I would love to, but—"

"I thought you said he was working on his novel," Katherine said.

Shit. I had. "Did I? Oh. I thought he was," I said, "but it turns out, he's away. My mistake."

Katherine sounded suspicious, but not enough to cause a scene, not yet. "Well, can you have him call me when he gets in? I'd love to hear his voice." That last bit was a lie, and an obvious one.

"Oh, sure, dear. I will do just that."

I didn't. I could lie too.

That had been over a week ago, and Katherine's level of suspicion had officially risen to scene-causing levels.

"Mom." Her voice was shrill. *"Where is Dad?"*

I took a deep breath and let myself sink into the chair, as if this could prepare me for the onslaught that was a few seconds away. "He's gone, dear."

"Gone? What do you mean—*gone?*" The honesty that Katherine had insisted upon had not, in fact, made her feel any better. I could have told her it wouldn't, but she wouldn't have listened.

"I mean, he's not here anymore."

A large bird flew past the windows, so close that its feathers nearly grazed the glass. Another sign that it was September. Hal and I had hung bird feeders when we first moved here, only to find our yard littered with avian corpses, their necks broken from crashing into our windows. We tried moving the feeders and applying painter's tape to the windows to keep them away, but soon learned that they weren't mistaking windows for open space but instead were intentionally careening into the hard outer walls of the house. Suicidal. Hal tried to tell me that it was normal, that birds just sort of did that sometimes, but even he had to admit that the frequency of the suicides was a bit much. So we took the feeders down. We still had our share of dead birds in September, but having fewer birds around during the year meant fewer corpses to clean up overall, which wasn't nothing.

"Did he leave?"

"I'm afraid he did, dear," I said, trying to keep my voice calm for both of us.

"Jesus Christ, Mom, why didn't you tell me? How long ago did he leave?"

An interesting question, one whose answer depended on one's definition of "leave." One might think that leaving is an all-or-nothing activity: one is here; then one is not here. However, experience would suggest that leaving occurs on a continuum, happening in stages. Had Hal left when he stopped sleeping in the master bedroom with me, choosing to sleep slumped over his desk instead? Had he left when he told me that he didn't want to live in this house anymore, that he didn't care if we took a huge loss in selling it or even if we didn't sell it at all, that he just needed to *get out*? Had he left when I put my foot down for once and told him that, no, we weren't selling, that I wasn't going anywhere, that this was our home? Had he left on one of those days when we didn't say a word to each other, just floated through the house on our own paths, apparitions following our own muscle memory? Or had he left the day he was gone, the day he decided he couldn't take it anymore, the door closing slowly after him but the tires of the taxi speeding quickly over the gravel in the driveway? (*Drive*, he must have commanded.)

Another deep breath. Katherine was not going to like this. "About a month ago."

"A *month*?" Katherine was yelling now. I moved the phone away from my ear. "He's been gone a whole *month*? And you didn't tell me? What the *fuck*, Mom?"

"Language."

"Where did he *go*? Where *is* he?"

"I'm not sure exactly." Hal didn't have any family left, and he had no friends in the area. He hadn't even seemed to have a fully formed plan when he walked out the door. He might as well be in the same space that Elias occupied after he vanished inside himself. He was simply gone. "He might have gone to a hotel, I think."

"You *think*? For a whole *month*?"

"I'm not sure, dear."

"This doesn't explain why he isn't answering *my* phone calls. Why is he ignoring *me*?" For a second, Katherine sounded like a child again, asking why she couldn't have a cookie before dinner. "I'm his fucking *daughter*, for Christ's sake."

"Language."

"Has he been in touch with you? Have you heard from him at all?"

"No," I said. "Not a peep." This was the truth. He went silent. I let him.

"So it doesn't sound like he just *left*," Katherine said, her voice high and panicked. "It sounds like he's *missing*."

I made a little hum of mild agreement. I supposed that was one way of looking at it.

"Do you think something happened to him, Mom?"

Semantics again. This depended on one's definition of "happened." Certainly, things happened to him—to both of us—all the time while we lived here. Terrible things, in fact. Especially last September. However, it was likely that fewer things were happening to Hal now that he was gone. I certainly couldn't imagine that there could be *more*. "What do you mean?"

"Like"—Katherine was choosing her words carefully—"do you think he got himself in some sort of trouble? You know, like . . . before?" She didn't elaborate. She didn't appreciate my disinclination to discuss the past but abided by it nonetheless, albeit reluctantly.

"Oh. No, I don't think so," I said. "But it's not impossible."

"And you haven't heard from him at *all*."

This wasn't a question, but I answered it anyway. "No, dear." I lifted a paintbrush out of an old cup and started chipping away at the dry paint on the handle with my fingernail. I wondered how much of this conversation would be circular.

"Jesus, Mom, you sound like you don't even *care*," Katherine said. "Doesn't this bother you at all? He's *missing*."

"Of course it bothers me." I watched a large chunk of paint fly off the brush after a satisfying flick of my fingernail. "I suppose

I've had some time to adjust." This was also true to an extent. With Hal so withdrawn in the months before he left, it was hard to even notice a difference in the house without him. It was as if he had always been gone. Besides, there was little point in concerning myself with an individual who was no longer in the house when there were many more concerning individuals who *were* actually in the house. And with September ramping up, the number of individuals in the house who warranted concern was about to increase.

But Katherine—who had never put up much of a fight about our various half-formed excuses regarding our being unable to host her for a visit over the years—didn't know anything about the number of concerning individuals in the house, so I wasn't going to tell her about any of *that*. There would be questions raised. Worries. Demands that I leave the house. Or, worse, demands that Katherine travel down here to view the horrors herself. No, none of that would do.

Katherine sighed. There was a silence, and for a pleasant second I thought I could end the conversation. "Why did he leave in the first place?" she asked.

He couldn't go through another September. "Oh, we don't really need to get into that, dear. He had his reasons. You know how he could get." I heard the dismissiveness in my voice and knew how ineffective this response would be even as I spoke.

"Yeah, I *do* know how he could get," Katherine snapped. "Which is exactly why you should be more freaked out than you are. Which is exactly why *I* am as freaked out as *I* am. Seriously, a whole month with no contact? With you *or* me? Something is fucking wrong."

I opened my mouth to admonish Katherine for her language yet again, but before my thoughts became sound, Katherine blurted, "I'm coming down there."

No no no.

"No no no," I said, a little too quickly. "You really don't need to worry about this. I'm sure he is just blowing off some steam. And before we both know it, he'll be back. And when he comes back, I promise you that you'll be the first—"

"I'm coming," Katherine said. "Someone needs to figure out what's going on, figure out where he *is*, and clearly you don't give a shit, so that leaves me. And I've got plenty of vacation time to burn."

I shook my head, not that Katherine could see me doing it. Katherine coming for an extended stay at the house—coming to stay at the house for the *first* time, in fact—in September, of all months, was a real worst-case scenario. I knew how to navigate Septembers. I knew who to avoid and how to avoid them. Katherine didn't. And for a novice, September would be a nightmare. So much of a nightmare that Hal—who had lived through two successful Septembers and a third, less successful September—had fled rather than face a fourth.

"Katherine, I . . . I can call the police about it. File a missing person report." I heard the desperation in my voice and hoped that she couldn't. "Let the police handle it. They'll do a much better job than you or I ever could."

"And the fact that you *didn't* file a missing person report *weeks* ago is exactly why I'm coming down." I heard a clicking sound in the background. Typing. Katherine was on a computer, likely on a travel website. The train was leaving the station. *Shit.*

When Katherine learned about the pranksters—or, worse, witnessed them firsthand—she would have opinions. She wouldn't be happy. She would want me to leave. And Katherine's insistence was just the kind of crowbar that might actually prove successful in that endeavor, which was exactly the kind of thing I didn't want. This was my home.

"Katherine, right now isn't a very good time for visitors around here," I said, grasping for any rationale more credible than the truth. Would sympathy work? "The house is in utter disarray. I haven't done much cleaning since your father left." Would logistics work? "None of the guest rooms are in any order and there is no food in the house." Would inconvenience work? "We have a leak in the roof that I've been meaning to get fixed for a while now."

None of it worked. "I'm coming." More typing in the background. "There is a flight out on the tenth. I'm booking it."

I was at a loss. Events would be noticeably increasing in severity by the tenth and only getting worse with each passing day. Angelica would have at least one friend (maybe more), Fredricka would be moving things about constantly, the blood would be everywhere, and the screaming—oh, the screaming. Elias would be pretty much the same, though. An upside.

"If you'll just give me until October"—I was nearly pleading now—"I think I could get the house in order." In October, everything would be calmer. There wouldn't be blood everywhere. Fredricka would be still. Angelica and all her little friends would be gone. The nights would be silent again. Sure, there would still be pranksters running around here and there, but it would be much easier to keep Katherine safely oblivious by then.

"Mom, I don't give a shit about the house," Katherine said, although she really, really should have.

"Katherine . . ."

More typing. "It's booked," she said. "I get in pretty late on the tenth, so I'll just stay in a hotel by the airport that night. I'll be heading your way on the eleventh."

So that was that. The one outcome of this conversation I wanted desperately to avoid. I pressed my eyes closed, searching for something to say. My mouth accomplished little aside from hanging open.

"I'll keep in touch," Katherine said. Now that she had gotten what she wanted, she no longer needed to keep talking. "Don't worry, Mom—we'll find him." She added this as an afterthought, as if to convince both of us that she was doing this for me instead of for herself.

I didn't even listen to the words I said in response, and the next thing I knew, I was sitting with my silent phone in my lap, dead eyes staring at nothing in particular. I couldn't be sure, but I had the sense that Angelica was in front of the basement door again, pointing. I gazed listlessly out the window, barely registering the large bird that slammed into the glass, snapping its neck and falling into the grass, a cloud of blood and feathers.

TWO

Things don't happen all at once, of course. They start gradually, changes occurring imperceptibly. You barely notice the differences, and once they make themselves known, they seem so small that you easily accept them, adjust your life in a minuscule way. Everyone can make minuscule adjustments. Then there's another change, a bigger one, but you can still adjust so easily. No problem, really. Then another change, another adjustment, and so on and so on, and before you know it, you're living a life that by all accounts should be unrecognizable but to you is just normal. Your life is that of a stranger's, but it doesn't bother you at all.

That is to say, of course the pranksters didn't show their faces immediately after Hal and I moved in. I wouldn't have stayed.

It started with things moving around when I wasn't looking. This might have been going on longer than I thought before I noticed it; since we were still unpacking, it was easy to lose track of where things were. Once we were settled in, we each assumed the other person had moved things without mentioning it. We became snippy with each other. *Why the hell do you keep moving the chair in my office?* Hal would yell down to me from the second floor. *You didn't need to change the sheets in the guest room. You saw me put fresh ones on yesterday,* I would yell back at him. Eventually the things we yelled at each other became somewhat strange, like *Why did you open every cabinet door in the kitchen?* and *What in God's name is going on with all the dead birds in the yard?* It became hard for me to believe Hal was the culprit. Hal found it a bit easier to carry on believing it was me, but that was his way.

There was also that sense of unease I felt in different parts of the house. I didn't admit to it initially, but sometimes rooms just felt wrong. It wasn't every room, and it wasn't constant, but from time to time, I would walk into a room and feel as if I had just interrupted two people in the middle of a fight. The air would seem angry, and there would be a distinct sense that I shouldn't be there. This happened sometimes in the dining room, as well as in Hal's office (Elias' former playroom or death room, whichever). And of course, the feeling was perpetually present in the basement. The immediate dislike I felt for the basement during the tour of the house only intensified after we moved in, and I certainly never got around to my plans of making the space any nicer. Hal, in his obstinacy, never fully admitted to it, but he avoided the place just as much as I did. We would find excuses not to go down there, or we'd send each other down on errands in our stead. If boxes needed to be moved downstairs, I would play the damsel in distress and appeal to Hal's manly strength to carry them. If something needed to be retrieved from the basement, Hal would claim that he was too busy and ask me to make the trek. Of course, once we'd learned more about the basement, we both overtly avoided it and both understood why. That, however, happened much later, right before the boards went up.

Eventually, the pranksters started to show themselves, but timidly. I would hear things: objects shuffling in the dining room when neither of us was in there, footsteps upstairs while we both sat in the living room. A quiet voice asking me if I wanted sugar in my tea. Figures spied out of the corners of my eyes, flickering out of sight once I turned my head. It was enough to make a person think they were losing their mind.

"I'm not sure we're alone here," I said to Hal. Hal was having similar suspicions, but of course would never admit them to me. What rational person would? Instead, he told me that I was letting my imagination get the best of me and that I needed a hobby.

After weeks of this, the whole process started to grow tiresome. The next time I thought I saw a shadow lingering to my side while I was in the dining room, I stood still, patiently keeping my eyes pointed forward, waiting for something to happen. The shadow remained visible in the corner of my eye, barely existing. I waited it out. It took several minutes, but the shadow appeared to be slowly shifting into a humanoid form—a head, a torso, and legs. It was tall, a full-grown person, and a large presence, from what I could tell. I felt my heart pounding in my ears, but not so much from fear as from triumph. These things that I thought were happening were *real*. I would tell Hal as soon as I could (and he would tell me I was crazy), but at that moment I had no idea how to act now that I had this information. So I continued standing there, eyes fixed on the center of the dining room table, the shadow—clearly a human figure now—getting closer and closer. I could hear myself breathing.

A voice, quiet and wavering—as if blown in by the wind— sounded in my ear. *Tea, ma'am?*

This was the first time one of the pranksters ever talked to me, and it took me by surprise. I whipped my head around to see my new companion.

The room, of course, was empty.

When I was a teenager, there had been a feral cat that lived in our neighborhood. For the longest time, I caught only glimpses of him scampering between bushes or out from underneath a parked car. I didn't get a good look at him until I came upon him lounging in a tree, and even then he was in the neighbors' yard. For reasons unknown to me, I embarked upon a mission of befriending this cat. I set a dish of canned tuna out for him and waited, but he never came. I left the tuna and went back inside. A few days later, the tuna disappeared. I left more, and we followed the pattern of me leaving food to be eaten by a seemingly invisible cat at an un- determined time. One day, I opened the door to catch him hun- kered over the dish, munching away. He looked up at me and scurried off. I started interrupting him during his meals more and more, and eventually he allowed himself to remain in my presence while he ate, choosing food over fear of contact. He still ran away when I got too close, but over time his boundaries shrank, until I was able to scratch behind his ears as he ate. Once, I thought I heard him purr. One day, I opened the back door to find a dead chipmunk on the doorstep, a mangled and bloody mess of fur. I have never been so moved as I was by that horror show. It was a sign that the cat had finally come to accept me as a friendly pres- ence in his life. He had left me a gift.

The first gift Fredricka left me was a cup of tea on my bedside table. I awoke and saw the cup, still steaming and with the correct ratio of sugar to milk, and immediately knew who was responsible. In all our years together, Hal had never once made me tea without being asked, and even then he usually did it wrong.

I tested my theory, anyway. I walked down to his office and sipped at the cup in the doorway. "Thanks for the tea," I said.

He didn't look up from his computer. "What tea?"

I smiled. "Never mind." It seemed that I had made a friend.

THREE

O h, Margaret," Edie said, "you're in a real pickle."

I had moved my self-pitying anxiety spiral to the front porch, a change of scenery for my misery following the phone call with Katherine. Our front porch was exactly the kind you dream about: large and encircling the house like a hug. Hal and I bought a row of rocking chairs to line the porch, and it was so pleasant to gently rock while staring out at the greenery of the front yard. If one is going to have an anxiety spiral, one might as well have a good view while it's happening. Edie, my neighbor, sat next to me now, rocking slowly and looking at me with concern.

"I sure am," I responded, my gaze still trained ahead. The day continued to hint at rain, bleary skies and an ominous wind pushing through, but no follow-through on the promise had yet occurred.

"What are you going to do?" Edie asked.

If I were being honest, part of the reason I had moved to the front porch was in the hopes that Edie might come over. I needed someone to talk to, someone with living, present-day thoughts and opinions. It was no more than five minutes before I spotted her trotting up our long driveway and waving at me the whole time, as if having read my mind.

We had met Edie soon after moving in. While Hal and I were still unpacking, in fact. She had arrived unannounced at our front door and greeted us with a cheerful shout that scared the bejesus out of both of us. Edie was a squat, motherly woman with close-cropped hair and a beaming smile. And boy, did she like to talk. She had plenty to say about our house *(How beautiful! I've always loved this house, always! I was so excited when the for-sale sign was taken down, couldn't wait to meet my new friends!)* and even more questions about us *(Where do you two come from? Was it hard to leave? How much was the final sale price on the house, if you don't mind my asking? Do you think you'll do any renovations? Oh, I hope not!)* that all came out within minutes of our meeting her.

"Can't stand that woman," Hal said to me after she left, but I found her to be pleasant enough and, over the weeks of her dropping by, grew to like her. These days, I would go so far as to say that she was my best friend, not that she had much competition. She was certainly nosy in a way that was occasionally overbearing, but I enjoyed her presence and—more important—the extent to which she was alive. Heart beating, blood pumping, knowing how to work a toaster, *alive*. These days, I had limited interactions with things that were alive.

"Not much I *can* do," I replied. "She's booked her flight. She's coming. When Katherine makes up her mind, there isn't much you can do to stop her."

"Like her father," Edie said. A little too personal of a statement, but not untrue. I couldn't fault Edie for being honest.

I beat my head against the back of the rocking chair. "Why

didn't I just keep lying to her?" I said. "I could have made something up. I could have just kept saying that he was busy or not at home."

"She wasn't really believing that anymore," Edie pointed out.

"Sure, but it might've bought me some more time," I said. "Maybe it could have gotten me through September, at least."

"You and I both know Katherine has been determined to talk to her father," Edie said, her soft face full of comfort. "If it weren't today she made you tell the truth, it would have been tomorrow or the day after." Still, I had seen Edie shudder at my mention of September.

"I know," I said.

"She can outlast you."

"I know." I sighed.

We sat and rocked in silence. I savored the moments I didn't have to think about Katherine or make any decisions. I closed my eyes, but I could feel Edie's gaze trained on me.

"Tea, ma'am?" Apparently, Fredricka had joined us on the front porch.

I looked up at Fredricka's large, broken face. "I'm fine for now, thank you." I glanced over at Edie, who was staring at Fredricka. "Would you like anything?"

"Oh, I'm good, thank you," Edie said quickly, eyes never leaving Fredricka. After Fredricka drifted away, nodding a farewell, Edie shook her head, as if trying to rattle something loose from her mind. "I don't know how you can look at her day in, day out. My God, her *head*."

I waved a hand. "You get used to it."

"I couldn't. And that *boy*. With those *eyes* just staring." Edie shuddered. She looked at me, insistent. "Katherine won't get used to it either, Margaret."

The momentary break in decision-making was over. "I know," I said. "She's going to have a fit."

"She'll want you to move." I heard a little panic in Edie's voice.

"She can't make me move." But even as I said the words, I had my doubts. Katherine was strong-willed. She had talked me into all sorts of things when she was younger, much to Hal's irritation. She had once gotten it into her head that she wanted a pet boa constrictor, and she had pestered me about it until I bought one for her. She named it Bilboa Baggins and kept it in a cage in her room, and our freezer was filled with dead mice for a couple of years. Hal didn't care for that. Katherine hadn't been allowed to bring Bilboa with her when she went to live with my sister, Noelle (*Why the hell did you even let that snake in your house to begin with?* Noelle asked me), so Bilboa lived with me and, to a lesser extent, Hal. I cleaned his cage and fed him frozen mice until I simply couldn't anymore, at which point I sold him to a neighborhood kid. When Katherine found out, she was *mad*. But she was fairly mad all the time by that point, so it all evened out.

It was time to make plans, do damage control.

"If she doesn't go up to the top floor, she won't see the blood," I said. "Maybe she'll be gone before it gets to the stairs." I put my head in my hands. "God, I don't know what to do about the screaming."

"Hopefully she's a heavy sleeper."

"Hopefully." She wasn't.

"Sleeping pills?" Edie looked at me, a criminal tinge in her eyes.

I laughed. "I'm not drugging my daughter."

Edie lifted her eyebrows. "It's a solution."

"I am *not* drugging my daughter."

For a minute we both stared out into the front yard, chuckling. A gust of wind rustled the grass. Somewhere in the back of the house, a bird slammed into a window.

I sighed. "I'll need to take the boards off the basement door."

Edie's head swung around. "Margaret, *no*."

"I know," I said.

"You know what will happen." Edie's eyes were wide. "And it's *September*."

"I know," I said. "But what is Katherine going to think if she comes here and sees the basement all boarded up? She'll get suspicious immediately."

"She'll also get suspicious if she sees the walls bleeding."

"I can try to keep her from seeing that. I can wake up early and clean it. I can keep her from going upstairs. I can make up some story about what the screaming is. Old pipes. I don't know. I can't keep her from seeing the basement door—it's right off the kitchen." I saw Edie's incredulous look. "I know it's risky, but there's no way around it. Besides, I've got the Bible pages up. I can call Father Cyrus. It's about time for him to come around again, anyway. Maybe that'll tide everything over."

"What if she wants to go down there?"

That would be a problem. But not a problem I could solve right now. "I'll cross that bridge when I come to it."

"But, Margaret, if she meets Master Vale . . ."

"She won't."

"How can you be so sure?"

"Because I'll die first." I heard the harshness of my voice and knew I should apologize for it. But when I looked over at Edie, she seemed to understand.

We spent the remainder of the time out front rocking in silence, staring out at the lawn together. Finally, the rain started.

FOUR

I met Hal when I was twenty-four and he was twenty-six. I had graduated college a few years prior and was in the middle of doing very little with my art history degree, while Hal was barely living off freelance-writing gigs. We met at a local gallery opening. He was writing a piece about the opening, and I had a single painting on display, which nobody looked at except for Hal, who doled out praise so liberally, it bordered on the disingenuous. He asked for my number and I gave it to him. We went out for a drink a few nights later.

I thought Hal was handsome. Some of my friends commented that he looked too thin, and they might have had a point; his too-big clothes draped off his lean body. But I liked his shaggy hair and his brown eyes and the way he smiled, crooked yet glowing. What I really liked was his excitement, his passion. He was the kind of person who could go on and on about anything—he could talk for *hours*, and I was happy just to sit and listen. He seemed to know a little bit about everything, which made me feel like I knew nothing about anything, but if I spent enough time with him, perhaps I could know a little bit about everything as well. I liked the way he laid claim to me after only a few dates, how when a male bartender complimented me on my blouse he wrapped his arm around me, as if to say, *Move on, pal. This one is taken.* And I suppose I *was* taken, in more ways than one.

For our third date, Hal took me to the movies. One of the theaters downtown was showing a rerelease of *The Exorcist* and Hal had never seen it. I had seen it once, several years back. I had never been much of a horror movie aficionado, but I remembered enjoying the movie in a general sense and feeling fairly entertained by it. Hal had a different opinion.

"Jesus," Hal said as we walked out of the theater hand in hand, "that scared the *shit* out of me."

I chuckled, focusing mostly on the feeling of his hand in mine. I liked when he intertwined our fingers and squeezed, as he had done just a moment ago. "I suppose it was sort of creepy."

"*Creepy?*" Hal laughed. "That little girl was *terrifying.* When she vomited all over that priest? Did that not scare you?"

"You know," I said, "they used split pea soup for that scene. The vomit."

"That doesn't make it less scary," Hal said. "It just makes pea soup more disgusting."

We turned left out of the theater and started walking down the street. It was late enough in the evening that most shops had closed, but the glow of signs and streetlights kept the sidewalk illuminated. It was late summer, and the nights were still warm. I hoped we could walk around forever, provided Hal kept his hand in mine.

"And the bit with the, um . . . crucifix?" Hal gestured. "That was fucked-up."

I laughed. "Definitely fucked-up."

"Didn't that scare you?"

I considered. "It bothered me," I said, "but I wouldn't say it scared me."

Hal shook his head and shuddered. "I'm going to be seeing that little girl's face in my sleep."

I hoped Hal wouldn't notice we had walked past our cars. I was afraid he would want to turn around, decide that the night was over, get in his car, leave. It was late—almost ten o'clock—but I wasn't ready for the night to be over yet. We walked past a restaurant that shone with red neon, lighting up Hal's thin face in the loveliest way.

"Also," Hal said, "I can't believe that priest died in the end. All that work he did for the little girl—"

"Regan," I said.

"Regan. And what thanks does he get? Thrown out of a window."

I swung our clasped hands together in between us like I was a child on a playground. "It was a sacrifice," I said. "He sacrificed himself to save Regan. He took on her demon and killed himself so she wouldn't come to any more harm."

"Captain Howdy." Hal exaggerated a shiver.

"Captain Howdy," I repeated, taking the opportunity to tickle Hal's side. He played along, shivering harder. We giggled. For the next few months, whenever we heard a noise in either of our apartments, I would say it was Captain Howdy coming to get us and Hal would fake a shiver and we would giggle and giggle. That joke faded with time, replaced over the next thirty or so years by new phrases and gags that only the two of us understood, but remembering it always brought a smile to my face.

I didn't know any of that at the time, of course. I was smiling simply because Hal's hand was still in mine. We walked in silence for a moment, grinning in the face of the future that unfolded before us.

"What I think is so neat about horror movies," I said, "is that they shine a light on what we think is scary. Not just ghosts and demons, but what we find *really* scary."

"How do you mean?" Hal asked. His eyes were on me, serious, dark spotlights that drowned out all the details in the periphery.

"These movies are so memorable because they play off things that we, as a society, find terrifying." I had taken a film studies class in college and, as a result, believed I knew all there was to know about film.

"You mean the devil?" Hal said, a smile darting across his face. "Seems like low-hanging fruit."

"Well, obviously, the devil." I chuckled. "Everybody is scared of evil things attacking them when they aren't going to church enough. I think this movie gets at a different kind of fear."

"Which is?"

"The fear of losing a child," I said. "Not physically, but emotionally. Captain Howdy *has* Regan. He's taken her over completely, turned her into some wicked thing. All parents fear the loss of their child's innocence—they'll go through hell to keep it from happening. And her mother is powerless except to watch it torn to pieces."

"It's not like any of that was Regan's fault," Hal said.

"I think that's what makes it the most terrifying," I said, enjoying the rare moment when I seemed to know more about a subject than Hal. "The lack of control. Neither Regan nor her mother did anything to cause it, and they certainly can't do anything to stop it."

"Not without being thrown from a window, anyway," Hal said.

"And I think that's the point," I said. "That's the decision that the priest made. In the face of the great, uncontrollable evil, he knew that his options were to let the demon take over Regan or to let it take him. He chose the latter. To him, it was worth it to stand up to her demon, to take on the evil himself if it meant that she could go free. He wanted her to have the life that ought to have been ahead of her."

"Regardless," Hal said, "it scared the bejesus out of me."

Hal and I arrived at a street corner. The light was red, so we waited to cross. This would have been a natural opportunity for Hal to suggest that we turn around and head back to our cars. Hal swung around to face me, taking both my hands in his. He smiled down at me—that crooked smile—and my heart sputtered.

"I'm sorry," I said, looking away from his gaze, the spotlights too bright for my eyes. "I'm prattling on."

Hal smiled wider. "I like it," he said. He squeezed my hands, bent down, and pressed his lips over mine. For a moment, the world flickered, a piece of film frozen on the projector in the moments before it starts to burn around the edges. Hal's lips were dry and there was a faint hint of popcorn on his breath, and I swear to Christ I heard my heart *sing*. I must have forgotten to breathe the entire time, because when we separated, Hal's hands still clutching mine, I was nearly gasping for air.

I had no idea what to say. I had forgotten all words. I looked up at him, smiling.

Hal smiled back. He squeezed my hands. "Do you want to go somewhere and get a drink?" he asked.

"Yes, I do," I said.

FIVE

Father Cyrus looked older than the house itself and moved at the speed of molasses. He didn't drive anymore, so he had one of the kids from the church drop him off, stopping at the end of the driveway in their souped-up sedan, music louder than Father Cyrus would have likely preferred. He maneuvered down the long driveway, a walking stick in one hand, a case of accoutrements in the other. His eyes were firmly planted on the uneven terrain in front of him but occasionally darted up at the house as if it were a predator.

He had understood the gravity of the situation when I called him. His voice had contained an extra tremor when he spoke to me, and he told me that he would be there the very next day, at three o'clock sharp. I could hear his heavy breathing pick up in pace as I thanked him and reminded him that, given the situation, I would need to remove the boards.

He made his way towards the house as I watched from the living room window, crashes and clatters sounding from back in the kitchen. Fredricka. Fredricka was upset with me and was be-having rather passive-aggressively about it, in my opinion. Earlier that day, I had sat her down as much as was possible, told her that Katherine was coming (of course, she already knew), and asked her in the kindest way I could if she could please make herself scarce during Katherine's stay.

She looked offended, an expression I had never seen on her broken face. "Does ma'am not want me to help?" she asked.

"It would be more helpful to me if you weren't around while Katherine is here. You can still be in the house of course"—a silly thing to say, as experience suggested Fredricka wasn't capable of leaving—"but not in the same room as Katherine. Please." I felt like scum; Fredricka was the only helpful prankster in this place. However, Fredricka was also the only prankster who listened to me even a little. I wouldn't be able to control Angelica and her friends, and could make Elias go away only temporarily by reunit-ing him with the bones of his mother, but I had a chance of at least keeping Fredricka out of the way, which wasn't nothing.

Fredricka looked as if I had insulted her ancestors. "Why?"

"I . . ." I struggled with the most tactful language. "I don't want you to scare her."

"Scare her?"

"Yes, you know . . . with your . . ." I gestured to my own head, pantomiming her wound. "It can be a bit scary. Not to me. I don't think it's . . . But other people might . . ."

Her brow furrowed.

"I . . ." I leaned forward. "Do you know what you look like?" It had actually never occurred to me that Fredricka might have been unaware of the volcanic split down her face. We had never spoken about it. I didn't want to come off as impolite.

"Ma'am?"

"You have . . . You have a very large . . ." I pointed at where her wound would have been on my own head before abandoning the cause altogether. If Fredricka didn't know, I certainly wasn't going to be the one to tell her. "Never mind. It's just . . . your presence will scare Katherine."

"But . . ."

"Please trust me," I begged. "It isn't personal, I swear. *I* think you're very helpful. *I* love having you around. But Katherine . . . I don't think she'll be able to see all of that. She'll just be scared."

As a final plea to drive my point home, I placed my hand on Fredricka's. Whenever I touched her, I was sent howling back to the last time she had been alive, and I saw the world through her eyes.

I saw the world through her eyes and I was in the dining room, the walls dark and unrecognizable, the thick smell of dinner—a roast—hanging in the air. I saw the world through her eyes, and although there were no windows, I knew it was nighttime and the flickering candles on the table cast jagged shadows that twitched and jumped on the wall. I saw the world through her eyes and there was a noise as someone shoved their way into the room, the swinging door slamming into the wall and shadows lilting to the side as the flames cowered in the wind. I saw the world through her eyes and a man with a wide, gleaming grin lifted his arms and, laughing, swung an axe into her head with furious strength. I saw the world through her eyes and I felt her skull collapse and heard a thick noise like a watermelon splitting in two. I saw the world through her eyes but one eye went dead, the other remaining trained on that man and his grin, laughter pouring from his mouth.

So, obviously, I tried to refrain from touching Fredricka whenever possible.

"For me?" I asked, shaking off the memory and trying my best to ignore the accompanying bloody nose I received whenever I touched her.

Fredricka agreed, but she was not happy about it. The sound of a plate shattering in the kitchen suggested that she might continue not to be happy about it for the foreseeable future.

Father Cyrus reached the front porch and ascended the steps at a pace that allowed me to open the door before he needed to knock. He gazed up at the house as a child might stare into the face of the boogeyman, then forced himself to meet my eyes and smile. "Hello, Margaret." His voice was like crinkled paper.

I smiled back. "Hello, Father. Thank you so much for coming out today."

With skin drooping from his face, pale hair barely clinging to his head in patches behind his ears, and a nearly ninety-degree tilt in his posture, Father Cyrus looked every second of his age. His knotted fingers gripped at my hands in greeting. "No bother at all. It was about time, now, wasn't it?" He looked away from me and the smile fell from his face as he crossed the threshold into the house, dropping my hands as an afterthought. "About time . . . ," he repeated, mostly to himself.

When that first September had been in its full rage, Hal and I had gone to the church for help. Neither of us was Catholic, or particularly religious at all for that matter—we were just desperate. Or, rather, *I* was desperate—Hal had spent most of the month pretending that nothing was amiss, and the fact that the pranksters tended to flee whenever he entered a room had certainly helped his cause. For longer than necessary, Hal had insisted that the screaming at night was just the wind and that birds smashing themselves into the side of our house was perfectly normal before he finally broke down and admitted that the river of blood cascading down our stairs was maybe more than just a leak and that the boy in his office wouldn't leave him alone. At this point, I had already had one run-in with the thing in the basement and was strongly advocating a trip to the church. Hal, finally, acquiesced.

Nobody believed us, of course. I couldn't blame them—I hadn't slept in days and certainly rambled on a bit too much about the regenerating blood and the dead children. I definitely didn't talk enough about the basement and I don't think I even mentioned the birds. Hal was unhelpfully silent, save for a tirade or two about the boy in his office. Everyone we spoke to looked uncomfortable for a while before validating our feelings, leading us in a prayer for peace in our new home, and wishing us well on our journey as they showed us the door. *Thank you for coming but kindly remove your crazy asses from our holy ground.*

"Maybe we should've told them we're Catholic," Hal said as we stood in the church parking lot, pondering our next move.

"I can't imagine lying to them would put us in their good graces," I replied.

We were still arguing over the merits of lying to holy leaders when we noticed Father Cyrus making his way over to us, walking stick in hand, at his usual snail's pace. "Excuse me," he said, his voice barely a gasp, "but I couldn't help overhearing that you two are having some trouble with your house."

Father Cyrus, apparently, was the last living priest to believe in the paranormal. He didn't look uncomfortable at all as I recounted our story; he only nodded as if I were telling him something he had known for a long time.

"You live in that old house on Hawthorn Street. Is that right?" he asked.

He was at our house later that afternoon. He'd still had his driver's license back then, so it was easier for him to visit at the last minute. I was beside myself, overjoyed that—at last—someone was willing to believe us, to help. I imagined that if there were a God, He'd had a great chuckle at how easily this lifelong nonbeliever tossed her faith over to a man in a dog collar at the first sign of things going bump in the night. At which point, I would have reminded Him that the bumping had gone on for several nights now and I was quite tired, thank you very much.

These days, Father Cyrus was well acquainted with the layout of the house. He set his bag on the kitchen counter and began to unpack his holy possessions—the usual: a Bible, a crucifix, a vial of holy water, a small silver bowl and rod (an aspersorium and an aspergillum, I had learned during one of these little visits). A tiny box that contained some significant relic—the bones of some saint or another, he once explained to me (specifically whose, I have since forgotten). He had obtained it during a trip to Italy years ago. *Very holy*, he explained. *It will help.* I remembered reading something about ancient merchants—pranksters of the past—selling fake relics to unsuspecting people, bones of chickens in place of bones of saints, but I doubted remarking on that fact would be helpful.

"Where is Hal?" he asked once he finished setting up.

I tried to keep my face flat. "He's gone," I said.

Father Cyrus nodded in understanding, placing a gnarled hand on mine. "Shall we pray for him?" he asked.

I smiled, forcing a small laugh that fooled nobody. "It's a little late for that, I think."

"It's never too late for prayer," Father said, but he didn't press the issue. "When will your daughter be in?" he asked.

"A few days," I said.

"And she's never been here before?"

"Never."

"And so we'll need to . . ." He let his sentence drop off as he glanced at the basement door, still boarded up.

I nodded.

Father Cyrus nodded back solemnly. He sighed, a shaky whine of air. "Let's get started, then."

Father Cyrus draped the crucifix around his wrinkled neck and stood tall. He lifted his hands in the air, palms outward, and closed his eyes. "In the name of the Father, the Son, and the Holy Spirit," he said, moving the ridge of his palm in a pantomime of a cross in the air.

I dropped my eyes and clumsily blessed myself in response. I was never sure if my hand moved in the right direction to shape the cross over my forehead and shoulders, but Father Cyrus never corrected me. "Amen."

"May the Lord God bless this house. Peace be with all who live here."

"And also with you." I knew my lines.

"Praise be to God, who fills our homes with his love."

"Blessed be the Lord."

Father Cyrus lifted his Bible, which yawned open in his hands. Whether it fell open to the correct passage was unclear. Father's eyes never looked downward as he read aloud to the room, left palm still hovering in the air, greeting the kitchen. "And now a reading from the holy gospel according to Luke . . ."

The process always began in the kitchen, as this room tended to be the least favored by the pranksters. It was the spiritual equivalent of dipping a toe into a pool before diving in. All Father Cyrus usually did in this room was a quick prayer. Typical house-blessing stuff.

It had been mid-September the first time Father Cyrus came over. He said his prayers in each room, kindly whispering at Hal and me when we missed our call-and-response lines. I trailed be-hind him like a lost child, wringing my hands and barely blinking as he sprinkled holy water on our nice antique furniture. Hal followed at a distance, occasionally giving my arm a nudge. *Let the nice priest work, Margaret.* The pranksters—annoyingly—were calm the entire time Father Cyrus was there. No Fredricka's bleeding head, Elias' biting fangs, or Angelica and her team of pointing children to be seen. Even the birds seemed to take a break from their suicide missions for the afternoon. We took Father Cyrus upstairs and pointed out the blood, but he couldn't see it.

"Goddamnit," Hal said. I slapped Hal's shoulder and shot him a look. We had *just* gotten this house blessed.

"You believe us?" I asked Father Cyrus, needing reassurance more than I ever had in my life. "We aren't crazy. I bet if you stayed the night, you would hear the screaming."

Father Cyrus lifted a palm and shook his head. "I don't need to see or hear anything," he said, and glanced all around him, as if there were pranksters in the room that not even Hal or I could see. "I can feel them. This house is dark. The things that live here, they blot out God's light."

Hal and I smiled and breathed sighs of relief.

Today, Father Cyrus came to the end of his prayer and poured holy water into the aspersorium. He bowed his head and whispered a little intercession to the bowl before lifting it and shuffling out of the room. I followed close by, ready to support him in place of his walking stick, abandoned against a counter.

Father Cyrus paused in the hallway, facing the front door. The basement door was to his left, but he didn't look at it. He closed his eyes and raised his hands, right hand still holding the aspersorium, as he prayed, his voice loud, too loud to give away a tremor. "Lord, defend us against the wickedness of the devil. Rebuke him and cast into Hell the evil beings who seek to harm your children. Amen."

"Amen," I said.

Out of the corner of my eye, I saw Fredricka pass between the dining room and the living room. She glanced at me and shook her head slightly. Still mad, I supposed. Fredricka always wondered why I bothered with Father Cyrus in the first place. I shrugged at her. What did she want me to do?

Father Cyrus moved forward and turned into the dining room, dipping the silver aspergillum into the holy water. "Lord, save this home." He flicked the aspergillum over his head like a whip, little flecks of water landing on the tablecloth.

"Lord, hear our prayer," I responded, trailing behind him. The dining room looked so different from how it had when Fredricka died in there. Instead of candles, a large chandelier hung from the ceiling. The dark wallpaper had been taken down sometime before we moved in and we had painted the room a deep maroon with gold detailing. At the time I thought it looked grand, but if I had to do it again, I would choose a color that reminded me less of blood.

That first night after Father Cyrus blessed the house three years ago, I slept like the dead. I awoke, disoriented and stiff, around noon the next day. The sleep deprivation had taken quite a toll. I checked the walls in the master bedroom—no blood. No blood on the stairs either. I couldn't remember any screaming in the night. The house was quiet in a way it had never been before. I made Hal swear that he hadn't heard the screaming either. Couldn't see the blood. Hadn't noticed the boy in his office. Hal had a habit of minimizing these sorts of things. I needed the truth. He swore it was over. Scout's honor.

Hal was convinced we had solved the problem once and for all. "We need to start going to church," he said.

Me, I didn't trust the quiet. It didn't seem like the rainbow after a storm—I had been in enough storms to know the difference. Rather, it was like the eye of a hurricane. Calm but hinting at chaos in a few short moments. These things, they don't go away so easily. These things, they only wait.

Still, we had a solid day and a half during which the house was ours again. I started on a new painting in my studio. Hal tapped away at a novel in his office, another one about cowboys. We had pasta for dinner. It was nice. Then, a couple days later, I found Fredricka in the kitchen rearranging plates.

"Tea, ma'am?" she asked, barely glancing up from her task.

"What are you doing here?" I asked. Perhaps my phrasing was rude, but I had almost started to believe that I might not see her again.

If Fredricka found my question rude, she didn't show it. "I live here," she said.

"But I . . . but we . . ." I mimicked the tossing of the aspergillum.

Fredricka's good eye rolled back in her head. "Ma'am would do best not to fall so readily for fancy men and their toys."

So that was that. Elias returned a few days later, much to Hal's dismay. A few days after that, we woke to find blood dripping down the walls again, and it was down the stairs in no time. Blythe, the woman who had been burned to death in one of the fireplaces, showed up again, howling and scratching at the walls. Her husband, Jasper, returned as well, but he was less of a concern, seeing as he had never done much of anything to begin with. The screaming returned, as did the dead birds, as did Angelica and her friends.

Father Cyrus crossed the foyer into the living room. "Cast away the evil from this house, and in your almighty power destroy it." Flick. Flick. Flick.

I followed. "Praise be to the Lord."

We had decorated the living room with charming antique sofas that were never quite comfortable enough to sit on. We had also bought a lovely old piano to serve as a finishing touch in the room, and I harbored fantasies of starting to play again. Unfortunately for us, Blythe liked to play as well, and the piano started playing when neither of us was in the room. A few isolated notes at first, but before we knew it, we were hearing full Beethoven concertos. Initially, I thought it was nice, but the music became constant and didn't stop during the night. It got a little old. We sold the thing—problem solved. There was still a large empty space in front of the picture window where it used to sit.

Father Cyrus walked through the living room and into my sunroom studio. This room tended to be free of pranksters and required no more than a cursory blessing. "As it was in the beginning," Father Cyrus said, flicking the aspergillum. I flinched, watching tiny droplets of water land on some of my unfinished paintings. I would need to paint over those spots later. More work.

We passed back through the living room and ascended the stairs, the wood groaning under our feet. The blood had reached midway down the second flight this morning, but the stairs between the first and second floors remained clean. Father Cyrus took each step carefully, painfully, panting and clutching the bowl of holy water with an unwavering grasp. I stayed by his side, hands hovering near his elbow in case he needed support. We reached the second-floor landing and Father paused to catch his breath. "Amen," he gasped, as if he had just finished a silent prayer, before heaving forward.

The first guest room. "Save this house, Lord." Flick.

"We trust in you, Lord," I murmured in response.

The second guest room. "Let the enemy be powerless over this place." Flick.

"Lord, protect us."

The bathroom. "Lord, send us aid in your holiness." Flick.

"Lord, watch over us."

The third guest room. "Lord, hear our prayer." Flick.

"Lord, hear our prayer."

Father Cyrus, pausing a heartbeat to take a deep breath, pushed open the door to Hal's office. Even though Father Cyrus had never seen Elias, he said he could feel Elias' presence in this room. I had a feeling that if Father Cyrus only waited patiently and let these pranksters grow comfortable with him, they would approach him in no time, stray cats creeping towards a dish of tuna. That was how it had worked with Edie. Unfortunately, Father Cyrus seemed to have no interest in being a dish of tuna.

Father Cyrus began moving through the room, dipping the aspergillum in the holy water. "Almighty Father, hear our call for help." Flick.

Fredricka still avoided this room in her cleaning, and the holy water left wet marks as it landed on the thickened dust on Hal's desk. I felt a twinge of something like sadness. Hal never would have liked to see his office in such an obvious state of neglect. I even spied cobwebs starting to form in corners.

"Strike fear into the hearts of those evil things that wish to bring harm into this place of peace. Give us the courage to fight against this devil." Flick.

Hal had decorated the room in dark wood and lined the walls with bookcases filled with vintage books, most of which he had never read. Copies of his first book—his first one that made us any money, anyway—were displayed prominently on the shelf behind his mammoth desk. His old desktop computer sat in the middle of the desk, dust turning it gray as it waited for him to return.

"By all the power you possess, cast this unholy presence out of your kingdom and redeem this dwelling through your Son, who lives and reigns with you, in the unity of the Holy Spirit, forever and ever."

"Amen," I said, tracing my fingers through the dust on the desk.

We made quick work of the third floor; the only rooms of interest were the master bedroom and the bathroom. There was no way Father Cyrus could climb the ladder into the attic. Not much happened up there, anyway. As we approached the landing of the stairs, preparing to descend to the one room we had neglected, Father Cyrus grabbed my hand. "Let us pray."

I knew the drill. "Our Father who art in Heaven—"

After all the pranksters returned following Father Cyrus' first visit, Hal and I concluded that he hadn't solved our problem. Still, we had nearly a week and a half of relative calm, and it was almost a month before things got back to the way they had been before. So, while Father Cyrus with his holy water and Bible weren't a cure-all, it seemed as if they acted as a Band-Aid on a larger wound. At this point, I couldn't complain about Band-Aids. Something needed to slow the bleeding, after all.

So, after another month, I asked him to come again.

That first year, there wasn't a schedule as to when I'd ask Father Cyrus back. I would let the pranksters stir up trouble until I couldn't bear it anymore, then have him over to buy us some solace. Then September rolled around again and everything was so much worse. By that time, I had figured out which of the pranksters were most affected by Father Cyrus. Fredricka was completely unaffected and dropped the pretense of disappearing after a few visits. Elias adopted a similar strategy, although his comings and goings were always much more erratic than Fredricka's to begin with. Blythe and Jasper were mildly affected, Jasper more so than Blythe. The basement and Master Vale, they seemed strongly affected, and ultimately they were what was in most need of controlling. It started to make a bit of sense. Fredricka was related to the goings-on in the basement only in an ancillary way, as were Elias and—to a lesser extent—Blythe and Jasper, so it stood to reason that they wouldn't be very affected by Father Cyrus' prayers against evil. On the other hand, Angelica and her friends were directly related to the goings-on in the basement, as was the blood, as were the screams. And Master Vale, he *was* the basement, so it went without saying that he would be affected. I was never quite sure about the birds.

So, after a bit of math and charting out various responses, I decided that Father Cyrus should come by at least once every other month. And, nonnegotiably, he should come by in September. Hal had shrugged, feigning nonchalance. *If it makes you feel better,* he'd said. But he had always reminded me to call.

"Amen."

The two of us had finished our prayer. There was a distinct tremble in Father Cyrus' hand. We took the stairs down to the ground floor one by one, my hand tight on his elbow for guidance. Father Cyrus was breathing heavily, and he seemed to take the stairs even slower than usual. I couldn't exactly blame him.

Finally, Father Cyrus and I stood in front of the basement door. For a moment, the only sound was the tremor of the aspergillum in the bowl he clutched in his hand.

"Do you think we should go ahead and take the boards off now?" I asked.

"While I pray," he responded. He looked at me. "Do you still have the holy pages on the inside?"

I nodded, then went to retrieve the crowbar from the kitchen. I had left it on the counter for this occasion.

Taking a deep breath, Father Cyrus raised the aspergillum

over his head with confidence. "I banish you from this home, unholy beast, in the name of God the Almighty." His voice was booming, all hint of tremor gone.

I wedged the crowbar underneath the topmost board and heaved with all my strength. I heard the wood crack as I yanked the nails from the doorframe.

"In the name of our Lord Jesus Christ, I command you to leave this dwelling."

The first board clattered to the floor. I felt flecks of holy water dance on my arms and face as I positioned the crowbar underneath the second board.

"In the name of the Holy Spirit, I cast you away from these children of God. It is Christ Himself who compels you, under whose might you are rendered powerless. Cower before him, O evil being." He dipped the aspergillum in the bowl again and flung the water, whiplike, at the door.

The second board fell to the floor, splinters spraying into the air.

"It is God the Almighty who commands you." Flick. "Our Lord Jesus Christ commands you." Flick. "The power of the Holy Spirit commands you." Flick. "All the saints and martyrs command you." Flick.

I wasn't even halfway through the boards and was already starting to breathe heavily. I took a moment to wipe the holy water from my brow before returning to my work.

Father Cyrus' voice amplified in intensity, achieving a volume I wouldn't have thought he was capable of anymore. *"Begone, you foul creature, you fiend who has wiled your way out of the gates of Hell. You will tremble in fear under the might of our Lord. For it is He who cast you down from the heavens and sent you to endless destruction. And it is He who will render you powerless yet again."*

The third board was proving to be a bit of a challenge. I grunted as I threw my weight against the crowbar. The wood splintered and I thought I heard something like a yawn echo just beyond the door.

"*I expel you, in the name of the Father.*" Flick. "*And of the Son.*" Flick. "*And of the Holy Spirit.*" Flick.

"Amen," I grunted, cracking into the fourth board. Holy water flecked into my eye.

"*Glory be to the Father.*"

Crack. "As it was in the beginning." My response was coming in puffs of heavy breath now. I could feel sweat dripping down my back. The splashes of holy water were starting to feel refreshing.

Father Cyrus lowered the aspergillum. He released a breath. "The Lord be with you."

The fourth board clattered to the floor, and I allowed myself a pause before attending to the final board. "And also with you," I panted.

"Let us pray." Father Cyrus bowed his head, but I continued working. One board to go—no time to pray. "Father God the Almighty, please hear the cries of your poor children. Lord, look upon this dwelling with pity and love and banish this foe back to the fires of hell. This we ask through Christ our Lord, and in His name we pray."

"*Amen,*" I grunted triumphantly, the fifth board collapsing to the floor. That yawning noise sounded again, just audible over my gasps. I leaned back against the wall to catch my breath. When I opened my eyes, Fredricka was standing in the kitchen, her expression unreadable. *Water?* I tried to mouth to her, hoping she wasn't too upset with me still.

Next to me, Father Cyrus put his hand on the knob of the basement door.

My eyes darted to his hand, then back to Fredricka. Her expression likely matched mine, horrified. She shook her head. I pushed myself off the wall to face him. "Father—," I began.

But he was already turning the knob. "Dear God, we ask that you keep this unclean being far from this home and grant all who dwell here peace in their days." The door opened with a groan, and I moved behind Father Cyrus, backing away. The Bible pages we had taped to the back of the door waved gently at the disturbance, their edges frayed. "We pray that the light and love of our Lord Jesus Christ shine down upon this home." I could smell it now, the heady air moving up the stairs, thick and slow as blood. "May we have no reason to fear the devil, for our Lord Jesus Christ is with us." Behind me, Fredricka was shaking her head violently now. "He who lives and reigns with you in the unity of the Holy Spirit, forever and ev—"

At that, Father Cyrus' body was pinned with a rigidity akin to rigor mortis. His arms stiffened and dropped like metal rods to his sides, the aspersorium clanging to the floor, holy water spilling all over the nice wood. The heels of his shoes left the ground, his toes now barely scraping the floor. His head wrenched backwards, eyes unblinking, mouth gaping, the vowels of the final words of his prayer grating out of his mouth with an ear-shattering volume.

This was new.

"What the hell do I do?" I hissed at Fredricka. As unprecedented as this was, it seemed like a bad sign. Fredricka was no help whatsoever, her mouth open and her head still shaking no.

With the care one takes to test the heat of a pot on the stove, I grazed my fingers over Father Cyrus' shoulder. "Father?" I needed to speak quite loudly to be heard over the rattle coming out of his throat.

As if my fingers corrected the skip of a broken record, the

sound stopped, his mouth frozen open in a silent scream. He hung there, rigid and unmoving. I was about to try touching him again when a gush of black fog erupted from his mouth, releasing into the air, buzzing. It was flies—a swarm of fat black flies exploding from his body and spilling out into the hallway. The flies landed on his neck and face, crawled into his nose and over his open eyes. A thick gagging noise sounded over the buzzing, coupled with a low scream that could have been coming from either Father Cyrus or somewhere in the basement. I couldn't quite tell.

"*Cut it out!*" I screamed into the basement, shoving Father Cyrus aside and slamming the door, my shoulder pressing hard into the wood, my hip jamming into the doorknob.

As soon as the door closed, Father Cyrus crumpled onto his hands and knees and vomited violently, coughing and gasping. I knelt beside him and rubbed his back, not particularly sure what had just happened.

Father Cyrus hacked and gagged through his final retches, falling to his side on the floor, chest heaving. He trapped my foot under his arm, somewhat uncomfortably. I patted his shoulder, waiting as his gasps quieted. My own breath needed a moment to calm itself as well, I found. Between the thickness of the flies in the air and the smell of his vomit in front of me, I was starting to feel a little nauseous.

"You maybe shouldn't have opened the door," I said.

Father Cyrus shifted on the floor, struggling to raise himself, a trembling hand underneath him. "This house is so cold," he stammered. I stood and offered a hand to help him up. He took it and pressed his weight against me but didn't meet my eyes. Instead, he turned to the kitchen, where his things waited on the counter. "So cold," he said.

He stumbled into the kitchen and began shoving his accoutrements into his bag. Crucifix, Bible, holy water—all tossed in with no semblance of care remaining. Guiltily, I lifted the aspersorium and aspergillum from the floor and walked over to him, offering them out like an olive branch. Still not meeting my eyes, he grabbed them from my hands and tossed them in, then closed his bag with haste.

His ritual wasn't finished yet. There was a whole other bit after he blessed the house, and we still needed to say the Apostles' Creed. I thought about pointing this out, but the hurried nature with which he snatched up his walking stick and hobbled towards the door suggested that my words would land on deaf ears.

I jogged along after him. "Thank you for coming, Father. I'm really sorry about, you know . . . the flies?" I opened the front door for him and he nearly leapt onto the porch. "That has never happened before."

"No need for apologies," he panted, already down the porch steps and heading for the driveway. "Call me if you need anything else. *Julio!*" This last bit was directed towards the driver of the car, still parked at the end of the driveway, a faint hum of rap music emanating through the cracked windows. *"Julio, we're leaving."* He dove into the car and they sped away, dust in their wake.

That all could have gone much better. I left the front door open for a minute, trying to fan away the flies that made their way to the foyer. These goddamn things would be in the house for *days*.

I looked up to see Edie hustling down the driveway, arms pumping as her body waddled towards me. "What happened?" she shouted. "I saw a car peel out of the driveway like a bat out of hell. I waved at them to slow down—there might be kids around, you know—but I think they actually *sped up*."

"It's fine," I said, still fanning at the flies. "Just a bit of a hiccup with the blessing."

Edie climbed the steps to the porch, panting from her jog down the driveway. "A hiccup? What do you mean?" She peered through the door and into the foyer. "What's with all the flies?"

"They came out of the priest," I said.

"You don't say." Edie sounded perplexed but unsurprised.

"He opened the basement door," I explained.

"Ahhh," Edie murmured, the sound of a person who had found the last piece of a puzzle. "He maybe shouldn't have done that."

I groaned, brushing away a fly that had landed on my face. "And now I have to clean up his vomit." I tried not to think about the stains the vomit and the holy water were going to leave on the nice hardwood floors and—unfortunately—the wall.

"Oh dear." Edie glanced past me into the house. "Will you need any help?"

"Oh, I couldn't subject you to that," I said, although not necessarily because of the vomit. Edie didn't like the house and avoided going past the front porch as much as she could. I decided to spare her the fright. I had frightened enough people today.

Edie gestured towards the flies. "What about with these?"

I sighed, glancing around at the swarm. "Actually," I said, "yes. If you don't mind." There really were a *lot* of flies.

Edie nodded and I left her at the front door shooing their thick black bodies away with both hands. I walked down the hallway, steeling myself. I had cleaned up plenty of other people's vomit before—including both Katherine's and Hal's—but that didn't make the task any more pleasant. However, when I reached the basement door, I found Fredricka on her hands and knees in front of it, scrubbing away at the floor, soapy bucket at her side.

"Oh, no," I said, trying to wave her away without touching her. "You don't have to clean this up. Really."

"It'll leave a stain," Fredricka responded, her scrubbing not even slowing as she spoke.

I felt terrible. I had already upset Fredricka by asking her to stay away while Katherine visited, and now she was cleaning up the vomit of a priest she didn't even approve of my bringing to the house. "I mean it, Fredricka. I'll clean it. It's my fault, anyway." Technically, it was the basement's fault, but Master Vale wasn't exactly going to climb the steps and clean up the vomit himself, so I was the next in line for blame.

"It's no trouble, ma'am."

I sighed. I knew a lost cause when I saw one. I grabbed a second rag and settled at her side, scrubbing away at the mess next to her.

We worked in silence for some time. Finally, Fredricka sat back on her heels, hands in her lap, and spoke, her gaze lingering on the remnants of the mess in front of us. "I will stay away when ma'am's daughter visits," she said.

I looked up. "Are you sure?"

Fredricka nodded. "I will still be around to help," she said, seeming to—on some level—comprehend that she was not physically capable of leaving entirely. "But when ma'am's daughter comes, I will keep my distance as best I can."

"Fredricka, I—" I felt at a loss. There is nothing like watching a person scrub up vomit that isn't theirs to make you realize just how much you ask of them. "I don't know what to say."

Fredricka was still looking away from me, her expression calm. "It is no burden," she said. "I don't want ma'am's daughter to be frightened"—she glanced at the vomit on the floor—"like he was."

I could have cried. I scooted closer to her. "This is so kind of you. I asked so much of you, and . . . this is just . . ."

Fredricka smiled about as much of a smile as she usually mustered. "Anything to help, ma'am. Needs must."

I flung my arms around her. With that touch, I was again sent howling back to the day she died, to the unrecognizable dining room, the thick smell of the roast, the jagged shadows of the candles, the grinning man, the swinging axe. I felt the weight of the axe sink through my—her—skull, felt it collapse, heard the cracking-watermelon noise, and saw the world fade out through one eye. It gave me a terrible headache, but I only hugged her tighter. My nose bled onto my sleeve. It was worth it.

SIX

Katherine called me midmorning on the eleventh to tell me she would get a later start than anticipated. Her flight had been delayed. She hadn't gotten to the hotel until nearly three in the morning. Blah blah blah.

"Take your time," I replied, trying not to sound thrilled at the delay.

She called me again in the early afternoon to tell me that getting the rental car was a debacle. She was stuck in traffic leaving the city. Blah blah blah.

"Take your time."

She called me again in the midafternoon to tell me that the traffic was terrible. She was about to run some Lincoln off the road. Blah blah blah. By this time, the majority of her language was profanity. She was not going to be pleasant when she got here.

"Take your time."

The house had been calm so far. No blood on the walls, no

screaming at night, and Angelica and her friends were gone. Fred-ricka also seemed calmer, tidying things in an orderly fashion in-stead of moving objects from room to room for no reason. It seemed as if Father Cyrus' blessing—aborted though it had been—had some impact, after all. I was thankful for the reprieve; we'd had a lot of work to get done in the days leading up to Katherine's arrival.

A few days prior, I dug up the bones of Elias' mother, which was always a laborious, multihour task. She had been buried out in the woods underneath a half-dead oak tree and was a pain in the neck to find the first time I dug her up, let me tell you. Since that first time, I had marked the tree with paint, a fuchsia M for "mother," making her easier to find. Still, the digging-up part was strenuous. My prime body-excavating years were definitely be-hind me. I always tried to rebury the bones in a shallower grave than the one her initial gravedigger (whoever that had been) had dug, but I still wanted the bones deep enough to avoid detection by any wild animal. Elias might not care for the idea of a fox chew-ing on his mother's ribs, were he to find out.

I was sweating and covered in mud by the time my shovel hit plastic. The first time I had done this, I'd had a delusion that I needed to treat the bones with some degree of respect, and I'd brought the nicest urnlike pot I owned—the kind you grow trees in before planting them out back—to carry them in as I hauled them back to the house. I placed them in the pot with care and reverence and then returned them gently to the dirt when I was finished. After the third time, I realized that trying to find a whole human skeleton in the dirt over and over was a monumental pain in the ass, so I bought a series of plastic bins from the Save Mart to serve as makeshift coffins. Small ones for the delicate finger bones, larger ones for the ribs and femurs. It felt a bit like organiz-ing a closet, only with human remains. It took just a few more times after that for me to determine that lugging several large bins full of human remains up and back to the house was also not particularly pleasant, nor was lugging the urnlike pot, which was heavy as all get-out. That was where the garbage bag came in, the thick kind that doesn't tear easily. Now the bins come out of the ground, the bones go into the bag, and the bag goes up to the house. I left the shovel and the empty bins by the tree as I turned back towards the house, garbage bag full of bones flung over my shoulder. I would be back soon.

I tracked mud all over the foyer and up the stairs, much—I'm sure—to Fredricka's annoyance. The most likely place to find Elias was in Hal's office. I unceremoniously dropped his mother's bones on the floor, calling out for him. He didn't appear, so I would have to summon him. I grumbled. After digging up his mother, I was fairly thirsty and in no mood for singing.

I sighed and cleared my throat. *"Sleep now, my darling. Don't you cry."* My voice was hoarse and off pitch, but it would do the trick. This was the song she used to sing to him, and it never failed to bring him about. *"Mommy's gonna stay with you all through the night."*

A puff of black mist started forming in the corner of the room. The bones began clattering on the floor.

I continued singing. *"Ne'er shall you worry. Ne'er shall you mourn. . . ."*

Elias hissed into existence in the corner, face already black, teeth gleaming, jet-engine noise sounding. He was never a fan of the beginning of this process. He moved towards me. I skittered out of his reach, eyeing the bones as they trembled.

"You won't see your little gray horse no more."

Out from the bones sprang a gossamer-thin form of a woman, skin drooping, empty sockets for eyes. She howled. Elias moved closer to me, his jaw unhinged like that of a python ready to devour a rat.

I continued singing. *"He ain't in the field. No, he's long gone. . . ."*

Elias looked to his right. He noticed the ghost of his mother emerging from the bones and his rattle quieted. His mouth folded back in on itself and his fangs vanished. His mother reached her skeletal arms out for him.

"But you'll see his sweet face again 'fore long."

I moved back to allow space for the reunion. Elias' charcoal face regained its normal hue, and his eyes lost their resemblance to a burning void. For a minute, he looked just like a regular child as he stepped into the open arms of his dead mother. She wrapped her cracking arms around him and her mouth fell open. In a weak, gasping voice, she sang, *"It all comes around with the moon and the sun, but Mommy's gonna stay here till all is done."* The two of them collapsed into each other in a stream of ash and the room was empty once more, save for the bones on the floor, now still.

The first time I did this, I thought for sure I had cracked the code. I told Hal I had solved the Elias problem once and for all and he wouldn't be bothering us anymore. It's almost laughable how naive I was, and not so long ago either. Elias was back after about a week, and up to his usual tricks, lurking in corners, sinking his fangs into passersby who got too close. A disappointment for sure. On the bright side, I learned that reuniting Elias with the bones of his mother bought me one Elias-free week, which wasn't nothing. Sometimes it was nice just to have one less thing to deal with.

I knelt down and started putting the bones back in the garbage bag. That song would be stuck in my head for the rest of the day. At the very least, I would be humming it the entire time I reburied Elias' mother.

As I trudged back down the staircase, I passed by Fredricka, on her hands and knees, scrubbing my muddy footprints off the floor. I looked behind me and saw that I was still tracking mud and—if we're being honest—trace particles of Elias' mother. Fredricka followed my gaze and might have looked frustrated if she allowed that emotion to register on her face. "I'm sorry," I said to her. Fredricka returned to scrubbing.

When Katherine finally arrived in the late afternoon of the eleventh, she was—as predicted—in an unpleasant mood.

"You would not believe how much goddamn construction there is by the airport," she said to me instead of hello, wrapping an arm around me in a cursory hug as we met in the driveway, just outside her rental. "They're putting in a new exit ramp, I think. Who the hell knows? Traffic was backed up for miles."

Fortunately for me, she was too wrapped up in her own irritation to notice how visibly nervous I was.

"And then there was a goddamn pileup on the northbound side of the road and I was stuck in *that* traffic forever. And the wreck was on the *other* side of the road, for Christ's sake. Everybody was just slowing down to gawk like a bunch of fucking morons."

"Language," I said, grabbing her bags.

Katherine would turn thirty in a few months, but she looked older. Her job, important and stressful, was starting to take a toll on her. I could see crow's-feet that wanted to appear around her eyes, and lines on her forehead that refused to vanish when her face stilled. Her hair, dark and stylish, appeared free of gray, but I wouldn't have been surprised if she dyed it. She certainly hadn't been afraid of hair dye as a teenager; her hair had often been defiant shades of blue, green, and once even pink.

For some reason, Katherine had dressed for her travels as if she were heading to a business meeting. She wore smart gray slacks that would easily compose one half of a power suit, and a silk blouse that was still neatly tucked in despite her lengthy car ride from the airport. I wondered what her teenage self might have said about her current outfit.

Katherine seemed to be studying me as well, charting the changes in my appearance. It had been several years since we'd seen each other in person, after all. Things had changed. "Your hair's gone gray," she said.

"Happens to the best of us," I replied. In truth, I didn't care much about the grays. I've always been somewhat neutral concerning my own appearance—I've never been anything special, not the kind anyone would think to feature in a magazine, but I had still managed to turn a head or two in the past. Hal's head, at least. Noelle used to snipe at me for having the sort of skin that looked decent enough without much makeup, but over the years, the lines had set in. Distinguished, one might say, if one weren't aware of how many of those lines were caused by lack of sleep. The grays too for that matter. Years ago, I might've considered dyeing my hair like my mother had when her hair started to go (*The silver stands out in hair like ours*, she once told me), but there didn't seem to be much of a point to upkeep these days. So instead I let the salt mix into the pepper and let my hair grow long—the opposite of Katherine's practice, it would seem.

"You've had a long trip," I said. "You'll want to settle in, I'm sure. Get comfortable." Change out of those nonsensical clothes and what I now saw were *heels* on her feet. Since when did Katherine wear heels?

Katherine pulled her duffel bag from my grasp and hoisted it over her shoulder. "If it's all the same, Mom, I'd like to get started figuring out what the hell happened to Dad. I'm so pissed I wasted most of the day in traffic." With that, she set off towards the house and I followed, wheeling her suitcase behind me.

Hal and I had been successful in keeping Katherine away from the house for the entirety of the four years we'd lived here. Luckily, we had Katherine's petty disinterest on our side. Ever since Katherine had left for college, it had been clear she had left for good. She made it a point to make her visits home as short as possible and arranged summer classes to keep her away at school, with no reason to return. She landed a good job immediately after graduating and threw her heart into it, quickly climbing the ranks and filling her time with work. She was now upper-upper management at some bank or another and had no time to visit. For a while it hurt our feelings, although I couldn't say I blamed her for her distance. Hal hadn't exactly made things easy for her, and although Katherine pretended not to be, she was always one to hold on to the tail end of a grudge. Still, once I had realized what life would be like in the new house, I drew a rare line in the sand. Katherine couldn't be in the house. It was too dangerous, too frightening. Hal and I living there was one thing—we knew how to handle the pranksters (*I* did, anyway); we weren't scared (*I* wasn't, anyway); we had figured it all out (*I* had, anyway)—but Katherine was another story. I was perfectly willing to make a heaven of any hell in which I happened to find myself, but I would be goddamned if I made my daughter endure it.

Hal tended not to like the infrequent occasions when I drew lines in the sand, but in this situation, he wasn't hard to convince. We came up with some half-hearted excuse for postponing the initial visit we planned for Katherine, and never made any serious plans for her to visit again. For her part, Katherine half-heartedly feigned disappointment and never brought up any serious desire to visit again. We spoke on the phone briefly yet regularly, readily accepted one another's excuses for not spending holidays together (*I'm doing Christmas with Claire's family* or *Your father and I are thinking about heading up to Maine for the holidays*), and we were mutually satisfied with the arrangement, albeit for different reasons.

As such, this was the first time Katherine was seeing the house. Even through her frustration, she paused outside and looked up, taking it all in. "Jesus, Mom. This is a beautiful house."

I stood next to her and smiled, following her gaze. The blue and white of the paint made the house stand out against the yellowing trees that surrounded it, and the turret was always impressive, whatever the season. The house could be a pain in the neck more often than not, but nobody could deny its beauty. "It sure is," I said.

We walked inside and Katherine mumbled a few other compliments, rare for her, about the house. "Original hardwood," I said as we ascended the stairs. "And you'll see in the kitchen— vintage stove. Still in working condition."

Katherine made small noises of appreciation, but her interest was already fading.

Choosing which room to put Katherine up in had been a feat. Each room was challenging in its own right. The first bedroom on the left was nice because it had a fireplace, which would have been enticing were it not for Blythe's having been chained up and burned alive in there. Blythe liked to come crawling out of the fireplace, skin melted by flames, charcoal limbs dragging her along the floor, leaving a trail of ash in her wake. She would get right in your face and scream, charred fingers scratching at your cheek— not exactly pleasant. Blythe was the reason we couldn't light fires in the house; she would raise hell whenever one was lit—howling, flinging open doors and windows, and bringing about tornado-like winds that would snuff out any flames we started. But who could blame her?

The second bedroom was the room where the man who killed Fredricka—that grinning man, Jasper—had been found dead in the closet. He'd killed Blythe—his wife—as well, but I was always more perturbed about Fredricka, given the substantially more pleasant nature of our relationship. The papers at the time said that Jasper had committed suicide, but once you saw him there, all crumpled in on himself and bent at those unnatural angles, you knew it hadn't been a suicide. Still, he didn't do too much besides spend his time in the closet, body bent like a dead spider's. When you opened the closet door, his head fell towards you, mouth agape, revealing those same gleaming teeth now shattered. One broken hand would rise, revealing the red head of a matchstick between his fingers. He flicked at it with a dried, cracked finger. It never lit. I didn't interact with Jasper very much. In my defense, I wasn't particularly interested in getting to know him, given what he had done to Fredricka and all.

The last guest bedroom was generally fine, although from time to time a large gash would appear on the wall, giving way to some sort of black void oozing something that looked an awful lot like blood but was definitely not blood. I wasn't too sure what it was all about, but I had a feeling it was best not to touch it.

So the second bedroom it was. Least of three evils, I supposed.

Katherine flung her bag on the bed with a sigh. I lingered in the doorway with her suitcase, on guard for any pranksters in the room. Jasper usually went away for a little while after Father Cyrus' blessing, but one could never be too careful around here.

Katherine checked the time on her phone. "I want to go down

to the police station today, file that missing person report," she said absentmindedly, scrolling through her emails.

"It might be a little late for that today, dear," I said. "It's a small town, not a lot of police officers."

Katherine was typing out an email, barely listening. "They can take our information," she said to her phone.

"They won't be able to get started on anything until tomorrow," I said.

I heard the *swoosh* from Katherine's phone as she sent her email. She stared at her screen, one hand on her hip. "Four forty-eight," she mumbled to herself.

"It's at least a thirty-minute drive to the station," I said. "And you've had such a long day in the car already."

Katherine lowered her phone, pressed her eyes shut. "Fuck." It was her way of admitting that I was right, and I would take it. She stood there for a second, eyes closed, before springing back into action, hands flung into the air. "Fuck. Fine, fine. Fuck." She ripped her duffel open and started pulling out clothes, begrudgingly settling into the room.

I held my breath as she moved towards the closet and wrenched the door open. Jasper was nowhere to be seen. I exhaled.

"Do you have any hangers in here?" Katherine asked, examining the closet.

"I have some upstairs," I said quickly, trying to minimize the amount of time Katherine would spend inside the closet. I retrieved a handful of hangers for her and left her to unpack. I was grateful for both the night's reprieve from a police investigation and a continued prankster-free household. Neither of those realities could be delayed forever, but I would take whatever calm moments I could get.

In the kitchen, a cup of tea, still steaming, was waiting for me. I lifted the cup to my lips. "Thanks, Fredricka," I said into the air.

"You're welcome, ma'am." I wasn't sure where Fredricka's response came from. I was grateful for our truce.

The day before, Fredricka and I had gathered up all the bird carcasses from the yard and tossed them into the garbage bag that previously contained the bones of Elias' mother. I didn't want Katherine to become unnerved by the birds, especially since after a few days they begin attracting ants. There had been more birds in the yard than I'd thought; collecting them turned into quite the chore. We burned the birds in a bonfire in the backyard, Fredricka holding the bag open and me tossing each feathered corpse, one by one, into the fire. Together, we watched the birds burn, their feathers singeing into nothingness as their bodies blackened. Our faces glowed orange with the fire in the diminishing dusk light. Somewhere inside the house, Blythe howled and roared, climbing the walls and scratching her nails against the ceiling.

"I'm really worried about Katherine's visit," I said.

Fredricka murmured in response, pushing a smoldering bird closer to the flames with a stick.

"I don't like that the boards are off the door," I said, watching a burning feather drift into the air.

"Needs must when the devil drives," Fredricka responded.

"I suppose," I said.

We stood in silence, the sky growing dark around us. The heat from the flames was a comfort in the chilling air. The fire cracked and spat, ashes lifting skyward. The flames started cooking the flesh of the birds, feathers completely gone now, and an aroma of charred poultry hung thick in the air.

"You know what we haven't had in a while?" I said. "Roast chicken."

"Mmmm," Fredricka responded. "I believe we have a chicken in the icebox. If ma'am wishes, I could prepare it for dinner tonight."

"That sounds good," I said, my mouth starting to water. "Perhaps with fingerling potatoes?"

"Of course."

"Oh, excellent," I said, taking Fredricka's stick to poke at another carcass, mostly eviscerated at this point. "I'm *starving*."

Today, I stood in the kitchen, tea nearly finished, and looked out at the remnants of the bonfire in the backyard. It had raged on for an hour or so while Fredricka cooked and I watched the birds turn to ash. It really had been a pleasant evening, after all. And the chicken had been delicious.

My pleasant recollections were shattered by the sound of crashing and clattering from upstairs. *Goddamnit*, I thought, leaving my teacup on the counter and dashing out of the kitchen. *This is happening too soon.* Father Cyrus had *just* blessed the house. True, he hadn't gotten to finish, but I thought I had at least a week before things started getting chaotic again. I sprinted up the steps. Who was doing this? Elias? Not due back for several days, at least. It couldn't be Angelica—she and her friends tended to stay gone the longest. Had Fredricka decided she was upset with me again? Even after our truce?

The noise was coming from Hal's office. Likely Elias, then. *What on earth did I excavate his mother for?* I thought. If I weren't going to get a week of peace out of the ordeal, I wouldn't have even bothered digging up the woman.

I burst through the office door, ready to give Elias a piece of my mind, even if I ended up getting bitten in the process. However, instead of Elias' chalky presence, I found Katherine yanking at the cabinet doors lining the lower halves of Hal's book-shelves.

"Katherine," I said, my voice a mix of surprise and relief, "what on earth are you doing?"

"All these doors are fucking *locked*," Katherine growled, pulling harder at the cabinets.

"Language."

"Locked." She pulled on the handles of a set of cabinets. "Locked." She grabbed at another set of handles. "They're all fucking *locked*!"

"Could you be careful with those, please?" She was yanking on the cabinets so hard I could envision the wood shattering.

"Why the hell did Dad lock all his cabinets?"

"I have no earthly idea."

"What the hell is he keeping in here?"

"I don't know. Drafts of manuscripts, perhaps? Signed copies of his books?" Both of these suggestions were unlikely.

Katherine swiveled around on the floor and started tugging at the drawers of his desk. "These are fucking locked too. God-*damnit*!" She slammed both palms against the top of Hal's desk, hard. A cup of pens tipped over.

"Jesus Christ, Katherine," I said, startled by her outburst. *"Language."*

"Is there a key anywhere?" She dug through the items on top of Hal's desk—the toppled cup of pens, a little bowl of paper clips, stacks of random papers. Her oncoming emotional outbursts had the same tells as her childhood tantrums. Raised volume of speech, rapid movements, inflexible insistence on getting what she wanted. When she returned home from her stay at my sister's and discovered we had gotten rid of Bilboa, she tore around her room, looking for him and shouting, *Where is he? Where is he?* long after we told her we had given him away. Then she threw things. And she was seventeen at the time, probably too old for all that.

"I'm sure there's got to be one somewhere."

Katherine stood, waving her arms about her face. *"And why are there so many goddamn flies in this house?"*

"Katherine—could you just calm down?"

Of course, nobody ever listens when you tell them to calm down. *"Fuck!"* Katherine screamed. "Fuck fuck *fuck!"* She snatched up a stack of papers, crinkling them in her hands and raising them high, preparing to hurl them across the room. The tantrum was nigh. I ducked in preparation.

Then, seemingly remembering she was almost thirty, Katherine stilled herself. She set the papers back on Hal's desk in a messy, crumpled ball, and took several long, deep breaths, her fingers sunk deep into her hair. She looked as if restraining herself from throwing things was causing her physical pain, but she breathed her way through it.

"Sorry," she said finally, not looking at me. "I'm sorry."

I blinked. This was progress. When she was a child, Katherine's tantrums had been legendary, both in length and in power. She had completely lacked the ability to calm herself or see reason, so it had been left to me to assuage her or just to hold on for dear life until the storm passed. Hal had always said I gave in to her tantrums too quickly. However, if the choice was either giving in to Katherine's demands or hours of vicious tantruming, I tended to choose the former over the latter. Somewhere along the way, it seemed as if Katherine had learned a way to resist giving in to her own temper, although her restraint looked wobbly.

I recovered from my shock. "You're tired," I said. "You've had a long day of travel. You clearly aren't in a good headspace to cope with setbacks." I motioned to the desk, a mess of spilled pencils and crumpled papers; then I moved towards her, reaching out a calming hand to place on her back. "Take the night off. Get some rest." My hand connected with the swell of her shoulder, and I took momentary joy in the warmth of her living body, as well as the nonoccurrence of ghastly death-day flashbacks following the touch. "Then tomorrow you can start up with a clear head."

Katherine's hands were still in her hair, but she nodded, taking long, purposeful breaths. "Okay," she said. "Okay, you're right." She lowered a hand and patted mine, a touch that didn't so much communicate appreciation of comfort as it did *Okay, Mom, that's enough of that.* I released her shoulder and she lowered both hands to her side, meeting my eyes at last. "And I suppose it's about dinnertime. Do you have any food around here?"

I smiled. "I have some delicious roast chicken leftovers."

THE CHICKEN WAS INDEED DELICIOUS, EVEN REHEATED. I PREPARED DINNER WHILE Katherine changed and likely sent more emails upstairs. Fredricka loitered along the periphery of the kitchen, whispering cooking tips and instructions for working the antique stove.

"You can take the night off, you know," I hissed at her.

"Ma'am will find a cup of fat in the icebox. It will keep the chicken from growing too dry," she responded.

After a while, Katherine joined me. She had finally shed her professional attire in favor of gray lounge pants and a Sex Pistols T-shirt, and she looked much more like the Katherine I remembered, the firecracker of a teenager trying desperately to be edgy.

Katherine found a bottle of red wine in the pantry. She had likely been looking for one, but was unhappy when she found it nonetheless. She grabbed it by the neck, held it in front of me. "Was Dad drinking again?" she asked, a question I didn't feel like answering.

"I think that may have been a housewarming gift," I said, which wasn't a lie. Our real estate agent had brought it over shortly after we moved in. Not feeling like explaining the decades of bad history this family had with that sort of thing, I hid the bottle away in the pantry. The fact that it had gone untouched all this time spoke more to Hal's dislike of red wine than to his sobriety.

After dinner, we lounged in the living room, on either side of one of the vintage sofas, and we enjoyed the sleepy haze that follows a big meal. Katherine twirled her fingers around her third glass of wine, swirling it and occasionally lowering her nose to the glass to inhale deeply before taking another sip. Sometime between when Katherine left for college and now, she had learned how to look proper while drinking wine. Lord knows she hadn't learned that from Hal or me.

Katherine must have started drinking when she was in college. Despite her punk rock inclinations and general air of rebellion, Katherine had been a surprisingly teetotaling teenager. She had been nettlesome and tempestuous, sure, but as far as I knew, she hadn't even had so much as a sip of beer at a party. She must have learned a lesson early on about the consequences of certain types of habits, and chosen instead to throw herself into her academics, a means of getting herself far away from such consequences. I told her once that I was proud of her for all that and she rolled her eyes at me. Somewhere along the way, she must've decided the habit wasn't so horrible, after all.

"The chicken was good," Katherine said, nose in her glass. "Very moist."

"Added in a cup of fat while it cooked," I said.

Katherine murmured in response and attended to her wine. We sat in silence, save for the buzzing of the occasional fly.

When I was pregnant with Katherine, I had been so excited to learn that I was having a daughter. I'd had my trepidations about having a child to begin with, especially considering the chaos that Noelle and I had experienced growing up. Our father, with his little ways, was often needier than Noelle and me combined, making him an additional child for my mother to raise. But finding out that I was having a girl had cast an exciting glow over the whole prospect. Katherine had been my little shadow when she was younger, running errands with me, crying if we had to be apart. It was nice.

"How's Claire?" I asked. I might as well take this opportunity to get to know my daughter again, before she busied herself with her work and her emails and her quest to find out what had happened to her father.

"Broke up," Katherine said into her glass.

"Oh. I'm so sorry, Katherine."

"Yeah. Well."

The air was tense. I needed to tread lightly here. We were five or six missteps away from an outburst. "When did it happen?"

"A few months ago," Katherine said.

Katherine and Claire had been together for a few years at least, although Katherine hadn't told us about her until they were serious, so it could've been longer for all I knew. Prior to Claire, Katherine had dated a few girlfriends with varying degrees of seriousness, none lasting longer than a few months. I always wondered what the common denominator was for all those brief relationships. Was it the type of women Katherine found herself drawn to? Was it a lack of desire for a longer commitment on Katherine's part? Was it Katherine's demanding nature or her tantrums, which must have grown tiresome to all women who were not her mother? Or was it something deeper, some flaw or brokenness within Katherine, something put there by Hal and me, despite our best efforts?

The length of Katherine's relationship with Claire had seemed like a good sign. Katherine was starting to calm herself, to settle. Katherine always spoke highly of Claire, albeit in her own guarded manner. Still, to those who knew Katherine—and I would argue that I knew her fairly well—it was evident that she cared deeply for Claire, more than she had cared for anybody in the past.

"She moved her stuff out," Katherine said, answering a question I didn't ask. "She's living closer to her parents now."

"Are you . . . okay?" I didn't know how this question would be received. Katherine and I had never really talked about her feelings in the context of romantic relationships, even when she had been a teenager. Of course, there had been more pressing issues in our lives at the time, and I struggled to remember if Katherine had even dated anyone during her adolescent years. She must have. I was just forgetting.

"I'm fine." Katherine took a long pull of her wine. That was that.

When she was younger, I had always thought Katherine more closely resembled Hal than me. She had his dark hair, his taut jaw, his piercing eyes. She definitely took on more of his personality than of mine, always preferring to be the one to set the rules rather than follow them. As I watched her on the couch now, I thought that she looked quite like me after all, her hard angles having softened with time, lines forming on her face just as they had formed over mine. And the way she tugged at her ear, absentmindedly—that was my mannerism, always had been. How funny that she should have picked up one of my quirks so unintentionally and kept it with her all this time, even through the distance, both geographical and emotional.

"Do you remember that time Bilboa got out of his cage?" Katherine asked.

Lost in my own thoughts, I was more startled by the sound of her voice than by the content of the question. Still, I blinked. "What?" I asked.

Katherine shrugged. "Random, I know," she said. "I was just thinking about him. Some nature documentary came on the other day. The narrator mentioned something about boa constrictors liking to have places to hide, and I thought, *Yeah, they sure do.*" She glanced at me. "Do you remember?"

I chuckled. "Yes, I do. You came out of your bedroom looking more guilty than I had ever seen you, and I thought, *She's really done something wrong this time.* The way you looked, I thought you might have killed someone."

"I thought you guys were about to kill *me,*" Katherine said. "That was the most scared I ever was to tell you guys something. And that *includes* coming out."

"You were just standing there, looking like you were about to confess to serial arson, and giving me a panic attack. And then you said—and I remember this exactly—"

"He's gone on an unexpected journey," Katherine and I said simultaneously, both starting to laugh.

"It took me so long to even figure out who you were *talking* about," I said.

"And then you went back to my room to *check,*" Katherine giggled, "as if I would have misplaced a five-foot snake in his own cage."

"We tore up the house looking for him." I laughed, picturing us racing around the old house, panicked. "And calling his name, for God's sake. Like he was a dog."

"Bilboa, Bilboa," Katherine mimicked, and clicked her tongue against the roof of her mouth. "C'mere, boy. . . ."

"You wouldn't think it would be so hard to find a giant snake," I said. "But how long did we look? Hours?"

Katherine's eyes started to glisten. Her wineglass was swaying. "And . . . do you remember . . . ?"

Oh, I remembered. I could barely get the words out. "Your father . . . peeling out of his office like it was on fire . . ."

"*Screaming . . .*"

"A full two octaves higher . . ."

"*That . . . goddamn hobbit . . . almost bit me. . . .*" Katherine wheezed, bent at the waist. Her laughter was contagious, and I gladly let myself fall victim to it. For several moments, the only sounds in the room were giggles and Katherine's occasional snorts.

Hal had been fairly mad about Bilboa, and the search party we had formed was fueled more by fear than by amusement at the time. I was relieved to see that Katherine had colored the memory with humor now, especially when it would have been so easy to paint it the usual dismal shade of so many of her teenage memories. Hal's discovery of Bilboa in his office had played a large role in his eventually convincing me to get rid of the snake, but I didn't need to mention that today.

Katherine dabbed at her eyes and nose, still giggling. She took another sip of her wine, properly aerated now after the jostling it had received. After a time, her chuckles and sighs and sniffs faded into silence.

"Claire said I was angry all the time."

Katherine's sudden words startled me more than any of the pranksters in the house ever had. I looked at her, blinking and soundless. She stared into the distance, clutching her wine like a security blanket.

"She said living with me was like walking on eggshells. That she never knew what would set me off. She said it made her tired." Katherine's mouth twitched, a frown trying to fight its way onto her face. "She said she didn't want to be tired anymore."

I knew the feeling.

"She has a new girlfriend now," Katherine said, her voice bitter. "Some fucking therapist or something. Someone well-adjusted who doesn't get angry, I bet."

I considered asking her how she knew this but thought better of it. My next move was crucial, and I could spot a bad response when I saw one.

"I tried, Mom. I really tried." Katherine's eyes were starting to glisten again, but she wasn't laughing. "I know how I am. I don't want to be this way. I've seen what . . ." She waved her hand as if to erase the sentence she had inadvertently started. "I went to therapy. I took medication. I cut back on the drinking. I thought I was getting better. But, apparently, I wasn't."

This was more information about Katherine than I had received in years, likely since she was a child. I felt lost and she still wasn't looking at me. I considered touching her, an attempt at comfort, but sometimes when you touched things around here, you regretted it.

Katherine's face was wet. She finished off her wine in a large gulp, then stared at the glass as she would have at an enemy. Her lips were starting to adopt a maroon hue.

Finally, her eyes, glinting and tinged with red around the corners, met mine. "I'm so scared I'm going to be just like him," she said.

When Katherine was younger, getting her to stop crying had been easy. She usually wanted something, and I could give it to her. A toy? Sure. A cookie before dinner? Ill-advised, but why not?

A five-foot boa constrictor that eats frozen mice and escapes periodically? Sounds like a fun adventure! I could get her what she
needed, bandage up any injury she had, tell her it would all be
okay, and usually be right. I didn't have many jobs in this world,
but keeping Katherine from crying was an important one. And
right now all signs would suggest that I had failed.

"Katherine . . ."

She gestured at her empty glass, made a crude mimic of a
laugh. "As if we needed any more evidence."

"Katherine . . ."

"I know *you'll* love me, anyway." Her mouth twitched. "But
will anyone else?"

I had lines here. Somewhere inside of me was the right thing
to say, the thing that would make everything better, stop Katherine from crying. The answer she couldn't get from therapy (she
had gone to *therapy?*) or medication (she had taken *medication?*).
My lines were in an old book somewhere, tucked far away on the
bookshelf of my mind and covered in dust. I had misplaced it.
Perhaps I had thrown it away years ago, not thinking.

I was too late. Katherine wrapped up her grief with a shake of
her head and a sharp exhalation. "Anyway." A tight laugh served as
the ribbon wrapping up the moment, never again to be undone.
"Might as well finish off the wine, I suppose." She launched off the
couch, glass in hand, and plodded towards the kitchen, finger swiping at her eyes. Apparently, cutting back on the drinking was not on
the docket for tonight.

There was no point in my saying anything now to make everything better. Katherine seemed done with show-and-tell and was
taking her toys back home to play by herself, as she usually preferred. Still, I searched my mind for something that might fix the
situation. Muscle memory and all.

"Mom," Katherine's voice called from the kitchen, "did you know you had a kettle boiling on the stove?"

Goddamnit, Fredricka. Talk about muscle memory.

"Oh, um . . . yes, I did." The lie was evident. "Water. For tea."

"It's really boiling. I think it's done. I'm going to take it off the stove, okay?"

"Yes, dear, that's fine."

Katherine walked back over to the living room. She stood in the entranceway, looking at me quizzically. "Sorry. I just get nervous leaving things on the stove when we're so far away from the kitchen. It's a quirk I have."

Of course I knew this was a quirk of Katherine's. Because it was a quirk of *mine.* Katherine had grown up hearing me fret over the stove, anxious about leaving the kitchen with pans on the burners for even a second. I'd go on about things catching fire, while Katherine and Hal just rolled their eyes at me. How many times had Katherine been making herself a grilled cheese and darted out of the kitchen for just a second—just to get something from the other room, she'd say—only to be sent back by me shouting, *Don't you leave that stove unattended?* Countless.

"I know, dear." *The stove wasn't unattended,* I thought. *Fredricka was there.*

Katherine was looking at me the same way I had looked at her when she was four years old and told me she could pour her own milk from the gallon jug into her cereal bowl. "Do you want tea?" she asked.

I sighed and lifted myself off the couch. I *didn't* want tea, but what kind of person would I look like if I said I didn't? A crazy woman who forgot about a kettle full of boiling water for tea she didn't even plan to drink. I decided to have a conversation with Fredricka later and tell her to calm down with the tea for a little while. She wouldn't like it, but she had already agreed to keep her distance from Katherine for me, hadn't she?

But when I got to the kitchen, I saw that Fredricka had left out the chamomile and a jar of honey, and that sounded pretty good, after all.

SEVEN

There are rules to these things. Everything is survivable.

After Hal and I learned that Father Cyrus' blessing was going to get us only so far, we needed to figure out our own solutions. Rather, *I* needed to figure out solutions; Hal was never particularly solution focused. I, however, was a bit of a pro.

The thing is, every situation, no matter how unusual, has rules. They might be strange rules, and they might be difficult to figure out, but once they are learned, they can be followed. And everything works out.

Charred remains of a woman crawling out of the fireplace with claws for hands—screaming and getting ashy footprints on the walls whenever a fire is lit? Stop lighting fires. Easy. Fires are lovely in the winter, but they aren't essential. You can do without.

Birds snapping their necks against the nice clean windows at all hours of the day and night? Get rid of the bird feeders. Fewer birds coming by to eat mean fewer birds sailing into loud and violent suicide missions that scare the bejesus out of everyone on otherwise quiet afternoons. Sure, you might have always dreamed of a lush backyard full of fat, chirping birds, but you also dreamed of a backyard free of mangled, ant-infested bird corpses. Compromises must be made. There are rules.

Milky-eyed boy hovering in Hal's office, biting anyone who gets too close? You might assume that rule to be simple—don't get within biting range. Hal, however, wanted a more lasting solution. That would be a bit trickier, especially since the boy doesn't talk. Some investigation will be required, a trip or two to the local library to browse through old newspaper clippings. It isn't ideal and it certainly seems like the behavior of someone who's more than a little off-balance, but the clippings reveal information about the boy's mother, so it's well worth the sideways glances. Sure, digging her up will never be the ideal way to spend an afternoon and her bones don't keep him away forever, but a temporary fix is still a fix. It's nice to feel a sort of control over these types of things. Control is important.

Some problems seem like problems, but they aren't actually problems. The children who arrive in September, Angelica and her friends, they aren't really problems. They appear one by one and point down into the basement. Some of them are *very* wounded, upsetting to look at, but just because something is upsetting doesn't mean it's harmful. You would be surprised just how many upsetting things aren't harmful in the end, if you consider the definition of "harm" in the strictest sense. The rule is to ignore the children and walk around them when they appear, not walk *through* them—that would be rude, and it tends to evoke a fairly strong vomiting reaction.

Jasper, the crumpled man in the upstairs closet, isn't really a problem either. He's hard to look at, sure, but he never leaves the closet and the matchstick that he keeps in those splintered fingers never catches flame, no matter how much he flicks it. It's terrible what he did to Fredricka and Blythe all those years ago, but you can live with something without approving of it—those are two different things. You can live with many, many things you find deplorable. Especially when there are rules.

Still, some problems don't have solutions, and the rule is just to cope. Take, for instance, the blood dripping down the walls every September. Logic would dictate that the rule should be to clean it up, but that course of action is never particularly effective. So it seems that the rule is simply to do nothing. Sure, you can investigate how far the blood makes it down the stairs as the days progress if you are feeling a spark of scientific curiosity, but in the long run, what good does that do? Knowing how much blood is on the stairs doesn't change how much blood is on the stairs. The best course of action is to simply try to walk around the blood and keep the bloody footprints to a minimum. You don't want to make the situation worse, after all.

September doesn't have a solution either, thanks to Master Vale down in the basement. Sure, Father Cyrus' blessing makes it better, an aspirin to quell a migraine, but the storm of September makes landfall every year like clockwork. These things are cyclical. It starts with the blood and the moaning, which turns into clotty red waterfalls and screaming. Angelica arrives, followed by more and more of her little friends—broken, devastated bodies of children darting around the house, pointing. Fredricka is a mess; Blythe is testy; things get out of place. The house becomes a conductor for chaos. Pranks turn vicious. There's only so much you can do during times like these. Best to keep your head on a swivel. Brace for impact.

That said, it isn't all difficult. There are nice times, times when everyone is calm and September is months away. There are times when Elias is easy to dodge and the birds give it a bit of a rest and Fredricka makes dinner and permits assistance with the potatoes. Those times are almost enough to make you think you've done it, finally made the house a half-decent place to live, with no screaming or bleeding walls or massacred children. Of course, nothing lasts forever—September is always right around the corner, exactly as planned. Still, if the rules are followed, the nice times can be even nicer.

But then there's the basement. There is really just one rule for the basement—don't go down there. Make sure the Bible pages stay taped to the back of the door, no gaps visible. Keep the door closed and boarded up at all times. Don't open the door, not even a crack. And definitely not in September.

These rules, they keep things in order. They make life bearable. You will find that everything, even the apparently unbearable things, can be bearable to some degree. It is all in how you handle them. The perspective you take. How quickly you can learn what to do and what not to do and act accordingly.

There are rules to these things. Everything is survivable, even this.

EIGHT

When I got up the next morning, Katherine's car was gone. Very likely, she had gone ahead to the police station and couldn't be bothered to wait for me to go along. I checked the clock—nine fifteen. She was eager.

Fredricka was making herself busy in the kitchen, taking advantage of Katherine's absence and humming a little song to herself. She had tea and toast ready for me, an assortment of jams lined up on the counter.

"It would seem ma'am's daughter has gone to the police," she said, not turning away from the dish she was drying.

"Filing the missing person report, I suppose." I sipped at the tea. English breakfast tea, two lumps of sugar. Just as I liked it. "God bless her for trying."

Fredricka made a small harrumph. I had a feeling she was not a fan of God. But then, if I were in her position, I doubted I would be either. She continued drying the dishes while I spread jam on the toast. Blackberry today. It reminded me of how Hal and I used to coexist together in the kitchen, me preparing some meal or another, him chopping vegetables or sometimes just reading a book at the table. Spending time together without paying particular attention to each other.

"Sleep now, my darling. Don't you cry," Fredricka sang. *"Mommy's gonna stay with you all through the night."*

When I woke up this morning, there had been a smear of red on the wall just above my head. I stood on the mattress to get a closer look. Blood. A single drop starting to ooze down the wall. "Shit," I had said aloud to nobody, or perhaps to many people, knowing this place. In a few days, the blood would be pouring down the walls. A few days after that, it would be flowing down the stairs in thick waterfalls. Would Katherine still be here then? Signs pointed to yes, unless a miracle happened. And this place didn't seem particularly prone to miracles.

"Ne'er shall you worry. Ne'er shall you mourn."

I had hoped Father Cyrus' blessing would stave off the storm longer than this. Perhaps the premature termination of his ritual had weakened the effect of the prayers, like expired medication. Or perhaps it was the boards, being taken off the basement door, one less barrier between us and Master Vale. Regardless, putting the boards back on the door was a nonstarter so long as Katherine was here, and I doubted I'd be able to coax Father Cyrus back over anytime soon. One must persevere.

"You won't see your sweet little sis no more," Fredricka sang.

I munched on my toast, leaning over the counter. "I wish Katherine wasn't involving the police in all this. It makes me nervous, having them poke around this house."

"Needs must—," Fredricka started.

"—when the devil drives," I finished. "I know."

Fredricka glanced at me out of the corner of her eye—her good eye—and smiled. *"She ain't in her room. No, she's long gone,"* she continued singing. *"But you'll see her sweet smilin' face 'fore long."*

A rapping noise came from the living room. "Your friend," Fredricka said. She collected my plate as I went to investigate. Indeed, there was Edie, face pressed against the living room window, peering inside.

"How's Katherine?" she asked as we settled into the rocking chairs outside. "I don't see her car."

"She went out this morning," I said, "to file a missing person report."

Edie made a humming noise. "That girl means business."

"She certainly does."

"I see you still have the flies." Edie motioned backwards into the living room with her head.

I groaned. "Tell me about it. They'll be in there forever."

"Laying eggs." Edie's nose crinkled.

"They came out of a human man," I pointed out. "While he was levitating. Can they reproduce like normal flies?"

Edie considered. "Fair question. Do you think they might not?"

"Who knows? I probably can't Google it."

"Probably not."

The day looked like it was going to be pleasant, blue skies with a smattering of clouds. I could hear birds chirping in the distance. It was a nice change from the sounds of birds suiciding on the side of the house.

"The blood is coming back," I said.

"Oh dear." Edie looked at me, her expression grave. "That's sooner than expected, right?"

I nodded.

"Do you think that has anything to do with . . . ?" Edie motioned at her mouth with her fingers, pantomiming flies buzzing out of a person.

I shrugged. "Maybe this house is developing an immunity to religion."

Edie snorted. "Wouldn't *that* be a hoot?"

Edie and I spent much of the remainder of the morning on the front porch, rocking and talking and laughing. It was enough to make me forget about all the chaos that reigned in the house just behind me. I was very thankful for Edie's friendship.

Before we moved here, before the struggles of marriage and life leapt in our way, Hal and I had talked and laughed too. We used to get on famously, Hal and I. We could talk for hours and hours about anything, from the pitfalls of organized religion to the staying power of forty-five rpm records. Of course, the way life had ended up going for us, we talked and laughed less and less as the years wore on. We started getting it back after Katherine left for college, before we bought the house. For a moment, it felt as it had right when we first started dating. Then we moved here, and there were arguably more things to talk about, but none of them were particularly humorous.

Katherine's car screeched into the driveway later that afternoon and the front door slammed behind her. I heard her stomp through the house from my studio, where I sat, paintbrush in hand, staring at a blank canvas. I had foolishly thought I could get some work in before Katherine got home and started tearing the house apart. Best-laid plans and whatnot.

"Goddamn small-town police," she yelled at nobody. "Good for nothing."

I sighed to the canvas. What could I paint here? I was still thinking of children's faces and found myself a little stuck.

Katherine leaned into the doorway of my studio. My back was to her, but I could've told you what she looked like. Arms crossed, face screwed up, eyes glowing fire. "I bet the only reason they even did the report is because they knew I wasn't leaving."

"You got the report filed?" I tapped my paintbrush against my mouth. Maybe a child playing, a wild smile, running through a field of red?

"No thanks to those cops. I basically had to bully them into it. Isn't it their *job*?"

"But you got it done. That's good." A child in the foreground, not playing anymore. In the background, a man, a wild smile. The child looking over her shoulder at the man. A field of red.

"Apparently, *grown men* can just *leave*. They're only 'missing' if they're a *child*. Apparently, it doesn't matter if they haven't been answering their phone, haven't been seen in weeks. Apparently, disappearing without a trace is a privilege of adult men."

"Your father certainly exercised that privilege." Now I was seeing just a door. The basement door, to be precise. Also red. I shook my head at the canvas. Too boring.

"I bet half the information is wrong. I didn't even know the answers to most of their questions."

"I could've come with you," I said, "if you had waited until I got up."

"Yeah. Well." Katherine didn't elaborate, but her message was clear enough. *You had a month to get the police involved and you didn't. Your work here is no longer needed.* "They said they'd be by the house in a few days to talk to you. They have some questions."

Now all I was seeing was red. No longer a field, just a canvas of deep red in thick, globby strokes.

"Oh," I said, doing my best to sound nonchalant. "They're coming to the house?"

"Yeah. God knows when, though. They said they'll call before they come. If I haven't heard from them by—"

"I can go down to the station," I said, perhaps a little too quickly. Who knew what this place would look like by the time the police came? Would they want to look around? Investigate? I had a feeling that cops might not be too keen on blood dripping down the walls of my bedroom, even if it wasn't Hal's. And what if they stumbled upon Fredricka, a walking crime scene? What if Elias returned and bit one of them? What if they wanted to look in the basement? No, none of this was good.

Katherine was on her phone, typing away. "No," she said absently. "They said they'll come down here to talk to you. I guess because this is where he was last seen."

I put down my brush. Painting was not going to happen in the foreseeable future.

Katherine finished up on her phone and placed her hands on her hips as if she were some sort of superhero. "Well," she said, "I don't want today to be a waste. I'm going to see what I can find in Dad's office." With that, she was gone, imaginary cape fluttering behind her.

As soon as she was gone, a bird crashed into the window, leaving a small smattering of blood and feathers in its wake. It actually made me jump.

KATHERINE WAS ALREADY BANGING AWAY IN HAL'S OFFICE BY THE TIME I MADE MY way upstairs, my studio cleaned and ready to be neglected until October. She knelt on the floor behind his desk, shoving papers aside and digging through the drawers. Apparently she'd managed to jimmy a few of them open, and I hoped not in a way that damaged the wood. So far as I could tell, she was still on her desperate search for a key. She hauled a handful of papers out of a drawer with a huff and flipped through them haphazardly.

"Nothing. Garbage. Meaningless." She slammed the papers on the desk, not noticing how close she set them to the edge. They fluttered to the floor, and I flinched. This was going to be hell to clean up once she was finished, and it was unlikely that Katherine would stick around to help.

"Anything I can do, dear?" I stealthily picked up the fallen papers, trying to arrange them in a stack. Someone needed to get to this mess before Fredricka. That woman had enough on her plate.

"You can materialize the fucking key." Katherine finished flipping through another handful of papers, then flung them onto the desk so they slid across the surface and flew onto the floor in front of me.

I bent over to pick up the new papers, and sorted them into the stack I already had in my hands. "I'm afraid I'm not much help there. I didn't even know he locked those cabinets."

Katherine disappeared behind the desk. She was all arms as she pulled random debris and homeless cables from drawers, scattering everything at her sides. "Yeah, and that just tells me he has something he wants to hide."

"He was always particular about who went into his office." One reason Hal didn't care for Elias and his unwavering insistence on lingering in this room.

"But he didn't use to lock everything up, did he?"

I honestly wasn't sure. I had never investigated. Unlike Elias, I'd only had to be told once to stay the hell out of Hal's office. It had been easier that way.

Katherine finished with the drawer and turned her attention to the top of the desk. She pushed more papers onto the floor. She shifted Hal's monitor to the side in a way that made me flinch.

She lifted the keyboard and kicked up the layer of dust that had settled over it. She waved a hand in front of her face, fighting back a sneeze.

"Don't you guys ever clean in here?" she asked, grabbing a cup of pens from the top of the desk and tipping it upside down. Pens clattered across the desk, then tumbled to the floor.

I closed my eyes, took a deep breath, counted to ten. I tried not to think about how angry Hal would be if he saw this scene.

Katherine lifted a letter tray off of the desk and shook it upside down over the floor. More papers scattered across the floor in a puff of dust.

Chamomile tea, I willed, wishing that somehow Fredricka could hear my thoughts. *When this is over, I need a cup of chamomile tea.*

Katherine sat back behind the desk. She gazed upon her mess.

"Fuck this," she said after a moment, hoisting herself from the floor and storming out of the room.

I gathered the pens one by one, putting them back in the cup. The letter tray had broken apart when Katherine tossed it to the side and I investigated the pieces, trying to fit the top of the tray back onto the bottom. It looked like a little plastic latch had broken, but maybe if I glued it . . .

Katherine burst back into the room. "Mom, did you know you have water boiling on the stove?"

For chamomile tea, I hoped.

"Anyway, I turned it off. Seriously, Mom, you need to pay more attention." Katherine herself did not seem to be paying much attention, even to her own words. She made a beeline for the cabinets behind Hal's desk, brandishing something in her hand.

The crowbar.

I dropped the letter tray. It cracked apart further. "What the hell, Katherine? Where did you find that?" I had stored it under the sink after the unfortunate basement blessing. Had she gone through the kitchen cabinets this morning? How much of this house did she plan on investigating?

"It was on the counter, Mom." She knelt down by the cabinets.

Goddamnit, Fredricka. She and I would need to have another conversation about our respective definitions of "helpful" behavior.

Katherine positioned the crowbar in between two of the locked cabinet doors. She slapped at the curved edge with the heel of her hand, firmly jamming the sharp point in between the doors. I saw the wood scrape and chip around it.

I darted to her side. "Katherine . . ."

Katherine made a twisting motion with her arms and the sharp edge dug deeper into the space between the cabinet doors. I heard a cracking noise as the wood started to splinter.

"Jesus Christ," I said. "Be *careful.*" We had spent a lot of money on those cabinets. They were exactly as Hal had dreamed—thick, bright wood, with ornate designs carved into the exterior of each door. Oh, Hal would be mad. He would be so mad.

Katherine wasn't listening. She grunted and planted a foot against the base of the cabinets, using her body weight as leverage as she yanked at the crowbar. More cracking noises. A shard of wood flew off the door.

"Katherine, wait!" Another shard of wood landed near my hand. "*Shit.* These cabinets were *expensive*, Katherine."

"Sorry." Katherine heaved, breath heavy as she struggled, not very sorry at all. "I don't think . . . there's any other . . . choice." She let out a yell, yanking at the crowbar with the strength of an Olympic rowing team and the door finally gave way, splintering around the lock and swinging open.

The cabinet was filled with empty bottles.

"Jesus Christ." Katherine's face sparkled with sweat. She wiped at her brow, eyes wide and mouth agape as she stared into the cabinet. She reached in and grabbed a bottle. Jack Daniel's. That was Hal's brand all right. Katherine turned her dumbfounded gaze towards me, handed me the bottle. Unsure of what to do, I took it from her. "Did you know?" she asked.

"I . . ." I didn't know. Hadn't known. After last September, Hal had spent increasing amounts of time in his office. He sometimes slept in here, slumped over his desk. He always kept the door closed, and—given how clearly he had expressed his feelings about people entering his office—that was as good as a dead bolt. I never bothered him. That was the rule.

He'd mumbled something or other about working on a new novel. I had an inkling that there wasn't any new novel—he never shared any details about it or let me read a few draft chapters like he usually did—but I believed him anyway. When Hal told you something, you listened. You believed him.

"I didn't know," I said quietly. For the first time since Katherine had arrived, I heard honesty in my voice. My voice wasn't that of a concerned mother trying to keep her daughter from being sad or afraid, but of a woman who had just learned something earth-shattering, like that mole people lived under the earth's crust and they were *not* friendly, or that stepping on cracks—in fact—*did* break backs.

Katherine let out a breath filled with the kind of relief of someone who had been expecting terrible news for quite some time and the world had finally delivered.

We sat in silence, both staring at the bottle. I turned it over in my hand. A tiny droplet of amber liquid moved about in the bottom, a leftover hardly worth remembering. How long had it taken him to finish this bottle, locked up in the office by himself? No ice in here, just warm whiskey, neat. Had he used a glass, or drunk straight from the bottle, not in the mood to pretend anymore?

Katherine's attention drifted back towards the cabinets. "Look at all these," she said, pulling the empty bottles out of the cabinet one by one. "One, two, three, four . . ." She handed the empties to me as she pulled them out. Unsure of what she wanted me to do with them, I started lining them up alongside the desk.

Katherine pulled open the adjoining cabinet door, free to move now that its partner had been unceremoniously broken open. This cabinet was filled with bottles too, also empty. "Son of a *bitch*," she hissed, yanking at the bottles with much less care. The glass clattered; a bottle tipped over and landed on the floor with the Jack Daniel's label faceup.

"Katherine, *careful*." I reached a hand into the cabinet to steady the wavering bottles. "We don't want broken glass everywhere."

Katherine was still counting. "Seven, eight, nine . . ."

Maybe I had known. The way you can know something without really being aware of it. The little part of you that, every day, is aware that, at some point in the future, your body will cease to be alive and the cause of it all could be natural and peaceful or violent and quite unpleasant indeed—but still you keep dusting the picture frames and going to the post office to pick up stamps, largely unperturbed by your knowledge. Living with Hal for so long, of course I knew what whiskey smelled like behind a closed door. I knew what it meant when Hal's eyes were only raised to half-mast and he tripped into walls. I knew what it meant when I heard wet, choking coughs coming from the bathroom late at night. I knew that, even though for years it had seemed that all this had been straightened out, these things were cyclical.

"*Son of a bitch.*" Katherine grabbed the crowbar from the floor and swung herself towards the adjoining cabinets. It took only one violent twist of her arms for the crowbar to crack the doors open.

More bottles. Empty.

"*Fuck.*" Katherine snaked her arm behind the bottles and pulled them out in one sweeping motion before turning her attention to the final set of cabinets. The bottles clattered and bounced on the floor. The fact that none shattered was something of a miracle.

Fredricka might have known too, not that we had talked about it directly. Fredricka and Hal had never formed much of a relationship, and she tended to steer clear of him, electing to do her chores only after he left the room. She rarely even referred to him by name, called him simply "ma'am's husband" when talking to me. One day, while I was sitting in my studio, trying to paint while ignoring loud thumping and crashing from Hal's office above, Fredricka appeared behind me. *A leopard cannot change his spots*, she said before moving into the living room to fluff the pillows.

Can't imagine why he'd want to, I thought. *The spots are part of what makes leopards so beautiful.*

Katherine cracked open the third set of cabinets. The door blocked my view, but, based on her reaction, I assumed this cabinet was filled with bottles as well. I busied myself with tidying the empties that clattered onto the floor while Katherine cursed beside me. It would seem I was done telling her to watch her language for the day.

Katherine held out a bottle to me, her fist clenched around its neck. This one still had whiskey in it, a band of amber that swirled around the bottom third of the bottle. "We found where he left off," she said.

I didn't count the bottles, but I'm sure Katherine had an accurate tally in her mind. She might've even been able to calculate how quickly Hal had been finishing off these bottles if she had known when he started drinking. I didn't know the precise date myself, but I had a sense he had begun immediately after last September.

Katherine pulled a book out of the cabinet and examined it, her brow furrowed. She handed the book to me. *The Shadows and You: How to Cope with Mental Illness.*

"What's *that* all about?" she asked.

"I have no idea," I said.

I was still staring at the book in my hand, cursing Hal for his lack of faith and his damning choice in literature, when I heard Katherine laugh beside me. It was a thin, desperate laugh, like she had been given the choice between laughing and sobbing and reluctantly chosen the former. I looked over at her, and she had a cigar box open in her lap. The lid obscured my view of its contents.

"What do you have there?" I asked.

She laughed harder, then tossed the container onto the floor in front of me. A rainbow of shimmering coins bounced from the box, glinting as they rained onto the floor.

"His goddamn AA chips," she said.

NINE

The police came by the next day.

The moaning had started up again the night before, and it seemed more insistent this time. With the moaning—before it gets to screaming—you can swear you hear your name, little whispered commands. *Margaret, help me. Margaret, come find me. Margaret, I need you.* It's very disconcerting. You'd think you could tune it out—like being able to sleep in the same bed as somebody who snores, which, incidentally, I had done for more than thirty years with Hal—but there is something in your brain that jolts awake when you hear your name. All that is to say, I did not get a very good night's sleep, and when the police arrived, I was in no mood.

I worried that Katherine might have been kept awake by the moaning as well, but when I descended the stairs, I found her sitting in the kitchen, seemingly well rested. She was scribbling in the notebook she'd been keeping since she'd arrived, filling it with theories about Hal's whereabouts. She barely noticed me when I entered.

There was no kettle boiling on the stove. I felt a petty, spoiled frustration over having to make my own tea and reminded myself that at least Katherine would have no reason to think I was constantly turning the stove on and leaving the room. Then I noticed three stacks of plates, usually stored in the cupboard, sitting out on the counter. *Uh-oh.* Fredricka must have reached the phase of her September shenanigans in which she felt compelled to stack objects. This would become only more of an irritant as the month continued and she switched from plates to furniture.

I tried to covertly move the plates back into the cupboard. "How did you sleep, dear?"

"Pretty good," Katherine said, not looking up from her notes. "What's with the plates?" She gestured with her pen.

Couldn't get anything past Katherine. "Oh, I was cleaning out the cupboards last night. Things get dusty when you don't use them, you know." I could hear the speed in my voice. "Anyway, I took them out and cleaned the shelves, but then I was too tired to put the plates back. Lazy of me, I know."

The clatter of plates returning to the cabinets temporarily overpowered the scratch of Katherine's pen on paper. "When did you do that?" she asked. "You went to bed before me."

"Yes. Well. I couldn't sleep." That at least was true. I smiled my best *trust me* smile, just in case Katherine was looking. She was not.

"Sounds rough," Katherine said to her notebook. "Anyway, the police called. They'll be by in a few hours to talk to you. So you might want to shower."

The blood in my bedroom was even more noticeable this

morning, not exactly the sight I had been hoping for when I opened my swollen eyes after a few short hours of broken sleep. I wiped the blood away with my nightshirt, but it didn't do much good. I wondered if I should start keeping bleach or stain remover in my bedroom, at least until Katherine left or the police wouldn't be coming by anymore. The thought of scrubbing away at a bloody wall—inhaling sharp smells of nickel and bleach—before having even a single sip of tea was not a particularly pleasant one, but sacrifices must be made.

As Katherine promised, two bored-looking police officers arrived within a few hours. Officers Jones and McDouglas. Jones was a stoic middle-aged woman with dark hair and a flat, no-nonsense mouth. Her baggy eyes landed on me and did little wavering from there on out. McDouglas was a less intimidating presence, with a jolly face and a potbelly protruding over his uniform belt. His eyes tended to focus on the house, looking with appreciation at our decor. I offered the officers something to drink. Jones declined but McDouglas accepted a glass of water. I took a glass from the stack that had appeared on the kitchen counter just a few minutes prior to their arrival.

McDouglas waved his hand in front of his face as he walked into the kitchen. "What's with all the flies?"

Jones sat down with me at the kitchen table, notebook flipped open, while McDouglas ambled about the kitchen. He didn't appear to be investigating anything in particular, just letting his eyes wander, killing time. Katherine joined us, although her presence was unnecessary.

"Name of the missing person?" Jones asked, pen ready.

"I already told you this," Katherine said.

"Harold Martin Hartman," I said. "He goes by Hal."

"Age?"

"I already told you this too," Katherine said.

"Fifty-nine," I said, ignoring Katherine.

"Physical description?" Jones asked, also ignoring Katherine.

"About six feet tall. Lean build, I would say. His hair used to be brown, but it's been gray for a few years now. He wears it short. No facial hair—could never stand it. Says it itches."

"Any scars? Birthmarks?"

"A mole on his right shoulder." There was also a circular scar on his ankle that looked suspiciously like a bite mark, but I decided to omit that one.

"What was he wearing when you last saw him?"

"Jesus, that was over a month ago," Katherine said. "How the hell is she supposed to remember—"

"He was wearing a dark blue shirt. Chicago Cubs logo. Kind of ratty—he's had that shirt for years. Blue jeans. He had this brown jacket with him—kind of a bomber style, you know, with the fur around the neck?" I smiled. Hal loved that jacket, loved it enough that it was the only thing he chose to take with him the day he left, aside from the clothes on his back.

Katherine looked at me, shocked.

"Good memory," McDouglas said from the other side of the kitchen, eyes out the window.

"What kind of car does he drive?" Jones continued. "And if you have the plate number that would be helpful."

Katherine snorted. Jones' eyes darted up from her notebook, eyebrow raised in question.

I sighed. "Hal doesn't drive."

"Anymore," Katherine added, eyes on me pointedly.

Jones waited for my explanation.

"I'm afraid my husband used to have a problem with drinking."

"Used to?" Katherine snorted again.

I ignored her. "Several years back. Anyway, I'm afraid he was, you know, intoxicated behind the wheel. I suppose a few too many times. And . . ." I waved my hand. *Catch my drift?*

Jones' lips thinned. She jotted something down in her notebook.

"It makes things easier, anyway," I said, although no question had been asked. "We just sold the second car. One less expense. You know how much money it takes to maintain a car. Gas, insurance, repairs. We could put that money towards something else."

"Jesus Christ, Mom." I *heard* Katherine's eyes roll.

Jones wasn't interested in extra details. "And Hal has been missing since . . ."

"August second. A little over a month ago."

"And have you had any communication with him since that time?"

"None."

"Have you tried to contact him?"

I paused. I hadn't. What would've been the point of that, anyway?

Katherine was looking at me like I had just told her I believed in Bigfoot, and, considering all the things I'd seen in this house, I supposed I might. "Mom?"

"Katherine tried to call him several times," I offered. "She said that the calls always went to voicemail. Then his voicemail was full."

"You didn't try to call him at *all*?" Katherine asked. Jones might have let my inadvertent admission slide, but Katherine wasn't about to.

"It happens sometimes," McDouglas said. He peered into the dining room. "I like the color you guys painted the walls in here. What's the name of it?"

"Tell me what was going on the day he went missing," Jones said.

I glanced at Katherine. This was the part I had been dreading. "Um, I would really prefer to talk about this without my daughter present."

"Absolutely not." Katherine looked like I had just told her where she could shove it.

Jones glanced between the two of us, pen in hand, no help at all.

"Katherine," I said, "some of this, it's personal between your father and me."

"Tough shit," Katherine said. "I want to know what happened to him, Mom. I want to find him." And that was that.

I looked back at Jones, who motioned for me to start talking. I sighed. "Hal and I had been having a disagreement."

"You mean a *fight*," Katherine said.

"You can let your mother tell it how she wants," Jones said.

"She probably meant a fight, though," Katherine said, arms crossed over her chest, pouting.

"A disagreement," I said.

"What were you two disagreeing about?" Jones asked.

"Hal wanted to leave," I said.

"Leave you?"

"No, leave the house. He wanted to move out, wanted us *both* to move out." Hal would never have wanted to leave *me*. Throughout all we had been through together, that was the one thing he had been insistent upon. Neither of us was going anywhere, least of all me. It was endearing. I chose to find it endearing.

"Why did he want to move out?" Jones asked.

"Yeah, why?" McDouglas called out from the foyer, where he was examining the wooden banister. "This house is fantastic. Are these the original hardwood floors?" I hoped McDouglas would keep his ogling limited to the first floor. A trickle of blood had probably already reappeared on the wall above my bed, and I had a feeling it might distract him from his sightseeing.

"He didn't like it here," I said. It was the truth—a very abridged version of the truth.

"And you didn't want to move," Jones said. It was a statement, not a question.

"Well, no, of course not. This house . . ." I sighed. "Are you a homeowner?" Jones nodded. "Well, you know how hard the whole process is. You find the perfect house, go through all the rigmarole of buying it—the bids, the loan applications. Neither of us really had a permanent home while we were growing up, so, having a home that was *ours*, that we *loved*, was important to us. We poured so much of ourselves into this house. We found all this furniture, decorated all these rooms. This house is *ours*. It is *us*, and it is so beautiful." I gestured around at the ornate kitchen cabinets, the perfectly painted walls, the—yes, *original*—hardwood floors. "This is our home," I said. This was the truth, unabridged. No pranksters were going to drive me out of my home. Not when everything was survivable.

"Right," Jones said. "The day he left, was that the first time you two had this . . . disagreement?"

Oh, we had been having escalating versions of this disagreement for months. Eleven months, to be precise, beginning immediately after last September. That had been our third September in the house, and I had believed that we had Septembers handled—or that *I* did, at least. Sure, we had made some mistakes last September, but mistakes were simply opportunities for learning. We would problem-solve, do even better this year. Hal disagreed. He wanted life to be normal, to be perfect, and he didn't seem to understand that that wasn't how life worked. He also seemed to think that we had almost died last September, but he was just being dramatic. We were fine in the end. We learned our lesson. Hal certainly learned, anyway.

"No," I responded.

"Tell me a bit about what your relationship was like. Before he left."

To use the word "relationship" seemed overly kind to me. Throughout our years together, Hal and I had waxed and waned in closeness and intimacy, distance and anger. However, towards the end of our time together in the house, Hal and I had existed together in the same way that I existed with Jasper in the upstairs closet or Blythe in the fireplace. Was that a relationship? Perhaps, using the broadest definition possible. Still, we had seen harder times, and the pranksters in the house were good reminders that things could always be worse. Hal had a difficult time seeing that, but I never did.

Katherine was watching me like she would the climax of an action movie, with the leading man dangling by his fingertips off a cliff.

"I suppose it wasn't very good," I said.

"What do you mean?" Jones asked.

"Well, when you have a disagreement like that, where no one is willing to compromise, I suppose it is easy for things to not be very good." I always excelled at compromising. In the face of Hal's rigid insistence, my strongest asset was my ability to bend. But when it came to this house, the possibility of leaving this place I'd made my home, I wasn't willing to bend. It was rare for me to set such a firm boundary. Hal didn't know what to make of it at first. "I suppose it was my fault," I said quietly. "I was being inflexible."

Katherine groaned.

"So—frequent disagreements, then?" Jones asked, pen scratching across paper.

"You could say that." Truthfully, the disagreements—loud, insistent, incessant—had died by early summer. Hal certainly knew how to be a broken record (Katherine came by it honestly, after all), but he also knew a lost cause when he saw one. He realized that, for once, I wasn't budging. He certainly gave it his all, and there was a desperation in his voice I had never heard before, but by the summer, he had retreated to his office, defeated. Working on a new novel. Allegedly.

"These disagreements." Jones was looking at me now, her brown eyes intent. McDouglas drifted back into the room and stood somewhere behind me, silent. "Did they ever get physical?"

I felt Katherine's stare.

"No," I said quickly.

I felt Katherine's stare change, pelting the side of my face like sleet.

"Before you moved here," Jones continued, "what was your relationship like?"

"Oh, it was good," I said.

Katherine snorted.

"It *was*," I said to Katherine. I could have done without the color commentary. "You were away, Katherine."

"Away at Aunt Noelle's, you mean?" Katherine aimed this comment like a handgun, barrel pointed at the bull's-eye.

"No, Katherine. You were away at college. Away at work. Away with *Claire*." She flinched at this last comment. *Both of us can shoot to kill, Katherine.*

Jones' gaze darted back and forth between us.

"Hal and I had our rough patches, of course," I explained. "All marriages do. I'm sure you understand." I glanced down at Jones' hand. No wedding band. Okay, maybe she didn't understand. "But we got through it. It made us stronger. And for a while there, things were good between us."

Things *had* been good. The third DUI, that was what had changed things. Hal needed to do a little jail time after that one and got his license revoked. The court made him attend counseling, something I hadn't been able to convince him to do for nearly twenty years, but I didn't exactly have the threat of incarceration on my side. If he had gotten a fourth DUI, he would've been looking at no less than a year behind bars, a prospect that motivated him to take sobriety seriously for a change. It was just counseling for the drinking initially, but he figured out that he liked it and had some things he needed to work through. He started going to AA meetings, got a sponsor, actually started earning chips beyond that twenty-four-hour coin. In his counseling, he learned skills to keep calm and actually used them. We started talking again, laughing. He reminded me of the slant-grinned kid, skinny and bursting with energy, I had met when I was younger. I didn't have to remember the rules anymore, although I still followed a few of them. Muscle memory.

All that had happened during Katherine's senior year of high school, and she had returned home from Noelle's house for at least part of it, so I knew she was a witness. She ought to have remembered, but she had likely not been paying attention. She had left Noelle's begrudgingly and had already moved away to college in her mind, months before she even graduated from high school. Hal once proudly showed her his six-month chip, and she looked at him like he'd told her he had been abducted by aliens. Katherine was not as ready a believer as I was, and was far less keen to forgive.

We had six years of bliss after Hal got sober. Katherine didn't come home very often, and when she did make brief visits, she didn't seem to see what we saw. Still, for those six years, we were happy. Everything was as it should have been from the beginning.

Then we bought the house.

I suppose I should be thankful. Not everyone gets six years of happiness.

"And what was his mood like the day he went missing?" Jones asked. "Was he angry?"

In my mind, I pictured Hal, with his faded Cubs shirt thrown on, brown jacket tucked under his arm, not a single bag packed. The sound of the cab idling in the driveway as we stood in the doorway. *Please*, he said. *Please come with me.*

"No, he wasn't angry," I said, a burning in the back of my throat turning my voice thick.

Hal had clutched at my hands, his face cracking. *No one deserves to live like this*, he said.

I swallowed the burning as best I could. "He was sad."

My words lingered in the air for a moment before Jones cleared her throat, relieving me of the necessity to elaborate. "And can you think of anywhere he might have gone? Any friends in the area? Family?"

"No, no family to speak of." Parents—dead. Brother—estranged. "No friends either. Hal and I were homebodies, I suppose." A habit we had picked up out of necessity—or, rather, Hal's insistence— back before the six years of bliss. After that, we hadn't so much needed the habit anymore but couldn't seem to shake it.

"Mom thinks he might have gone to a hotel," Katherine offered.

"At least at first," I said. "I don't know what he might've done after that."

"Do you have access to his financial records?" Jones asked. "Credit cards, things like that? Do you share an account?"

"Oh, shit, that's a good idea," Katherine said, already typing, phone in hand.

"I—," I said.

"It might let us know where he's been," Jones explained.

"We do share an account—"

Katherine already had the website pulled up on her phone and had managed to correctly guess our username. "Mom, what's your password?"

"Katherine," I hissed, "financial records are private."

"Is it Bilboa123?" she asked. "With a capital B?"

I remained silent.

"The password I made when I set up your email before I left for college?" she asked. "That's what it is, isn't it?" She typed it in. "Jesus, Mom, you need to update your passwords."

"Language." I sighed.

"Okay, okay." Katherine was giddy. "Five days ago, we have a purchase of eighty-seven dollars at the Save Mart."

"That was me," I said. "Groceries."

"We also have a purchase of twenty-seven dollars, same day . . ."

"Also me," I said. "Gas."

"We don't really need to—," Jones started, but Katherine was already going, scrolling excitedly on her phone.

"Utility bill, another utility bill. Wow, Mom—it is really expensive to heat this place. Don't you have fireplaces? You could probably save— Wait. Here's something from the night he went missing. An ATM withdrawal. For . . . a lot of money."

She lifted the phone and showed it to Jones. Jones' eyebrows rose. I saw Jones' gaze dart over my shoulder. I didn't need to see McDouglas' face to know that the two had shared a look.

Katherine's shoulders slumped. She scrolled back through the remaining charges. "And the rest of these are all your purchases, Mom. I guess he paid cash from this point on."

"Sometimes, when people leave, they expect to get frozen out of shared accounts," Jones explained, her face full of infuriating sympathy. "Especially when there have been . . . disagreements."

"They make a big cash withdrawal right away, expecting it to be the last one they can get for a while," McDouglas said behind me. "I'm sorry, ma'am. Sometimes people do nasty things when they leave their homes."

I was about to tell him that I wasn't concerned in the least about what had compelled Hal to withdraw the money, when a thought forced its way into my mind—*Needs must when the devil drives*—so clearly that I could have sworn it was Fredricka speaking. It was her voice, and it even sounded louder in my right ear than in my left, as if she were standing in the corner of the room and had been this whole time. Before I could stop myself, I whirled my head around. *Get the hell out of here, Fredricka.* Of course Fredricka wasn't there. It was just Katherine and me and the police officers, who were now sharing a different kind of look.

"What the hell are you doing, Mom?" Katherine asked.

"I . . ." I cursed myself as I turned to face forward once again. "I thought I heard something."

Jones kept her eyes on me and smiled in a way I'm sure she thought was reassuring. I saw her pen jerk almost imperceptibly as she made a notation in her notebook, a little scribble that she didn't want me to notice.

The officers had a few more questions for me, none particularly noteworthy. I was shaken by what I thought might have been a Fredricka sighting, and my answers sounded disjointed and off. The officers seemed to notice and kept their eyes on me even as they prepared to leave.

"Thank you for taking the time to speak with us, Mrs. Hartman," Jones said.

"We'll let you know if we find anything," McDouglas said, oblivious to the fact that he had used the word "if."

"I'll walk you guys out," Katherine said, a clear ploy to get some time with the officers without my presence.

As soon as the front door closed, I drifted after them, my footsteps silent against the floor. I pressed my ear to the door.

"I understand, ma'am," I heard a male voice say. McDouglas. "But I'm afraid there isn't a lot we can do here."

"You can *find* him," I heard Katherine insist. "You have information to go on. You know he couldn't have gotten far. He doesn't have a car or a license."

"We'll do what we can." A female voice. Jones. "But your father is an adult, and if he wanted to leave, he has the right to do so."

"He didn't *want* to leave." The officers didn't know it because they hadn't raised her, but Katherine was barreling towards a tantrum.

"According to your mother, he did," Jones said. "They had been fighting about that very topic: your father *wanting* to leave. And then he left. Voluntarily, it would seem."

"But . . ."

"It sounds like your parents had some difficulties in their relationship," Jones said. "And from what I can tell, it sounds like you know that too."

"They did, but—"

"That can be a hard reality to face." McDouglas now. He must have been assigned the role of Good Cop. "I know I always hated seeing my parents fight when I was younger. But sometimes people are just better off apart than they are together." If McDouglas had raised Katherine, he would have known that this Good Cop act wouldn't work on her.

"It isn't a matter of me hating to see them fight," Katherine spat. "I've seen them fight. A *lot*."

Thanks for that, Katherine.

"Their relationship was shit," Katherine said. "And I swear to Christ, I *wished* he'd leave. I even *prayed* for him to leave, which ought to tell you something."

"Ma'am—"

"But he *never left*," she continued. "He never did. Not once, not even for a day. He may have been a piece of shit, but he was god-damn *loyal*."

"Even the most committed relationships reach their breaking point." Jones now, voice soft to counteract Katherine's increasing volume.

"And without any communication?" Katherine was not to be dissuaded. "Just dropping off the face of the earth like that?"

"Sometimes people who leave don't want to be found," Jones said. "They skip town. They ditch their cell phones. They pay for everything in *cash*." This last comment was pointed.

"But"—Katherine was pleading—"no communication with *me*?"

"You told us earlier that you hadn't had much communication with your father in general before he went missing," McDouglas said.

"You said that your relationship with him was poor." Jones now, apparently ready to remember things Katherine had already told her.

"Yes, but—"

"Is it *possible*"—Jones' voice was even more pointed now—"that he is not interested in reaching out to you, given how little you two communicated previously?"

"You're not *listening* to me." Katherine's voice was wet. Even through the closed door, I could practically see her foot stomp. "Something is *wrong*."

"We understand how upsetting this is," Jones said.

"It's difficult to have a loved one leave and not know where they went," McDouglas said.

"We'll do our best to look into it as much as we can." Jones.

"We just don't want you to get your hopes up." McDouglas.

"Do us a favor and look after your mother." Jones, her voice quieter as she walked away.

"She seems like she might not be doing very well." McDouglas, even farther away.

"We'll call you if we get any leads." Jones, her voice tiny now.

Through the door, I could hear Katherine's deep, forceful breaths. She was managing to remain calm—perhaps the therapy was paying off after all—but I could still hear all the tells of a storm rapidly approaching.

I backed away from the front door, thinking it best to keep my distance until she wore herself out. When I turned around, there was Angelica, pale skin and devastated face, standing by the basement door. She lifted her knobby arm and pointed at the basement.

Shit.

TEN

The next afternoon, I found myself in the passenger seat of Katherine's rental car, a sensible sedan that Katherine was currently pushing to the limits of its acceleration capacity. I had told her to slow down three times already and it was doing just as much good as it had when she was sixteen and learning to drive.

Katherine had her phone in her hand, GPS pulled up. She was not looking at the road. "There's another bar just a mile away," she said. "It's called Happy's. Do you know it? Did Dad ever mention it?"

Katherine had recovered faster than I'd expected after the police had left the day before; perhaps the breathing had helped after all. She burst through the door a few moments after I shooed Angelica away from the basement door (sometimes, if you ran at Angelica and her friends, they scattered like terrified pigeons). Katherine stomped down the hallway with red eyes, a wet face, and a renewed sense of purpose.

"Fuck the police," she said, sounding remarkably like a song that Hal and I had once told her that she was not, under any circumstances, to blast from the car stereo anymore while she drove around the neighborhood. "If they aren't going to take this seriously, we will." Katherine reasoned that all alcoholics needed alcohol, which meant that she planned to visit every bar in town, on the off chance that somebody had seen Hal. She also planned, much to my dismay, for me to accompany her.

"Shit, we missed it," Katherine said, hurling the car into a U-turn at what felt like eighty miles an hour with barely a cursory glance at oncoming traffic.

My forearm slammed into the armrest. "Katherine, *slow down*," I said for the fourth and definitely not final time.

The car shuddered as it swerved through the road, finally slamming to a halt in Happy's parking lot. My seat belt jerked against my shoulder as I flew forward, braced for impact. Dust settled around us. Katherine was out of the car before I even had a chance to catch my breath.

Sleep the night before had been virtually nonexistent. Angelica returning so soon after Father Cyrus' blessing had me rattled, and I had spent the remainder of the evening looking over my shoulder, petrified that Angelica or one of her friends would be in Katherine's view. What if Katherine followed one of them into the basement? That would be a catastrophe. I spent the night awake with worries spinning through my head, pointless yet insistent. Then of course there was the moaning, louder tonight. It hadn't developed into screaming just yet, but the mentions of my name were more frequent. *Margaret, come down here. Margaret, we need you. Margaret, come find us. Margaret, come see what he did to us.* I didn't wake up so much as give up in the morning, my puffy eyes opening hopelessly to the sunrise as I accepted that sleep was not on the docket. And of course, there was a waterfall of blood on the wall behind me. Of course.

On top of all that, Fredricka was getting increasingly squirrelly. As if the stacks of plates and cups in the kitchen weren't enough, I had descended the stairs this morning to find that she had taken all the cushions off the couches and arranged them neatly on the floor. It also looked like she'd moved all the couches three or so inches to the left, judging by the grooves in the carpet. Not sure what that was about. It was challenging to move the furniture back and replace the cushions quietly before Katherine came downstairs in the morning, but if she had heard me, she didn't give any indication. One benefit to sleepless nights—completion of morning chores before breakfast.

Still, the whole of it didn't exactly make me a particularly peppy travel companion. By the time I made it into the bar after Katherine, she was already holding Hal's photo in the face of a confused-looking bartender.

"Have you seen this man?" she demanded. "He's my dad. He's missing. He's an alcoholic."

"Former alcoholic," I said, finally making my way to her side.

"*Current* alcoholic," Katherine corrected. "Have you seen him?"

"Lady, I don't remember what I had for breakfast this morning, let alone every person who drinks in this bar." The bartender had an armful of liquor bottles he was restocking, and didn't seem keen on pausing in his task.

"Can you just look at the picture?" Katherine's voice was shrill.

"Please?" I asked. "It would mean a lot to us." The bartender caught my eye, and I tried my best to communicate my apologies for Katherine's behavior while moving as little of my face as possible.

The bartender walked over to us, glanced at the photo. He sighed. "Like I said, I don't really remember. But I don't think he'd've come here. Happy's usually has a . . . younger crowd. You know what I mean?"

I looked around at the grimy decor, beer pong table, and lack of chairs, and I knew what he meant.

"Are you sure?" Katherine asked, pushing the picture even closer, unwilling to accept no for an answer even if no was, in fact, the correct answer.

"He's sure," I said, pulling her arm away and turning her towards the door. "Your father wouldn't be caught dead here." Hal didn't like to drink in bars at all, much preferring the comfort of his own home, but Katherine, thus far, had ignored this little fact.

Back in the car, Katherine crossed Happy's off her list, cursing. We were early in our search—four bars down, countless to go—but she was already frustrated. Perhaps she imagined that Hal had frequented every bar in this town, or that other patrons were so familiar with his face that they shouted his name when he entered, a regular Norm from *Cheers*.

"Next up is a place called . . . the Salty Nurse," Katherine read. "It's about a mile away." She turned the key in the ignition and, I swear, managed to lurch the car into motion before the engine even started all the way. Certainly before I had my seat belt on.

I wanted nothing more than to be back home, cup of tea in hand.

I was not particularly interested in seeing the inside of whatever excuse the Salty Nurse had for a bathroom once we arrived, but we had been out for a couple hours now and there was no holding it anymore, as well as no convincing Katherine to make unnecessary pit stops in favor of restrooms that didn't boast condom machines and broken soap dispensers. The bathroom in the Salty Nurse was particularly seedy—unmentionable stains, toilet paper everywhere, and a broken lock on the lone stall door—but it would have to do. I wiped down the browning toilet seat with tissue before I sat down and leaned my hand forward to act as a barrier between myself and the bobbing stall door. The inside of the stall was peppered with graffiti—scribbled-out phone numbers, people's names surrounded by either hearts or expletives, and tracings of genitalia. Just to my left, a limerick had been carved into the wall.

There once was a man named Vale
Who the wee ones thought was so frail
But he had them all snowed
And he took 'em below
And one by one made them all wail.

Well, *that* was interesting.

The Vale family had once been well-known in this town, but these days the name seemed limited to the occasional mention in a few old newspaper articles I'd read back when I thought research would help anything. I'd never really heard the townsfolk go around with the name on their tongues, and certainly not with any sort of foreboding connotation. As far as I could tell, *I* was the only one who knew of Master Vale's horrors, and that was only because I had firsthand evidence. Was I mistaken about Master Vale's reputation? Was he some sort of local boogeyman, the one that teenagers whispered about at sleepovers and that parents threatened their children with if they didn't eat their vegetables? *Be careful or Master Vale will come and take you away.*

I doubted it. Based on the articles I read, nobody seemed to have ever drawn a connection between Master Vale and the missing children. Likely, I was the only person to connect the dots, and I had been given generous assistance from the batch of pranksters taking up residence in my home.

Somehow, I had a feeling this limerick had been composed for me. It felt self-centered, but I knew. I knew the way I knew that, outside the bathroom door, Katherine was making enemies with a bartender and growing increasingly unpleasant. As far as I was aware, this was the first time any pranksters had tried anything outside the house. Not that I had given them a lot of opportunities—I did my best to leave only when absolutely necessary—but I might have noticed Fredricka moving food at the grocery store or blood running down the side of the bank. I couldn't help but wonder what this meant. Nothing good, likely. But then, as Fredricka sometimes said, it's an ill wind that blows no good.

Katherine pounded on the bathroom door. "Are you almost done in there?" Time to go, apparently.

We passed by the bar on the way out. The bartender was busy counting money at the till. I stopped in front of him, letting Katherine walk ahead.

"This is a weird question," I said, voice low, "but you wouldn't happen to know anything about the limerick written on the wall of the women's restroom, would you?"

He looked up at me, brow furrowed. "What?"

"Mom, let's *go*." Katherine was out the door.

Back in the car, Katherine crossed the Salty Nurse off her list and careened out of the parking lot. The next bar was eight or so miles away and Katherine intended to get there in under five minutes.

An urge to return home tugged at my mind like a child on a mother's sleeve, light but insistent. I wanted to be in my studio painting, the sunlight making the walls shine a brilliant yellow. I wanted to sit in the kitchen sipping tea while Fredricka puttered about. I wanted to rock on the front porch and gossip with Edie. Most things about the house weren't particularly terrible, after all. The blood and the birds weren't so bad. The pranksters weren't so bad. Following the rules wasn't so bad. However, speeding around in this car was bad. Bothering bartenders in these grimy bars was bad. Being outside the house was bad. Nothing inside my home was bad. Everything was rule-bound and predictable and survivable.

Katherine hit a speed bump without slowing and I heard the axles shudder.

"How many bars do we have left?" I asked, bracing myself against the dashboard.

"A lot," Katherine replied.

The next bar was called Boomer's, and the bartender was female, so Katherine was a little nicer and took a little more time asking questions. While she chatted, I walked around, surveying the decor. The bar boasted several framed prints of nature that had been painted over with various monsters. A quaint image of a lake with the Loch Ness Monster erupting from the water, fangs gleaming. A bucolic scene of a tree-lined valley with an alien spaceship beaming up a cow. A peaceful forest being torn apart by a dinosaur, a bloodied villager in its teeth. Idyllic scenes rendered disastrous.

"Wow, I'm really sorry about your dad," the bartender said. She leaned towards Katherine, exposing her cleavage. "That must be awful."

"He's a motherfucker," Katherine said.

"Language," I called from across the room, preoccupied by a painting of Godzilla frolicking across a field of tulips. I quite liked this one.

The bartender studied Hal's picture. "I don't think I've seen him, though. He doesn't look familiar."

"Join the club," Katherine grumbled. "Apparently, he's a goddamn ghost."

"Maybe you could give me your number?" The bartender

blinked her doe eyes at Katherine. "And if I see him, I could give you a call?"

The next picture—a hill of lush grass, the same color green as our backyard. Lying across the grass, the red bodies of several children in various states of dismemberment. One of the children—a girl, pale skin and flowered blue dress blotched with red—had something horrible that had happened to her skull.

Katherine shoved the photo into her back pocket. "Don't bother," she said. "He's probably been drinking somewhere else." She turned, uninterested in the bartender's frowning face watching her leave. "Let's go," she called to me.

"That bartender seemed to have eyes for you," I said to Katherine once we were back in the car.

"Not interested." Katherine was staring at her notebook, her expression pained. "The next bar is ten miles away. It's called"—she sighed—"the Wet Hole. Jesus, who *names* these places?"

The urge to return home tugged harder. I had never been one to venture far from home, even before we'd moved. Sure, I might have been more sociable in my early twenties, before I met Hal, but soon into that relationship, I learned that sociability was not sustainable. So I adapted. I went grocery shopping, ran errands as necessary, went to my job when I had one. That was it. It wasn't so much a rule—not like staying out of the basement was a rule—but it made things easier, *much* easier. These days, especially with Hal gone, there's no real need to stay at home anymore, but I go on following the rule anyway.

Sleep now, my darling. Don't you cry. . . .

When the song first drifted into my consciousness, tickling my brain long enough to catch my attention, I thought it was only in my head. Like Fredricka's voice yesterday a loud thought in my own ear.

Mommy's gonna stay with you all through the night. . . .

Then I realized the song was playing on the radio. And Katherine was singing along to it.

"Ne'er shall you worry. Ne'er shall you mourn," Katherine sang softly. *"You won't see your poor ol' pop no more. . . ."*

I stared at Katherine, my mouth agape. I had a feeling this song had something to do with me as well, just like the limerick in the bathroom stall.

"What?" Katherine asked once she noticed my eyes on her.

"Where the hell did you hear this song?" I heard the sharpness of my voice but had little control over my reaction.

"Jesus, I don't know." She was immediately on the defensive, looking at me out of the corner of her eye like I was punishing her for something commonplace, like breathing. "I think you used to sing it to me when I was a child?"

"I *never* sang this song to you," I said.

"Okay, fine. Christ." Katherine stopped singing and faced forward, both hands on the wheel. Her eyes kept darting towards me as she assessed the situation, formed conclusions. In the silence, the song kept playing.

He ain't in the barn. No, he's long gone. . . .
But you'll see his sad face again 'fore long. . . .

I rubbed my temples. "Can you drop me back off at the house?" I asked. "I'm not feeling well."

BACK AT THE HOUSE, THINGS FELT RIGHT AGAIN. AS RIGHT AS COULD BE EXPECTED, anyway. After Katherine dropped me off at the front door, grumbling and barely even slowing the car for me to hop out, I walked inside to find Angelica standing by the basement door, pointing, as always, and all the kitchen chairs stacked on top of the table. Fredricka's work, clearly.

Good to be home.

I took the chairs off the table while Fredricka made tea, taking a break from rearranging the silverware drawer to be helpful. I sipped tea at the kitchen table while Fredricka moved the saucers into the utensil drawer and the utensils under the sink.

"How was ma'am's outing with her daughter?" Fredricka asked, placing a spatula next to a jug of bleach.

"Tiring," I said.

"Young Katherine seems to be quite assertive in her manner," Fredricka said.

"'Assertive' is one way of putting it," I mumbled into my teacup.

Afterwards, Fredricka went upstairs to the guest rooms to move all the pillows from one room to the next while I went outside with a pair of gardening gloves to gather up the dead birds that had accumulated over the past few days. Despite the sun, the day was growing chilly—autumn was fast approaching—and a wind rattled the trees. Quite a few winged corpses dotted the yard, and I was dismayed to learn that they had attracted bugs. I lifted each bird tentatively by a clawed foot, ants and other crawlies dropping from it as I walked, and tossed its feathered body into the woods. I would have preferred to burn them as Fredricka and I had done before Katherine arrived, but I had a feeling Katherine would ask questions about the funeral pyre in the backyard when she returned.

Katherine's car pulled into the driveway a few hours later. I had hoped to find time for a quick nap while she was gone, but I ended up spending the remainder of the afternoon following Fredricka around and ensuring that her nervous reorganizing wouldn't raise too many concerns from my houseguest.

"Any luck?" I asked Katherine as she stormed through the door and up the stairs.

"The bartenders in this town are fucking morons," Katherine shouted, slamming the door to her room. So, that was that.

Katherine got in the shower shortly thereafter and I tried to rest in the living room. If I knew Katherine, I would have at least thirty minutes before she came back down the stairs. I lay back on the couch and shut my heavy eyelids.

"What would ma'am and her daughter like for dinner?" Fredricka was standing over me.

Crap. I hadn't even thought about dinner.

"Perhaps I can fry some chicken?" Fredricka offered.

"No, I can make dinner," I said, lifting myself up. Yet another way Fredricka had me spoiled—I rarely had to do any sort of meal preparation of my own. Fredricka was a damn good cook, although her repertoire was limited to recipes that were popular around the time of her death.

"I can at least skin the chicken. Get the batter prepared," she said. "Young Katherine would not have to see me."

"You're very helpful, Fredricka," I said, moving towards the kitchen. "But you don't have to worry about it. I can handle dinner." There was a high probability that I would just order us a pizza.

"*Mom!*" Katherine's voice came screaming down the stairs from the upstairs bathroom, overpowering the sound of the shower behind her. "*Do you have the faucet running or something? I just lost all the hot water up here.*"

I walked to the foot of the stairs. "No, I don't," I called up. "It's an old house, Katherine."

"*Are you sure? It's fucking freezing in here.*"

I was about to call back up to her, but I noticed a sound over the din of Katherine's shower. A rushing sound of running water, coming not from the upstairs bathroom but from the kitchen.

That couldn't be good.

In the kitchen, the sink was running, both handles turned and pouring at full blast. I hadn't done that, and I had a feeling that Fredricka hadn't either. Much to my dismay, the liquid coming from the faucet—splattering and foamy—wasn't water. It was blood. Or something that looked an awful lot like blood, anyway. The sink was filled nearly to the brim with the viscous substance, millimeters away from overflowing.

"God*damnit*," I hissed, rushing over and turning off the faucets. A few lingering drops of thick red fell from the spout. The blood inside the sink slowly settled and stilled. I saw my own confused face staring back up at me from the gleaming surface. It smelled like a butcher's shop in here.

"*Thanks, Mom. That's better,*" Katherine's faint voice called from the bathroom.

The pool of blood had a calm, unmoving surface. The drain stopper sat next to the faucet, undisturbed. The drain was open, but something was blocking it.

With a sigh, I rolled up my sleeves as far as they could go and sank my arm into the sink. The blood was warm and enveloped my arm completely. I felt the dense liquid sink under my fingernails as my hand made its way to the bottom of the sink. There—something was stuck in the drain all right, something soft and meaty. I pulled it out, my arm coated in gore. It was a chunk of something that looked an awful lot like flesh. Human flesh? Animal flesh? Some questions are best left unanswered. I gagged. I don't consider myself to be a squeamish person—I'm a mother, after all, and the walls of my bedroom bleed regularly—but everyone has their limits. The blood started draining. That had solved the problem, at least. I walked to the back door, trying my best not to drip blood all over the floor, and flung the chunk of flesh into the backyard as hard as I could. Not an ideal solution, but I couldn't have rotting meat stinking up the kitchen trash. The flies would *never* leave then.

I heard the shower turn off upstairs.

The blood covered my arm up to the elbow and was rapidly drying. The sink looked like a crime scene. I hadn't kept blood droplets off the floor. Shit shit *shit*.

I rushed back over to the sink and—saying a little prayer to the patron saint of normal plumbing practices—turned on the faucet. Regular, clear water. Thank God. I scrubbed the blood off my arm with a sponge. I might not be able to get all of it out from under my fingernails, but I could at least try. Thin streams of red poured off me and swirled down the freshly cleared drain.

The bathroom door opened and Katherine's footsteps moved into her room, the door closing behind her. She was getting dressed, probably, and would be downstairs any second.

I wet a cloth and scrubbed at the trail of blood droplets that led from the sink to the back door, drying the floor with my sock. No time to do things properly. I set to work on the sink, where the real horror show was. Thick clots clung to the white porcelain and the whole thing was stained with red. I ran the faucet, water as hot as it could get, and scrubbed madly at the blood. The steaming water stung my arms, but I ignored it.

I heard Katherine's footsteps heading down the stairs. The sink was mostly clean. The cloth I was using looked like a murder weapon, even after I wrung it out. I wrinkled my nose. This was one of my better dish towels—I wished I had thought it through before I used it to wipe up blood. *Oh well*, I thought, tossing it into the trash. *Needs must, I suppose.*

By the time Katherine entered the kitchen, I was rinsing my hands, my arms clammy and red from the water.

"What do you want to do for dinner?" Katherine asked, reaching into the cabinet for a glass.

"Oh, let's just keep it simple tonight," I said, looking for something on which to dry my hands and realizing I had just used my last dish towel to clean up blood. "I was thinking we'd just order a pizza." Somewhere, Fredricka was likely frustrated with me.

Katherine walked over to the sink to fill her glass with water. "Sounds good to . . . What the *hell*, Mom?" Katherine's glass clattered into the sink as she grabbed my forearm with a tight fist. "What are *those?*"

Along my arms, standing out in stark contrast to my pink skin, were streaks of little white scars, healed but improperly so. They were tooth marks—fang marks, rather—but it was difficult to tell from their length and their winding pattern. The scars were from Elias, and mostly from that first year we lived here. I had gone through a phase of problem-solving wherein I tried to befriend Elias. He had not taken well to that course of action, and the results were charted out on my arms. Lesson learned.

"Did *he* do this to you?" Katherine demanded, holding tight to my arm. Her eyes could've shot flames.

For a blurry moment, I thought she was referring to Elias. *How the hell does she know about Elias?* I thought. Then I realized what she meant. I pulled my arm away from her grip.

"Of course not, dear," I said, pulling my sleeves back down over my arms. "Don't be silly."

"Don't minimize this," Katherine said. "Don't you think I have a right to be concerned, considering . . . ?" She gestured over her shoulder to a past that was standing right behind her.

"Of course, you have a right to be concerned." This was going to turn into a fight. I could tell. "But you've no reason to be. Those marks are nothing."

"Those aren't *marks*. They're *scars*, and from a pretty bad injury from the looks of it." Katherine was glaring at me. "What the hell happened?"

"It's really nothing, Katherine," I said. "You're making a bigger deal of this than you need to."

"So *that's* how we're playing it," Katherine snapped. "I can't wait to hear the story you come up with for this. Fell down the stairs? Did the cat we don't own attack you?"

"I don't think I care for your tone." She was really backing me into a corner.

"Go ahead. I'm all ears." Katherine leaned back against the counter, teeth bared in a vicious smile. She gestured for me to start talking.

"If you must know, these marks—"

"Scars."

"—are from gardening." It was weak. I knew it. One look at the lawn and anyone could tell that the amount of gardening I did was zero. My heart was pounding. I couldn't think.

"Gardening?" Katherine laughed, fake and angry. "That's the lamest story I've ever heard. You must be out of practice, Mom. But I suppose there aren't a lot of people who come all the way out here to ask about how you got hurt."

"Jesus Christ, Katherine."

"But then you always were a shitty liar. *I had a bad dream and plumb fell out of bed. I bumped into the counter and it must've bruised my arm. I stepped on a rake and the handle hit me in the face.* Do you remember that one? That was one of my personal favorites. Like in your imagination we live in a Three Stooges movie."

"I'm not lying to you," I lied. "These marks—"

"Scars."

"—are really from gardening. I got my arms all cut up on some rosebushes." We didn't even *have* rosebushes. This was not going well. What was I supposed to tell her? *Don't worry. These are tooth marks from the little dead boy who lives here and bites you when you get too close to him. I got too close to him, is all. It's all my fault, really.* "It's all my fault, really," I said.

"There it is!" Katherine shoved herself from the counter, flinging her hands in the air. *"There* is the classic line! *It's all my fault.* Christ, you ought to get that inscribed on your fucking tombstone."

"I have no idea why you're angry with me," I said.

"Do you think I enjoy sitting here and listening to you lie to police officers?" Katherine was nearly shouting now. "Do you think I enjoy sitting here and listening to your bullshit? Trying to convince everyone that Dad's alcoholism was no big deal, really. That you guys were having cute little *disagreements.* I lived through those fucking *disagreements,* Mom. I know what they look like."

You don't know, I thought. *You have no idea. Because I kept you safe from it. Because I did what any good mother would have done and I protected you.*

"And you're just acting like the most innocent person in the world, trying to make everyone believe that you guys just had a little rough patch, no big deal. Nothing so bad you had to send your own *daughter* to live with your sister for a while. Otherwise the state was going to come and take her away from you. Nope, nothing that bad. Just some *disagreements.* You handled it."

I did handle it, I thought. *Just imagine what you would have seen if I hadn't sent you away.*

Katherine was practically snarling at me. "And now you're sitting here telling the cops that everything was hunky-dory over here while you've got those goddamn *scars* on your arms. Jesus, Mom. Dad must have really upped his game once you guys moved in here. Bruises and black eyes are for suckers, huh, especially when he can *really* leave a mark?"

"That's *enough*," I said. "You have no idea what you're talking about."

"Of course not, because God forbid you *tell* me anything," Katherine said. She was standing too close to me, chest squared, face red. She reminded me of Hal. "You think you can paint a perfect little picture of how life is, how you want me to see it. You must think that I'm the biggest idiot on the planet, that I couldn't see what was happening back then, that I can't see what is happening here."

You can't *see what is happening here*, I thought. *It will scare you too much.*

"I protected you," I said, my voice filled with ice.

"You couldn't even protect yourself." Katherine snatched her car keys off the kitchen counter with a scrape. "Fuck this," she said. "I'm going out."

I hadn't moved since she started yelling. I was a statue, standing by the sink, watching her leave.

Katherine grabbed her purse and jacket. She paused by the kitchen door, not looking at me. "I hated you for staying with him," she said. "And now I hate him for leaving. How was it that *he* was the one with the strength to leave in the end?" And with that, she was gone, the door slamming and tires squealing beneath her.

She was wrong, so wrong about so many things. Hal wasn't the strong one, not in this house. He didn't have the fortitude to keep living here, couldn't weather another September, couldn't even muster the courage to follow the rules. He might have been the strong one in the past, the one with the muscles and the lungs and the demands, but this house, the things that lived here, had overpowered him. In the end, I was the strong one. I was still here, and Hal had fled, whimpering with his tail between his legs. In the end, Hal was weak.

Fredricka came up beside me. "Fried chicken for dinner, ma'am?"

I sighed. "That sounds lovely."

ELEVEN

Of course Hal didn't start putting hands on me right away. I wouldn't have stayed.

It didn't even start with hands. It started with words. This might have been going on longer than I thought before I noticed it; Hal had always had an unpredictable temper, even before we got married. Once we were settled in, with Katherine on the way, I assumed Hal was stressed with work and I was stressed with pregnancy. We became snippy with each other. However, Hal had a real knack for it. With his writer's mind, he could come up with the most creative insults to throw your way, things that wriggled into your brain and you found yourself repeating back to yourself later, wondering if he had meant what he said or if he was just angry. He always kept his words just close enough to the truth that a part of you couldn't help but agree with him. Maybe he was right that I would never get a real job and he would have to support me until the day he died. Maybe he was right that he only loved me out of kindness—a charity case, really—and that nobody else could ever be expected to be as patient and forgiving as he. Maybe he was right that I would end up just like my father, babbling and incoherent, with only a resentful spouse around to keep me alive. He would apologize the next day of course, but I never could blame him. It became harder to believe that he was speaking nonsense.

The first time Hal put his hands on me when he was angry, it wasn't even that bad. We were disagreeing about something or other, perhaps about how Katherine spilled juice on the sofa and I should've had the foresight to stop her. He was yelling, and I'd had just about enough of it and gone to walk out of the room. He grabbed me by my arm, swung me around, and gripped me by the shoulders. *You do not leave when I am talking to you.* That was the first time and I barely thought anything of it. He left bruises, but they were faint and faded in a day or so. He apologized the next day, but I barely remembered what for. And anyway, I *had* been trying to leave when he was talking to me.

Eventually, Hal putting his hands on me became commonplace. Grabbing at my arm when I wasn't facing him, shoving me against walls when he didn't like my tone, pushing me down when I said something wrong. Relatively loose grips I could easily escape, until, one day, I couldn't. Open hands, until, one day, they were closed. Marks on my arms and torso only, places that could be easily covered up with clothing, until, one day, they weren't. It didn't happen daily, of course, most of the time not even weekly, but it was regular enough that I could no longer write it off as an isolated incident. He would apologize the next day, but sometimes he really didn't need to. I had been there for the whole escalation, after all. I saw how I had drawn it out of him.

After a while, the whole process started to grow tiresome. One of us needed to make some compromises. And my ability to bend was my strongest asset.

Take, for example, my sister, Noelle. Noelle was the kind of person with opinions—strong, loud opinions—and she had plenty of them about Hal. Hal *hated* Noelle and had plenty of opinions about her as well. I had to hear Noelle's opinions—verbose, insistent—whenever she called and Hal's opinions—furious, pummeling—afterwards. It was always the same.

One day, the phone rang. It was Noelle, her number bright on the caller ID. Hal was in the room within seconds, not speaking or acting, just staring, his eyes lighting fires. Waiting to see what I would do.

I tried an experiment. I let the phone ring and ring. It went to voicemail. I deleted the voicemail.

"Who was that?" Hal asked, already knowing. Testing me.

"It was Noelle," I said. "I don't want to talk to her." I was very good at tests.

The fire in his eyes fizzled out. A little smile flitted across his face. He walked over to me, wrapped his arms around me tight, almost crushing. "Good," he whispered in my ear.

I smiled, wrapped my arms around him in return. It would seem I had made a rule.

TWELVE

Margaret, you look terrible," Edie said as she joined me on the front porch. It was regrettably early in the morning, with the sun barely peeking through the trees, and I had given up on sleep.

"I *feel* terrible," I said. My head throbbed and my eyelids felt like they weighed fifty pounds apiece. Every bone in my body was stiff. "It was loud last night."

"Oh dear," Edie said. "Is it full-on screaming yet?"

"Not quite, but it's about to be." I rubbed my temples. "I'd say by tomorrow night we'll have arrived at screaming." At least with the screaming the speaking would stop. *Margaret, you can't hide from us. Margaret, we'll get you.*

Edie looked worried. "Do you think Katherine heard?"

Interestingly enough, Katherine hadn't come home last night. I stayed up in the living room waiting for her, drinking cup after cup of tea, but I gave up around one in the morning. The moaning had been raging for a little over an hour at that point, but I deluded myself into thinking I might be able to tune it out and get some sleep.

Edie surveyed the empty driveway. "I see," she said.

"There was a bartender," I said. "At a place called Boomer's. I'm guessing that's where she ended up."

"Ah," Edie said.

"It's just as well. There's no way she would have slept through the ruckus last night."

"Did *you* get any sleep?" Edie looked the part of the concerned matriarch, the kind who offered sweaters when you weren't cold and food when you weren't hungry. The kind I had tried to be for so many years.

The moaning had died down around dawn and I thankfully closed my eyes, determined to get some sleep, even if only twenty minutes. I felt myself sinking down into oblivion as soon as my eyes shut, but was awakened sometime later—it could have been seconds or minutes; I couldn't tell—by a jet-engine noise.

I opened my eyes to find the burning caverns of Elias' pupils staring into mine. His jaw was unhinged like a snake's, fangs pointing down at me, ready to close on my face. Inside, his maw was viscous blackness, oozing like oil. He smelled of rot.

"Jesus Christ," I had cursed, rolling away just in time. Elias sank his teeth into my pillow and howled. He disappeared into nothingness, leaving behind a torn pillow dotted with darkness. I supposed I would be throwing that pillow away. It was hypoallergenic too—what a waste.

Anyway, that ordeal had woken me right up.

"Not much," I said.

"Did you and Katherine get into it last night?" Edie looked sympathetic.

"More or less," I said. "She saw the marks on my arms. The ones from Elias."

Edie nodded. She was well aware of my attempts to befriend Elias. She, in fact, was the one who told me it was time to abandon those attempts.

"She thinks they're from Hal. She thought that we were back to fighting before he left."

"I see," Edie said. Edie and Hal had never been particularly close. They had barely even interacted. Hal didn't care for Edie, and Edie never seemed interested in pursuing the relationship. Edie knew about Hal, about our colorful past. I could tell she disapproved in a motherly, protective manner, but she never pushed the issue like Noelle or Katherine or a few nosy police officers had tried to. I was grateful to her for that.

"It's a pickle," I said. "I don't want her to think that way about her father. God knows he gave her reasons to be upset with him, but he really changed. Especially these past few years." *Especially* since moving in here. "She's already having trouble with how he used to be. I hate to give her reasons to be even more upset, especially when they aren't true."

"Well"—Edie looked thoughtful—"which would you rather her believe: that you and Hal were fighting or that you live in a house filled with dead people?"

"Good point." I was grateful for Edie, for the time we spent together, rocking on the front porch. Before moving here, I had spent so much of my time alone and friendless—friends weren't against the rules per se, but they made it difficult to follow the rules, and following the rules had been my top priority. When we moved here and Hal had gotten so good at using his new therapy skills, I figured I could bend a little and made a friend in Edie. Hal didn't like it, but didn't cause nearly as much of a fuss as he used to.

Besides, Edie and I mostly just sat on the front porch and talked, so Hal could listen in on our conversations if he ever felt so inclined. I'm not sure he ever felt so inclined, but I know he preferred to have the option.

"Speak of the devil," Edie said, nodding towards the driveway. Katherine's rental car was ambling down the long stretch of gravel. It was the slowest I had seen her drive—she must not have been looking forward to returning.

Edie waved.

Katherine emerged from the driver's seat, looking disheveled. Her hair was a tangled mess, finger combed and sticking up in places. She was wearing a shirt I hadn't seen her wear before and certainly not the one she had left the house in. She held her bra in her hand. She jogged quickly up the front steps with her head down, glancing at me out of the corner of one eye before darting into the house and out of sight.

Edie and I rocked in silence for a moment, the awkwardness of the situation lingering in Katherine's wake.

"It looks like she might not have gotten much sleep last night either," Edie said.

I chuckled at that, and Edie accepted the invitation to laugh along with me. "Regardless," I said, "it's better than her staying here. I would rather she be kept awake by . . ." I waved my hand in the air.

"The bartender?"

"I was trying *not* to say that." I slapped at Edie's chair and she snorted. "But yes—I would rather she be kept awake by the bartender than by all the ruckus over here."

"*Well*," Edie said, "there's always my first suggestion."

I narrowed my eyes at her, a laugh still light on my breath. "I am not drugging my daughter."

"Okay, okay," Edie said, hands up in surrender. "But just think about it. When it gets worse." She looked at me, her face suddenly serious. "And it'll get worse, Margaret. It always does."

After Edie left, I went back inside to make myself some breakfast. Angelica stood by the basement door, and I shooed her away. Fredricka had rearranged all the furniture in the living room, and I would have to move it back at some point today, but right now I couldn't be bothered. I heard the water running upstairs—Katherine was taking one hell of a long shower. I glanced at the sink in the kitchen—no blood this time, thankfully.

I made myself some toast and was about to take my plate into the living room to eat when I saw a little boy standing in the kitchen. He was about six—younger than Elias, skinnier too—and had hair that had once been blond but was currently gray with dirt and debris. His clothes were torn and his face was sallow. He raised a trembling arm and pointed in the general direction of the basement door.

This one was Julian. One of Angelica's little friends. There was a thing about Julian, but I couldn't quite remember—

With his other hand, Julian lifted his tattered shirt to the middle of his chest, revealing a gash that ran from hip to hip, opening like a gaping mouth across his stomach. As if no longer held back by the shirt, his intestines tumbled out of the gash, dropping onto the floor in a splattering heap. Blood started leaking from his mouth.

Oh, right. *That* was the thing about Julian.

"He's down there," Julian coughed.

I looked down at my plate of toast smeared with thick raspberry jam, and suddenly lost my appetite. *Thanks, Julian.*

KATHERINE CAME TO FIND ME AFTER HER SHOWER. I WAS LYING ON THE COUCH IN THE living room, an arm over my eyes, exhausted from having just moved all the living room furniture back to its correct location.

Katherine stood in the center of the room, not talking. I lifted my arm to look at her. She had her head lowered and was staring to the side, reluctant to make eye contact. Still, I could see that her eyes were red and swollen. Her hair was damp from the shower and she wasn't wearing makeup. She looked tinged with regret, and I had a feeling not very much of it had to do with me.

"I'm sorry about last night," she said, her voice a tinny echo. "The things I said."

I sat up. "Oh, Katherine, there's no need to apologize."

"No," she said, still not meeting my eye, "I mean it. I'm really, really sorry."

"It's all right," I said. "No big deal. Water under the bridge."

"I promise it'll never happen again." She looked ashamed, pitiful. She looked so much like Hal.

I THOUGHT KATHERINE WOULD BE TIRED ENOUGH FROM HER ADVENTURES THE NIGHT before to keep from continuing her investigations, but she chugged an irresponsible amount of caffeine and proved me wrong. Her hands drummed the steering wheel out of time with the blaring music on the radio as we careened out of the driveway, gravel spewing behind us. I clung to the roof handle, my head throbbing.

"We struck out with bars," Katherine shouted over the music. "But I'm trying a different tactic today. Hotels!"

On the radio, some rock band was yelling exclusively in vowels about something or other. The bass made the car rattle.

"He had to have stayed at a hotel at least those first few nights," Katherine said. "Might even still be there—God knows he took out enough money. Someone has to have seen him."

The radio switched to a car dealership commercial and it was so much worse.

A traffic light a block ahead of us turned yellow and Katherine floored it. I clenched my eyes closed and said a prayer to nobody in particular that we would both make it out of the car alive.

"There are a couple small motels near the center of town, and then a bunch of big hotels closer by the highway. Hopefully we'll get lucky and won't have to drive that far out," Katherine said. "Besides, the cheapest places are the motels. At least that's what Tabitha . . ." She trailed off, realizing her admission. The bartender. She glanced at me to see if I had noticed. I pretended I hadn't heard her, which I barely could anyway.

"Cheap" was an understatement for the first place—an old cinder block building by the name of Value Lodge. The light for the letter U had burned out in the neon sign. We walked through the thick smell of cigarette smoke and stale alcohol as we entered the main office. In one of the rooms nearby, a couple was either having enthusiastic sex or murdering each other—it was difficult to tell which.

"I don't think I've seen him," the acne-faced kid working the front desk said to Katherine as he studied Hal's picture. "But I just started working here a few days ago. I can ask Bill. He's been here for longer. He might know."

"Great," Katherine said. "Can you get Bill?"

The kid turned his head and looked me square in the eyes. "He's down there," he said.

I blinked. "What did you say?" I asked.

The kid looked flustered. "He's down there with his family today. Down in the next town over. He won't be in again until tomorrow."

"I guess we'll come back tomorrow, then," Katherine said, shooting me a strange look out of the corner of her eye.

Back in the car, my body grew a mind of its own, trying desperately to slip into sleep. My head bobbed up and down as Katherine told me about the next motel. She made comments about my strange behavior at the Value Lodge, but her words were coming in fuzzy.

The car hit a pothole at full speed and I jerked awake, neck snapping up hard enough to give me whiplash.

"I mean, if we act like weirdos, they won't want to help us," Katherine was saying.

"Of course, dear," I mumbled, the world already growing hazy in front of my eyes. The radio was too loud for me to fall into a complete sleep, but I could feel the edges of the world blurring around me. An indiscernible amount of time later, the car slammed into park at the next motel.

"We're here," Katherine called at me, already out of the car.

I followed her through the parking lot, rubbing at my eyes. This place was called the Paradise Motel, although it hardly looked the part. Longer-term tenants sat outside of their respective rooms, smoking cigarettes. There was a surprising number of stray cats milling about, sniffing at pieces of trash.

A bell jangled as we walked into the main office. Inside, twangy music played softly over invisible speakers. A young man in a hat sat behind the counter, engrossed by his phone. "Help you?" he asked, not looking up.

Katherine pulled Hal's photo from her purse. It was starting to wear at the edges. "My father has been missing since the beginning of August. We think he may have stayed in a motel around here."

As Katherine spoke, I walked around the lobby, trying to keep myself awake with movement. The brown walls of the office were bare, save for a few pictures and a framed map of the town; a smattering of brochures for local attractions was displayed on a nearby shelf. There was a small arrangement of various toiletries for purchase by forgetful guests: travel bottles of toothpaste, single razor blades, sanitary napkins. My eyes rested on a small pack of sleeping pills and I heard Edie's voice in my mind. *It's a solution.*

"No," I said, shaking my head with a half smile. I hadn't meant to say this out loud, but I did, anyway. Luckily, Katherine and the man weren't paying attention.

"He doesn't look familiar to me," the man was saying as he studied the photo, his eyes finally off his phone. "But let me get Ted. He might've seen him." The man looked over at me. "He's down there," he said.

I blinked at the man. A question started to form in my open mouth, but the man turned back towards Katherine.

"By the pool," he said. "Fishing out leaves. I'll radio for him." He picked up a walkie-talkie from the desk and said something unintelligible to Ted while I shook my head, trying to jostle myself back to life. I wasn't thinking straight.

Ted, a portly man in a stained gray shirt, joined us with a young woman in tow. She had long brown hair and chomped on gum. "I brought along Angelica," he said. "She has a good memory."

I shook my head again. That was a coincidence.

Katherine ignored me and pushed Hal's picture towards them. "Like I was telling— I'm sorry, what's your name?"

"Julian," the man in the hat said.

I blinked. This might not be a coincidence.

"Like I was telling Julian," Katherine continued, "he's been missing since August. He doesn't have a driver's license, so we don't think he went far out of town. We think he might've stayed in a motel around here."

Angelica looked at the picture and snapped her gum. "He doesn't look familiar to me."

"He probably paid in cash," Katherine offered. "Like, only in cash."

"You're describing most of the people who stay here," Julian said. He was back to fiddling with his phone.

"Yeah," Ted said. "I don't think I've seen him either. But a lot of our customers keep to themselves. I can keep an eye out for him, let you know if I see him."

Angelica was still leaning over Hal's picture, but her eyes were pointed directly at me. *He's down there*, she mouthed.

Ted handed Hal's picture to Julian and told him to go make a copy of it. Julian sighed, deeply inconvenienced, before grabbing the picture and disappearing into a back room.

"My sister's husband ran off too," Ted said, looking sympathetic, to Katherine, "so I know what you're going through." He turned his eyes on me and his expression flattened. "He's down there."

"Well, we're afraid he might have gotten in some trouble or something," Katherine was saying, frustrated by the insinuation that Hal had simply *run off*, but I wasn't listening to her because I finally heard the music that was playing through the speakers.

It wasn't the same recording we had heard on the radio yesterday, but it was the same song.

Wake now, my darling. Open your eyes.
Mommy must leave now. Don't you cry.

Angelica was still staring at me. Julian returned with Hal's photo and he was staring at me too.

Ne'er shall you worry. Ne'er shall you mourn.
You won't see your darling mommy no more.

That urge to return home flooded back, tugging on my mind with new insistence.

She ain't in the kitchen. No, she's long gone,
But you'll see her old face again 'fore long.

Katherine was thanking the employees for their time, shaking their hands. Apparently, she'd figured out being nice was a viable strategy when asking others for favors. That might have been another thing Tabitha had taught her last night.

It all comes around with the moon and the sun,
And no one escapes when the time has come.

"No problem," Ted said. "If you want to check back, you can ask for me. The name is Ted Vale."

The bell on the door chimed behind me as I fled from the office, leaving Katherine to stare after me in confusion. I was no more than two steps into the parking lot when I came face-to-face with one of the tenants who had been seated in a plastic chair outside his room, smoking, when we'd arrived. He was dressed in a grimy undershirt and baggy shorts. He had a blank expression on his unshaven face and a lit cigarette still dangled in his limp hand.

"He's down there," he said.

"Jesus Christ." I pushed past him and waited by the car for Katherine to return.

Katherine drove us out towards the highway to ask around a few of the other hotels. I waited in the car. When Katherine stopped at a gas station to fill up, I went inside and asked the attendant for two packages of DoZZZe-Rite, the extra-strength kind.

"THAT'S ODD," EDIE SAID TO ME AS WE ROCKED TOGETHER ON THE FRONT PORCH. THE sun was dipping low behind the trees and the sky glimmered with pink and dusty blue—cotton candy colors. Katherine was upstairs in Hal's office trying to hack into his computer on the off chance he had saved a document entitled "Where I Disappeared To" directly onto his desktop. She was frustrated with me for being unhelpful at the hotels earlier but was trying not to break her promise about yelling at me within the same twenty-four-hour period in which she had made it.

"It sure was," I said. "Nothing like that has ever happened before, I don't think." My eyes were half closed against the dull headache that lingered behind their sockets. It was likely I'd have this headache until October.

"Is it another September thing?" Edie asked. "A new one?"

"Who knows?" I stifled a yawn. "Lord knows Hal and I never ventured out very often. Maybe September shenanigans spill out into the rest of the world too and we just never had a chance to notice."

"At least Katherine didn't notice all the hullabaloo," Edie said. "One less thing to try to explain to her."

"She noticed *me*," I said. "I'm sure she thinks I've got a screw loose."

"She's not wrong." Edie poked at the arm of my chair, grinning at a joke we both knew wasn't funny, given my family history. I chuckled out of obligation.

The sky was a richer pink now, the blue giving way to blackness above. I saw the first stars peeking out as the sky darkened. The screaming was coming—soon, soon, soon.

"Have you thought about taking some sleeping pills yourself?"

Edie asked. "You really look like you could use a good night's sleep."

"I can't," I said, "not with Elias lurking around. I don't want to wake up with bite marks all over my face. What would I tell Katherine then?"

"Good point."

"I just got those DoZZZe-Rite things as a precaution, anyway." I looked pointedly at Edie. *I'm not drugging my daughter.*

"Right," Edie said. "Just a precaution." She didn't believe me, but I appreciated her pretending.

When I walked back inside, all the pink was gone from the horizon. Stars dotted the sky, and I wondered if it was too much to hope for a peaceful evening. I closed the front door behind me and froze.

Katherine had come down from her room some time ago, and she stood in front of the basement door. The *open* basement door. The yellowed pages of the Bible we had taped to the back of the door were fully visible, tattered edges fluttering from the door's being disturbed. Katherine's palm lingered on the handle and she peered down into the darkness quizzically, her nose crinkled slightly at the smell. A vision of Father Cyrus—frozen in possessed rigor mortis, a cloud of flies streaming from his gaping mouth—flashed through my brain, followed by a picture of Hal's shredded leg as he had limped back up the stairs after that third September. I saw Katherine lift her foot, sliding it towards the first step.

"NO," I screamed, lurching into action and sprinting towards Katherine. She looked up at me, her face full of surprise. I wrenched the door from her grasp and slammed it, *hard*, the force of it fluttering my hair.

"What the fuck?" Katherine said. She looked too stunned to

be angry, but I had a feeling it was only a matter of time before she found her way there.

"Do *not* go down there," I shouted, momentarily forgetting my goal of keeping Katherine from thinking I had a screw loose.

"Why the hell not?"

With the door closed firmly behind me, my body blocking her from danger, my panic had lessened just enough for me to realize my misstep. The wheels in my head struggled to crank over the rapid pounding of my heart. "It's . . . not safe."

"What do you mean?" Katherine asked. "And what is with that shit on the back of the door?"

"Mold," I gasped. It was all I could think of. "We had a leak down there ages ago. A bad one. And now there is mold. Everywhere."

Katherine raised an eyebrow, undecided on the extent to which I was full of it. "Mold?"

"*Black* mold," I said. "We had a person come look at it. An inspector." I didn't even know if that was a real thing. "He said it was very bad and we shouldn't go down there. For our health." I went to guide Katherine away from the door, into the kitchen, but out of the periphery of my eye, I saw Angelica and Julian standing in there just behind Katherine's back, staring at us and pointing straight ahead, at the basement. Julian's intestines had already spilled out onto the floor. We would be continuing this conversation right where we were, then.

"Is that what that smell is?"

"Yes, it is." She was believing me. Thank God. "Awful smell, isn't it? It really is very bad in the basement. That's why we keep the door closed at all times. And *never* go down there." I guided her towards the living room, taking care that she didn't turn around to look into the kitchen. I could see Angelica's and Julian's heads turn, their gazes following us as we left. They lowered their hands.

"You should really get that taken care of, Mom." She still sounded skeptical, but she was going along with it, and we were moving away from the basement—safe, at least for now.

"I think Hal found the number for someone," I said as we walked down the hallway. "I'll have to find it in his things."

In the living room, Fredricka had taken all the cushions off the couches and stacked them vertically in the center of the room. Katherine didn't need to ask the question—her face said it all.

Goddamnit, Fredricka.

"Oh, sorry about the pillows," I said, walking over to the pillow tower and grabbing a few off the top, trying to sound as if this sort of thing were normal. My adrenaline was fading, and I was too tired to come up with another excuse off the top of my head. Katherine said nothing and helped me return the cushions to the couches, her wary gaze pointed at me the whole time.

Later that night, I crushed up two DoZZZe-Rite tablets and mixed them in with Katherine's tea. I watched her bob and blink on the sofa for twenty minutes before excusing herself and going upstairs to bed.

Even later that night, the screaming started in earnest.

THIRTEEN

Four Septembers ago, the screaming started in earnest as well. Hal could sleep through a freight train's barreling through an air horn factory, and he was snoring next to me as if nothing were amiss. I was wide awake, watching moonlight glisten off the blood cascading down our walls. If you looked with enough imagination, you could envision shapes in the shadows on the blood, like you were cloud gazing. I thought I saw an approximation of Edvard Munch's *The Scream* on one of the rivulets, but there was a chance I just had screaming on the brain, given the circumstances.

We hadn't contacted the church or even found Father Cyrus yet, but we would in just a few short days. Until then, there was nothing but the screaming.

Hal gave a snort and rolled over, his shoulder digging into my arm. I felt a stab of irritation at his body for behaving properly. I hadn't slept in three days.

The nightly moaning and shrieking and screaming and *Help us, Margaret* were unnerving at first, but after a few nights of all that, it became more tedious than anything else. The lack of sleep certainly wasn't helping.

"To hell with this," I said, shoving Hal off me and hoisting myself from the bed. If I was going to be wide awake, I might as well be wide awake downstairs, having tea in the kitchen. The screaming wasn't any louder or quieter down there, so it didn't make much of a difference where I was. Interestingly, the screaming was equal in volume throughout the house, which seemed to suggest that it wasn't coming from one place in particular but rather was emanating from the house itself. *Everything* was screaming, which also happened to be how I felt about the headache I had been nursing for the past few days.

As I neared the bottom of the stairs, several of the pale children who periodically pointed towards the basement door darted in front of me and I nearly leapt back up the stairs. I sighed, frustrated more at myself than at them. I should have known better than to let those children—*pranksters*, as I had started calling them—give me such a fright. Even if they didn't ordinarily run. Or yell. *He's coming.* I took a nice, deep breath before I resumed descending the stairs, more cautious this time, in case the pranksters decided to pull anything else.

It was when I reached the first floor and turned towards the kitchen that I saw him. The basement door was open and standing in front of it was what looked like a man, but not quite right. He was impossibly skinny and tall, too tall—even the brittle manner in which he hunched over couldn't hide his height. He was pale as moonlight, with whips of tangled white hair twisting in clumps around his milky scalp and angry red lesions dotting his skin like craters. His limbs, which looked too long for his body, were skinny and twisted as tree branches. His whole body seemed to be twitching out of time with itself, flickering like an old movie.

I froze, staring at him. I didn't yet know who this man was, but I knew he was the reason I didn't like going into the basement.

His head lolled about on his shoulders, his gaze drifting absently around the hallway until finally coming to rest on me. His eyes, milk white and red rimmed, met mine.

Having never encountered a similar situation before, I wasn't sure what to do. I stood there, motionless. The world blinked into silence, as if someone had hit PAUSE on a CD player. The only noise was the thrumming of my heartbeat in my ears.

The man turned his twitching body towards me. His hunch lessened and he expanded upwards, glaring down at me even from so far away.

Tentatively, I inched my heel backwards.

His legs were stick-thin and unsteady as a marionette's as he started moving towards me. He jerked and twitched, his skinny arms reaching for nothing. Yes, there was quite a number of sores on his body. I could see that clearly as he moved closer.

Run? I suggested to my legs, but the air hung heavy, dreamlike, and my muscles were reluctant to comply.

The man flew to life, spasming body lurching forward, his too-long limbs twisting into right angles as his narrow frame convulsed across the floor. With his movements, the screaming sprang back into sound and pounded into my ears from all around me. The man's eyes were wide, and his mouth was open, a handful of rotting teeth bared to me, and I heard his breath rasping as he came at me, at me, *at me.*

"*Shit.*" My body finally remembered how to work, and my feet sputtered backwards, carrying me swiftly towards the front door. I wasn't so foolish as to turn my back on this man, not when I could see his spindly fingers reaching out like talons as he raced towards me. For a wild second, I thought he was going to catch me. I felt the sharp jab of the doorknob in my back. I clutched at it with both hands, madly trying to unlock the door and turn the knob with sweaty fingers as this nightmare of a man closed in on me.

Somehow, I got the door open, screaming as I threw myself outside. I slammed the door in the man's raging, oozing face and everything went silent. No screams, no rasping breath. Nothing but the sound of my own shaky breathing and the chirping of crickets. I took a few steps back, my eyes darting to a front window. It seemed peaceful inside. But things weren't always what they seemed.

There was a chance everything would be fine if I went back in, but I wasn't about to risk it. It was chilly outside and my pajamas were thin, but I was nowhere near being in danger of freezing to death and nothing was coming for me out here. Besides, the night air was pleasant enough, the wet smell of earth thick around me, and the stars shone in the sky, reminding me that there were calm constants everywhere. I wrapped my arms around myself and sank down in one of the rocking chairs (we had just bought them a month earlier), letting my breathing return to normal. Who the hell was that? What did he want? I tested out various answers in my mind, none of them particularly reassuring.

I sat there until the sky turned a pale blue and the birds awoke to resume their mission of crashing against the windows and dropping dead. Soon, Edie came waddling down the driveway, wide hips bouncing and hand waving in an enthusiastic greeting.

"What are you doing up so early?" she chirped before getting a closer look at me. "Oh no, Margaret—what's wrong?"

I had known Edie for only a few months at this point, and I was just starting to consider her a vague acquaintance instead of a minor annoyance. Hal certainly disliked her, and I had to admit that she stopped by awfully frequently for my taste, but I was out of practice with having friendships. Looking back, I don't think I'd had a true friend in years. I barely even spoke to Noelle anymore, and she was my own sister.

It's a funny thing about being alone. You never really notice it when it's happening. You're aware that nobody else is there, but you're so busy with yourself and the little things you do to occupy your time—the painting, the housework, the occasional errand. And then there was Hal, obviously; he counted for something. But as with wading into cold water, you acclimate to the relative solitude until it doesn't even bother you anymore. You don't realize that your hands and toes have grown numb until there is a sudden burst of warmth that sends needles through your extremities. That is to say, Edie's single question was enough to jolt me into the realization that, for the past several years, I'd had no one.

I'm ashamed to admit it, but I started crying.

Edie rushed over to me in a bustle of maternal concern. "Tell me all about it," she said.

There are some things you just don't talk about. It's not that people don't ask, but rather that they don't want to know, not if they want to keep seeing you as a sane, rational human being. The things that went on in this house—the blood, the screaming, the pranksters, that tall man with his wooden limbs and needle fingers—nobody wanted to hear about them, let alone go on talking to you afterwards. No, best to keep quiet, to handle these things internally.

"Just let it out, Margaret," Edie said.

And, much to my surprise, I did.

It felt like a fever breaking, like setting down a heavy object after carrying it for miles and miles, like finally reaching the shore after a long, cold swim. Once I started talking, I couldn't stop. By the time I finished, Edie was sitting in the rocking chair next to me, staring at me with unblinking eyes.

At this point, Hal believed only about a third of the words that came out of my mouth. He saw the blood, but wondered if it wasn't some sort of leak. He barely heard the screaming, what with his Olympic-level heavy sleeping. He saw the pranksters only out of the corners of his eyes as they fled from him. There was Elias, but this early on in our time here, I was used to not being believed.

"Wow," Edie said. "You've been dealing with a lot, Margaret."

"Yes," I said, feeling my headache lessen for the first time in days. "I suppose I have." I shook my head, wiping at the remaining tears in my eyes. "It's not so bad, though. I've got it under control."

Edie looked at me like I'd told her I could jump to the moon. "It's hell, Margaret. No one deserves to live like this, to go through all that," she said. "At the very least, nobody deserves to go through it on their own."

I could feel my tears wanting to start up again, but I swallowed them down. I had grown accustomed to solo trips through hell over the years. It seemed counterintuitive to invite company. "Thank you," I heard myself say, and I was surprised to find that I meant it.

Edie smiled. She seemed to understand, in a way. She asked me about the pranksters, what I knew about them, what I thought they were on about. I didn't have a lot of answers.

"Do you think they mean you harm?" Edie asked.

I considered. "The housekeeper—Fredricka—I don't think she does," I said. "She just seems like she wants to be helpful. The folks in the upstairs bedrooms are a sight, but I don't think they want to hurt me. I think they're just upset. That boy—the one with the face? He hurts, but I think he just doesn't like his personal space invaded."

"Who does?"

"The children don't seem like they want to hurt either," I said. "I think they're trying to tell me something."

"And what about that man," Edie asked, "the one who chased you?"

"I think he's a problem," I said. "I think he wants to hurt." I thought for a minute. "I wonder if he's what the children are trying to warn me about."

Edie looked afraid. "Do you think you'll move out? You and Hal?"

I felt a stab of affection for her and realized that I might miss her if I left, even with all her visiting and meddling. We might just be friends.

I grinned at her. "They'll have to drag me out of here in handcuffs," I said. Edie looked relieved.

Inside, I could hear Hal shuffling around, calling my name. It was unusual for him to wake up and not know where I was. "I'm out here," I called, "with Edie." *That* would keep him inside.

We rocked for a moment in silence. I would need to go inside and start breakfast soon.

"Do you think we should get in touch with a church?" I asked Edie.

Edie shrugged. "Couldn't hurt."

FOURTEEN

The next morning, two more of Angelica's friends—Charles and Constance—showed up on the landing of the second floor. They were new arrivals, a nice little midmonth gift on the Advent calendar of September. Charles and Constance were twins, or at least looked a lot like twins. They usually showed up together and were remarkably similar, what with their dirty hair cropped around their shoulders, their little tunics made from the same fabric, and their matching stab wounds in their stomachs, arms, and faces. Constance's mouth was slashed open at one end, creating a garish grin that stretched nearly to her ear. They pointed downward, towards the basement door. Blood slowly leaked from all the various openings in their skin.

I'd just finished scrubbing blood from the walls and the top of the stairway and was in no mood. I shifted the bucket of bloody water I was lugging downstairs to one hand and shook my free hand at them. "Shoo," I whispered. Behind them, I saw Blythe's spindly fingers wrapping around the doorframe of her room, her blackened face peering out at me, mouth long and fierce. "You too," I hissed. She yowled and slammed the door. The twins vanished inside themselves with a sob.

Honestly, everything in the house made such a racket. I hoped the sleeping pills that Katherine didn't know she had taken had made her a sound sleeper.

In the kitchen, Fredricka had turned the table completely upside down and stacked all the chairs on top of one another. Every cabinet was flung open, and it looked like she had broken a few plates. I set the bucket down with a plop, bloody water spilling out onto the floor. Oh well. What was one more element added to this cleanup, anyway?

"Fredricka," I called, slowly removing each chair from the stack and placing it in the center of the room, "any chance you can come help me with this?"

Fredricka appeared—or perhaps had always been—to my left, holding a plate in her hand. "Yes, ma'am?"

"This mess." I gestured. "You made it. Can you help clean it?"

"Of course, ma'am." Fredricka lifted the plate as if to place it in a cabinet, but was actually standing about ten feet away from the cabinets, so the plate crashed to the ground, shattering and adding to the debris.

There was my headache again, back like clockwork.

"Never mind," I said.

"I can help," Fredricka offered.

"You can help in October," I said. "Right now just try your best not to do anything destructive."

"Of course, ma'am," Fredricka said. "I'll make some tea." She moved over to the stove, turned all the burners on high, and vanished. Flames leapt into the air.

Jesus Christ. I turned off the burners. I would make tea later.

Right now the priority was cleaning, and Fredricka was making me feel like a dog chasing after its own tail. After returning the kitchen table and chairs to their rightful orientation (Christ, that table was *heavy*), I emptied the bloody water into the sink, watching the swirling mess turn red to pink to clear, and felt thankful that the pipes hadn't been clogged with any unidentifiable chunks of flesh since that one time a few days ago. Or was it a week ago? Time was getting fuzzy.

I dried out the blood bucket and placed it under the sink, where I discovered that Fredricka had hidden a decent number of my winter sweaters. I left them there; it was best to prioritize which parts of Fredricka's messes needed rectifying, and sweaters under the sink were a low priority. It was unclear where she had hidden the cleaning supplies that had been under the sink just this morning, but I was sure I'd find them soon.

I picked up the shards of broken dishes off the floor. It looked worse than it was—Fredricka had broken only four or five plates and I still had plenty up in the cabinets, or wherever Fredricka had moved them to. I tossed the shards into the trash, then gathered up the bag to take it outside. Charles and Constance stood in the kitchen doorway, holding hands and blocking my exit.

"Move," I said.

"He's down there," they said. Constance's mouth was bleeding.

"For the love of God." Usually, I tried to avoid walking straight through the pranksters. They were just going about their business and I thought the act seemed rude, especially when there were more productive ways of communicating. But it was seven in the morning, and I was already tired of this. Needs must. Devil driving. All that.

I pushed through the twins, passing through their joined hands. They wailed and vanished, but not before I felt my body punctured by stab after stab after stab—invisible blades sinking into my skin in rapid, frenzied succession—and heard the faint sound of screaming that almost could have been confused with laughter. Doing this always set my body off course, and I collapsed to my knees, coughing and gagging up nothing. In my clumsiness, I dropped the trash bag, garbage and ceramic shards spilling out across the floor. "Son of a *bitch*," I said to the new mess.

Angelica to my right. "He's down there."

So I cleaned up the mess (this one I couldn't blame on Fredricka), carelessly tossing bits of debris and plates into the bag, now a little torn from the broken edges. Clutching the bag by its tattered top, I exited the house and tossed it into the large can outside.

The yard was absolutely *riddled* with dead birds.

By the time I got back into the house after cleaning up all the bird carcasses, properly rotting and thoroughly ant infested, my hands stung from a dozen tiny bites and Elias was standing by the door staring.

"Elias, I am in *no mood*," I snapped.

"What?" I heard Katherine call from the living room. Goddamnit. She was awake already.

Elias gave a howl and vanished just before Katherine rounded the corner. "Who are you talking to?"

"You," I said, forcing a smile and trying not to pick at my hands. "How did you sleep, dear?"

"Like a log," Katherine said. "I actually still feel a little groggy."

"I'll make some tea," I said.

"Jesus, Mom, what happened to your hands?" Katherine grabbed at my hands, inspecting the ant bites.

I snatched my hands back, perhaps a little too roughly. I tried to conjure back a smile. "Oh, don't worry about it, dear. I was just outside. Gardening. I happened upon a colony of ants. They seem to have gotten the better of me."

"You were gardening at eight in the morning?" A valid question.

"Well, you know how hot it gets at midday," I said. It, in fact, was not particularly hot at midday anymore, not in September. "Do you prefer tea or coffee?"

"Do you even *have* coffee?" Katherine asked. Another valid question.

I stopped in the middle of the kitchen, remembering. "No," I said.

"I'll have tea, then," Katherine said, sitting down at the kitchen table, her gaze wary. "Are you feeling okay, Mom? You seem . . . scattered."

"Oh, I'm fine, dear," I said, picking up a rag and scrubbing at the kitchen counter. I thought I still saw a smudge from Julian's intestines near the sink. "I must just be a little groggy from sleep too."

"You look tired," Katherine said. "Like, really tired."

"Oh, I'm fine," I said. I went to throw the rag in the trash can but realized that there wasn't a bag in the can. Also the trash can was gone. Fredricka must have moved it sometime in the past thirty minutes or so. I looked around the room for a bit—where in the *hell?*—before remembering that I didn't need to throw the rag away, could just rinse it in the sink. I chuckled at myself.

"Mom?"

Oh, right—Katherine was still there.

"Yes, dear?" I said.

"Tea?" She looked worried. She didn't seem so much like she wanted tea but rather seemed to want to see if I was capable of making tea without burning the house down. Well, I would have her know that I was very capable of making tea.

Except the tea bags were missing.

Hands on my hips, I stood by the spot near the stove where I usually kept the tea bags. If I were Fredricka, where would I have moved them? The possibilities were limitless. She could have put them in the mailbox for all I knew.

"It's okay, Mom. I don't need it," Katherine said. She stood up from the table. "Listen. I was going to go back into town today and check out some of the hotels we didn't get to yesterday. Will you be okay here, by yourself?"

I'm not by myself, I almost said out loud. "Well, of course, dear," I said instead. "But I can always come with you if you'd like."

"No," Katherine said quickly. "It really seems like you need to take it easy today. Maybe get some sleep?"

I was a little irked by her insinuation that I was not fit to accompany her on her investigation. It was accurate, but really— who was the mother here? Still, I didn't particularly *want* to join her out and about today, especially not after the unusual events of the past two days. And sleep sounded marvelous.

"All right, dear," I said, and Katherine went upstairs to shower. When she was gone, I surveyed the kitchen for the tea. "Fredricka," I said, "where the *hell* did you hide the tea bags?"

"Who are you talking to?" Katherine called from upstairs.

"No one, dear." Shit shit *shit*.

FIFTEEN

Shortly after that business with the man on the stairs, I decided it was high time I learned a little more about the house. Father Cyrus had already come and gone, as had September in all its chaotic glory, but there were still pranksters around and the basement still brought about that dreaded feeling, even more so now that I knew the man was down there.

It wasn't that Hal didn't believe me about the man by the basement stairs, but he believed me only in a vague sense, like someone might loosely believe in UFOs without ever seeing any evidence. Still, Hal didn't share my desire to learn any more about the house; he had never been the type to delve deeper into a situation, to really grasp its underpinnings. So I was alone in the library, stacks of old newspaper clippings surrounding me. I had a good laugh at myself for being the type of person to squint over a microfiche reader, jotting down notes about murders past and getting sideways looks from the librarians. I might as well have been a character in a movie.

There wasn't enough information to form a linear story, but there were enough bits and pieces that I was able to fill in at least some of the blanks.

"A lot of things make more sense," I said to Edie later as we rocked on the front porch and sorted through my stacks of photocopies and microfilm printouts. Edie shared Hal's disinclination to learn more about the history of the house, but she was at least willing to listen.

"Here's what I can piece together." I held up a photocopy of a newspaper article, its grainy images nearly obliterated by time. "This house was built in 1882 by this family—the Vales. They seemed well-known in town. Once I started searching for the name, there were little blurbs about them everywhere. George Vale was a doctor, and his wife, Penelope, was on all these planning committees for dances and the like. The townsfolk seemed to love them—there are all sorts of glowing things written about them in the paper. Even their *children* seemed to be town celebrities. Their son—Vernon—was active in the church, and their daughter—Violet—had a piece written about her debutante ball." I passed the piece of paper to Edie, who turned it over in her hands and pretended to be interested.

"Do you think the man you saw on the stairs is George?" Edie asked.

I showed Edie a picture of George in the paper. Even in the blurry, faded black-and-white photo, you could tell that George was somewhat short and fairly girthy. "I don't think so," I said.

Edie chuckled.

"There were some discrepancies about the family in these articles," I continued. "Some articles said that George and Penelope had two children and others said three. But I never saw any children's names mentioned aside from Vernon and Violet. I chalked it up to errors on the newspaper's part at first. But when I looked up their obituaries, that's when things got strange."

"Strange how?" Edie asked. "Did they die under suspicious circumstances?"

"Sort of," I said. "The whole family seemed to die around the same time. Like, within a month or so they were all dead, even the children. George died first—a heart attack."

"Not *that* suspicious," Edie said, pointing at his picture.

"Right," I said. "But then Penelope died a few days later. Because the family was such a big deal and George had just died, there was a longer article about it. The newspaper said that she had been outside gardening and had a seizure, but some family friend was quoted as saying that she had had no history of seizures and had been in tip-top shape."

"Grief?" Edie asked.

I rolled my eyes. "Everything is survivable."

"Not seizures, apparently."

"Fair point," I said. "But get this—a week later, Vernon died." I handed Edie the article. "Their nanny said he was playing ball in the yard with some friends and collapsed. Just like that. She said he hadn't been feeling well but was trying to soldier on, being the new man of the house and all. They never figured out what happened. And *then*"—I handed Edie yet another article—"Violet disappeared, just walked off into the woods. She was found a week later, propped up against a tree. She'd been nibbled at by some wild animals, but the article says that wasn't what killed her. It says she died from dehydration or exposure to the elements or something. Like she just sat down and died."

"That's odd," Edie said.

I pointed at the articles. "And look at the *dates*."

Edie peered at the blurred text. "September." Her eyes widened. "Do you think that's what all the hullabaloo was about last month?"

"Maybe," I said.

Edie made a sad noise. "A whole family. Dead in under a month."

"Interesting you should say that." I shuffled through the papers. "Because it turns out, that wasn't the whole family." I placed an article in Edie's lap.

Edie read it over, then looked up at me. "They had another son?"

"Well," I said, "*Penelope* did. Theodore Vale." It had been nearly impossible to find out anything about him, but I had been able to piece a few things together. "She had him before she and George got married. Their marriage announcement said her last husband died. I guess George adopted him."

"That's nice," Edie said.

"Not quite," I said. "Theodore Vale's place in his family seems uncertain. He wasn't in any family photos. He wasn't mentioned whenever the family was written about. Hell—I couldn't find a record of him having attended *school*. Both Vernon and Violet had little articles written about them when they were born, and Theodore wasn't mentioned in either. But he had been there all along."

"That's strange." Edie's brow furrowed. "Why do you think he was left out?"

I shuffled through my papers. "I have a theory about that," I said. "A few months after everyone died, someone wrote an article about the Vale family. They talked about the tragedy of their deaths, the summer of youth stolen away, blah blah blah. The house and everything went to Theodore Vale, and the article had a thing or two to say about him." I handed Edie the article. "First of all, Penelope wasn't telling the truth when she said her last husband had died. Apparently, there *was* no last husband. Theodore was born out of wedlock."

"So?" Edie asked. "Who cares?"

"George Vale, apparently," I said. "A close friend of the family said that he was enraged when he found out that Penelope had lied, that she had been with another man outside of the bonds of marriage. That he had given his family name to a *bastard*."

Edie rolled her eyes. "Men."

"Right?" I said. "Also, even though the Vales had this reputation in town as being the perfect family, there are excerpts from a few of Violet's letters that told a slightly different story. Apparently, George was a bit of a dick. Violet talked about him not allowing her to eat the week before her debutante ball, so she could fit into her dress. She said that Vernon got low marks in school once, and George beat him so bad he couldn't walk for days."

"Oh my." Edie's eyes widened.

"But in another letter," I said, skimming through the article, "Violet says, *Oh, it's not as bad as all that. At least it isn't as bad as Teddy gets it.*"

"Theodore?" Edie asked.

"I guess so," I said. "Not that Violet had any sympathy for him. Here, she says, *He draws it out of father with his wicked little ways. It is in his nature, after all, being a bastard.*"

"*Jesus,*" Edie said.

"I know," I said. "Different times, I suppose. It seems that Theodore Vale had a rough life. But . . ." I shuffled through more articles until I found the one I was looking for—it had a grainy photograph of the house, taken just after the Vale family died. It was faint, but in the living room window, I could just make out a figure—a tall, skinny man with arms that were too long for his body; he was staring out at the world with an expression that time had erased. I pointed to the figure. "That is *definitely* who I saw."

Edie blew out a breath. She didn't seem to care for the man in the photograph.

"The article says a lot more about him," I said, "and most of it isn't good. Some of the former staff were interviewed—Theodore Vale fired most of the help after his family died, apparently. They said he was vicious and ill-tempered, would lash out at them for the simplest mistakes, insisted everyone call him Master Vale. They said that he didn't seem to grieve his family's death at all, that he said it was time he got what was rightfully his."

"Well"—Edie shrugged—"they didn't seem to treat him very nicely, now, did they?"

"The article got a little weird after that," I said. "Apparently, a few townsfolk thought that Theodore Vale had had something to do with his family's deaths, that he was involved in some sort of witchcraft or devilry. There doesn't seem to be any actual evidence of that, though. I think they were just saying it because, it says here, they never saw him at church."

"Old-timey folks and their superstitions," said Edie.

"And then it gets really bad."

"Oh?"

"A while later, children started to go missing." I grabbed an article and pointed at a large photograph of a doe-eyed girl sitting by her infant brother. "That girl. That's the one I've been seeing. The one who points at the basement."

Edie peered at the photograph. "Are you sure?"

"Positive. I saw her every day for a month straight. I practically saw her in my sleep, if I'd been sleeping at all. That's her." I looked at the article. "Her name was Angelica."

"Did they ever find her?" Edie asked.

"No," I said. "They never found any of them. There were three . . . four . . . five . . ." I flipped through the articles, counting. "Six children missing in total. None of them found. The advertisements would show up in the paper from time to time—*Have you seen this child?* But as far as I can tell, nothing came of them."

"That's terrible," Edie said. "To lose a child and never know what happened."

"*I* know what happened," I said. "Every single one of these children, I've seen them. They were here, in this house. Last September. They look just like they did when they died. This one"—I shuffled through the papers until I found the picture, then held it up for Edie to see—"named . . . Julian. He was disemboweled. These two"—again holding up a picture—"Charles and Constance, they were stabbed. This kid"—another picture—"his arm was cut off."

Edie waved her hand at me. "I get the point," she said, gone a touch pale. "Was Vale ever found out?"

"No," I said. "The children were spaced out across the years. A few children gone one year, a few more the next."

"How can you be so sure it was him?" Edie asked.

I gestured toward the house. "Who else could it've been? All these kids disappearing, one after another, starting right after Theodore Vale takes over the house? And then reappearing in this same house, all together? Speaking of—" I shuffled through the papers. "Guess when the children went missing each year."

"September?"

"Exactly. There is something about Theodore Vale—*Master Vale*, I guess—and Septembers," I said. "Anyway, I have his obituary here. Apparently, he wasn't paying off his debts, and when someone from the bank came around to check on him, they found him dead inside the house. They think he had some sort of disease. It says he had wasted away to basically nothing and had sores all over his body. He had long since fired all the house staff at that point, so he was all alone, with no one to care for him."

"Don't tell me you feel *bad* for that man." Edie chuckled.

"Not really," I said. "But he had a hard life. Think about it— neglected and abused, despised by your parents, who refused to acknowledge you while your siblings got all the adoration? That must really have an impact on a person."

"He killed children," Edie reminded me.

"I know that." I waved my hand at her. "I'm just saying that when you consider the kind of life he had . . ."

Edie rolled her eyes but let it rest. Edie knew how I was, given my own family background.

"So, what else did you find out?" Edie asked.

"Nothing near as exciting," I said. "There was an article written in the 1910s, when that man in the upstairs closet went insane and killed Fredricka and his wife and then supposedly himself, but I already knew about all that. Otherwise, the house has mostly just been empty. I keep finding real estate listings for it, as the property of the bank. People buy it and then disappear."

"Are there any pictures? Do you recognize any of the former owners?"

"No pictures." I frowned. "And not a lot of names either. Here's something—in the 1940s, the place was owned by a widow and her son. I can't make out the woman's name, but it looks like the child was named Elias. They went missing after a few years, and the sheriff was quoted saying they couldn't afford the payments anymore and split town."

"Do you think that's the boy you keep seeing?" Edie asked. "The one that bites?"

"It must be," I said. "I haven't seen his mother, though. Not sure what that's about."

"She must be around here somewhere," Edie said.

"The last article written about the house was in the mid-nineties," I said. "At the time, the house had been recently purchased by someone, but the article didn't say who. But then, a few years later, I found a real estate posting about the house again, back as the property of the bank."

"Oh dear," Edie said.

I told all this to Hal later, but he wasn't particularly interested in any of it. He didn't find my deductions about the children revelatory (*Haven't you been saying they look all cut up?* he asked. *Of course they were murdered.*), nor was he especially interested in the backstory of Master Vale (*What does his father being a dick have to do with us?* he asked). He was not at all sympathetic about Elias, saying only that the boy gave him the heebie-jeebies when he stood at the end of the hallway and stared like that, eyes full of nothing, and Hal definitely did not care for all the biting. *I would have left him too if he had bitten me like that,* Hal said when I told him about Elias' mother, and he was not receptive to my reminders that the problem could be prevented by staying out of Elias' space (*That's not the point,* Hal said).

"Will any of this get these things out of our house?" Hal asked me. "These things you say you're seeing."

"I don't think they're going anywhere," I replied. And that had been the end of that.

"Do you want to hear something funny?" I asked Edie.

"Sure," Edie said.

"Guess when Master Vale died," I said.

Edie smiled, already knowing. "When?"

"September thirtieth."

Edie laughed. "Of course."

SIXTEEN

Of course, I knew that I wouldn't be able to get any sleep while Katherine was gone. Fredricka broke a few more plates, and it was difficult to tidy up with Angelica and Julian and Charles and Constance crowding around me and periodically chanting, *He's down there. He's down there. He's down there.* Blythe started making one hell of a racket upstairs, and when I went to her room to shush her, I found her on the ceiling, pounding both fists against the plaster and howling. I yelled at her to quiet down and she unhinged her jaw and shrieked at me before vanishing into the fireplace and I hoped that would be the end of that. While I was up there, I noticed that the black hole in the third guest room had grown considerably and seemed to be pulsing, so I just closed the door and locked it. The wall of the upstairs hallway had started bleeding a little even though it wasn't supposed to start up again until later that night (really, was I the only person in this house who followed the rules?), so I grabbed the blood bucket and cleaned that up, and just when I finished, five big birds shattered their necks on the back window in quick succession, so I went outside to stay ahead of the curve on body disposal. All this time, Elias was hovering about five feet behind me. He followed me from room to room and hissed. I came back inside and found that Fredricka had managed to move one of my dressers into the living room and stacked the drawers in the dining room, and let me tell you, *that* took a long time to move back. Afterwards, I tried to take a nap on the couch but Angelica and all her friends lined up beside me and chanted, *He's down there. He's down there. He's down there*, over and over again until I burst up and through their bodies and felt the phantom pains of stabbings and disembowelings and hammerings and whatever the hell happened to Constance's face, and this time I actually *did* throw up all over the living room floor, so I had to grab the blood bucket again to clean up my own vomit and that was it for sleep for the afternoon.

That is to say, when Katherine returned home that evening, I was fairly exhausted. I sat myself on the kitchen floor and stared at nothing as I sipped the first cup of tea I'd had all day. I had finally found the tea bags about thirty minutes before. They were in the upstairs bathtub.

I was somewhat grateful that Katherine was home. The pranksters seemed to calm down when she was around. Like feral cats, they kept their distance around strangers, saving the yowling and scratching for people with whom they were familiar. I'm sure they would eventually grow comfortable with her, as they had with Edie, but for the time being, they saved their pranks until Katherine was out of the room, a welcome respite from today's chaos. I wondered if it was time to dig up Elias' mother again, or perhaps cajole Father Cyrus into making another visit. Both of those endeavors would be difficult with Katherine here, but Lord knew that I could use some help.

I heard Katherine coming before she even entered the house, talking loudly on the phone as she turned the lock in the front door.

"Right, and what I'm telling you is, it's suspicious," she was saying. "He wouldn't just abandon his belongings like that."

There was a pause as whomever Katherine was talking to chattered away.

"Yeah, I get that," she said. "But he left all his things. If he really snuck out because he couldn't pay, he would have at least taken his stuff with him, right?"

Another pause.

"I'm just saying, go by and talk to Bill. He was the one that cleaned up the room, and—"

Pause.

"No, he said there weren't any signs of a struggle, but he's not a *cop*, is he?" I could hear Katherine's voice growing irritated.

Pause.

"*Thank* you. That's all I'm asking," Katherine said with a sigh. "Value Lodge—do you know where that . . . Okay. The name is Bill Franklin. F-R-A . . . Okay."

Pause. Katherine was walking down the hallway to the kitchen, and I could hear the chirping of her call through her phone's tinny speakers.

"I appreciate it," Katherine said. "Thank you, Officer."

The squeak of the voice through her speakers sounded female. She was talking to Officer Jones, then.

Katherine strode into the kitchen, pressing END on her phone. "What are you doing on the floor?" she asked, setting her purse on the counter, phone still in hand.

To be honest, I wasn't particularly sure why I was on the floor. I had simply found myself there. My best guess was that I couldn't have been bothered to walk to a chair when it was time to sit down. All I knew was, I was happy for the tea and the sitting, regardless of the location.

I heard myself respond, but I wasn't really listening. It didn't matter, anyway, because Katherine was done waiting to tell me her news.

"That guy, Bill," she said, "from the Value Lodge, he gave me a call while I was out. Said he remembered Dad. Get this—he had read Dad's books. He's a *fan*."

I made an approximation of laughter.

"I didn't know Dad *had* fans," Katherine said, shaking her head. "Anyway, he had *such* good information. Since he recognized Dad and all, he paid attention to his comings and goings." She pulled her notebook out of her purse and started riffling through it. "He said Dad booked a room for three nights and paid cash, like we thought." She pointed at me as she said this, as if I were a coconspirator with her in the solving of this mystery, the Dr. Watson to her Sherlock Holmes. "He said he saw Dad out and about a lot that first day, hailing cabs, going into town. He said he wondered why Dad didn't have his own car, being an author and all—I didn't tell him. Don't worry. I know how you are about that." She rolled her eyes, as if family privacy were unfathomable.

I felt my head growing foggy. This was turning into quite the long version of a story I had already heard about half of when she was on the phone.

"Anyway," Katherine said, "after that first day, he didn't see any more of Dad. He said he was kind of disappointed because he was hoping to have a conversation with him." She rolled her eyes again. "Can you imagine—someone actually *wanting* to talk to Dad?"

I did something like nodding but I had a feeling I got the speed all wrong.

"But get *this*." Katherine flipped through her notes. "Dad never checked out. Bill said he thought that maybe he just missed him, that Dad checked out overnight or something, but there was no record of him settling up and the key was never returned. They knocked on the door, and nothing. So they went in. Guess what they found."

All of his things. I'd heard this part already. I thought about answering her, showing her that I was following. It's what Dr. Watson would have done. I might've responded. I wasn't sure.

"All of his things," Katherine said. I must not have responded, then. "A change of clothes, a thing of shaving cream, a razor. Even his goddamn *toothbrush*. Bill even said that there was a half-eaten sandwich in the mini fridge growing fuzzy things. And a Jack Daniel's bottle, of course."

"Of course," I said to my tea. I hadn't meant to say it out loud, but I did.

"They thought that maybe he was still staying there, trying to cheat the motel out of a few nights' pay, but he never came back. So they gathered up his things, cleaned out the room. Bill said they usually just trash things that guests leave after them, but because he's a fan, he wanted to keep them, kind of a souvenir." She gestured with her thumb behind her. "He dropped them off at the motel for me, everything except the moldy sandwich and the Jack Daniel's, that is. He said he'd ask around with some of the other employees, the folks that worked the night shift when Dad went missing. See if they know anything. Said he'd give me a call if he learned anything."

"Of course," I said again, because I felt like I was particularly good at saying it. What was that thing Sherlock Holmes always said? The thing he was famous for saying?

"I've got Dad's things out in my car," Katherine said. "I've already gone through everything—nothing helpful, unfortunately. I was hoping he had left his phone. I guess he took that with him when he left the motel. You can have a peek if you'd like. Maybe you can find something I didn't."

"Elementary," I said.

Katherine raised an eyebrow. "Is that a yes?"

I nodded, sure to get the speed right this time.

"This is good, right?" Katherine asked. "It's not a lot, but we know he stayed in a motel for a few days. Then something happened. He left. Or maybe someone took him away? Whatever it was, it had to have happened suddenly, right? Or else he would've taken his things with him."

The game is afoot, I thought. *That's another thing Sherlock Holmes says.*

"The police don't seem to think it's all that suspicious," Katherine was saying, "but I think it's suspicious as hell, isn't it?"

With great power comes great responsibility, I thought. *Is that a thing Sherlock Holmes says?*

"I mean," Katherine was saying, "they're telling me that people leave things in motel rooms all the time. But not *all* their things, right? Not their clothes and razors and toothbrushes? And certainly not their *alcohol*? Dad especially."

"Spider-Man," I said.

"What?" Katherine said. "Did you say something?"

Shit. I was saying things out loud again. "I'll go look at his things," I said, hoisting myself off the floor. I didn't want to get up—I had been quite enjoying my little sit—but perhaps moving would decrease the amount of nonsense coming out of my mouth for the time being.

"I think this is a real breakthrough," Katherine said, following me to her car. "I think we're one step closer to finding the motherfucker."

There was a thing I said to Katherine when she said words like "motherfucker." What was it? And what was that thing that Sherlock Holmes always said? The thing he was famous for saying? I had forgotten already.

In the trunk of her car, Katherine had Hal's things stacked in a box, an empty case of liquor—this box in particular used to carry Jack Daniel's.

"Yeah," Katherine said, "the irony is not lost on me."

As Katherine said, there wasn't much of Hal's in the box. He hadn't taken very much with him the night he left. The toothbrush in there had barely been used, and it wasn't the one he kept at the house—he must have bought it after he left. Same with the razor (sharp, cheap) and the shaving cream (not his usual brand). He must've bought himself a change of clothes as well—the clothes in the box were the ones he had been wearing the night he left. I grazed my fingers over the soft denim of his jeans, the tough leather of his jacket. God, he loved that jacket. I picked up his Cubs shirt. The fabric was baby soft from years of wear, and I could see the trunk light shining through the faded blue fabric. I lifted the shirt to my face, sniffed it. It didn't smell like him anymore. It smelled like mothballs and old carpet and just a hint of cigarette smoke. I felt a stab of disappointment. I had hoped to smell him again.

Katherine was watching me, her face a mix of emotions I might not have been able to decipher even if I hadn't been operating on God knows how many nights without sleep.

"I shouldn't have left," she said.

I raised an eyebrow at her. "Today?" I asked.

"No," she said. "When I was a kid. When you sent me to live

with Aunt Noelle. I shouldn't have gone. I shouldn't have left you"—she swallowed—"with him."

I rolled the worn fabric of Hal's shirt with my fingers. Katherine was forgetting that she almost hadn't left. She had dug her heels in, as she was wont to do. She chased after us, shouting at Noelle and me as we hurriedly loaded her things into Noelle's car—mostly Noelle doing the loading, as I was in a bit of a state. Katherine had had plenty to say to me, plenty of questions, plenty of refusals, plenty of opinions about why she ought to stay. That time, however, I wasn't backing down.

"I always felt bad," Katherine said. Her eyes were on the trunk of her car, staring at the box of Hal's things, which barely interested her. "I should have stayed. I should have tried to help you. To protect you."

Katherine had said all that in the driveway of our old house as well, standing next to Noelle's idling car as I tried to push her inside. She told me that it wasn't safe for me there. She told me that the terrible things that had happened, that had been happening for years, would happen again and again. She told me that it would get worse after she left. She told me that she had to stay, that she could help protect me.

Katherine, of course, had been wrong. Yes, these terrible things that had been happening for years were likely to go on happening in her absence. Yes, they might even get worse. These things are cyclical—I knew that. But that didn't mean I wasn't safe, and it certainly didn't mean that it was Katherine's job to protect me.

"Claire always told me I shouldn't feel guilty," Katherine said. "She told me I couldn't have done anything to protect you—not really, anyway. She told me that standing up to him would have been dangerous. I was just a kid. He was a full-grown man, and an alcoholic at that. He could have seriously hurt me. Still"—she tapped at her head—"it's there."

I had lines here, surely. I could've told her that Claire had been right—of course Claire had been right. Katherine couldn't have stayed, couldn't have stood up to Hal, and certainly not when he was as gone as he was. The sorts of things he had done when he was like that weren't the sorts of things that Katherine could have been permitted to endure. *Nobody* should've been permitted to endure them, honestly, not unless they knew how to survive. My brain, however, was far too tired to turn any of that into sound. I could only touch at Hal's shirt, staring at the outline of my fingers through the fabric, my mouth useless.

"If we find him," Katherine asked, "will you take him back?"

I looked up from the shirt, startled. "What?"

"Would you take him back? Let him come back?"

"Of course," I said. "Why wouldn't I?"

"You'd be within your rights not to, you know," Katherine said. "I wouldn't blame you. Nobody would. He certainly gave you enough reasons not to take him back, what with the drinking, and the . . ." She gestured to my arms.

"He's my husband," I said.

"This could be your chance, Mom," Katherine said, her eyes eager. "Maybe he's giving you a chance."

This was all moot, of course. I had already made my choices, and they felt permanent.

Katherine shook her head. "You should have come with me," she said. "That day. You should have left for Aunt Noelle's with me. Noelle would've let you stay as long as you liked. You know that." Her eyes were shimmering in the dim light of her trunk. "You could have *left*, Mom. You could have gotten away from him."

Katherine was forgetting again. She had said all this fourteen years ago as well, sitting in the back of Noelle's car, while I did my best to say my goodbyes without tears, which would have irritated my already swollen eyes. She told me I should come with them. She told me that she would share her room at Noelle's with me or even sleep on the couch if needed. She told me that I could start over, that these terrible things that happened to me wouldn't happen anymore. She asked me to go. Begged me to go.

For a moment, I saw Hal again, the day he left, standing on the porch not ten feet from where we stood, these clothes on his body instead of boxed up in the trunk of a rented sedan. Looking at me, pleading, *Come with me.*

Katherine's eyes were insistent, shining on me in the dark like spotlights. "Why didn't you *leave*, Mom?"

Please, Hal had said when he left, *we need to end this.*

Please, Katherine had said when she left, *come with me, Mom.*

I'll end it without you if I have to, Hal had said, *but God, Margaret, I don't want to.*

He'll just keep doing it, you know, Katherine had said. *You know you have to leave, Mom.*

Why? Hal had asked, his expression almost identical to Katherine's as he asked me why, why, why. *Why in God's name do you want to stay?*

I'd always thought it was a silly question, why I wanted to stay here, in this house. This house was everything I'd ever wanted. Sure, it wasn't perfect, but sometimes it actually *was*. Or at least as close as anything could come to perfect in this life, which admittedly was not very close. It wasn't horrible every single day—so few things ever are—and when it wasn't horrible, it was almost lovely. I knew how to survive here, and I always had the sense that if I just survived long enough, if I just played by the rules well enough, I could make it into a perfect home once and for all. I just needed to work a little harder.

I loved this house. And you didn't give up on the things you loved.

Katherine was looking at me as if she expected an answer, one that made sense. I tried to shake the cobwebs from my head. "People can change, Katherine," I said. I nodded towards her. "*You* can change. You're changing." It was true, I realized. I caught fewer and fewer glimpses of the uncontrolled, tantruming child Katherine had once been. The anger was still there, hot and leaping, but I could see her trying to steady it, to keep hold of the reins.

Katherine shook her head. "Barely," she said. "I'm *barely* changing, and it's *hard*, Mom. Half the time I'm so fucking *angry* and . . ." She wiped at her nose. "I never put my hands on her, you know. On Claire. I promised myself I'd never do that. It was the one fucking promise I managed to keep, apparently." Katherine glanced up at me, her eyes red. "You know, when I was a kid, I thought we were the only ones who had problems like this. Everyone else's parents seemed so fucking *happy*. No yelling. No mom with mysterious bruises shoving you out of the house when Dad starts drinking too much. I thought that it was just us, that there was something wrong with *us*. Then I got older and I learned that shit like this happens everywhere. I learned how these stories go. And this little fairy tale you've concocted"—she gestured up towards the house, tall and beautiful in the night—"with your house and your healing and your happy ever after—*it isn't real*."

I blinked at her. The house was as real as things tended to get. *Too* real, if I were being honest. "What are you talking about?" I asked.

"That's not how these stories end," Katherine said. "Husbands who drink, who beat their wives, they don't just wake up one day and decide to stop. It was sheer dumb luck that Dad got that DUI, that he was forced into counseling, that he actually decided to *listen*. I don't know how well he did controlling his anger, but we all know how his sobriety worked out." Her eyes darted to the box, in her trunk, boasting the logo of Hal's favorite pastime. "These stories don't end happily, Mom. They end with somebody dead."

"All stories end with somebody dead," I said. That was how the story of every single person who lived in this house had ended. None of them seemed to be happy endings, but they were endings all the same, and all remarkably similar when it came down to it.

Katherine huffed out a breath, exasperated. "So, that's your take on it?" she asked. "If he comes back, you'll just stay with him forever, just waiting for him to beat you to death?"

Fourteen years ago, when I told her that my leaving wasn't up for consideration, Katherine had been angry. She had cried, sure, but they were angry tears, and her face was pure rage. She had a whole host of things to say to me, various opinions about what an idiot I was: that this was my chance to escape and I was letting it pass me by; that I was *choosing* to let these awful things happen to me from this point forward; that I *deserved* these awful things happening to me if this was the choice I was going to make.

I could see the anger coming back today, the clenched fists and the reddening skin. However, today the anger never quite made it to the surface; it sank back down, defeated, as Katherine's eyes went pink and her mouth tugged into a frown.

She shook her head. "No one deserves to live like this," she said.

No one deserves to live like this, Hal had said to me that night as he was begging me to get into the cab with him.

No one deserves to live like this, Edie said to me that morning on the porch, watching me sob over Master Vale.

It sounded like a bit of a broken record all of a sudden: people telling me what I did and didn't deserve. It might've been the lack of sleep, or the day filled with blood scrubbing and bird carcasses, or the incessant headache that was pounding against the interior of my skull, but I was a bit done with quite a lot and the words were coming out of me before I could even contemplate their usefulness.

"Of *course* no one deserves to live like this," I snapped, although I was no longer certain to whom in particular I was talking. "Of *course* this isn't a hell anybody wants to walk through, least of all alone. But none of that exactly matters, now, does it? It doesn't change reality. And *this*"—I gestured around myself, waving my arms at the car, the house, the night, only half of which I was actually certain was completely real—"is reality. There's no sense in bellyaching over it if it can't be changed. One does what one must. *There are rules.*"

"But *you* can change it, Mom," Katherine said. "Didn't you just tell me that people can change? *You* can change."

I hadn't the first clue what she was talking about. I changed all the time. I was flexible. I bent. I had changed little by little, steadily over the years, until by all accounts I was a person who should have been unrecognizable but to me was just who I was. I ought to have been a stranger to myself, but it didn't bother me at all.

"You can do things differently this time," Katherine said. "If we find him, you can choose not to take him back." She shook her head, her exasperation returning. "God, Mom—why would you *ever* take him back?"

The lack of sleep was steadily making itself known to me. My head throbbed, and I was fairly finished with this conversation. "Would you take Claire back?" I asked, knowing the answer.

Katherine's eyes flashed fire. "That's not the same."

"Of course it's the same," I said. "It's love."

Katherine grabbed at my arm, pulled my sleeve down to my elbow, revealing the scars from Elias' teeth. "This isn't love, Mom," she said.

I looked at the marks on my arms. "Oh, that's just Elias," I said.

Katherine blinked, still holding my arm. *Who?*

Shit. I was saying things out loud again. "Everything is survivable," I said.

Katherine dropped my arm. She seemed finished with this conversation as well. "Not everything," she said.

I said nothing. I found myself completely out of responses.

I hadn't said anything more to Hal as he stood on the porch that night either, the cab idling in the driveway. He seemed to have nothing else to say as well, and after a few silent moments, he turned and got into the cab. He looked at me once from the window, then up at the house, his expression changing. Then he turned and said something to the driver. As the cab sped away, I closed the front door behind me. Fredricka made me some tea and I sat in the kitchen and chatted with her as she scrubbed the countertops.

"Do you want any of this crap?" Katherine asked. She had a look like she wanted to light all of it on fire.

I gazed at Hal's Cubs shirt, his jacket. I might have been feeling something like sadness, something in the same neighborhood, anyway. But the only feeling I could identify with any degree of certainty now was exhaustion. "I suppose not," I said. I tossed the shirt back into the box.

Katherine slammed the trunk and the last traces of Hal disappeared from sight. That night, Katherine drank from Hal's partially finished whiskey bottle, which she had retrieved from his office. I watched a thin film of sweat form around her temples and a light sway creep into her gait. She could barely stumble up the stairs by the time the DoZZZe-Rite took hold.

SEVENTEEN

There are rules to these things. Everything is survivable.

Once it was clear what sort of life Hal and I would be living together, what with his anger and his hands, I knew I needed to figure out some solutions. With Hal, there were all sorts of rules for all sorts of situations, and I was an expert at following them.

Most of them were no big deal at all. Don't go into Hal's office or touch his things. Don't contradict or disagree with him—as much as it can be helped, anyway. Be sure he knows where I am at all times, that I have no time unaccounted for. And so on. Some were trickier than others. Not talking to men anymore, not even small talk with a cashier, was certainly tricky (as it turns out, men are *everywhere*), and not talking to Noelle was nearly impossible. Still, it was feasible, all of it.

The rules weren't foolproof by any means. Sometimes they didn't work; sometimes troubleshooting was needed. And when Hal had been drinking, the rules went out the window altogether. Nothing was particularly effective. I could perfectly follow the rule of letting him know where I was at all times, texting him before I left for the store, while I was there, and when I left with an estimated time of arrival that was precise down to the minute, and he would still be upset that I was at the store in the first place and also that I didn't remember to buy oranges. I could ignore the seventh call in a row from Noelle, having gone over a month without speaking to her at all, and he would be upset that she called in the first place, or seemingly that she even existed. Nobody can create rules for these situations—they're too specific, too arbitrary. So the rule was to do nothing. Brace for impact. For an evening, the house would become a conductor for chaos. I charted the progression of the storm, from slurring to yelling to stumbling to fists to unconsciousness to teary, heartfelt apologies that came either much later that night or the following morning. Clockwork.

Mind you, it wasn't all difficult. There were good times, times when things were peaceful and everyone got along. There were times when Hal and I laughed over dinner, times when the three of us all went for ice cream and had a lovely evening, even Katherine. Once or twice, Hal and I even managed a weekend away at the beach, when Katherine was off on a school trip or staying over at a friend's. I never really knew how long the good times would last—sometimes a few days, sometimes a few months—so it was best to enjoy the moments when they were around and not to worry about the future. When they lasted for a while, it was almost enough to make me think I'd solved it, that I'd finally figured out the right combination of behaviors to keep everything happy, blissful. Of course, nothing lasts forever—that's just the cyclical nature of it all. However, if the rules were followed, the good times could last longer.

With Hal, the most important rule of all was about leaving—don't do it. Don't mention it. Don't even think about it. If I had to pick just one rule to follow, it would be this one. Hal wasn't afraid of many things—or at least he wasn't before we moved here—but this was his biggest fear. It turned him into a cornered animal, lashing out, snarling with angry terror, unpredictable. But it never really mattered, because I wasn't going anywhere. The trick was never to let Hal suspect I was thinking of it, even though I wasn't. And definitely not when he'd been drinking.

That is all to say, I understood the rules and I knew when I needed to start playing by them. And I can't tell you how I knew it, but I had a feeling that the house and Hal had the same sorts of feelings about my leaving. The thought had nibbled at my mind for a while, the way you can tell when there's a tiny bit of gravel in your shoe. I never liked to spend time away from the house and always made sure to return as quickly as possible. I once left a full cart of groceries in the middle of the aisle when I spied how long the checkout lines were. No thank you. Sometimes even walks down to the mailbox had me hustling along, nearly jogging my way back to the front door. If there was a rule to it, it wasn't particularly complex or even explicitly stated, but it was clear—*don't*.

Okay, I thought. *I won't.*

And that was all before Katherine came, before her little jaunts to bars and hotels brought limericks and paintings and songs. Little reminders everywhere of the pranksters disapproving of my extended trips away, signaling me to go back home. Nothing objectively threatening about any of it, but added together, it had the feel of a large person looming just behind me, scowling. There was something it was meant to communicate. *We see you, Margaret. We know where you are.* It wasn't a particularly coherent message, but it was certainly a noticeable one.

If you ever leave, Hal once said to me, *God as my witness, I will find you. Wherever you go, I'll find you.*

I don't doubt it, I said.

Truly, I'd never understood what the fuss was about. I'd had no intentions of leaving Hal back then and I certainly had no intentions of leaving the house now. I loved it here. Sure, the house had its little idiosyncrasies and headaches, which could certainly get dangerous at times, but I loved it all the same. After all, if we didn't love something, flaws included, what sort of love would that be? Yes, there were rules galore, but they were all feasible. Survivable. The house didn't have to waste its time on little messages and subtle threats when I stepped out the door—I wasn't going anywhere. I would stay here until I was pried out with a crowbar.

This is my home, and I am excellent at following the rules.

EIGHTEEN

We had been just under three Septembers in when Hal started to change. He stopped sleeping. He was tired, certainly, but he didn't come to bed at night, choosing to stay awake, pacing. He seemed disoriented, rubbing at his eyes and ears, asking me to repeat myself when I hadn't said anything. I shrugged and carried on with my day. It was unusual, certainly, but if I allowed an unusual thing to grind everything to a halt in this house, I would never get anything accomplished.

I was in my studio painting a lovely scene of children playing in a field—most of their limbs still intact—when Hal approached me, his eyes glued to the floor. He looked like a child reluctantly admitting to breaking an antique lamp, and only because he knew he'd be found out anyway.

"That man you said you saw," Hal said, "the one from the basement. What did he look like?"

I had seen Master Vale only a handful of times at this point, but he was memorable. "Tall," I said. "Taller than you'd think a human ought to be." I considered. "I don't think he's human anymore, though. Depending on your definition." I waved a hand, then continued. "He's skinny, nearly all bones. He doesn't look like he ought to be able to hold himself upright."

"Does he have sores?" Hal asked. "All over his body?"

"Yeah," I said, wrinkling my nose. "Pretty gross, isn't it?" I grinned at Hal. "Have you seen him? Master Vale?" This seemed like wonderful news. Perhaps Hal could help me speculate on Master Vale's origins, fill in the gaps the newspapers had left. Perhaps I'd finally have a sort of partner in crime in all of this.

Hal wasn't smiling. "When he talks to you," he said, his voice wavering, "does he sound"—he tapped at his head, as if the voice had burrowed itself somewhere in the center of his brain, a tick digging under skin—"wrong?"

"Wrong?" I asked.

"Like he can't quite speak at all," Hal said. "Like he's laughing."

My brow furrowed. I had never heard Master Vale speak before. I had heard barely any of the pranksters speak. At this point, Angelica and her friends hadn't started notifying me about the basement ad nauseam yet, and the only prankster I had heard speak actual words was Fredricka.

"He talks to you?" I asked. "What does he tell you?"

Hal's eyes were wet. His lips shook. "To get out of his house," he said.

"Well," I said, "we live here now."

Hal shook his head. He stared at the window, glaring at the yard as if it had personally wronged him in some manner. I could see his fear morphing itself into anger already, painting his face red, curling his fingers into fists. Hal was familiar with anger; he preferred it. It was like a warm blanket to him, something soft and smelling of home.

"We have to do something, Margaret," he said.

"Easy," I said. "We play by the rules."

But that wasn't what Hal meant.

NINETEEN

The next morning (or, rather, early afternoon), Katherine sat groggily at the kitchen table, nursing her third cup of tea while I washed dishes. That is, I did something akin to washing dishes. I wasn't putting a lot of thought or effort into it, but I was rubbing a sponge over a dish and that was in the ballpark, anyway.

"I didn't think I had that much to drink," Katherine said. "I thought I only had two glasses. Maybe three. But I feel like shit."

I wondered if I ought to have slipped her only one DoZZZe-Rite tablet, given the whiskey and all. Still, it was nice to have a bit of time when Katherine wasn't dragging me along on her little investigation. More freedom to deal with the pranksters without any pesky but valid questions. I said nothing.

I had actually drifted off to sleep for a moment or two the night before, despite the screaming. I fell into a dream almost immediately, a terrible dream that Master Vale had found Katherine and had her pinned to the floor, gnarled hand planted firmly on her chest, pressing her down. His rotted teeth bore down on her in a manic grin. When she parted her lips to scream, he hissed a stream of flies into her open mouth and she started gagging. That thing was happening to me where I couldn't move or scream, like I was floating in a vat of honey. I heard a little croak escape my mouth and Master Vale's oozing head snapped in my direction, and all of a sudden it was Hal's face, broken and wrong. He howled at me and Katherine howled through the flies and her head was split in two like Fredricka's and finally, *finally*, I howled back and jerked into consciousness and was awake, likely forever.

No matter. I had chores to do.

This morning had brought the arrival of another one of Angelica's friends—a boy named either Thomas or Tobias. I could never remember. He was a lanky lad with a mess of dark hair and a dirty face cut through with vertical lines from his tears. One of his arms had been removed in a very haphazard and imprecise manner. His remaining arm could still point, though. I spotted him on the second-floor landing while cleaning the blood a little lower down the stairwell than I would have liked. I expected only one more of Angelica's friends—I had completely forgotten that one's name—to show up this month, and we would have a real full house. That would be a touch overwhelming, but it wasn't anything I hadn't dealt with before.

"Have you been washing that one dish this whole time?" Katherine asked, finally rising far enough out of her funk to be perceptive. I looked down. Why, yes, I had been. There wasn't even soap on the sponge. But the tap was running, and it wasn't blood coming out. Small favors.

"No," I lied. I dried off the probably not-clean dish, and went to put it back in the cabinet. Inside the cabinet was a pile of dirt.

Wonderful. I set the dish next to the dirt. I would deal with that later.

Katherine rubbed her forehead, staring down into her half-empty teacup. "There's not enough caffeine in this shit," she said.

This morning, the tea bags had been outside on the rocking chairs. At least I had known to look for them.

"You don't have an aspirin, do you?" Katherine asked. "I checked the medicine cabinet upstairs but there was just a bunch of spoons in there. Why do you keep spoons in there, by the way?"

Goddamnit, Fredricka.

"I think I have some in the master bathroom," I said. I darted down the hallway, hoping to avoid both her question and the chance of her following me upstairs. There was actually only about a twenty percent chance that the aspirin was still in the bathroom instead of, say, crammed behind the hot water heater, and my search would go better without Katherine hovering behind me, that concerned expression planted on her face. With all my remaining mental faculties dedicated to figuring out where the hell the aspirin might be, I turned towards the stairs without looking where I was going. I hadn't even realized I'd walked straight into Elias until I heard the jet-engine noise and felt the cold blackness overtake me.

I was in time, however, to watch his fangs sink into my forearm.

"*Jesus Christ,*" I shouted before I could stop myself. Saying things out loud again. I clamped a hand over my mouth, as if that would take the words back from the air.

Elias' biting me produced an effect slightly different from whenever any of the other pranksters touched me. I didn't see the world through his eyes like with Fredricka or feel what it felt like when he died like with the other little pranksters but instead just sank into a pit of blackness and anger. I imagine that was still what it was like when he died, but it was a bit trickier to grasp. It also made it very difficult to focus. I tried to tug my arm from his mouth, but he had latched on tight, and his fangs sank deeper into my skin with each twist of my forearm. In between flickers of angry blackness, I could see blood pooling between his teeth, dripping onto the floor. Shit shit *shit*.

"Mom, what happened?" Katherine was running down the hall towards me.

Shit.

Shit.

Shit.

"Katherine—*no*." My voice sounded too panicked to claim nothing had happened. The blackness was still flickering in and out. I shook my head, trying to stay rooted in the here and now. "Nothing happened. Don't worry."

But Katherine was already around the corner.

Elias was still latched onto my arm. I was half in the *now* and half in the *then*, trying with all my might to focus on Elias and his fangs while remnants of an inky void and directionless rage danced behind my eyes.

"What is— Holy *shit*, Mom," Katherine said, her eyes wide.

"Katherine," I said, blinking away the blackness, "I can explain. You don't need to be afraid. I didn't want you to know. But it's okay." I looked down at Elias, who was making a noise like fading propellers. "It's all okay."

"What the fuck happened to your *arm*?" Katherine shouted, moving towards me, hands out to grab my arm.

"*No*," I said, my free hand outstretched to stop her. The blackness flickered around me, and I was only somewhat sure where Katherine was even standing. "Don't come any closer. I mean, it's safe. Don't worry. Just . . ." I tried to back away, but Elias still had ahold of me and he wasn't budging, the bastard. Although if he was intent on continuing to bite me, at least he wouldn't be biting Katherine. Silver lining.

"What do you mean, it's safe?" Katherine asked, not paying attention to my warnings, confusing as they admittedly were. "You're bleeding all over the place. How the hell did you cut yourself?" Her eyes darted all around me.

I blinked, looking down at Elias. The burning holes of Elias' eyes seemed to meet mine, although it was hard to tell for sure, especially when the image was interspersed with strobes of void and rage. "Do you not . . ." I blinked some more. "Do you not see him?"

Katherine looked at me like I was speaking German. "See *who*, Mom?"

"I . . ." My brain was foggy. None of this made sense. Elias was right *there*, plain as day, very real and very toothy. He growled at me, his lips curling, revealing more of my blood caught in his gums. Yep, he was there all right. As for me, I was only partially there, still caught in limbo between Elias' angry past and my confused present.

"Who are you talking about, Mom?" Katherine moved closer. I jumped back the best I could, given the trap my arm was in. My hand was still out flat, practically touching Katherine's stomach to keep her away.

"It's nothing," I said too quickly. "But don't come closer. Please." To my left, I could see the other pranksters drifting over. Angelica and Julian and Charles and Constance and Thomas or Tobias or whoever. My eyes darted to them, then back to Katherine. Could she not see them either?

"What are you looking at, Mom?" Katherine asked, her worried gaze following mine. "Did you see someone in here?" She strode past me to peer into the living room, walking right through the line of pranksters. They parted like the seas for her but kept their eyes on me.

She couldn't see them.

I stared at them in disbelief, almost forgetting about Elias on my arm. Almost.

"Mom, there's no one here," Katherine said. "You have to tell me what happened. How did you hurt your arm?" She grabbed at my forearm with both hands, yanking it from Elias' mouth painfully and bringing me back into the here and now, the dark and the anger a rapidly fading memory. Elias made that noise and bared his fangs again, turning his nightmare maw towards Katherine.

"NO," I yelled, pushing Katherine out of the way. Elias' teeth gnashed against air and he howled in rage, finally disappearing into himself and letting us be for the moment.

"What the *fuck*, Mom?" Katherine snapped, stumbling backwards. "I'm just trying to help you. Did you . . ." She had the look in her eyes that Hal and I must have had when we confronted her about smoking cigarettes as a teenager. "Did you do this to yourself?"

Jesus Christ. This was all out of hand now. "Of *course* not."

Katherine had me by the other arm, the one that wasn't bleeding. "I'm not fucking around, Mom. There's nothing here that could have cut you. I'll ask you again." Her eyes were fire. "Did you do this to yourself?"

"I didn't . . . I would *never* . . ." But what could I tell her? It wasn't like telling her about Elias—the little dead boy she couldn't see who bit me sometimes—would buy me any more sanity credits in her eyes. She had me between a real rock and a hard place here, and my brain was still trying to turn its grinding wheels around everything that was happening, and Christ, my arm *stung*.

And Christ, my arm was *really* bleeding now.

"*Christ*," I said.

Katherine looked down at my arm. "Oh, fuck," she said. "Okay, where is your first aid kit?" Not waiting for my answer, she tightened her grip on my arm and dragged me up the stairs, towards the bathroom. "We need to get that cleaned up. Do you have hydrogen peroxide? I don't know if you'll need stitches. If you do, I'm taking you to the emergency room right *now*."

"This is all . . . silly," I said, fully aware that it wasn't particularly silly but unable to think of anything else to say. I watched my blood drip onto the stairs as we ascended. The irony was palpable.

The pranksters stayed at the bottom of the stairs, watching us.

"I'm not joking," Katherine was saying. "If I think for even one second that you need stitches, I am— *Jesus fucking Christ*." Katherine stopped so abruptly in the door of the bathroom that I nearly tripped into her back. She stood at the door, eyes wide, mouth gaping.

In the bathroom sink, piled in a haphazard, glistening stack, was every single knife from the kitchen drawers. Paring knives, butcher knives, carving knives, even a butter knife.

I ran a hand over my forehead. "Goddamnit, Fredricka," I said.

Katherine turned to face me, her expression a mix of confusion and fear. She pointed at herself. "I'm *Katherine*," she said.

"Yes, I know that, dear," I said, brushing past her to gather up the knives. I hoped that Fredricka hadn't filled the kitchen drawers with dirt too, or I wouldn't know where to put these.

Katherine darted in front of me, blocking me from approaching the sink. "Stay the *fuck* away from those," she said. She pushed me back to the bathroom door. She looked around, considering what her next move ought to be, before yanking a towel—one of the nice guest ones—off the rack and gathering the knives into it one by one.

"Careful," I said.

"You're one to talk," she snapped. She wrapped the towel around the knives and held it away from her body in a fist. She stared at it for a moment, unsure what to do next, before pushing past me and disappearing into her room. It would seem that the knives would be living in there for the time being, although given the propensity for things to move around in this house, it was unlikely to make much of a difference.

Katherine emerged from her room, knifeless. "Don't even *think* about going in there after them," she said, pointing a finger at me. She started down the stairs. "Are there any knives left in the kitchen?" she called up to me. She didn't wait for a response.

Meanwhile, I was alone in the bathroom, bleeding all over the floor. I stared down at my arm without really seeing it. What had happened just now?

Fredricka appeared in the doorway, holding a lamp. "Does ma'am require assistance?"

"Jesus, Fredricka," I said. "What the hell was with the knives?"

Fredricka ignored the question. "Can I help?" she asked.

I sighed. "You can help me get cleaned up, I suppose."

"Of course, ma'am," Fredricka said. She dropped the lamp and it shattered.

"What the hell was that?" Katherine yelled from downstairs.

I flinched. "Nothing," I called out. Fredricka moved past me and started rummaging through the cabinets. Looking for bandages, I hoped.

I heard Katherine walking back down the hallway, towards the stairs. *"I heard something crash."*

I turned to Fredricka. "Get out of here," I hissed.

Fredricka pulled a box of gauze out from under the sink, not looking at me. "Ma'am's daughter cannot see me."

She might have been right about that, but I didn't want to risk it. "I'm serious, Fredricka. Get out of here. You're going to spook—"

"Who are you talking to?" Katherine said from the doorway.

I turned to look at Katherine, then turned my head behind me to look at Fredricka. She stood by the sink, still and stoic. *See?* her expression seemed to say.

"I . . ." I wasn't sure how to explain much of this.

"And what the hell is going on in the kitchen?" Katherine said. "Nothing is where it's supposed to be. Why the hell are your socks in the utensil drawer? And where the hell are the utensils? Why are you moving things around?"

I closed my eyes, thinking. I hoped that Fredricka could somehow sense the curses I was hurling at her in my mind. "I . . ."

"Fuck. You're bleeding everywhere." Katherine finally remembered my arm. She noticed the gauze on the counter. "Oh, good," she said, pulling me over towards the sink. Fredricka stepped out of her way. Katherine didn't see her.

"Do you have any hydrogen peroxide?" Katherine asked.

I looked over at Fredricka. *Well?*

"In the attic," Fredricka said.

"No," I said to Katherine. "I don't think I have any."

Katherine turned the faucet on full blast. She grabbed my bloodied arm. "This is going to suck," she said.

And it did.

TWENTY

Seeing Master Vale had really lit a fire under Hal, and that third September, Hal decided he was going to take matters into his own hands.

"We have to fight him," he said to me. "We have to take our goddamn house back."

So many of Hal's solutions involved fighting.

I didn't think it was the right way, but Hal was insistent. I dug out my old research about Master Vale and the missing children and taught Hal everything I had pieced together over the years. We sat at the kitchen table, my crumpled printouts and clippings spread in front of us.

"The bastard *has* to have some sort of weakness," Hal said.

I wondered if "bastard" was the best term to use, given what we knew about Master Vale's upbringing, but I kept my mouth shut.

It was early in the month. The screaming was still just moaning, and the blood was relegated to the third floor. Angelica was around, but none of her friends had arrived yet. There were two ways of looking at this—with deep dread for the terrors that were to come or thankfulness that they were not yet upon us. I took the latter approach; Hal took the former. I had long known that Master Vale was the biggest of the problems in September, but for the rest of the year, he was manageable. I caught him roaming the house a few times, and he gave chase whenever he saw me, but thus far, I'd been able to outrun him. Sure, he'd whispered a few threats into Hal's ear, but he hadn't exactly *done* anything other than piss Hal off. As far as I was concerned, Master Vale was survivable, a problem controlled.

Hal, of course, saw things a bit differently. He seemed to take Master Vale's presence as a personal threat—whether to his safety, status as master of the house, or general sense of sanity, I hadn't the foggiest—and he was not willing to stand for threats. Me, I didn't think that anything the pranksters did was meant to be personal. This was their house first, after all.

"What about fire?" Hal asked. "We could smoke him out."

"We don't want the house catching fire," I said.

"Well," Hal said, "maybe a little bit of burning will be what it takes to get him out of here."

"I am not having you burn this house down," I said.

Hal made a little grumbling noise but went back to flipping through the papers, letting the issue drop. I could hear Fredricka moving about in the dining room, cleaning nervously. She was still acting helpful for the time being. She might even make us dinner later. I hoped for a pot roast.

"What about something with his family?" Hal asked. "Like you did with that boy?"

"Elias," I said.

"Yeah," Hal said. "Dig up their bones or something."

"That doesn't exactly make Elias go away permanently," I said. At this point, I had excavated Elias' mother only two or three times. I tried to reserve that trick for special occasions, like the start of September.

"Maybe we can *make* it permanent," Hal said, "if we're forceful about it. You go up there with that boy and just sing a little song. Maybe with that freak downstairs, we don't sing to him. We let him know he needs to leave us the hell alone." Hal might have been eight years out of therapy and ten years sober, but he had never quite given up the idea that all problems can be solved with the right amount of muscle.

And despite the fact that Hal was eight years out of therapy and ten years sober, I still never strayed very far from the rule of not arguing with him. That wasn't to say we never disagreed, but I found gentler ways of doing so and picked my battles. A very small number of battles.

"Regardless," I said, riffling through the papers until I found the stack of obituaries for the Vales, "they aren't buried out in the woods like Elias' mother. They're buried in that big cemetery in town. You know, the one by Saint Dymphna's?"

Hal grunted at the obituaries.

I pointed. "Here's a picture of George and Penelope's grave marker." George and Penelope, apparently set on being a fixture in the town even after death, were buried under a statue of a giant angel, arms outstretched underneath its flowing wings. Their names were inscribed clearly on the stone below the angel. "I think it'd be tough to sneak bones out from there."

Hal grunted again. "I guess grave robbing is still beneath us."

I considered that what I had been doing with Elias' mother was technically grave robbing, but I didn't want to split hairs.

"Maybe something else to do with his family," Hal said. "If it has an impact on that boy—"

"Elias."

"—it *has* to have an impact on what's-his-face." Hal poked his thumb in the direction of the basement.

"Master Vale."

Hal raised an eyebrow at me. I could see an old irritation throbbing in his head. He didn't like that I called the man downstairs Master, that I was reverent enough to give this man in our basement a name or any sort of attention. Years ago, this might have been a bigger issue. However, Hal's therapy was telling him that it was irrational to feel jealous of a man who had been dead for over a century and wished to seriously harm both of us. Hal listened, albeit reluctantly.

We didn't solve the problem that day. The best solution we could come up with was finding something that could reconnect Master Vale with his family (*I don't think he'll be happy to see them*, I said. *That's the point*, Hal said), but we had no idea where to start looking for something like that, or even what we'd be looking for. Hal scoured a few antique shops in the area on the off chance that some Vale family heirloom was on display, but didn't have any luck. Eventually, he started poking around in various corners of the house (pointedly avoiding the basement) and managed to find something hidden under some floorboards in the attic. I wasn't particularly happy he was prying up floorboards, but I decided it was a battle I wasn't willing to fight.

"*Look.*" Hal beamed, holding the item out for me to examine— a long object made of thick wood, faded pale with time and use and coated with dust. On one side was a handle, with finger grooves molded into the wood; the other side was wide and flat.

"It's . . . a paddle?" I asked.

"Yes," Hal said, scrubbing some dust off the wood. "And look right here—the initials G.V. And look what's written there."

Inscribed along the side of the paddle were the words "Master of the House."

"Do you think George beat his children with this?" I asked, turning it over in my hands. I wasn't so sure I enjoyed holding such a thing. I was also wondering if Hal had put the floorboards back in place in the attic, or if that was to be my responsibility.

"Maybe," Hal said, looking at the paddle as if it were a holy relic. "I suppose there weren't many spare-the-rod sorts of people back in those days."

"It looks *really* worn," I said. If Violet's letters about George Vale were to be believed, he got quite a lot of use out of the thing indeed. The middle of the paddle—the part that had likely come into contact with the most skin—was dim and faded, the wood smooth.

Hal took the paddle from me. He smacked it against his palm like a batter about to step up to the plate, certain of a home run in his future. "All the better," he said. "I bet just one look at this and old Vale downstairs will turn tail and run."

Something told me that Master Vale was not the turning-tail type, but I said nothing.

By this point, September was in full swing, and Hal insisted upon going down into the basement to confront Master Vale as soon as possible. I wondered if we'd ought to wait until October, but the compromise we reached was that we would do it during the day instead of at night.

We developed the sketches of a plan. We would go down into the basement, find Master Vale, and then . . . show him the paddle.

"Do you think we'll have to *hit* him with the paddle?" I asked as I stood outside the basement door with Hal, flashlight in my hand. To me, there seemed to be many details still to iron out.

But Hal already had his hand on the doorknob. "I don't think so," he said with absolutely no evidence to support his opinion.

So down we went.

The basement door creaked open. We hadn't yet put the boards or the Bible pages up—that would come later. Hal flicked the light switch and an insufficient yellow glow illuminated what lay below. Nothing but stairs in front of us.

The basement was ancient and unfinished: dirt floors like back in the old days, plain brick walls, and exposed wooden beams that gave us a peek into how the house was supported. Cobwebs clung to the corners in huge clusters. I didn't even want to think about what sort of critters lived down here. There were no windows, making me realize that doing this during the daytime, as I'd insisted, had minimal advantages. The air was thick and clammy, and there was always that *smell* that we couldn't quite place but that seemed like an indication of something very wrong.

Hal descended the stairs first, the paddle slung over his shoulder like a baseball bat. I followed him with the flashlight, my hands feeling very weaponless all of a sudden. I felt like a fool, but I clung to Hal's shoulder with my free hand, desperate to stay close.

We reached the bottom of the stairs and looked around, trying not to show each other how nervous we were. The basement was huge, spanning the entire footprint of the house, and in the dim light and with the support beams obscuring the view, it was difficult to see from one side to the other. From where we stood, the basement seemed empty, save for a few boxes, but I wouldn't have described it as calm or still. It felt like the moments before a thunderstorm hits, when the air is sweet and unmoving but the sky is black and you know you had best get to shelter *fast*.

"Do we just . . . call out for him?" I asked.

Hal and I had the exact same amount of information about and experience in this endeavor, but Hal was the sort of person who had answers when I had only questions. "Not just yet," he said.

We didn't move. We stood by the stairs, looking around, our bodies like tightly wound springs. I thought I saw the lights flicker, but I might have been mistaken about that. I could hear Hal breathing next to me, heavier than he would have liked, probably.

"Should we look around?" I asked.

"Yes," Hal said, as if lingering, motionless, by the stairs for a few moments before moving had been a very precise part of his plan and had nothing whatsoever to do with nerves.

We started moving slowly, turning first to the left of the stairs to examine the portion of the basement directly underneath the living room. I shone the light into the dim section of the room, revealing only dirt and cobwebs. The light landed on a glimmering spiderweb with a large spider sitting in the middle of it. I crinkled my nose. The lights flickered again, and for a split second, only the white beam of the flashlight was visible. I wasn't mistaken this time.

"Where are you?" Hal said. It would have been a cry for Master Vale, had he not said it so quietly, barely loudly enough for even me to hear.

We turned back to the stairs to examine the other half of the basement. The only sounds were the scrapes of our footsteps on the floor and our shaky breathing.

At the far side of the basement, there was a brick wall carving off something that could have been a separate room if any of the house's previous owners had been brave enough to renovate. The entrance to that room was large and open, but we could see only darkness inside, and the remainder of the room was obscured from our view. I had a feeling we were saving that section of the basement for last.

We shuffled around the middle of the basement, me shining the flashlight into corners and Hal smacking the paddle against his palm. "*C'mon,*" I heard Hal whisper—not to me.

We heard something rustle to our left and I shone the light at the source of the noise—a mouse scurried along the wall.

"Do we have mice?" I whispered.

The lights flickered again. In the darkness, we heard something that sounded like a scream silenced abruptly.

Hal and I caught each other's eye.

No point in delaying it further. We turned towards the little room on the far side of the basement. Hal lifted the paddle in the air at his shoulder, prepared to swing. I held the flashlight in front of me. Inch by inch, we drifted towards the darkness inside the room.

The lights flickered again. Again. Each flicker brought a second of a scream, snuffed out as soon as the light returned.

The smell was definitely more noticeable now, practically visible. There was a palpable sense of *not okay* surrounding us, a sense that we had ignored several warnings and it was now too late. If you had asked me, I would have said it was no longer daytime outside. But then, if you had asked me, I would also have said it was no longer *now* outside. I wasn't sure how, but something felt very much like *then* in this basement.

The lights were flickering faster now, the screams connecting to form a continuous sound rather than a punctuated one.

We walked inside the little room.

Of course, there he was, blinking into existence as the lights worked into a frenzy, the time frame of the world around us shifting from *now* to *then*. There was a light dangling from the ceiling above him in the *then*, and we could see the room clearly even in the dimness. He had a whole workstation set up in the little room, with various tools and sharp things hanging from the walls and a wooden table in the center. On the table, tied down by the wrists and ankles, was Angelica. She was wearing her not-quite-blue-anymore dress and her dirty hair was everywhere. She wasn't screaming just yet, but it looked like she ought to be at any moment. Angelica rolled her head to the side and caught my eye. She didn't seem particularly surprised to see Hal and me standing in the doorway. She had been directing us down here for quite some time, after all.

Master Vale stood in the corner, his back to us. He seemed to be considering the tools on the walls, making a decision. He had one arm tucked behind his back, with his other hand hovering in the air, wavering in front of his shining gadgets. Choosing. The screaming noise was coming from him.

His entire body seemed to brighten as he made his decision. He lifted a large hammer from the wall, the metal head thick and heavy. He tested the weight of it in his hand as he turned around.

Now that we could see his face, we realized that he hadn't been screaming at all. He was *laughing*. His red-rimmed eyes were wide with delight, those of a child on Christmas morning. His rotting teeth were bared in a grin that seemed as if it would split his lips at the corners. He was overjoyed. He was ecstatic. He walked towards Angelica, the hammer in his hand. He seemingly couldn't see us, or at least was too distracted by the task in front of him to care about our presence.

Hal was frozen next to me. He had stopped breathing normally, instead taking in small sips of air with tight little gasps. The paddle had lowered to his side but I could still see it shaking in his hand.

We should do something, I thought. *We need to intervene. We need to help Angelica.*

But I knew anything we did would be futile. After all, this was *then,* not *now.* What had happened to Angelica had happened a very, very long time ago. I knew how this story ended. I had read the newspaper clippings. I knew about her disappearance. But most of all, I had *seen* her. I knew what had happened to her head.

Master Vale stood by Angelica's side. His laughter was louder now, a shrill, piercing sound that seemed to be hurled from his very core, snapping through his parted teeth and seeping out his bulging eyes. He started to raise the hammer.

Angelica didn't look at him. Her eyes were still on me, her face placid.

Stop looking at us, Angelica, I thought. *Look at him. Do something. Struggle. Run away. Don't let the thing that is about to happen to you happen.*

But I knew how difficult running away could be.

Master Vale held the hammer high above his head. He hadn't blinked in what seemed like ages. His mouth was a shriek, pure sound.

Then the thing that had happened to Angelica's head happened.

Her mouth opened. I couldn't tell if in surprise, pain, or just reflex. If she made a noise, it couldn't be heard over the sound of Master Vale. She didn't stop looking in my direction, but one of her eyes wasn't quite solid anymore.

And then it was all over for Angelica.

I heard Hal make a little noise next to me, a kind of choked gasp. My own breathing sounded much louder—*too* loud, really.

Knowing how this story ended didn't make watching it any more bearable.

When Master Vale was finished with his hammer—and it was quite clear when his job was done—he let his hand drop to his side. The hammer clanged onto the floor. His face was still a mad slash of delight but his laughter was a low wheeze now, his thin shoulders rising and falling heavily with his breath. He looked satisfied, proud, like he had just painted a masterpiece. He leaned forward over Angelica and planted his hands on either side of her head, fingers digging into her skin like needles. He lowered himself down to her, his mouth gaping and teeth bared, pale gray tongue leaking a string of drool as it stretched out to taste and—okay—*that* part I didn't see coming. There was only so much you could tell about someone's death from looking at their shattered skull, I supposed. My stomach lurched.

Hal screamed.

Master Vale's head snapped up. His nightmare eyes met mine. The smile fell from his face and was replaced by a snarl. He bared his teeth. They were covered in blood.

Shit shit *shit*.

Master Vale pushed Angelica's head aside and straightened to his full height. He made a sort of hissing noise and slowly started towards us, crossing from behind the table. He licked at his teeth, his mouth leaking red.

I began backing up but Hal, gulping, stood his ground. He held up George Vale's paddle. His hand trembled.

"Hal," I whispered, tugging at his shoulder, "we need to leave."

"Theodore Vale," Hal said, his voice loud but wavering, "do you recognize this?"

If Master Vale recognized it, he gave no indication. His long legs walked him closer. He was starting to grin.

"Hal . . . ," I said.

"This is *our* house," Hal said, his voice increasing in conviction, but only by an ounce, "not yours. It's time for you to get out."

Master Vale's grin was wider now, and he was starting to laugh again. The noise rattled out of him, as thin as the wind.

I tugged harder at Hal's shoulder. "We need to leave *now.*"

Behind Master Vale, the table with Angelica was fading, going back home to *then*. Now it was just Master Vale and us. The lights flickered out, and the basement seemed hopelessly dark. Now there was just the beam of my flashlight, and I was having a difficult time holding it steady.

"*Get out of our house and leave us alone,*" Hal shouted.

Master Vale was quite close indeed. Hal craned his neck to look at him, raising the paddle even higher in an effort to seem intimidating. It didn't work.

"*Go away right now,*" Hal shouted, "*or I will beat you like your father did.*"

I let out a little whimper.

Within seconds, the smile on Master Vale's face was replaced by rage. In one fluid motion, he raised his open hand and smacked the paddle right out of Hal's shaking fist. It clattered across the room, useless.

"*Run,*" I screamed to Hal, my feet already moving me backwards. This plan was not going to work. I raced towards the stairs, stumbling over dirt and uneven ground in the darkness. There was the sound of cursing behind me, Hal finally coming to his senses and following after me. I didn't need to look back to know Master Vale was behind us. I heard Hal's body bump into support beams as he ran, heard him curse and cry out. The flashlight I was still somehow holding was waving wildly, the light erratic. It didn't matter. We just needed to get to the stairs, get out of the base-ment, and never come down here again.

"*Margaret*," Hal called out. I was at the stairs already, but I turned around, shone the light in his direction. Hal was on the ground. He had fallen. His fingers dug into the dirt as he tried like hell to pull himself back up and resume running, but Master Vale had him by the legs, his needle fingers stabbing into Hal's calves. Master Vale pulled Hal back with a powerful motion and Hal's fingers left grooves in the dirt. "*Margaret, help!*" Hal cried. His face was desperate, tearstained.

Fuck. For a moment, I didn't know what to do. Then some-thing in the corner of the basement caught my eye. The paddle. I dropped the flashlight and rushed over to it. I closed both fists against the wooden handle, felt the weight in my hands.

The beam of the flashlight cast light only across the floor. I could barely see Hal's body, only his white face and groping hands as he screamed and fought against Master Vale. Master Vale's face was all grooves and shadows, but his eyes and teeth gleamed through the darkness. Snarling, Master Vale lifted his head and—with a mouth that seemed *too* wide—sank his rotted teeth into Hal's leg.

Hal screamed.

And then I was there, paddle in my hands, swinging like I was trying to win a prize at the strong man game at the county fair. The paddle connected with the side of Master Vale's head with a wet *thunk*, and his teeth were wrenched from Hal's leg. His thin body bounced to the side and Hal pulled himself free, scrambling to his feet in a half crawl, half sprint towards the stairs. I was right on his heels.

When we reached the stairs, we could see the door—still

open; light shone down at us. Upstairs, it was still daytime, still *now*, only a few feet away. We scrabbled up the stairs, our legs barely remembering how to work. I dropped the paddle in favor of a two-handed grip on the railings, pulling my shaking body up step by step.

The door slammed shut.

We heard a growl behind us, at the bottom of the steps.

Hal threw his body against the door, both fists clutching the doorknob. He twisted and pushed. The door was shut tight.

Master Vale was behind us. He crawled up the stairs, long limbs bent like a spider's. That scream-laugh of his started again. His bloody mouth re-formed into a cracking grin.

I pounded my hand against Hal's shoulder. *"Open the door,"* I screamed.

"I'm trying," Hal barked. His voice was broken, more tremor than words.

Master Vale was halfway up the steps.

I turned, pushing my back into Hal's body, trying to create more distance between us and the nightmare man crawling his way up the stairs. Hal slammed his shoulder into the door over and over, each impact loud and rattling. It sounded like his arm might break before the door did.

That scream-laugh was so loud, it knifed its way into my ears, sliding into my brain. Master Vale was only feet away. He grabbed at me, gnarled fingers scraping at my shoe. I kicked his hand away but he reached out farther.

"Fuck." Hal's cries were desperate and shrill. He reminded me of Katherine as a child.

Master Vale's fingers grazed my ankle. I felt a whirlwind of confusion and shaking and bellyache and hunger and choking and a sick, inexplicable laughter that all must've been reminiscent of the day he died.

Suddenly, on the stairs below us there was a figure barricading us from Master Vale with its body. The figure was small yet powerful, unmoving.

Elias.

Elias stood so close to me on the steps, we were nearly touching. His ashen face was placid as he stared down at Master Vale below him. Master Vale gnashed his teeth at Elias, hissing like an animal. He crept closer up the stairs.

Elias' face opened. His eyes went red and his jaw gaped and his fangs glistened and that jet-engine noise made the doorknob shake behind us. Master Vale's body stiffened, his back arched like an angry cat's. Air rattled through his throat, gasping his reply at Elias' audacity. His fingers like claws, he swiped through the air towards Elias' face, and I remembered Angelica's head again—it was a very similar motion.

Elias sank his teeth into Master Vale's hand, pockmarked with lesions and pus and now something black and oozing.

Master Vale let out a noise that was definitely not laughter anymore. He wrenched his hand from Elias' mouth and scampered back down the stairs, crawling across the dirt of the basement until he disappeared into the blackness, gone.

The door opened and Hal and I, a pile of profanity and ragged breathing, tumbled back into the bright daylight of the kitchen. Hal slammed the door behind us, not giving a second thought as to whether Elias needed to follow. I was sure he was fine.

We lay on the kitchen floor for several minutes, panting and cursing and—in Hal's case—bleeding everywhere. The sunlight shone through the windows and there was a faint chirping of birds outside, punctuated by the occasional slams of feathered bodies hitting glass. It was *now* again, solidly *now*.

"I don't think the paddle is going to work," I said.

Hal let out a string of profanities in response.

I helped Hal up to the bathroom to deal with the mess of his leg. I sat him on the toilet lid and knelt in front of him, washed the blood off his leg, and applied liberal amounts of hydrogen peroxide while Hal kept up his cursing and periodically punched at the wall. Master Vale had left a jagged semicircle of knobby teeth marks along Hal's ankle, as well as several scratches along his calf. It didn't look like stitches were needed, but it didn't look pretty. Lord knows what kind of infection one might catch from the dead man in one's basement.

By the time I wrapped his leg in gauze, Hal looked defeated. He stared down at his hands in his lap and took sad, deep breaths.

"What are we going to do now?" he asked someone, possibly me.

I wrapped the gauze around his leg one final time and taped the edge down securely. I stared at my handiwork before looking up at Hal. His eyes were bloodshot, his face slack. He looked lost.

"We play by the rules," I said.

Later that day, we called Father Cyrus back. He gave us a Bible and we tore the pages out of it to hang on the back of the door. Father Cyrus flinched the whole time but understood that it was for the best. We found some boards and nailed the door shut, Father Cyrus saying one last emphatic prayer as the final nails sank into the wood. And that was the rule from that point forward. Never remove the Bible pages from the back of the basement door. Keep the door closed and boarded up at all times. Don't open the door, not even a crack. And definitely not in September.

Hal was silent the whole time Father Cyrus was there, save for when he needed to recite his parts of the call-and-response prayers. His eyes kept twitching over his shoulder. He rubbed at his ears. After Father Cyrus left, Hal shut himself in his office. *Working on a novel.* Or something.

A FEW DAYS LATER, WE SAW ELIAS AGAIN. WE WERE MAKING DINNER IN THE KITCHEN, me at the stove and Hal at the table, and we noticed him staring at us from the corner. Hal shook himself out of his stupor just enough to smile at Elias. Elias seemed to have our backs, after all.

"Hey, kid," Hal said. He stood up from the table and walked over to Elias, then bent down, so the two were at the same height. "I just wanted to say thank you. For what you did down there." He reached out a hand, his palm open, a kind gesture.

Elias bit him.

TWENTY-ONE

Back in the present day, the marks from Elias' teeth were on *my* arm, covered by a clumsy layer of bandages. My arm ached dully, a mosquito buzzing at my consciousness. I was too tired to care. My whole body ached these days—my arm would have to get in line. I sat in the hallway, my back against the basement door. There was something comforting about blocking it with my body.

Upstairs in her room, Katherine was having a loud, sobbing conversation over her phone.

"I *know* it's not okay for me to call," she was saying, her voice a shrill whine, "but things are fucked-up over here and I need to talk to you."

There was a pause.

"I don't care if it's not a good time," Katherine said. "I just really need to talk. Give me five minutes. *Five minutes.*"

Katherine had always been a reckless child, and I couldn't count the number of times I bandaged up her injuries—scraped elbows and bloody knees and the like. I had gotten it down to a science, sitting Katherine's crying frame on the toilet and cooing gently to her as I got out the bandages. While I cleaned her wounds, I would sing her a little song—some song I could no longer remember but was definitely not the one about the moon and the sun and everything coming around again that had been stuck in my head for days now. By the time the bandages were applied, Katherine would have a little smile poking through her wet face. I would kiss her forehead and tell her she could go get a cookie. I had made everything all better, a proper mother.

"The question I have isn't even for *you*," Katherine was saying. "It's for your therapist girlfriend."

Katherine was somewhat less skilled in caretaking. She hadn't cooed softly or tried to sing me a little song. She had cried and sniffled as she muddled her way through the bandaging. I'd thought about correcting her, telling her that the caretaker didn't cry; the caretaker wiped up the tears of others. Instead, I held my arm still as best I could and made suggestions about the tightness of bandages. *I know what I'm doing*, she'd said, although she hadn't. When she was finished, I told her that it would be okay, but she said nothing in response, retreating into her room with her phone in hand, already mid-dial.

"Look, Claire," she was saying, "I don't really have time to . . . I *know* because I still follow your fucking Instagram, remember? That doesn't matter right now. Just . . . Will you let me ask her a question?"

When I'd walked back downstairs from the bathroom, the basement door was wide open. I slammed it shut without looking into the basement. I didn't need to see if anyone was on their way up the stairs. I just needed to keep them down there. Perhaps it was time to put the boards back on the door. Katherine already thought I was crazy. What was one more offense? Just put it on my tab.

"*Fine. Block me.* I don't give a shit. Just let me ask her a question."

So Katherine couldn't see Elias. That was clear. She hadn't been able to see Angelica and company either, it seemed, and she had made no mention of Fredricka in the bathroom. This wasn't entirely unprecedented, I supposed. The pranksters certainly had their favorites—namely me. Edie didn't have any trouble seeing the pranksters after a while, but Father Cyrus had never seen them, not in all the time he had spent in the house. Most of the pranksters always darted out of Hal's way, but I'd assumed that he could *see* them. Couldn't he? Or would he have walked right past them just like Katherine did? Still, Hal had never had any trouble seeing Elias, and he'd *certainly* had no trouble seeing Master Vale. The pranksters were fickle, it would seem, in who could see them and who couldn't, and my muddled brain was having trouble making heads or tails of that at the moment.

"*Thank you,*" Katherine said, sniffing. "I'm just . . . I'm just really worried, is all. Yeah, put me on speaker. I don't care."

Still, I thought, Katherine could see the knives in the bathroom sink. I hadn't done that—Fredricka had put them there. She could see the other products of Fredricka's restlessness too—the stacks of pillows, the rearranged dishes, the boiling kettle on the stove. Could she see the blood on the walls, unlike Father Cyrus? Could she hear the screaming, or did she think it was the wind, like Hal had at first? My head throbbed.

"I think there's something wrong with her," Katherine was saying. "Like, more wrong than usual."

Angelica drifted into the hall, coming to rest directly in front of me. As I was sitting against the door like this, she was a few inches taller than me. Her remaining eye stared down into mine, not exactly menacing but not particularly comforting either.

"Katherine can't see you," I said to her, or perhaps to myself. Angelica didn't seem to care either way.

"I'm worried she might've lost it," Katherine was saying. "We've got that family history, you know. Her father. He spent a lot of his life in hospitals. I think he killed himself. I don't know. Mom never talks about it."

Julian appeared next to Angelica, his intestines making his shirt look lumpy.

"Katherine can't see you," I said to him.

"How would I be able to tell if she was . . . you know . . . ," Katherine asked, *"not all there?"* She was trying to dip her voice lower but she had never been particularly skilled at that trick.

Charles and Constance, holding hands as usual, appeared on the other side of Angelica.

"Can't see you," I said, pointing at Charles with a tired finger. "Can't see you." I pointed at Constance.

"Or maybe she has dementia?" Katherine asked. "She seems really out of it. She's not remembering things. But isn't she too young for that?"

Thomas or Tobias or whoever sidled up next to Julian.

"I regret to inform you," I said to what's-his-face, "that she cannot see you either."

Katherine was silent, listening. "Today was the first time," she said. "But there have been signs. Things haven't been right with her since I got here. She keeps calling me by different names, people I've never heard of. She is always glancing away, like she's seeing something in the corner of the room that isn't really there. I think it's been going on for a while and she's kept it from me. She does that—keeps things from me."

Another boy appeared next to the twins, the final one I could expect to arrive this year. His hair was a dark mess and his clothes were bloodied and torn, just like the others'. I remembered him from previous Septembers but I couldn't think of his name for the life of me. It might have started with a J, or possibly a W. Anyway, he didn't have legs anymore and he pulled himself around on his forearms.

"I can't say with certainty," I said to him, "but I feel like Katherine can't see you either."

"It might have to do with my dad leaving," she was saying. "I can't— I don't have time to get into their fucked-up relationship. Claire can tell you, I'm sure. But she kind of needed him in this way that didn't make any sense. She says it got better but I don't think it actually did. You should see her fucking arms. And now he's gone and she's . . . she's not okay."

I surveyed the scene in front of me—Angelica and her head, Julian and his intestines, Charles and Constance and their lacerations, Thomas or Tobias or whoever and his arm (or lack thereof), the boy with no legs and the trail of blood he was leaving behind him. They circled me, all clear exits covered. They stared down at me, their empty eyes making it unclear if they were seeing me at all. Slowly, deliberately, they each raised an arm in unison, pointing directly at me. I considered whether I ought to be worried.

"I don't know," Katherine said. "I thought he might have done it to her but now I'm worried that she did it to herself. Is that a symptom of anything? She's never done that before—I don't think, anyway—and I'm just . . ." Her voice dropped off. "I'm just really freaking out over here."

I chose not to be worried. Worrying takes effort, and one must be selective about where one expends effort these days.

The pranksters went on staring and pointing, staring and pointing.

I gestured behind me with my thumb. "He's down there," I said.

Katherine had gone silent again. "Okay . . . okay . . . ," she said periodically, as if taking notes.

Fredricka appeared behind the pranksters. "Shoo," she said, waving at them with her hands. They drifted away, disappearing back inside themselves after a moment. Fredricka motioned for me to slide over, and sat down next to me, her thick smock draped around her on the floor. She pressed her back into the half of the basement door I was no longer covering. "Sometimes one must be direct with the little ones," she said.

"If she *is* crazy," Katherine was asking, "what do I *do*?"

"Did you ever have children, Fredricka?" I asked. Fredricka never spoke about her past. Most of her comments to me were limited to the state of the house, her thoughts on my actions, and the occasional proverb. I was usually the one who talked, telling her about my life and my thoughts and my plans for the day, even if she did little else but listen and offer me tea. Sometimes that's all you need.

"I can't remember," Fredricka said. "That was a long time ago."

"You would have made a good mother," I said.

"Children are certain cares, but uncertain comforts," said Fredricka.

"Okay," Katherine was saying, "but how will I know that it's come down to that?"

"Well," I said, "my child thinks that I'm crazy."

"You're not," Fredricka said.

I chuckled. There was something ironic about the dead woman—the one with the terrible split that ran down the front of her skull and through her eye, the one who had just shooed away a handful of bloody and dismembered children who insisted upon telling me about the monster in the basement—assuring me that I, in fact, was not crazy. "Thanks," I said.

"And what if she doesn't want to go?" Katherine was asking. "Can I make her?"

I leaned my head back against the doorframe. I was so, *so* tired. "Do you think anybody deserves to live like this, Fredricka?" I asked.

"We all deserve more than what we are given," Fredricka said. "So much more." Judging by the state of her skull, I'd say she was right.

I put my hand in hers and saw the whole scene from the night she died—the candles and the dining room and the laughing man and the axe and the watermelon sound. I felt blood trickle out of my nose and my head throbbed, but it was worth it because sometimes you just need somebody to hold your hand, somebody who might have been a mother once but couldn't quite remember.

TWENTY-TWO

'll not sit here and tell you that Hal was the only person in charge of setting the rules—although, admittedly, he was the reason that the vast majority of them existed. I set rules as well. Or at least I set one, the most important one. The rule was this: the situation with Hal and me—our disagreements and our oh-so-slow changes and the ever-developing rules and Hal's unpredictable anger—Katherine was to be spared all of it.

To be honest, I thought the rule was so fundamental, it would never even have to be spoken. For most of our lives together, Hal seemed to understand. The rules never applied to Katherine. Hal kept his fists far away from her, even when he was drinking, bless him. Sure, Katherine knew when Hal was upset with something or other I didn't know I had done (she had ears, after all), and Hal would certainly yell at Katherine when she tested his patience a bit too much (what parent doesn't?), but he never turned the full brunt of himself towards her. He seemed to view Katherine as my responsibility, a checkout clerk to my shift supervisor, and any perceived deficits in Katherine's behavior were up to me to manage. It made sense, really. Any complaints with the checkout clerks ought to be taken up with the supervisors, anyway. It was all perfectly fine by me—I had excellent managerial skills. I could listen, receive feedback, adjust the way I managed Katherine accordingly, and Hal would keep his hands to himself. I thought Hal and I were on the same page with all that.

The day I found out I was wrong was a fairly typical day. It might've been a Tuesday. Katherine was fifteen or sixteen at the time, and Hal was only on his second DUI. I had gone through my usual routine of texting Hal when I arrived at the grocery store, at least three times while I was in the store (you'll find there is a lot to say about grocery shopping if you think about it), when I checked out (in the line with the female cashier, of course), and when I got stuck in a bit of congestion that might delay my arrival back home. Hal responded to only a few of these texts, but his responses weren't as mandatory as the texting—the *open communication*. So I wasn't alarmed when I pulled into the driveway and started to unload the groceries from the car. But I became alarmed as I heard the faint sound of Hal's voice drifting through the walls of the house.

Yelling.

For a moment, I assumed he was yelling at me, and I searched my memory for what I could possibly have done wrong. I had told him about this grocery trip *yesterday*. I engaged in so much open communication. I returned home exactly when I told him I would. Had he found out that the male deli clerk had smiled at me? Did Noelle call while I was away, even though we hadn't spoken in ages? I braced for impact.

When I entered the house, I realized he wasn't yelling at me, after all.

Katherine's bedroom door was open.

When I was a child, I had a friend who got ahold of some fireworks. We were setting them off in her backyard and she held on to one a little too long and it exploded in her hand. It was a *bad* explosion despite the colorful sparks, loud and bright and hot and bloody. Anyway, that was what it felt like in my chest just then. I ran down the hall.

I could hear enough words to piece together what Hal was on about. Apparently, some new friend had dropped Katherine off after school—a *male* friend. Hal's opinions of males who weren't him had been well established, and I could tell by the sluggish nature of Hal's consonants that he had been drinking, which only strengthened those opinions.

"I will not have any daughter of mine driving through town like some goddamn WHORE," Hal was screaming when I got to Katherine's room.

I could tell by the scene that Hal's tirade had started abruptly and had been going on for some time. Hal was halfway in Katherine's room and closing in fast. Katherine had tucked herself into a corner, her back to the wall, knees bent as if trying to somehow push herself through the wall and into the yard behind it. This was a fairly new situation for Katherine. She'd been reprimanded before, but never like this. This was the sort of thing that was typically reserved for me. I'd thought Hal and I were in agreement on that.

"Dad, I already *told* you . . . ," Katherine was saying. That was a mistake, arguing back. You didn't argue back, especially when Hal had been drinking. Katherine didn't know. She'd never had to follow the rules before.

"YOU'RE FUCKING HIM, AREN'T YOU?" Hal screamed at her.

Katherine's mouth opened and closed. She looked more confused than I had ever seen her. At fifteen or sixteen, Katherine had already figured out a thing or two about herself and her romantic inclinations. She hadn't gotten around to telling us yet, but a mother knew these things, and with Katherine it was fairly obvious. Hal was less observant. I figured Katherine was working herself up to making the announcement, but this was not the moment she wanted to choose.

"What?" Katherine stammered.

Don't make Hal repeat himself. That was another rule. Oh, Katherine.

"YOU IMPUDENT CUNT," Hal yelled.

I saw Hal puff his body up, his shoulders rolling back, chest protruding. His hands were fists at his sides and he glowered down at her. I didn't need to be able to read tea leaves to tell what was coming next. Hal lunged forward, fist raised high. Katherine screamed.

"NO," I shouted, hurling myself at Hal. I got him in his midsection like a football player, knocking him off his balance and pushing him to the ground. He hadn't even noticed me coming at him, and he went down hard, bouncing once on his side before rolling onto his back. I was on top of him, pinning his arms with my hands, his thighs with my legs.

It was only a matter of time. Seconds, likely.

I turned to Katherine, who looked as if she were prepared to cry just as soon as she became less terrified. *"Run,"* I said.

"Mom?" she said.

"Get out of here," I said. *"Go next door. Run."*

Katherine ran.

She left just in time. With a grunt, Hal threw me off him. I slammed into Katherine's dresser, her little knickknacks clattering above me. A bottle of lotion rolled off and hit me on the shoulder. I leapt to my feet with speed, putting as much space between Hal and myself as I could. I needed distance between us while I expressed my opinions, even if only for a moment, which was all the time I was likely to get. Hal was on his feet.

"You do *not* treat our daughter like that," I said. There was a fierceness in my voice that I had never heard before.

It was a rare line in the sand for me, perhaps one of the first I had ever drawn. I hardly ever outright disagreed with Hal—that was the rule. I knew how to handle Hal, after all. I wasn't scared. I'd figured it all out. But Katherine was another story altogether. I was perfectly willing to make a heaven of any hell in which I happened to find myself. But I would be goddamned if I made my daughter endure it.

"Excuse me?" Hal's shoulders rolled back, his chest puffed out, his hands fists at his side. He was glowering down at me. He moved to close the distance but I darted back. I still had more to say.

"You can do whatever you like to me," I said, my voice loud, firm, confident, "but you do not—*do not*—lay a hand on our daughter."

"Are you telling me how to discipline my own child?" Hal wasn't a cornered animal now. He was a starving lion. He was a pack of wolves. He was a circling hawk. And in all those metaphors, I was a rabbit with a wounded leg. But I wasn't frightened, and I wasn't going down without a fight. And let me tell you, a fight was coming.

"You heard me," I said. "And if I ever—*ever*—catch you treating Katherine like that again, I swear to Christ, I will take her away from you. I don't care if you kill me, but with God as my witness, you will *never* see her again. *Do you understand me?"*

Hal must have understood me. His hand met my face with a thundering crack—open palm but *hard*, hard enough to knock me to the ground. There was a ringing in my ears and my head felt shaken loose. My hand rose to my face, which was hot and stinging. I blinked through the disorientation and saw his feet in front of me.

Things got much, *much* worse from there.

But everything is survivable. And I did survive, of course. So far, my survival rate has been excellent.

Afterwards, Hal left the house to go continue his evening at a bar somewhere and I lay on the floor outside of Katherine's bedroom, breathing and surviving. I was very aware of the breathing because it hurt quite a bit and it seemed that I needed to do a lot of it—more than usual, it appeared. But breathing is a success, and we never take time to celebrate the little successes, do we?

It was time to make plans.

Standing didn't seem like a viable option, as I was still dizzy and throbbing and couldn't see out of my left eye. Crawling wasn't comfortable and I was sure I was making quite the mess out of the carpet, but it was the lesser of two evils at that moment. I dragged myself to where my purse had fallen by the front door. For a moment, I thought about the groceries slowly going bad out in my car, but I pushed that thought aside. I had more pressing problems. I felt around in my purse until I found my phone. I could barely see, but I knew by heart the number I wanted to call.

It's a funny thing about being alone. You never really notice it when it's happening. Of course, you're aware that nobody else is there, but you are so busy with the little things. You've become acclimated to solitude, but it only takes one little thing to jolt you into the realization that for the past several years, you have been completely alone in all of this.

Noelle picked up on the first ring.

"Margaret?" she said. "What's wrong?"

Speaking would give it all away, of course, because my lips were thick and my tongue wasn't right and my mouth wasn't doing the best job of moving. But you don't really have a choice over the phone, now, do you?

"Hi, Noelle," I said, lying back down on the floor.

"Jesus Christ," Noelle said, "what happened?"

"I need a favor," I said.

"Oh my God." Noelle sounded panicked. "Do I need to call the police? Do you need an ambulance?"

"No," I said. "Please, don't."

"Jesus, Margaret, you sound—"

"I need you to come over here right now," I said. "I need you to get Katherine. You need to take her."

"Margaret—"

"It isn't safe for her here," I said. "Please."

There was a pause. Noelle was still thinking about the police, I could tell. But finally, she sighed. "I'll be right over," she said.

After I hung up, I stayed on the floor, the phone pressed against my chest. It was wet; I would probably need to wipe it off before the blood dried on it. Soon, sooner than I'd have liked, I would need to stand up and take care of some things. I would need to gather some of Katherine's things for Noelle to take with her. I would need to do something about my face before Noelle showed up and once again started talking about calling the police. I would eventually need to do something about the carpet, but not yet. One must prioritize in these situations. I could lie there a little longer, celebrating my success.

TWENTY-THREE

After Katherine finished with her phone call and had what sounded like a nice long cry followed by some nice long deep breaths, she came downstairs with a renewed sense of purpose and a notebook full of scribbled-on pages. I was still sitting in front of the basement door with Fredricka, although I had stopped holding her hand. There were only so many times you could feel an axe sink into your head before the whole process grew tiresome.

Katherine stood in front of me, not seeing Fredricka or the pranksters who had resumed milling about the hallway, periodically reminding me about the basement. "Your nose is bleeding," she said.

"I suppose it is," I said. From what I could tell, it had bled down my face and onto my shirt. No matter. I was an expert at cleaning blood out of fabric.

Katherine reached a hand out to me. "Get up, Mom," she said. "I've got some questions for you."

I grabbed her hand and she hoisted me to my feet. She accidentally pulled me through Julian, and I felt a knife slice through my gut, invisible intestines spilling out onto the ground. I clutched at my stomach, wincing.

"What's wrong?" Katherine asked.

"Nothing," I said.

Julian seemed unfazed. He looked back at me, pointing at the basement door. *He's down there.*

"Wash your face off," Katherine said, gesturing at the sink. "Then sit down at the table with me."

I stumbled over to the sink. The spot where my stomach wasn't being disemboweled emanated a dull throb. I picked up a dishrag and turned on the faucet.

Blood again, thick and dark.

I looked at the blood, then over at Katherine. She had already taken a seat at the kitchen table and was reviewing her notes, moving her mouth as she read.

"Can you see this?" I asked, pointing at the sink. I didn't want to alarm her, but if there was any chance I could avoid washing my face with blood, I was willing to risk a little alarm.

Katherine looked up at me, barely paying attention. "What?" she asked.

I looked back at the blood pouring out of the faucet. "Never mind," I said. I turned the faucet off and rubbed at my nose with the dry rag. Better safe than sorry. Hopefully there wouldn't be any flesh stuck in the drain this time.

I sat down opposite Katherine. Her expression told me I hadn't gotten all the blood off my face, but neither of us could be bothered to do anything about it.

"This is going to seem weird," Katherine said, "but I have some questions for you. Just answer as honestly as possible, okay?"

"Sure," I said. My guts still hurt.

"There are no wrong answers," Katherine said. "And nothing bad is going to happen." She was reading from her notes. She had been told to say this.

"Sure," I said again. I had a sinking feeling that something bad was going to happen.

"Okay," she said, grabbing a pen and settling in. "First question. What day is it?"

This seemed like a question that had a wrong answer. "Tuesday," I said.

Katherine's brow furrowed. "It's Friday," she said. She made a note in her book. "Next question. What is today's date?"

If I had gotten the day question wrong, there was a good chance I would get this question wrong too. I did some math. Katherine had gotten in on the eleventh. She had been here for . . . six days? "The seventeenth?"

Katherine blinked at me. "Mom," she said, "it's the twenty-fifth."

The twenty-fifth? It didn't seem like that much time had passed since Katherine arrived. I tried my best to remember what had filled all those days, but parts were missing—jigsaw pieces that had gotten lost underneath the couch, waiting to be discovered years later, when they no longer mattered.

"*Mom.*"

I looked at Katherine. "Yes?"

"Did you hear my question?"

Apparently not.

Katherine exhaled. "Where are you right now? Like, the address."

"Three thirty Hawthorn Street," I said. "The old Vale house." This last part came out of my mouth without permission. *Interesting*, I thought. I had never referred to the house as such before.

"The old *what?*" Katherine asked, eyebrows raised.

"*No,*" I said pointedly, more to the house than to Katherine. "*Not* the old Vale house anymore. *My* house."

"Okay," Katherine said, not looking any less worried. I was mostly just proud of myself for getting the question right. Small victories, really.

He's down there. Julian was suddenly at my immediate right. I hadn't even seen him appear. I jumped, clutching my chest. *Jesus Christ, Julian*, I thought.

Katherine didn't see Julian, but she saw me flinch. "You okay?"

"Perfectly fine, dear," I said, perhaps a little too breathlessly.

He's down there. Angelica was at my immediate left. These pranksters were going to give me a heart attack.

Katherine was saying something.

"What?" I asked.

Katherine's eyebrows lifted. Asking her to repeat herself twice was not the best of moves, but I had little choice here. "Count backwards from fifty by fives," she said.

The boy with no legs dragged himself into the room, a trail of blood following behind him. This close, you could tell that he still had bits and pieces of his legs, but not enough for it to really matter.

Katherine was watching me expectantly. That's right. I was supposed to do something. Something involving the number five.

"Five," I said. I wondered if Katherine could see the stains the boy with no legs was leaving behind him.

"*No,*" Katherine said. "Count *backwards* from *fifty* by fives."

"Oh," I said. The boy with no legs shifted his weight onto his side and raised his arm, pointing. *He's down there.*

When I looked away from the boy, Katherine was still staring at me. She waved a hand at me. *Whenever you're ready . . .*

"Fifty-five," I said. On my right, Julian was standing so close to me, I could see his face in the corner of my eye, inches from mine. *He's down there.*

"*Backwards,*" Katherine interjected, trying hard to keep her voice quiet. "*Backwards* from fifty."

Charles and Constance walked from where they had, apparently, been standing behind me and crossed through the kitchen, holding hands. They looked back at me. *He's down there.*

"Forty . . . ," I started. Whatever part of my brain was usually responsible for math was finding it a little challenging to properly function with so many dead children demanding my attention.

"By *fives.*" Katherine was really struggling to keep her voice down now. Her words wavered a bit, although it was difficult to tell if that was from anger or something else altogether.

Julian had crawled up onto the kitchen table and squatted on all fours nearly directly in front of me, his intestines drooping inches from my hand. I scooted my hand away from his dangling bowels.

"Forty . . . ," I tried again. I was having a little trouble remembering the number I was supposed to subtract by, as well as how to subtract.

"Jesus Christ," Katherine said, scribbling in her notebook. "Never mind. Let's try this one. I'm going to name three things. After I'm done, just repeat what I said. Okay?"

I had to lean around Julian to see her. I wanted to swat at him, but I didn't care to experience the sensation of being disemboweled again so soon. I also had a feeling that swatting at nothing wouldn't help Katherine's perceptions of my mental stability. "Okay," I said.

Katherine set her notebook on the table. She looked me straight in the eyes. "He's. Down. There."

"What?" I said.

Katherine looked distressed. She flipped through her notes. "Shit. I don't know if I can repeat it. Can you just . . . just tell me what you remember?"

He's down there, Julian said.

Standing on the back of my chair, leaning over me so her dirty hair dangled in my face, was Angelica. *He's down there*, she said.

Thomas or Tobias or whoever drifted into the room. *He's down there*, he said.

"He's down there," I said. That was wrong. That was definitely wrong. But what else could I say? What else could anybody say in this house, apparently?

Katherine looked up from her notebook, brow furrowed but eyes wide. "No," she said. "What? No. I said: clock, wheel, tulip. Mom, did you hear any of those words?"

"Clock . . . wheel . . . something." It was devilishly hard to concentrate with Angelica dangling over me like this. Part of her head was swinging loose and I really didn't want it to touch me. I tried to duck lower, avoiding both her and Julian at the same time. I could only imagine what I looked like.

Katherine flipped to a blank page in her notebook, scribbled something, then tore the page out. She handed it to me. "Read this and do what it says."

I read the page. Written on the paper, in Katherine's scrawling handwriting, was: *He's down there*. I looked back up at her. This seemed like a trick.

Katherine was staring at me with urgency. "Well?"

"It doesn't . . ." I looked back down at the paper. "It's not telling me to do anything."

"Jesus Christ." Katherine grabbed the paper from me and held it up in front of my face, pointing at it with a finger gone unsteady. "Can't you read this?"

He's down there. The pranksters helped me read by reciting the words in unison.

"I . . ."

Katherine looked at it. "It says, *Lift your hand.*"

"Oh." I squinted at the paper. It still read, *He's down there.* "I see," I said, although I certainly didn't. I lifted my hand, albeit not very high, what with all the various body parts around me I didn't want to touch. In any case, I had a feeling this would be considered cheating and wouldn't count.

The boy with no legs crawled underneath my seat. I moved my feet away from him, not interested in feeling what it was like to have my legs removed so carelessly. Somehow, Angelica had both her hands and feet balanced on the top of the chair, and she was leaning over my shoulder.

"Fuck." Katherine scribbled in her notebook. "Do you remember the three words I asked you to remember earlier?" She tried to ask this with hope.

"Um . . ." My eyes were stuck on the boy underneath the chair, and I tried to be sure we both stayed as far away from each other as possible. I definitely remembered Katherine saying some words earlier—one of them had to do with something round, perhaps—and I remembered what I *thought* I'd heard Katherine say, but there didn't seem to be much chance of me remembering what she'd actually said.

"Ring?" I tried, leaning over a little more because Julian was directly in front of my face now. "And . . ." There was little doubt in my mind that, whatever test this was, I was failing it spectacularly. I wasn't sure what the consequences of failing would be, but I didn't think I would like them.

Katherine cursed. She tapped at her paper with her pen, moving her lips as she did something that seemed like counting. She paused, then recounted. Her breath was starting to come in a touch fast. "This is not good, Mom," she said.

"Will that be it, dear?" I asked, eager to gain a little distance from the pranksters crowding around me. We had, apparently, reached the part of September when everybody forgot the importance of personal space. The pranksters were reminding me a bit of Hal, who—right after we first got married—liked to make a game out of distracting me while I was on the phone by poking me and tickling me and blowing in my ear. He considered it a victory if he got me to giggle or squirm or in any other way draw a confused *What's going on, Margaret?* from the person on the other end. I had to say, it was *much* cuter when Hal did it.

"No. Mom. Fuck." Katherine rubbed at her temples. "Have you been forgetting things lately?"

"I don't think so," I said to her through Julian's head.

"You know, like forgetting you had the kettle boiling?"

Oh, right. Katherine still thought that was me. "That was one time," I said.

"Five times," Katherine said. "That I've counted. I feel like every time I walk into this room there's water boiling on the stove and you're nowhere to be found."

Goddamnit, Fredricka.

"I don't know how to ask this," Katherine said. From the side of Julian's face and through Angelica's hair, I could just make out that Katherine's head was in her hands. "Are you . . . like . . . seeing things?"

Julian's intestines were leaving a puddle of something brownish red on the kitchen table. The twins moved in on my right and Thomas or Tobias or whoever moved in on my left.

"I'm not sure what you're talking about," I said. I wished I could swing my arms at the pranksters, run at them until they scattered and left me to concentrate on this conversation with Katherine, which seemed like it was gearing up to be an important one. However, I had a feeling that Katherine would take that sort of thing as evidence that her theories about me were correct.

"You know what I mean," Katherine said, waving a hand in the air. "Seeing things. Things that aren't really there."

"No," I said, and it somehow felt like both the right and the wrong answer.

"Mom, that's bullshit," Katherine said. Her voice was growing wet. "Earlier today, when you hurt your arm, you asked me if I could see *him*. Who were you talking about? Were you seeing something that wasn't really there?"

Who could argue that Elias hadn't really been there? I had the marks on my arm to prove he had been, after all.

"All the things I see are really there," I clarified.

Katherine swallowed. "So you *do* see things."

"I see *you*," I said, which was actually a lie because all I could see was Julian's face inches from mine and Angelica's one remaining eye hovering just above my head. If Thomas or Tobias or whoever had an arm, it would have been pressed against me right now—that was how close he was standing. But if I scooted to my right, I would bump into Charles, and Julian's head would obscure my view of Katherine entirely, and I would have Angelica's hair in my face. And if I looked any odder, Katherine was *definitely* going to think I was crazy. More crazy than she already thought I was.

"That's not what I mean," Katherine said. "It's just . . . you've been acting so goddamn strange ever since I got here. You say things that make no sense, you're moving stuff around the house with no rhyme or reason, and you're always looking around, like you're watching something out of the corners of your eyes. You never seem like you're fully paying attention, like you hear some-one else talking and you're listening to them, not me."

He's down there, the pranksters chanted.

"I'm listening," I said.

"Mom, these questions I've been asking you—they're to see if you're, like, *all there*," Katherine said. I could just make out her finger tapping at her own head. "Like, that you know where you are and can do simple stuff like remember things and follow directions. It gives you a total score that's supposed to tell you how you're doing. Your score is . . . *not good*."

Angelica's hair brushed against my nose, giving me little tickles of *hammer* and *laughter* and *that thing that happened to her head*. "I'm sure it's no big deal," I said.

"I'm not trying to be an asshole here," Katherine said. If I could see her properly, it seemed as if her eyes would be red, wet. "And I know you and I haven't always . . . Our relationship hasn't been the best. . . ." She took a breath, deep and shaking. "I don't want anything to happen to you, Mom, and I'm . . . I'm really worried, okay? I think I need to get you some help."

I tried to blow Angelica's hair off me, but it bounced right back. *Hammer. Laughter. Pain. Eye or lack thereof.* The sensations were just enough to drown out my heartbeat, the rate of which was starting to pick up. "Don't be silly, dear," I said.

"I'm serious," Katherine said, and she certainly sounded it. "I think . . . I think I have to take you to a hospital."

"I'm not sick," I said. *And I'm not leaving this house.*

"I think you *are*," Katherine said. "At least, I think you might be. I don't know. This is all way the fuck out of my knowledge base. But that therapist Claire is dating said . . . Well, it doesn't matter. But considering your family history, your dad . . . well, I think it's time to go to the hospital."

Katherine and I had never talked about my father before. She had never even met him, as he had moved himself on long before she was born. Noelle must have told her about him while Katherine was staying with her all those years ago. Katherine must have been under the assumption that because my father had spent some time in hospitals, I must need to spend some time in a hospital too. That was all a silly misunderstanding, though, because the things *I* was seeing were real.

Meanwhile, the boy with no legs was trying to pull himself into a chair, and let me tell you, *that* was a sad sight. Angelica had taken up a nonstop whisper into my forehead. *He's down there he's down there he's down there he's down there.*

"You're making a big stink about nothing," I said. I might have been talking loudly—it was hard to tell with all the ruckus. My voice was certainly unsteady and coming out much faster than was strictly necessary. "I'm fine, Katherine, really. Your grandfather's problems have nothing to do with me." Julian bounced closer and his intestines plopped onto my hand and my stomach lurched and I jolted away from him, all of which was incredibly bad timing.

"Okay," Katherine said, wiping at her eyes once more before slapping her hands on the table with finality. "Maybe I'm not being clear. We're going to the hospital. *Now.*"

"Katherine . . ." My stomach hurt.

She was on her feet, gesturing at me. "Up."

"Katherine, I am not going to the hospital." Lord knows what kind of ruin this place would fall into with me gone, and this trip to the hospital did not sound like a quick there-and-back. A sick panic snuck its way into what felt like my still–partially disemboweled stomach. "It's almost October," I said.

Katherine waved her arms in the air. "That nonsensical bullshit is exactly what I'm talking about. Get up. We're leaving."

I certainly didn't mean to stand up but I felt something wet land on my head and realized it was Angelica's eye dripping on me, and one can be expected to take only so much at a time. I burst from my chair, arms out, and drove my body straight through Angelica and Julian and the boy with no legs and Thomas or Tobias or whoever and, believe it or not, even managed to flail an arm through Charles. And all at once I felt the hammer and the disembowelment and the knives and the arm wrenched from its socket and the legs crudely taken elsewhere, and I tumbled to the ground—no legs, after all—and vomited. Talk about bad timing.

Well, I'm not sure if you would call what I did *vomiting* in the traditional sense, because I didn't have much food in my stomach. Instead, I coughed up quite a large quantity of swollen, dead black flies.

"What the *fuck*, Mom?" Katherine gaped at me, eyes bulging. For a moment, it looked like she might join me in this vomit party. She swallowed. "Are those *flies*?"

I examined my vomit. "It would appear so," I said, wiping my mouth. My whole body hurt. I wasn't entirely convinced that I still had both legs and all of my arms.

"Have you been"—Katherine's voice was thick, nauseated—"*eating* flies?"

Trust me, I was just as surprised as Katherine to see those flies. "I can understand how you might think that," I said. I felt something on my tongue and pulled it off with a finger. It was a wing.

"*Hospital.*" Katherine was screaming now. "*We are going to the fucking hospital. Now.*"

I remained on the kitchen floor, leaning on the one arm I was sure I still had. "I understand why you're upset," I said, doing my best to cling to the single shred of control I had over the situation. "But really—"

"How do you think you still have a choice in this?" Katherine yelled. *"This is not your fucking decision."*

"Language," I said. I had very little else to say anymore.

"Get off the goddamn floor and get in the car, or so help me God, I will DRAG you out of this house." Katherine's chest was puffed out, her shoulders squared. She was glowering. *"Do not fucking test me on this."*

I raised a hand, palm open, a white flag. "Hal . . . ," I said before I realized it.

Katherine's eyes widened. Her mouth fell open. She looked as if she'd accidentally staggered into Julian—an inadvertent disemboweling. *"What* did you just—" She was interrupted by a ringing sound. Her phone cheerily chimed away in her pocket, unaware of the scene it was interrupting. Katherine lifted her phone, blinking at it as if not quite sure what it was. When she saw who was calling, she snapped to attention. She looked at me, her expression telling me that this conversation was on a time-out, not over.

She answered the phone. "This is Katherine Hartman," she said, her voice odd. She paused as the caller spoke. "Listen," she said. "Is this urgent? I'm kind of in the middle of an important—" She went silent. Her eyebrows rose.

"Oh." She blinked. *"You do?"*

She looked down at me, her brain whirring with decisions.

"Do I have to come down *right* now?" she asked. "It's just . . . Fuck. Okay."

Silence. She closed her eyes, pursed her lips together.

"Okay," she said. "No, I get it. Okay. Okay. *Fuck.*"

Silence. Katherine opened her eyes and exhaled, then stared at the ceiling.

"Yeah," she said. "I'll be at the station in twenty minutes." She turned back to her notebook, still on the table. She grabbed her pen and scratched something on the paper, underlined it twice.

"Right," she said. "I'll see you soon." She pressed END on her phone. She looked over at me, then picked up her notebook and moved towards her purse.

"I have to go," she said. "The officers— Well, they say they've found something. I don't know what it means. They wouldn't tell me." She gathered her purse and dug out her car keys as she looked back at me. I was increasingly remembering that I had legs and two arms, and I shifted my weight so I was sitting up, balancing myself on both of the hands I luckily still had. "I'll be back soon," Katherine said, her tone indicating that this was not meant to be a comforting statement so much as it was a warning. *Don't try to burn the house down—I'll be here with a hose before you can even smell smoke.* Katherine gestured at me with an index finger. "This isn't over," she said.

Nothing is ever over. We get only a respite. But respites aren't nothing, and I was getting one right now—however brief—as Katherine darted out of the house. The tires of her car squealed as she pulled out of the driveway. Small favors all around.

TWENTY-FOUR

Katherine likely wouldn't be gone for long and I had plenty to do in the meantime. I made quick work of cleaning up my fly-filled vomit, then grabbed a shovel and a trash bag. It was long past time to dig up Elias' mother again.

I ran through the backyard and into the woods, ignoring the dozen or so dead birds that had accumulated since the last time I cleared out the bodies. I would handle the birds later. My top priority right now was calming Elias the hell down. I needed to calm everybody the hell down, every prankster in the house. Katherine couldn't see them, but she could certainly see *me*, and what she was seeing made her think I needed to be hospitalized. I needed to start looking sane, and *fast*.

I found the tree marked with the fuchsia M and started digging with an urgency I didn't think my tired body could muster. The clock was ticking.

The weather was cool this afternoon, a breeze dusting through the trees, but I soon worked up a sweat as I shoveled mound after mound of dirt away from what was now a well-trodden grave. My clothes were nearly black with dirt and my skin was caked in muddy sweat. I wiped the moisture off my forehead with a dirty hand. I would need to take a shower before Katherine arrived home so she wouldn't start asking difficult but valid questions about my appearance. When the shovel finally struck the plastic of the bins, I dove into the hole and started digging with my hands, scraping at dirt with my fingernails and yanking the lids off the bins while they were still in the ground. I tossed pieces of Elias' mother into the garbage bag as I found them—femur, rib, spine, skull. When I was fairly certain I had gotten most of her—surely the ritual would still work even if I was missing a piece or two—I twisted the top of the garbage bag closed and headed back for the house. I left the shovel in her grave. I would be back later to bury her, possibly after Katherine went to sleep, but probably in October.

I considered just keeping the bones in the house from this point forward—digging the bins out of the ground and storing them in some closet somewhere. Maybe Jasper could share his space. I always reburied Elias' mother after the reunion ritual because I wanted to be respectful, but I couldn't imagine that storing her in the house somewhere was any more disrespectful than what I was doing. Besides, I had already progressed from transporting her bones in a nice urnlike vase to a garbage bag. Did any of it really matter at this point?

This is how these changes start, I thought. *They happen slowly.*

My thoughts regarding how best to respect the bones of Elias' mother flew from my mind as I entered the house. All six pranksters stood in the hallway, sullen faces and empty eyes fixed directly on me. Together, they raised what arms they had and pointed at the basement door.

The door flew open.

The bag of bones clattered to the floor as I rushed to the door and slammed it shut so hard I felt the house shake. I turned back to the pranksters, my breath coming in a bit more ragged than I'd have preferred. They stayed statue-still in their little line, their faces placid. They were still pointing, all six of them.

The door started to fly open again.

I caught it, slamming the thing shut and shoving my shoulder against the wood before the door made it open even a foot. The door lurched against me, hurling itself open, and my muddy feet slipped on the floor. I caught the doorknob and regained my balance. I threw myself at the door, pushing the whole of my body weight against the thing. I barely got the door settled back against the doorframe before it screamed open, shoving me aside with a strength one rarely sees in doors. I pushed back, my mud-slick hands slipping against the wood.

A smell wafted up from below, something thick and sour and wrong. I caught a flicker of light, and the faint sound of a scream-laugh, before I heaved the door shut again.

The door lurched and jolted. The wood slammed into my cheek, and for a moment, I saw stars. I turned myself, digging my heels into the floor and pressing my back against the door with all the strength I had in me, which admittedly was not a lot at this point.

The pranksters still stood in a line, now in front of me. Pointing. They were absolutely no help.

Just behind the door, the scream-laughing started up again. It seemed to be getting louder.

The doorknob dug into my back. My shoes squeaked along the floor. I dug my fingernails into the doorframe, anything to hold myself in place. The door pushed and pushed. The pranksters pointed and pointed. It seemed I was fighting a losing battle, which was on par with most of the battles I was fighting these days.

Fredricka drifted past the pranksters, seemingly oblivious to my struggle. She was carrying an armful of family photos that had been hanging in the living room and went to hang them in the middle of the hallway. The spot she chose did not actually contain a wall, so each frame fell to the ground with a crash. I flinched at the sound of shattering glass.

My shoes skittered on the floor. I regained my balance, shoving myself against the door so hard my teeth rattled. "Can you do something?" I asked Fredricka. "Please?" My voice shook with the effort.

Fredricka nodded and drifted over to the back door. She lifted the garbage bag that contained the bones of Elias' mother.

Shit. "No," I said. "Something to *help.*"

Fredricka nodded again. "Of course, ma'am." Then she drifted down the hallway with the bones, disappearing around the corner to put them God knew where.

"*Goddamnit, Fredricka,*" I shouted. The door shoved itself against me. I shoved myself back. Behind me, the scream-laughing was definitely louder. There were footsteps, soft but sure, coming up the stairs.

He's coming, the pranksters told me in unison.

"I know," I snapped. I turned again, pressing both hands to the door. The smell was so bad it was practically a taste. The footsteps were midway up the stairs. The scream-laughs were somehow even closer.

"*Stop it,*" I shouted. "*Stay down there.*"

Footsteps. Closer.

I dug my feet into the ground. I pressed myself so hard against the door that I thought my wrists might break. *"Stay away,"* I shouted.

The footsteps were at the top of the stairs now. He was close enough to reach out knobby fingers and turn the doorknob. I pressed my eyes closed.

"STAY AWAY," I screamed.

The doorknob started to turn.

"No," I shouted, and sprinted into the kitchen, barely even noticing as I ran partially through Julian in the process. I yanked one of the chairs from the center of the room, where Fredricka had inexplicably lined them up, and raced back into the hallway. I shoved the chair underneath the doorknob, wedging the legs of the chair against the floor just as the door started creaking open once more.

The knob rattled. The chair squeaked against the floor. Then all went still and silent. The pranksters milled about the hallway, looking bored.

I collapsed against the wall, panting. I was drenched in sweat, and the dirt caked across my body had turned to mud. My stomach still felt sliced open from running through Julian.

Fredricka drifted back down the hallway. She held, for some reason, a single tea bag.

"Where," I panted, "did you put the bones?"

Fredricka studied me with curiosity.

"Elias' mother's bones," I said, and swallowed through the air I could barely breathe. "I still need them."

"What bones?" Fredricka asked. She dipped the single tea bag into empty air.

"Never mind," I said, heaving myself off the wall. My legs seemed to be made of water.

Fredricka pointed at the door. "It's not over," she said.

But I already knew that. I knew that Master Vale wasn't going to stay still forever—nobody ever did, especially in this house.

I needed to act fast, put some water on these embers before they flared up again. The boards needed to go back on the basement door; that much was clear. I should look over the Bible pages on the back of the door before I put the boards up, make sure none of them needed to be replaced. Perhaps I should also consider putting some on the front of the door. The walls too. To hell with looking sane.

Most important, it was time to call Father Cyrus, and I was more than willing to beg. I was sure that not even Father Cyrus could deny that Master Vale trying to shove his way out of the basement was a glaring sign that priestly intervention was overdue. I could refresh the Bible pages on the door and put the boards back up before he arrived, which would, I hoped, ease his mind a bit, because I needed him to come *today*, in the next hour if possible, in the next five minutes if miracles were real.

I grabbed my phone from the kitchen counter with shaking hands, and was barely able to hold it steady as I dialed.

"Saint Dymphna Catholic Church," said the voice on the other end. Young, cheerful—a receptionist.

"Father Cyrus, please." My voice wavered.

There was a pause. "Um . . ." I could hear the receptionist thinking, weighing options. "One moment, please."

The phone clicked to hold, and I heard music, soothing synthesizer tones of a nondescript song. I took several deep breaths and waited as patiently as I could for the receptionist to put Father Cyrus on the line. The calming music played on. I had just identified the words to the little tune (*It all comes around with the moon and the sun. . . .*) when a voice clicked back onto the line. Not Father Cyrus—a much younger person, polite yet worried.

"Hello?" the voice said.

"I'd like to speak to Father Cyrus," I said.

The man on the other end paused, taking in a breath. "I'm afraid Father Cyrus passed away," he said.

My legs were water again. "What?" I said.

"He's no longer with us," the man said as if his phrasing were the part that I had trouble comprehending. Little did this man know, I was very familiar with death these days.

"When?" I asked, bracing myself for the more pressing question on my mind. *"How?"*

"Just a week ago," the man said, his tone calm, almost mesmerizing. It was the voice with which he delivered condolences, and it was practiced to near perfection. "The services were on Sunday. I'm sorry you missed them. If it helps, it was a beautiful—"

"How did he die?" I asked. *Did it have anything to do with flies? Did I somehow kill this man with my prankster house and my tricky basement?*

"It was his time," the man said. "I'm sure you know, Father Cyrus was with us on this earth a good many years. He lived a long life, full of service to—"

"Was he sick?" I asked. "Did something happen?" *Were there flies?*

"I'm afraid I must respect Father Cyrus' privacy," the man said. "But I can tell you that it was very peaceful when he went."

There might have been flies, I thought.

I was at a loss as to what to say next. What would I do now? The only person at that goddamn church who was willing to believe me and help me with my prankster problem was now on the side of the pranksters.

"So," I said, unsure exactly how to phrase my question, "Father Cyrus had been . . . helping me. Helping my husband and me. With our house. He came over just a few weeks ago, and . . ."

"Ah." The man's voice was tight.

"We need him to come over again," I said. "We need his help. Someone's help. I don't suppose you have anyone else—"

"Were you one of the ones Father would visit to"—the man seemed to be searching for the phrasing least likely to end in a lawsuit—"say a prayer for the house?"

One *of the ones?* "Yes," I said.

"And did he tell you there was . . . something wrong with your house?"

He hadn't *had* to tell us that. We'd already known. "Well," I said, "not in so many words . . ."

"Ma'am," the man said, his voice smooth as a lawyer's, "the church wishes to offer you its deepest apologies. You see, Father Cyrus, he wasn't well. He hadn't been well for many years."

"What do you mean?" He seemed well enough to me, minus the flies.

"I'm afraid he had become senile," the man said. "It happened slowly, over the course of several years. But it was really quite pronounced by the end. He had been such a fixture in our church family for so many years that we kept him here."

My mouth hung open. Sure, Father Cyrus was old, but he had seemed sharp as a tack every time I saw him. And he sure had hustled out of the house the last time he was here.

"We didn't want him performing any of his duties in an official capacity anymore," the man explained. "He was really quite ill towards the end. It wouldn't have been right. But he kept finding little ways of eluding us. He paid one of the youths in our church, Julio, to take him on his little . . . errands . . . from time to time."

Perhaps this was why Fredricka had never warmed to Father

Cyrus. Perhaps she knew that something was off about him, that he was fraying at the edges.

"He became fixated on the paranormal," the man said. "He thought he could perform . . . *exorcisms*"—the man whispered this word—"on *places*. Of course, the church rarely performs exorcisms at all anymore. It is quite an archaic ritual, and we know so much now about psychiatry. Really, ma'am, the church was *very* displeased when they learned of Father Cyrus' practices."

But he was helping, I wanted to say. *And now there's nobody to help.*

"Honestly," the man said, "we at the church didn't even know what Father Cyrus had been up to until a few weeks before his death. Julio came to us after the last little *errand* Father tried to conduct. He suffered quite a bad fall there, and Julio's conscience finally got the better of him. He told us everything. Let me tell you, we were *shocked.*"

You should have been here, I thought. *Then you would have really been shocked.*

"I can assure you," the man said, "that we put a stop to it right then and there. We told him—although I'm not sure he understood; he was quite disoriented there at the end—that he was not to leave church grounds without one of us again, and he was *not* to perform any more of his little *errands*. Perhaps his behavior was a sign of how far gone he was, because he died just a week later."

And there were flies, I thought.

"You have my vow," the man said, "that Father Cyrus was the only member of this church who behaved in such a way. His behavior does not reflect the views or practices of Saint Dymphna Catholic Church. I might even say that it did not reflect his merit as a man of the cloth, given the advanced nature of his dementia.

We hope you will not think ill of us, and we hope you are still willing to be a member of our congregation."

This man seemed to be working hard to keep my five dollars in the collection plate. Little did he know I hadn't set foot in a church since Hal and I had begged them for help, and before that, I couldn't remember the last time I could have been considered a member of anyone's congregation.

"So what you're saying," I said, "is that you can't help me."

It didn't really matter what variant of *No, I can't* he said to me. I hung up the phone and leaned against the kitchen counter, stunned. With Father Cyrus gone, my options for damage control were limited. It had taken Hal and me so long to find anyone in the church who believed us, and now, apparently, our only advocate had been suffering from advanced dementia and was dead. What were the odds of my being able to find another priest, perhaps one less senile, willing to help me?

Fredricka drifted back into the room and began turning the remaining kitchen chairs upside down, one by one.

"He's dead," I told her.

"So are many things," she said, not looking up from her task. She had a point. Perhaps I shouldn't have expected any sort of sympathy from her.

"What do I do now?" I asked, slumping back against the counter.

Fredricka paused briefly at the kitchen table. She looked up at me, her face stoic as always. "What you must," she said.

The silence was broken by the squeal of tires in the driveway. Katherine was home, and all problem-solving must be put on hold. I set my phone on the counter and pushed myself towards the kitchen table. I had to right each chair that Fredricka had turned upside down, and I needed to do so before Katherine came into the room and started asking more questions. I left the chair in front of the basement door where it was, though. That one wasn't going anywhere. Katherine could just go on thinking I was crazy. I heard the slam of the car door and Katherine's rapid footsteps up the front porch. She was in a hurry. I wouldn't have time to clean the broken picture frames off the floor.

The front door flew open. I heard the doorknob bang into the wall behind it, sure to leave a dent. Katherine sprinted down the hallway and into the kitchen. When she found me, righting the last chair, she was short of breath.

"Mom," she said. Her eyes were wide and wild, her expression slack, shocked. She took me in, looked me up and down. "Why the fuck are you covered in mud?" She looked at the floor. "And why is there glass everywhere?" She looked behind her. "And why is there a chair in front of the door?"

I chose to ignore these questions for the time being. "What is it, dear?" I said, standing tall next to the table and crossing my arms over my chest. I couldn't quite tell what her face was expressing, but I had a feeling that we had moved past taking me to the hospital for the moment.

She shook her head, then moved on. Apparently, there were more pressing issues at hand. "The police," she said, catching her breath, "they found something."

"About Hal?" I asked. "That's good, right?" Of course, this depended on one's definition of "good." Katherine and I seemed to have different definitions of "good" these days. Katherine tended to consider the learning of new information, particularly information related to myself and Hal, to be good, although she didn't seem to regard the information itself as good once she had learned it.

"They went down to the Value Lodge," she said. "They talked

to some of the employees. They found the guy who was working the night shift when Dad was there. Dave . . . something."

"Oh?" I said.

"That last night Dad stayed at a motel," Katherine said, clutching her purse in a white-knuckled grip, "the one before he stopped paying, abandoned his things. Dave said he saw Dad leave. He said he saw Dad get into a cab."

"So he left," I said. "We knew that already." Katherine had a box of his abandoned things in the trunk of her car to prove it.

"The police found the cab driver," Katherine continued. Her voice was a thin thread, ready to break at any moment. "They talked to him. They said he remembered Dad."

"He did?" I asked.

"They found out where he went."

"And?" Based on Katherine's expression, I had a feeling I ought to be panicking, filling up with fear like a boat taking on water. Katherine certainly looked like she was drowning, gasping for air as the bow of her ship sank underneath dark waves.

"The cab took him back here," she said, her voice murky, underwater. "That last night—the last night anyone saw him—he came back to this house." She was staring at me, her eyes unblinking, rimmed with terror.

I looked out the kitchen door, down the hallway. From the front windows, I could see the bright strobe of red and blue lights illuminating the driveway.

TWENTY-FIVE

As you might imagine, the police had all sorts of questions for me.

There were four of them this time—Jones and McDouglas plus two new officers, fresh-faced lads whose uniforms seemed too big for their bodies. One of them, the skinnier of the two, was named Price. The officers kept referring to the other one as Coop, but there was no way that was his given name. Everyone seemed to be looking at me out of the corners of their eyes at all times.

"Been doing a little yard work?" McDouglas asked me as soon as he saw my muddy appearance, his face full of suspicion.

"I think you've had a bloody nose, ma'am," Coop said to me, gesturing above his lip while trying to avoid eye contact.

I rubbed at my nose, where the blood had long since dried. Oh well.

Coop and Price went upstairs to poke around, and I tried to pay attention to Jones' questions while simultaneously worrying about the extent to which the officers could see the blood.

The officers repeated Katherine's account of all the new information they'd learned. They'd chatted with both Bill and Dave, it turned out, plus a couple other employees at the motel who managed to remember who Hal was simply because Bill wouldn't shut up about him. According to the group of them, Hal had stayed at the motel for about one day and spent most of the time coming and going. Nobody was sure where Hal had gone each time, but someone said he had seen Hal unloading two large containers out of the back of a cab in the early evening. They couldn't tell what was in the containers, but said they looked heavy. Nobody asked questions. *People tend to keep to themselves 'round here*, Bill had explained, and Hal certainly had seemed to, staying in his room with the blinds drawn long after Bill's shift ended and Dave's started. Dave estimated that it had been about midnight when he noticed a cab pulling up in front of Hal's motel room. He peered through the glass of the office door, and—sure enough—saw Hal dart into the cab, with those two large containers of something or other in his hands. He said he hadn't seen Hal anymore after that, and it was a few days later that they'd found his room abandoned.

Dave didn't get a license plate number, but that was no bother for the police. In a town this small, tracking down which cab company responded to a midnight call to the Value Lodge was simple. The cab driver remembered Hal, not because he knew about Hal's books or anything, but because it was late and Hal had had those two big containers. "Can't tell you what was in them," the driver told the police, "but it smelled like gasoline. My cab stank for the rest of the night."

The cab hadn't dropped Hal off exactly at the house, but instead half a mile away. The cab driver thought this was odd. "It looked like I was leaving him in the middle of the woods," the driver had said. "Nothing around for miles. I told him I could drop him closer to where he was going, but he insisted. Walked away lugging those two big containers of his." The driver had watched Hal walk down the road a little ways, and seeing as our house was the only one on this street, it wasn't difficult to guess his destination.

"I'm going to need to ask you some more questions about the night Hal left," Jones said to me, notepad out. Her eyes were sterner than they had been the first time we spoke. I offered her a seat at the kitchen table but she remained standing in the hallway. I stood with her, although I would have much preferred to sit down.

"Of course," I said. When the police showed up the pranksters had scattered, spooked by all the new activity in the house. A good thing too—I had a feeling this conversation with the police would warrant my full attention.

McDouglas ambled into the kitchen, surveying the scene. He had been loitering in the living room and the dining room earlier, seemingly not looking for anything in particular so much as looking around, making mental notes of everything. "It's a bit of a mess," he said. "I don't remember things being in such disarray the last time we were here." He looked at me, his eyebrows raised. "Everything okay?"

"I'm going to need you to recount the events leading up to the night Hal left," Jones said.

"Well," I said, my brain feeling a bit like a jigsaw puzzle scattered across the table, "we had been having disagreements."

"Yes," Jones said. She already knew this part.

"About the house," I said.

"Yes."

"Hal wanted to leave," I said.

Hal wanted to do more than leave. Hal wanted to destroy

everything. Ever since that ill-fated encounter with Master Vale in the basement, Hal hadn't been quite right. He was silent and twitching, and he had locked himself in his office, angry at nothing and everything. Plotting. He was determined to show the pranksters in the house who was boss once and for all, and he had decided he wasn't going to waste his time coaxing Master Vale into submission through sentimentality. He decided that he was going to use brute force.

We have to burn it down, he said to me. His voice was a wobbly whisper, as if the things that lived in this house could hear him. Which they could.

"He wanted to leave," Jones repeated.

"Jesus Christ," Katherine moaned. She was pacing the kitchen, hands in her hair. "You've already *had* this conversation."

"Yes," I said, ignoring Katherine, "he wanted to move out. He didn't like it here."

You are not burning this house down, I had said. The first time we'd had this conversation, we were side by side in bed—back before enough repetitions of this conversation ensured that we no longer shared a bed. I had looked around the room, the spacious master suite with the hand-selected furniture, original hardwood floors, and—opposite us—grand picture window shining with moonlight. Who would ever have wanted to burn this down?

"Why didn't he like it here?" Jones asked.

Margaret, Hal had said, his voice low and insistent, *the things that live here are evil. You know this.*

I thought of Fredricka and all her helpful company. I thought of Jasper, who did little besides lie in a broken pile in the closet. I thought of Blythe, who had calmed down considerably once we stopped using the fireplaces and moved the piano out of the house. I thought of Elias, who was harmless so long as you respected his personal space. I thought of Angelica and her friends, seasonal and cyclical, who were mostly just annoyances. The only thing in this house that was evil was Master Vale. Not a high percentage of evil, all things considered.

"He didn't like it," I repeated. I couldn't think of a convincing enough lie. Everything was too busy. Coop and Price returned from upstairs.

"The rooms are a little messy up there," Coop said to Mc-Douglas. "I saw a stack of dishes on top of the toilet. And it looks like there are a bunch of pillows that have been ripped apart." His eyes darted to me for the briefest of moments. "Not sure what that's about."

"It smells like bleach," Price said. "There are worn spots on the walls, like someone has been trying to scrub something off."

McDouglas nodded at the two of them, his mouth a line. He kept his eyes on me.

"Jesus," Katherine muttered. She was on what seemed like her hundredth lap of the kitchen, arms wrapped around herself. "They need to be checking the woods. I don't know what they're doing looking around in here."

"He just . . . didn't like it?" Jones raised her eyebrows at me, unconvinced.

"This seems like an awfully nice house," McDouglas said, "ignoring the present state. What's not to like?"

Margaret. Hal's voice had dipped into little more than a shaking exhalation. In the dim light peeking through the bedroom window, I could see that his eyes were wide, his face terrified. *These things are going to get us in the end.*

I had looked at Hal, my face bold. I didn't whisper. *Not if we play by the rules.*

"He just . . ." I couldn't quite explain. "He was used to me going along with things. With what he wanted. But I wouldn't do it this time."

"And why wouldn't you?"

"I . . ." I looked around. I had already explained to them what this house meant to me. I gestured absently. "This is my home."

This is our home, I had said to Hal. There had been a time when I thought Hal was my home. I thought that, of all people, he ought to understand.

No, it isn't, Hal said. *It's their home. And it needs to burn.*

Jones sighed. "All right. Let's skip ahead to the night Hal left. Tell me what you remember."

I'm going to do it, Margaret, Hal had said. *I need you to help. Come with me. Please, come with me.*

"He decided he was going to move out," I said, "with or without me."

I'm not leaving, I had said to him. I was standing in the kitchen, leaning against a counter, munching absently at a sleeve of crackers. I was comfortable. I was happy—reasonably so, at least.

Please, Hal had begged. *I'm ending this. I'm getting gasoline. I'm getting matches. I am coming back, and I am burning this place to the ground.*

"Tell me about his mood," Jones said.

The night he left, Hal had gotten down on his knees, clutched at my hips. *I'll end this without you if I have to, but God, Margaret, I don't want to. Don't make me do this without you.*

I'm not going anywhere, I said. I considered that I ought to be sadder, but what would the point of that have been? Hal wanted to leave and I wanted to stay. We could both get what we wanted, a beautiful final compromise.

You'll have to leave eventually, Hal said, looking up at me with wet eyes. *I'm not lying to you, Margaret. I'm ending this.*

Do what you must, I said, and nibbled at the edge of a cracker. Needs must when the devil drives. I could almost *hear* Fredricka say it, even though she was nowhere to be seen.

"He wasn't angry," I said to Jones. "He was sad."

I heard a creak of wood on wood as Price wriggled the chair out from underneath the basement doorknob. Out of the corner of my eye, I saw him open the basement door. I swung my body in his direction, eyes wide.

Price examined the back of the door. "Are these Bible pages?" he asked.

Jones' eyes were on me. "Something wrong?"

"There's mold down there," I said, the only thing I could think. "Black mold."

"I'm sure he'll be fine," Jones said, voice stern, eyes never leaving me.

"It's not safe," I said, my voice barely a whisper. The pranksters were shy when visitors came over and could, apparently, choose not to be seen at all, but I had no idea what Master Vale would think about an intruder in his space, especially so recently after he had tried to come upstairs. He was probably itching for some company, and not in a hospitable way.

"You were talking about the night Hal left?" Jones said, pen still resting on her notepad.

Price disappeared down the basement steps. Coop followed just behind him.

"He left," I said, my voice tight and nervous, eyes flitting to the open basement door. "He called a cab, got in, and left."

I can't believe this is the choice you're making, Hal had said to me, standing on the front porch, the cab idling in the driveway.

I had said nothing in response, only stood in the doorway and watched him. He was making choices too. He always failed to see that.

"And did you see or hear from him again?" Jones asked.

"No," I said.

Nothing had happened that first night Hal was gone. I stayed up late, drinking tea with Fredricka, chatting while she cleaned the kitchen. There was no word from Hal the following day and I was surprised the house didn't feel quieter in his absence. I supposed that, given how much he had kept to himself over the past few months, I had gradually gotten used to the silence. Fredricka made a roast for dinner, and I turned in early. It all felt very right, as if this was the way it had been meant to be all along.

It was a little after midnight when I woke up to somebody moving through the house. It wasn't one of the pranksters—they tended to be quiet, unless they were shrieking at you—and besides, I could recognize Hal's footsteps. I heard the front door close behind him and listened to him stomping around the first floor. His feet were heavy and slow, like he was carrying something cumbersome. I heard a scrape and a thud as he set whatever he was carrying on the floor. I hoped he hadn't scratched the wood.

The moonlight shone through the picture window and my eyes adjusted quickly to the dim light. The bedroom was empty, save for myself, and the door was shut. I heard Hal's footsteps approach the stairs. He lifted himself up one step, two steps, then paused. It was silent for a moment, and I pictured Hal standing on the stairs and looking up, making decisions. Then I heard his footsteps turn and walk down the stairs and back through the first floor. Whatever he was considering, he'd changed his mind.

I heard a scrape and a grunt as he lifted the heavy object. His slow footsteps traversed the first floor, accompanied now with the occasional groan as he lifted the object. Quiet but distinct wet splashes.

Slowly, the thick smell of gasoline wafted up to the bedroom.

He set the object—a gas can, I assumed—down in the hallway. It sounded lighter now. Footsteps in the kitchen. I heard a squeak as he opened a cabinet to retrieve something. Then he walked to the basement door. I heard him grunt, heard wood cracking and popping as he pried the boards off the door. Then a creak, the door opening. I pictured him standing in front of the gaping mouth of the basement, staring down into the darkness, his hand on the doorknob, Bible pages fluttering next to him. There was another scrape and another grunt as he lifted the gas can, and I heard his footsteps fade into the basement.

Silence.

He was too far away for me to hear what he was doing now, but I could picture it nonetheless. The first floor already properly doused in gasoline, he was going down to the source of all the trouble. It wouldn't be long now, I supposed, before I started smelling smoke. I wondered if Hal planned to flee up the basement steps and out the front door. Would he watch the house burn down from the driveway? Stay until it was nothing but a pile of ash in front of him? Or would he sprint down the road, leaving the memory of the house and all its pranksters far behind? Regardless, one thing was certain—he would not be coming up the steps to get me.

Be that as it may, I thought. I wasn't leaving, not out the front door, anyway. I faintly wondered what might happen to all the things in this house that didn't leave, after there wasn't any more house. Would they fade away into nothing, disappearing inside themselves like they did sometimes, just not reappearing? Or would they find some way to stay? Haunt a nearby rock, perhaps.

Something made me think it would be the latter. The things in this house, they didn't seem shaken so easily by something so trivial as fire. I supposed I wasn't either in the end.

Perhaps, afterwards, I could join them. We could all move in circles together, kicking up a fuss in September.

I took one last look around the bedroom, taking in the way the moonlight shone against the hardwood floors, the ornate furniture. This really was a beautiful house. I rolled over in bed, pulling the covers up around me. I closed my eyes. Things weren't so bad. I was home.

I drifted off to sleep, full of peace.

"Can you think of any reason he might've come back here?" Jones asked.

I shook my head, most of my attention still drawn to the basement. If I wasn't mistaken, I heard a startled cry sound from the direction of the steps.

The next morning, the morning after Hal had returned with the gasoline, I was only partially surprised to find that I opened my eyes. It was a beautiful morning, and the sunlight beamed through the window, making the room glow in a nearly heavenly manner. I raised myself up, looking around. The bedroom was undisturbed, the door still closed. Everything looked as it should have. I pinched myself. It hurt.

I walked slowly, so slowly, down the stairs. The house was bright, yet quiet. All was still. I could smell the gasoline heavy in the air. I walked into the living room, holding my nose. Yes, Hal had gotten this room all right. I saw wet stains on the furniture and sighed. It would take *forever* to get the smell out of the upholstery.

"I need you to be very honest with me," Jones said. "Did you see Hal back at this house after he left?"

That morning, I walked out of the living room and back towards the kitchen, towards the basement. The boards from the door were scattered across the floor and the crowbar was propped up against the wall. The door was closed. I hadn't heard Hal close the door last night, but it was closed now. From the looks of it, it had slammed so hard that a small crack snaked down from the top of the door and nearly midway to the doorknob.

"Jones? McDouglas?" A tiny voice sounded. It was Price's. He had walked back up the basement stairs and was standing in front of the door. His face was white. He looked seconds away from being sick.

Truth be told, I hadn't even needed to see that the basement door was closed. I already knew. I likely knew before Hal even left, before he even thought about the gasoline, why the house was still standing. It's a bit of knowledge you can never quite put your finger on, a fact that isn't quite real, like the way you know when someone is watching you, like the way you know it might rain later even when the sky is blue. Like I knew even before the sonogram told me that my baby would be a girl, and her name would be Katherine.

Ah, I had said to the basement door. *So that's how you feel about* that.

I hammered the boards back up over the basement door. I never went down there again. There are rules to these things, and consequences for breaking them.

"What is it?" Jones asked Price.

Price's lips moved wordlessly. He stared at us. He raised one arm, pointing down into the basement. "He's down there," he said.

Jones' eyes widened. Her notebook flipped shut. It would appear that the questions were over.

McDouglas sprang into action, one hand touching the gun on

his belt, the other suddenly wielding a flashlight. He darted down into the basement just as Coop ascended the stairs, looking equally as nauseated as Price. He coughed into his sleeve. His eyes landed on me.

"My God," he said, "what did you *do* to him?"

Katherine cried out and sprinted towards the basement. Coop blocked her way, positioning his body in front of the doorway, his arm outstretched to keep her from coming any closer.

"That's my *father*," Katherine yelled, struggling to get around Coop's body.

"Trust me," he said, blocking her with his arm. "You don't want to see him."

Katherine pulled away from Coop but didn't try to get past him. Instead, she paced in tight circles in the hallway, lost. She pulled at her hair, her face torn. *"Oh God,"* she said. "Has he been down there this whole time?"

Price nodded at the floor. "It would appear so, ma'am."

Katherine stopped in front of the officers. She looked at them, her eyes red and wet. "And he's . . . ?"

Coop nodded firmly. "Yes," he said.

Katherine bent in two. She screamed something indiscernible, something about *Jesus* and *fuck* and *no*.

I had lines here. I should comfort her. I should do something—hug her or tell her it would be okay or offer her tea. But all I seemed to be able to do was watch the scene play out in front of me: actors on a stage, stumbling through their lines.

Jones hadn't taken her eyes off me the whole time. The notebook was gone. Her hands were on her belt.

McDouglas went up the stairs. His hand was still gently touching the gun on his belt. His face was stoic. He caught Jones' eye, nodded at her. "We're gonna need to call Homicide."

"Homicide?" Katherine asked.

Jones nodded at McDouglas, then turned back to me. Handcuffs materialized in her hand. "Margaret . . ."

Wait.

I snapped back into being, my brain spinning again. I took a hasty step away from Jones and her handcuffs, my palms out in front of me. *I mean you no harm.* At my sudden movement, all officers touched their hands to their guns, poised and ready for action.

Katherine looked around wildly. "What's happening?" she asked.

"Wait," I said. "I can explain."

"I would advise against that," Jones said, taking a slow step towards me, "because everything you say can be held against you in—"

"I know," I said. "But *that*"—I gestured at the basement—"wasn't me."

"It wasn't you?" McDouglas asked. "Who was it, then?"

I sighed. It was time for honesty.

"It was the *house*," I said.

Five confused faces stared back at me, four of them belonging to people who were looking for a reason to draw their weapons and fire. Jones took another step towards me, and I shuffled backwards. I was well inside the kitchen now, the officers carefully following.

"The what?" Jones asked.

"The *house*," I said. "Well, not the house specifically. Master Vale. It was Master Vale who did that, I promise."

"Mom?" Katherine said. "What the fuck are you talking about?"

"I know how it sounds," I said. "But I swear to you, Hal went into the basement—he shouldn't have done that. He was trying to . . . and Master Vale got him."

Price looked at Jones. "I didn't see anyone else down there."

"Margaret," Jones said, her voice calm. She had maybe taken a class in this, in speaking calmly to people who sound off their rockers. "Who is Master Vale?"

"He used to live here." This was not going to be received well, but the truth was my last option. "Back in the eighteen hundreds. His family built this house. The Vales. You've heard of the Vales?" The officers gave no indication. Katherine looked like she was about to snap into pieces. "He was one of their children. Well, Penelope's child, anyway. He's not mentioned in the papers much. I think they were ashamed. He was born out of wedlock and—" I shook my head. "Different times."

McDouglas had quietly looped around to my side, so he stood between me and the back door, prepared in case I tried to flee. He needn't have worried—I wasn't going anywhere.

"He lived here in the eighteen hundreds," Jones repeated.

"He isn't a nice man. Wasn't a nice man." I was never sure of the proper tense. Master Vale both *is* and *was*, and likely *would continue to be*. "He killed the pranksters. I'm sure of it. I've seen it. Sort of. They come and go. In September."

Coop and Price exchanged an incredulous look. They were out of their element. The academy hadn't properly trained them for this.

"Pranksters?" McDouglas asked.

"The children," I said. "The ones who went missing all those years ago. Angelica and Julian and the others. They're here too. They're not bad, though. I think they just want to warn me."

"Jesus Christ, Mom," Katherine moaned. "You need to stop talking."

"No," I said, connecting dots in my mind. "I think they wanted to *tell* me."

"Margaret," Jones said, "I just think you need to come down to the station. . . ." She extended her hand, the one with the handcuffs.

I wasn't being convincing. Maybe I should start at the beginning. "There are things that live in this house," I explained. "People that used to live here. Bad things happened to them. But they aren't bad people, not all of them. Some of them want to help. Like, there's a housekeeper . . . and a boy . . . Elias." I rolled up my sleeves, showed them my scars, my bandages. "See?"

Jones' eyes widened.

"Mom," Katherine hissed, *"stop talking."*

"Elias isn't bad," I said. "He just bites." I held my arms out and took a step closer to Jones, so she could get a better view. Now Jones took a slight step backwards. The mud from the grave had gotten into the cracks in my scars, and the exertion had caused my more recent wounds to reopen and bleed through the bandages. It all looked a lot worse than it was.

"I . . . ," Katherine said in a thick voice as she looked at Jones. "I think she did that to herself."

"Katherine can't see him," I explained, "but he's there."

"The older scars, I thought Dad did that to her," Katherine said. "But now I don't know." She hugged her arms around her chest. "I don't think she's well."

"Margaret," Jones said, "how did you get those injuries?"

"I *told* you," I said. No one was listening. "Elias did them. I wasn't paying attention. I'm so tired. The screaming, you see. Anyway, I didn't see him there and he bit me. Elias isn't the problem, though. It's Master Vale."

"She's talked about this Elias person before," Katherine said to Jones. "That's what I mean—I think she's seeing things."

I didn't appreciate Katherine talking about me as if I weren't here. "Hal could see the pranksters too," I said. "Well, he could see some of them. Sometimes. He could see Elias. He didn't like Elias. But it was Master Vale that Hal *really* didn't like." I smiled. Full honesty now. "That's what Hal was doing. He was going to burn it all down. He thought he could get rid of Master Vale once and for all. But . . . Master Vale got him." I could feel tears springing to my eyes as I said this. I had never spoken it out loud before, not even to Edie, although Edie seemed to know, anyway. "If he had just followed the rules . . ."

"Rules?" McDouglas asked.

"That little test I did with her," Katherine was saying. "It was supposed to assess her mental state or something. See if she knew where she was and what day it was. She did *really* bad. I think she's been losing time."

"We had rules," I said, wiping at my eyes with a dirty wrist. "You don't go near Elias. You don't light fires. You just ignore Angelica and the other children. You *don't go in the basement*. That's where he lives, Master Vale. Things get bad in September. Hal was afraid of September. But we would have been fine if we had followed the rules. We deal with Elias. We call Father Cyrus over. We—"

Jones and McDouglas exchanged a look. "Cyrus?" McDouglas asked.

"Yes," I said, remembering that he was dead now too. "If he were here, he would tell you. He knew about the house. But—"

"Margaret, Father Cyrus was very sick," Jones said, her expression one of pity.

I looked up at her sharply. "You knew Father Cyrus?"

"We got calls about him all the time," McDouglas said. "The church thought they could handle him, but he needed to be in a home. He was constantly wandering away. He was obsessed with the supernatural, convinced there were demons everywhere. He would break into people's houses and people would come home and find him trying to perform some sort of exorcism in their living room. I can't *tell* you how many times we—"

"That's . . . No," I said. "I mean, that's what the church said, but . . . that's not right. He was . . . that is, whenever I saw him . . . he was fine. And I saw him just a few weeks ago. He . . ." I remembered his fit by the basement door. "I think Master Vale tried to get him too. He opened the door and . . . flies came out of his mouth. That's why there are so many flies in here." I waved my arms around excitedly. They had seen the flies. They had even *mentioned* the flies the last time they were here.

"Ma'am," Price said timidly, "the flies are here because there's a dead body in the basement."

"You should see the number of flies down *there*," Coop added.

"I think she's been eating the flies," Katherine said quietly. "She vomited earlier, and—"

"Margaret, did Father Cyrus try to convince you your house was haunted?" Jones asked.

"No," I said, "he was the only one who *believed* us." I looked at Katherine pleadingly. I needed somebody to believe me. "You haven't seen *any* of them? Not Elias? Not Angelica and her friends? There is a broken man who lives in the closet in your room upstairs. . . ."

"There's a *what*?" Katherine asked.

"His name is Jasper. Don't worry. He doesn't do much. He just flicks a match, and it never lights. He tried to burn the house down too. Have you seen him?"

"I haven't seen anything," Katherine said.

"What about the blood?" I asked.

"The *blood*?"

I looked around at the police officers. "Did any of you see the blood? There's blood that pours from the walls upstairs. I clean it, but it keeps coming back. Did you see it?"

Their incredulous looks told me that they had not seen the blood. The pranksters' inclination to choose who could and couldn't see them was tremendously inconvenient at the moment.

I looked back at Katherine. "And I don't suppose you heard the screaming? I know you're a heavy sleeper, and what with the sleeping pills—"

Katherine's eyes widened. *"Sleeping pills?"*

Oh, right. She didn't know about that. I looked away, sheepishly. "Um . . ."

"What do you mean, *sleeping pills?*"

"I'm sorry, dear," I said. "I didn't want you to be bothered with all this. The screaming gets pretty bad by the end of September. I didn't want it to keep you awake. So . . ."

"So you slipped me fucking *sleeping pills?*" Katherine was not taking this news well. "You *drugged me?*"

"Just a little bit," I said. "It's only DoZZZe-Rite. We can talk about it later, if you'd like." I ran my hands through my hair, thinking. My eyes darted around the room, looking for something, *anything* that might convince the officers that these things I saw were real. My eyes landed on a pile of mud near the back door, the spot where the garbage bag containing the bones of Elias' mother used to lie. Where had Fredricka hidden those bones? It was risky, but worth a shot.

"Elias' mother," I said, gesturing at the back door. "Her bones are somewhere in the house."

Four hands on guns again.

"No," I said, hands up. "I didn't kill her. She died ages ago. Master Vale was behind it in some way. I can't be certain. But she is—was—buried out back."

Everyone's eyes were on me. Nobody seemed to believe me.

"I feel bad about digging her up," I said. "I really do. But when I dig her up, Elias goes away for a bit and things get a little more peaceful."

"Where did you say the bones were?" McDouglas asked.

I looked around the room wildly, craning my neck to peer down the hallway. "I don't know," I said. "They were in a garbage bag. I don't mean any disrespect. I used to keep them in a vase whenever I—" I shook my head. "Not important. Fredricka moved them. I don't know where she put them. If I can just—" I took a step forward towards the hallway, meaning to go look for the bones, but three bodies suggested to me that this was a bad idea.

McDouglas glanced over at Coop and Price. "Did you boys find any garbage bags up there?" he asked. "Possibly filled with bones."

Coop shook his head.

"Nope," Price said. "We would've told you."

I sighed. "No," I said, "you probably just didn't see it. Fredricka likes to hide things *inside* other things." I turned and started opening up cabinets, rummaging through the hodgepodge of trinkets Fredricka had moved into them. Clothing. Picture frames. A small lamp. Several—and I mean *several*—piles of dirt. I turned back to the officers, and waved an arm at the cabinets. *"See?"*

Everybody looked concerned. I glanced back at the cabinets. It would have been much more convenient if there had been bones in them.

"My grandma used to do stuff like this," Price said quietly. "Towards the end. She would rearrange things. Stack things."

"I know how it sounds," I said. "But I swear to you I dug her up just earlier. I grabbed each of her bones with my bare hands and tossed them into the garbage bag. Her femur, her ribs, her spine, her skull. They were all *there*." I ran my hands through my hair, which felt like a coarse, dirty tangle. "Where the *fuck* did Fredricka put them?"

"Is that why you look like that, Mom?" Katherine asked, gesturing to the length of my muddy body. "Were you . . . trying to dig up a dead body or something?"

"Or maybe getting ready to bury a dead body?" Coop muttered. Jones shot him a look.

Jones moved closer. "Margaret, you can tell us all about this once we're down at the station. We promise, we'll listen. We'll give you all the time you need to make sure we understand."

This was going poorly. I needed something on my side, some piece of concrete evidence to convince them that I wasn't crazy.

"Edie!" I exclaimed.

"Oh *God*," Katherine groaned, hands over her face.

"Edie has seen them too," I said, clapping my hands together. "She'll tell you. Call Edie over. She'll set everything straight."

"Who is Edie?" Jones asked. I could tell by her expression that she thought there was a good chance that Edie wasn't real. Luckily for me, Edie *was* real.

"She's my next-door neighbor," I said. "We're close friends. She comes over to see me every few days. She knows *everything*. And she's seen these things too. She knows they're real. Call Edie."

Jones and McDouglas exchanged looks. "Your next-door neighbor?" Jones asked.

"Yes," I said. "Call her. She'll tell you."

"Mom," Katherine said, "who the hell are you talking about?"

"*Edie*," I said. "My friend Edie. She lives just next door. She walks over all the time."

"Ma'am," McDouglas said, "you don't have any neighbors out here. The closest house is nearly ten miles away."

I turned to look at McDouglas, my brow furrowing.

"Where would she have walked from?" he asked.

I stared at him. He was right. We didn't have any neighbors out here. That was one of the things Hal and I liked about the house. And yet . . . he wasn't right. Right? Because Edie came over to chat with me, her plump figure waddling down the driveway three or more times a week. She came from somewhere. But where? I felt like my brain was skipping like a needle on a scratched record.

Jones looked at Katherine. "Have you met this Edie person?"

"No." Katherine shook her head slowly. "Nobody has been here except you guys."

"You *have* seen Edie," I said excitedly, remembering. "That morning you came back from . . . the bartender's." I whispered this last word and I saw Katherine look around, face flushing. "When you drove up the driveway, Edie and I were talking on the front porch."

Katherine stared at me.

"You walked right past us," I said. "Edie waved at you."

Katherine's face didn't look quite right. "Mom," she said, "you were sitting alone on the front porch that morning."

The scratched record in my brain skittered again. "No . . ." I frowned. "That's not right. Edie was there."

"No, Mom," Katherine said, "you were alone. I remember because I thought it was strange that you were just sitting there, not doing anything. I thought you might have been waiting up for me. It made me feel awful that I had left."

"No . . . ," I said, but the record in my brain wouldn't advance any further. This made no sense. Edie was *real*. She was my only friend, my only *living* friend. I told her everything. I hadn't had a person in my life to whom I could tell everything in so long.

I pushed past Jones and walked out of the kitchen and down

the hallway. Out of the corner of my eye, I saw Price and Coop touch their hands to the guns on their belts, waiting for me to do something dangerous.

"Margaret," Jones called after me, her voice a warning, "where are you going?"

"She lives next door," I repeated. I needed to see. I needed to see if there were houses next door. If I could just peer down the road, I could see where she might have come from.

I stopped when I got to the front door. There was Edie, peering in through the window. She was smiling, but the smile looked sad. She tapped on the window with a finger.

I turned back to the officers lining up behind me. I pointed at the window, grinning triumphantly. *"See?"* I said. "That's her."

None of the officers said anything. They looked very, very worried. Coop and Price kept glancing at Jones and McDouglas, looking for guidance.

"Mom," Katherine said, her voice vibrating, "what are you seeing?"

I pointed harder. *The woman in the window, obviously.* "Edie," I said. "She's on the front porch. She must have seen the police cars and come to check up on me."

"Margaret." Jones' voice was a body of still water. "There's nobody there."

"What?" I turned to look out the window again and suddenly Edie was inside the house, standing in front of the window. I flinched, startled. "Jesus, Edie," I said, hand on my chest. "How did you get inside?"

I heard Katherine moan obscenities behind me.

"Margaret," Jones said, "who are you talking to?"

"I'm sorry, Margaret," Edie said. "I wanted to tell you. I really did."

"What are you talking about?" I asked her. "Edie, I need you to tell the police that I'm not crazy. They don't believe me about the things in this house. But if you tell them you've seen them too . . ."

I'd never seen a smiling person look so sad. "I just enjoyed your company so much," she said. "And you seemed like you really needed a friend. I wanted to tell you, but you were so happy thinking that I was . . . well, you know. So, I could never get up the courage."

"Edie," I said, "what do you mean?"

I could hear the officers behind me moving closer but taking care not to get too close, not yet.

"Mom." Katherine was sobbing. "You need to stop this *right now*."

"I was afraid you wouldn't want to be friends anymore." Edie smiled at me. A tear was caught on the swell of her cheek.

"Margaret." Jones' still voice came from behind me. "Can you tell us what you're seeing?"

"Edie . . . ," I said. I could feel tears starting to form in my own eyes.

"I lived in this house before you and Hal," Edie said, the tear drifting down the curve of her cheek, down her face. "When you did all that research into the house, I was certain you'd find out. But I suppose my name never made the paper."

"You were the person who bought the house in the nineties," I breathed.

Behind me, Katherine was still crying, still asking me to stop.

"It was so lonely here," Edie said, her smile flickering in and out. "I never could find a way to live with the things in this house, not like you did. They terrified me. And it was so, so lonely." Her voice cracked.

"Edie," I whispered, "what did you do?"

Her smile returned, but only slightly. "Sleeping pills," she said.

I felt like I was filling with water again, sinking. Everything around me was heavy and blurry. Things moved more slowly underwater. I reached out and took Edie's hand and saw the world through her eyes: saw the master bedroom as she had decorated it, full of pinks and flowers; saw the light fading in the corners; felt the cloudiness sink into her brain, murky and thick but not yet powerful enough to dull the stab of sadness that rested in her heart.

Edie smiled at me and squeezed my hand. She gazed around the house, into the living room, down the hallway, up the grand stairs. "This really is a beautiful house," she said.

"I know," I replied.

"Margaret." A hand was on my shoulder, soft, practiced. *I'm not going to hurt you. I just want to talk.* "Why don't you come back into the kitchen with us?" Jones asked.

I released Edie's hand to face what was likely a very concerned audience. I was aware that my tears had cut lines into the dirt on my face.

"Mom," Katherine said, "your nose is bleeding."

I touched my hand to my face and examined my fingers. Indeed, my nose was bleeding.

"That happens when I touch them," I explained. My explanation didn't seem to relieve anyone's worry.

I let Jones' gentle hand guide me back down the hallway, away from Edie. I looked behind me. Edie still stood in front of the living room window, a small smile on her face. She waved. I waved back. Jones' hand became firmer on my shoulder, guiding me faster.

"Nobody here thinks anything negative about you," Jones said, nothing but compassion in her voice as she led me to the kitchen table and directed me into one of the chairs. She sat down in the chair next to me, her body facing mine, her hands clasped on the table. *I'm your friend here.* "We all just want what's best for you."

"Your daughter told us about your . . . behavior," said Mc-Douglas. "She told us about the things you're saying you see. The weird things you've been doing around the house. Moving things. Forgetting about things." Whatever class Jones had taken that made her good at talking to crazy people, McDouglas hadn't taken it.

"I'm not seeing things," I said, but the fight was out of me.

"Margaret," Jones said, "nobody else can see what you're seeing. When you were over by the living room—did you see someone there?"

I looked up at Jones. I said nothing.

"Did you see that friend you were telling us about? Edie?"

I nodded.

"You know we didn't see anyone there, right? None of us."

"Sometimes people can't see them," I said, but now that I thought on it, it seemed as if most people couldn't see them. Edie was the only other person who saw every single one of them, just like me, and it turned out, she was a prankster herself.

"They're not *real*, Margaret," Jones said, leaning forward.

"They're . . ." I wasn't sure how to finish that sentence. Hal had seen the pranksters—some of them, at least. He and I had gone into the basement and tried to fight Master Vale. Master Vale had bitten a chunk out of Hal's leg, and Hal hadn't been the same after that. He'd locked himself away in his office, with his whiskey.

Or was that before? Had he started with the whiskey even before last September, and I just hadn't noticed? Time moved funny around here, in stutters and cycles. It was hard to know when things had happened, but they would certainly happen again.

Jones cleared her throat, contemplated her next few words. "Katherine tells us there's a history of mental illness in your family?" She phrased this as a question, but she knew the answer.

My eyes landed on Katherine, who looked away. Apparently, she had been in more communication with the police than I had thought. They were all quite chummy, it would seem.

"Something like that," I said. "But I'm not crazy."

"Are you sure about that?" McDouglas asked.

Jones glanced over at McDouglas. *I have this handled*, her expression said.

"Nobody who is crazy thinks they're crazy, Mom," Katherine said.

"These things you're seeing," Jones said, her face kind, "they're all in your head."

"I can touch them," I said. I could also walk straight through them, but that didn't seem to help my case.

"That can happen sometimes when people see things," Jones said. "The things seem very real to the person experiencing them. They talk to the person, tell them to do things, threaten them. But they *aren't* real."

I thought about Fredricka asking me about dinner. I thought about Edie keeping me company on the front porch. I thought about the pranksters pointing and pointing at the basement. I thought about Elias. I thought about Master Vale. "Threatening" was certainly a word that could describe those last two.

"If I'm being honest," Jones said, "I was worried about you that first time we visited the house. Your thought process seemed scattered, nonlinear. You seemed distracted. I wondered if you were seeing something else in the room but were trying to hide it from us."

"I wondered that too," Katherine breathed. She was standing next to Jones now, a co-interrogator. And me, I had no one on my side anymore. "I know you know I was worried earlier today, Mom, but I've been worried for a *while*. Even before I came here, when we talked over the phone, I could tell that something was off about you. Officer Jones has it right. *Scattered*."

"I . . ." I wasn't sure what to say. I was fine. I *thought* I was fine, anyway.

"Katherine tells me you don't spend much time out of the house," Jones said. "And when you two ventured out, you seemed paranoid. She told me you would get fixated on little, unimportant things. Graffiti on a bathroom stall. The names of hotel clerks. A song playing on the radio. She said you seemed to think that these things were messages for you."

"They were," I said. They *were*. Right?

"Sometimes when people see things that aren't really there," Jones said, "they get paranoid, think that people—even strangers— are watching them, out to get them. They think that things are trying to communicate with them in some way, like through television commercials."

"Or a song on the radio," Katherine interjected.

"And with Hal," Jones said. "I know your relationship was hard. Katherine told us about the abuse. And you know that we know about the alcoholism. You know, people with mental illness often find themselves in abusive relationships. I don't know what it is. Maybe there are just certain types of people who prey on weakness."

"That's not really . . ." But I wasn't sure how to finish that sentence. I wasn't weak. I was flexible, accommodating.

"I know you and Hal were fighting, Margaret," Jones said. "You said so yourself. Was it as bad as Katherine thinks it might've been after you two moved here? I don't know. But it certainly wasn't marital bliss, was it?"

I shook my head. It certainly wasn't.

"Did the fighting have anything to do with your mental illness?" Jones asked. "Katherine told us about that book she found in his office. *The Shadows and You.* Was he insisting you get help, go to a hospital?"

He had been insisting I *leave*. But leave . . . to where? I was having trouble remembering.

"But you didn't want to go anywhere," Jones was saying. "You wanted to stay here with him. In your home. You didn't want to go to any hospital."

I certainly didn't.

"And then *he* wanted to leave," McDouglas said. "That must've been difficult."

"We understand how you must have felt," Jones said. "How you must have reacted. You two had been together for— How long? Thirty years? And then Hal wants to leave? After all he's put you through?"

"You were willing to put up with his alcoholism and his abuse," McDouglas said, his voice sad. "And he wasn't willing to put up with your mental illness? What an asshole."

"Of *course* you were upset," Jones said. "Of *course* you lashed out."

"It was Master Vale," I said, but my voice was barely audible. My eyes were fixed on the table. The world around me was foggy again. Everything they were saying somehow made both no sense and all too much sense. My own father had seen shadows, had talked about the government bugging our lamps. Sometimes he forgot things. Sometimes his words didn't make sense. Sometimes he had to go away for a little while. Taking a vacation, my mother said. When he returned, he would be dull and his hands would shake. He wouldn't talk about the shadows or the bugs for a while. But he always started up again. These things are cyclical. These things are also hereditary.

"Right," Jones said. "But if Master Vale is in your head, who actually did that to Hal?"

"But I don't . . ." My voice was shaking. "I don't *remember* it." This was true. I didn't remember killing Hal. But I could tell you exactly what he looked like down there. I knew he was in the back corner of the basement, in that little room where we had found Master Vale. (Or had we? Had Hal and I gone down there? Or had that been just me? Just something I dreamed up?) I knew he was crumpled up against the wall, his body broken, limbs bent in on themselves. I knew his shattered face was twisted in horror. I knew that, just like Jasper, he had a matchstick in his hand, never to be lit.

"Sometimes when people do terrible things, things they wouldn't do if they were of sound mind, they don't remember much of it," Jones said. "Sometimes they don't remember any of it at all."

It would have been an easy thing to do. Hal had been drinking the night he came back, of course. And he never had come up to the bedroom to ask if I wanted to leave with him. He would have been focused on his task down there in the basement, and not in his right mind. I was quiet when I moved, always had been. He wouldn't have heard me. And he had left the crowbar at the top of the stairs, so easy to grab. It made sense to wait until he was in that little room in the basement. He wouldn't be able to see me coming. I would have him cornered. He wouldn't be able to defend himself, not from the first blow. The first blow was critical.

"Does he have a matchstick in his hand?" I asked, eyes still on the table. "Hal? Down there?" I had so many visions in my head and no way to tell which ones were real. I needed confirmation.

Jones looked at Coop and Price questioningly.

Coop nodded. "Yes, ma'am, he did."

I set my jaw, nodding slightly. "And what happened to him," I asked, "does it look like a human could've done it? That is, a person all by themselves?"

"Jesus," I heard Katherine hiss.

Coop looked uncomfortable. "It's hard to tell," he said. "It looks like there's a lot that happened to him."

I nodded again.

Jones reached across the table, laying her hand gently on mine. "Margaret—are you remembering something?"

"People who see things," I said, "do they kill people?"

I heard Katherine let out a sharp, shaky breath.

"Not usually," Jones said. "But in very extreme circumstances, it's possible."

I figured I could consider these circumstances extreme. In my mind's eye, I could see the pranksters fading, drifting from transparent to nearly invisible. With no trace left behind, it was hard to say if they had even been there in the first place. I looked at the scars on my arms. They *did* closely resemble the scratches Hal used to leave on me in those early days. Now that I examined them closely, I couldn't see how they came from teeth at all.

"People who see things," I said, "do they hurt themselves?"

"Sometimes," Jones said.

I looked around the room, saw what utter disarray the house was in. The cabinets were still thrown open from my search for the bones, revealing the smattering of random objects that lay inside. The sink was a grimy mess, covered in mud and debris. There was dirt everywhere, dark footprints and handprints covering most surfaces. And the *flies*. God, how had I gotten so used to the flies? This did not appear to be the kitchen of a woman who was doing well.

"People who see things," I said, "do their houses look like this?"

Jones surveyed the kitchen. "Yes," she said.

I looked up at Katherine. She was crying. She had been crying a lot today, the thing I was supposed to keep her from doing. Right now all evidence would suggest I had failed. I supposed I had been failing at quite a large number of things these days.

Jones gripped my hand more tightly. "Margaret, we want to help you," she said. "We need to take you down to the station, to arrest you, but now that we know what you've been experiencing, we can make sure you go somewhere with people who know how to treat you. These things you've been seeing, they'll go away with medication. We can be sure you get that medication, get the care you need."

"You probably won't even go to prison," McDouglas said. "They'll put you in a facility where they treat people like you, people whose mental illnesses got out of hand. They'll help you get well while you're there."

"Please, Margaret," Jones said, "let us help you." She sounded so sincere. And I was so, so tired.

I was still looking around the kitchen. I would miss this place. This room in particular, even if it was a mess. Slowly, I nodded. "Okay," I said.

Katherine put her hand over her mouth. Her emotion was unreadable but palpable.

Jones smiled. "Okay," she said. She released my hand and the handcuffs materialized again. Her eyes flitted down to the cuffs, then back to me, her expression apologetic. "We have to," she said.

"I understand," I said. I stood up and turned around, hands behind my back.

Jones motioned for Coop and he moved behind me, taking her handcuffs and placing them over my wrists. The metal was cold, pinching.

"Margaret Hartman," McDouglas said, positioning himself directly in front of me, "you are under arrest for the murder of Harold Hartman." He said other things too, things about me remaining silent and something about an attorney, but I wasn't listening. I was trying to take in every last detail of the kitchen, trying to ignore the cold click of the cuffs around my wrists. I wondered if they would have tea where I was going.

"Not too tight?" Coop asked. He kept a hand on the cuffs.

"It's fine," I said.

"You're doing great, Margaret," Jones said, moving through the kitchen, towards the hall. She nodded at McDouglas. "I'll go call this in." She disappeared down the hall, the front door creaking open as she stepped onto the porch, off to warn the station of my arrival.

McDouglas turned to Katherine, who still had her hand clasped over her mouth, tears wetting her palm. "You can follow us to the station, if you'd like."

Katherine nodded, releasing her mouth. She grabbed her purse from the counter.

McDouglas exhaled, looked at me. "Ready?"

I wasn't. But it would appear I had little say in the matter. "I suppose," I said.

Coop's hand tightened on the cuffs, and he pressed a palm to my back. He turned me and we began walking out of the kitchen, heading down the hallway. Price followed just behind, with Mc-Douglas bringing up the rear.

Katherine—purse tucked under her arm, car keys already in hand—jogged forward until she was in step with me. She took a deep breath and squared her jaw, a soldier ready for battle. "It's going to be okay," she said, although it was unclear if she was speaking to me or herself. "We're going to figure something out."

"Katherine," I said. Her eyes met mine. She looked quite like me after all, her hard angles having softened with time, lines forming on her face just as they had formed over mine. She was all grown-up, I realized. An adult who took deep breaths even when she felt like wailing. "I'm so sorry about all of this."

She looked away, blinking and swallowing. "It's okay," she said, although we both knew it wasn't. We were halfway down the hallway now—I could see the blue of the day outside through the open door. Just past that, Jones was partway to the cruiser, glancing back at us to be sure we were following. The time to say the things I wanted to say was limited.

"I didn't want to tell you about any of this," I said. "I didn't want you to be afraid. I shouldn't have kept it from you. I should have told you."

"Yeah. You should have," Katherine said. A deep breath in, out. "But I know how you are. You were trying to protect me."

"I was," I said, although it would seem my protecting days were over. No one could protect Katherine from whatever was about to happen to me after we left the house and I got into the back of the police car. The weight of all of this would fall squarely on Katherine's shoulders, and I wasn't sure how I could shield her from it.

My eyes were wet. "I don't know what to do now."

Katherine glanced at me, putting on a smile that almost looked like courage.

"What you have to," she said. "After all"—she faced forward again—"needs must when the devil drives."

I stopped walking so abruptly that Coop bumped into my back. He made a startled noise.

"Margaret?" McDouglas said. "Let's keep going, huh?"

"What did you say?" I asked Katherine.

Katherine was a few paces ahead of me, not realizing that I had stopped. She turned to look at me, her face questioning. "Needs must," she repeated, unsure if she ought to be answering me, "when the devil drives."

"Where did you hear that?" My voice was little more than an exhale.

Katherine frowned. "I don't know," she said. "I just know it, I guess. It means, like, when you have to do something unpleasant—"

"I know what it means. But I had never heard it"—I breathed—"until I came to this house."

"I'm sure you heard it somewhere before, Mom," Katherine said, but I could tell by her expression that she had just placed where she had heard it as well.

"No," I said, a sharp, clattering exhalation.

"Margaret"—McDouglas stepped closer—"what's the problem?" His tone suggested that there wasn't supposed to be any problem, but that wasn't how any of this worked.

That was when the moaning started.

It was almost inaudible at first, faint as the whistle of the wind, and for a moment, I thought it was in my head. But the noise persisted, picking up in volume and conviction and working its way towards a sound that would become screaming within minutes. I could feel the moaning rattle something deep inside my chest, the way bass notes rattle the box of a speaker. Katherine's face told me that the noise wasn't in my head. I turned to see Mc-Douglas glancing around in confusion, and Coop and Price looking scared.

"Are you doing that?" Katherine asked me. "Are you making that sound?"

I shook my head. It was clear the moaning wasn't coming from me. It sounded as if it were coming from both nowhere and everywhere simultaneously, pouring out of the walls of the house itself. It sounded as if the house had finally had just about enough of everything and was ready to let us all know it.

"What the hell is that?" McDouglas said, hand on his belt.

Click.

The cuffs on my wrists sprang open and clattered to the ground. I felt the cold air and the lingering sting of the sharp metal on my newly bared wrists. Slowly, I moved my hands from the small of my back and examined my freed wrists, turning towards the officers as I marveled at this new development.

Coop and Price drew their weapons.

I raised my hands in the air. "That wasn't me," I said.

"Everything all right in there?" Out of the corner of my eye, I saw Jones turn around. She started moving back towards the house, her hand touching at her holster. As soon as she saw the officers with their weapons, she started moving faster, jogging up the porch steps and towards the door.

The door slammed shut so hard the house shuddered.

"The *fuck?*" Coop shouted.

The doorknob jiggled. The sounds of Jones banging on the door and shouting at us to open up were just barely audible over the moaning. I could tell from here that the door wasn't locked, but I wasn't about to move closer to investigate, not with three guns still aimed at me and an ever-increasing moaning suggesting that the guns were likely to be the least of my concerns very soon.

A liquid noise started to my right, the sound of something wet moving—like water over rocks, except the liquid seemed thicker than water and slower as well. I turned and saw blood pouring down the stairs, more blood than I had seen in any previous September. The gleaming red substance ran down the stairs in globby rivulets, a grotesque waterfall. A thick, meaty smell came with it, like pennies and rotting flesh. Within moments, the blood began to pool at the bottom of the stairs, inching towards us.

Katherine screamed.

All five of us stepped backwards, trying to stay out of the way of the thick red ooze. I pressed my back into the wall behind me, cornered. I was no stranger to getting blood on my feet, but this seemed like an entirely new ordeal. Coop and Price pointed their weapons at the stairs, as if that would do any good. I couldn't blame them for being so upset. They likely had zero experience with houses that bled, and besides, even I could admit that this was *quite* a lot of blood.

"What in the *hell*—," McDouglas started.

Thud.

A loud noise from the side of the house, the living room. We all jumped, whirling towards the offending wall, searching for the cause.

Thud.

This noise came from the front of the house, near the door. We all swung our heads around again, looking for nothing. Katherine inched back down the hall, away from the sound.

Thud.

McDouglas swallowed. "Jones?" he called. But the sound couldn't have come from Jones—the sound of her fists could still be heard clearly against the door, and this new noise was too far up the house. Katherine and the officers glanced around, but I stayed still.

Thud.

Thud.

Thud.

The sounds came faster and louder, attacking us from every side. I remained planted against the wall, doing my best to remain calm as the pounding closed in on us. The officers whirled their heads around so fast that they might have given themselves whiplash. Coop and Price ducked down, as if they could see some offending entity that was causing the violent noises. They needn't have bothered. I knew what was causing the pounding.

"The birds," I whispered.

Thud thud thud thud thud.

From all angles, birds—large and black and angry—screamed their way into the sides of the house. We could see them through the windows, careening down against the house in their vengeful suicides. They screeched and cawed as they approached, but we could barely hear them over the moaning and the pounding and the little whimpers that Coop and Price seemed intent on making. The birds slammed their weight into the walls, the door, the windows. They left smudges of blood after they shattered their necks, feathers lingering in the air after each carcass plopped to the ground.

"What the hell is happening?" Coop yelled.

The moaning was much louder now—guttural, angry. It was as if it wished to slide a knife into my eardrums and drown out all sound that wasn't itself. It was coming from everywhere, and it was spiteful.

"Margaret?" McDouglas said as if I had something to do with this.

Just underneath the moaning and the birds and the screaming of the officers, far too faint to be of any consequence, were pounding and shouting. Jones was still at the door, hammering against the wood with both her fists now and ripping at the doorknob, screaming at us to let her in. Nobody else seemed to hear her, and I had a feeling that her being outside was far preferable to being inside, birds and all.

"Sorry," I said to Jones, who didn't have a chance of hearing me.

From out of the kitchen, behind everybody, darted Angelica. She ran full tilt, her mouth open but soundless, her stringy hair whipping about and her dirty dress fluttering behind her, her skinny little arm gesturing back towards the basement. Her head was cracked open and her eye wasn't right and she ran like something awful was chasing her.

Everyone screamed. I had to admit, Angelica even startled me a little as well. I hadn't expected to see her anymore.

Coop and Price pointed their weapons in front of them, prepared to fire. They tracked her with their guns but mercifully didn't shoot. Angelica snaked between the lot of us and disappeared into the living room.

They can see her now, I marveled.

Julian leapt down from the banister of the stairs, landing on all fours, his intestines splattering onto the ground. He perched on the floor for a moment, his hands and heels in the pool of blood in front of us, his knees near his ears, the yawning hole of his abdomen twisted in on itself. He opened his mouth in a snarl, pointed at the basement, and scurried away like an animal. Coop and Price, shouting obscenities, swung their guns after him.

The moaning was definitely screaming now.

"What the fuck is happening?" Katherine yelled, whirling around amid the onslaught of pranksters darting about.

"Margaret," McDouglas said, his tone suggesting that if I didn't stop this nonsense right now, I would be in *big* trouble. I didn't know what to tell him. This was new.

A jet-engine noise sounded to my right and Elias erupted into the room in a whirl, his mouth a spinning kaleidoscope of teeth, howling loudly enough to overpower the screaming. His black eyes were full of rage and somehow looked at all of us and none of us simultaneously. He flew through the room, snapping his teeth at anyone he could reach, seemingly intent on drawing as much blood as possible.

I grabbed at Katherine's arm, pulling her away from Elias' path of destruction. None of these pranksters were particularly violent—just a lot to look at—but Elias warranted distance.

"Stay back," I warned everyone, although nobody seemed especially keen on approaching the hurricane of a boy howling his way through the hallway. Two of the officers cleared a path, pressing themselves against a wall, and Price half jumped onto the stairs, slipping a bit in blood as Elias whirled past him, a maelstrom of rage.

Katherine screamed and leapt into the air, half crashing into my shoulder. Behind her, the boy with no legs was dragging himself into our midst, scrabbling and falling as he lifted his arms to point at the basement. He was a little slower than the others—an unfortunate effect of his lack of legs—and we all got quite a good look at him as he slid through the room. He left a trail in the blood as he pulled himself through, like a tire cutting through mud, but the gory debris he usually left in his wake was masked by the mess already on the floor.

I saw Price aim his weapon at the boy. I was about to shout something about the futility of Price's actions and plead with him not to put a bullet hole in my nice hardwood floors, when a screech from behind him turned his attention away. Blythe was crawling down the side of the banister, clinging to the wooden balusters like a rodent. Little flakes of ashy charcoal floated off her crisped skin and landed in the blood. She pulled her slim torso over the top of the banister and shrieked at us, her jaw long and her blistered lips revealing an expression full of malice. You would have thought we had a fire lit. She leapt from the banister to the ceiling and scurried away towards the front door, evoking from McDouglas a string of profanities that would have rivaled even Katherine.

All this time, the birds pounded against the walls, loud and incessant; they sounded seconds away from breaking their way into the house. The screaming was earsplitting, rattling the insides of our brains. I couldn't hear Jones anymore—either she had run for cover or the birds had gotten her. Coop and Price whirled around like madmen, pointing their guns at everything, nearly falling over as they slipped in the blood, which was now everywhere. Katherine clung to my arm with a bone-splintering grip, cursing and jumping at each new terror that presented itself. McDouglas was watching me, seemingly expecting me to wiggle my nose and turn this whole mess off.

"I don't know how to stop this," I told him, my voice barely audible.

The screaming had now reached that place—the place where you couldn't really tell if it was screaming or laughing. The laughter seemed like a bad sign. It seemed to foretell something very, very exciting that was about to happen, depending on one's definition of "exciting." History would suggest that the house and I had different definitions of "exciting."

Then it all stopped.

Silence hit the house like a brick, a wall of nothing where there had once been sound.

The birds stopped.

The pranksters vanished.

The blood stilled, settling on the floor in calm puddles. The scream-laugh echoed in my brain, but the only real sound to be heard was our ragged breathing.

The silence seemed like a creature in and of itself. It was like a feral cat huddled in a corner, equally likely to purr as you pet its head as it was to sink its fangs into you. In these situations, I'd learned that it was in my best interest to simply wait and see.

Coop and Price lowered their guns. Everyone was wide-eyed, open-mouthed. Katherine had one hand tight on my arm, the other clutching her keys in a white-knuckled grip. She was apparently ready to use them as weapons if needed. McDouglas peeled himself off the wall, turned to me.

"What the *fuck* was—"

He didn't have time to finish.

It happened to Price first.

It was challenging to put into words, exactly what started happening to Price. When bodies do new things, things they were never designed to do, language fails. The best way to describe it is like when a spider is sprayed with insecticide. There is a certain way that spiders die, an unnatural way—twitching and contorting, limbs twisting in double upon themselves. They bend onto their backs, writhing and breaking, their bodies good for nothing except playing out the end of their little lives. They stay like that after they die, lying on their backs, bodies dried out, bent in odd, damaged ways. They don't look like spiders anymore after that—they look like pained husks, broken bellies laid bare to the world that placed them in such a predicament to begin with.

That is to say, what happened to Price was unpleasant.

It started with his arms. His fingers and wrists twisted inward towards his chest, bending in on themselves until the bones gave in. His wrists cracked at sharp angles, jagged protrusions suddenly visible underneath his straining skin. The skin of his right wrist tore, revealing a blade of white amid red, red, red. He stared down at them with wide, shocked eyes, as if he didn't yet comprehend what he was seeing. Then the bones in his forearms snapped—splitting down the middle like dry branches in the fall—and he understood. He screamed. Blood squirted out of him as his skin popped open in harsh lines, spraying onto the walls and the floor and a little bit on Coop's sleeves.

Price's legs cracked beneath him and he fell like a tree, tipping backwards and catching himself against the wall, sliding onto the bloody floor as his body convulsed. His ankles turned themselves inward at that same sharp angle as his wrists, the hems of his pants protruding and slick with blood. When his shins snapped, his pants tore open, the splintered bone stabbing through the thick material of his uniform.

I shot an arm out in front of Katherine, as if we were riding in a car and the person in front of us had slammed on their brakes a bit too suddenly. I had absolutely no idea how I meant for the action to help in this particular circumstance, but it seemed the only action my body was physically capable of. Muscle memory, I supposed.

Coop screamed Price's name, crouching on the floor next to him. He put his hands out, palms towards Price's body. He looked like he wanted to touch Price, to help him, to fix him, but was afraid of what might happen if he attempted to do any of those things.

The sound Price's femurs made as they splintered was memorable. Price's legs were now jagged lines and his limbs were curving into his core, bracketing like a cage. His whole body twisted and shriveled, his skin looking surprisingly dry and wrinkled considering the amount of blood pouring out of him.

Price was screaming. He was nearly louder than the house had been just a few moments ago. I had a sense that I ought to be screaming as well, but it would seem that I was no longer able to produce any sort of sound. Instead, I kept myself pressed close to the wall, arm still out in front of Katherine, my unblinking eyes glued to the thing that was rapidly becoming a disassembled version of Price's body.

Next to me, Katherine was making a wailing noise—part cry, part profanity—intermittently muffled as her hands flew up over her mouth.

Price's chest caved in on itself with a shattering noise. A pit formed in the center of his body where his ribs used to protect the delicate organs underneath. The cage of bones curled in and snapped and ruptured something that contained quite a bit of blood. Price's face twisted and broke, snapping directly down the middle. His screams changed, taking on more of a gurgling quality. Everyone in the room was saying some variant of "Christ" or "fuck." I still seemed unable to produce noise. I stared on, my eyes wide but my mouth closed.

And then it was all over for Price.

The silence reentered the room, unwelcome but barely noticed as everyone filled the space with gasps and sobs and Price's name and curses and questions that were likely never to be answered. Coop began backing away from Price's body. He had little flecks of Price's blood across his face and hands. He was whispering something under his breath that I couldn't quite make out. Whatever it was, he was saying it over and over and over.

Then Coop's arms started to snap, the cracking noises of his bones breaking the momentary stillness that had settled in when Price's body was no more. Coop stared at his twisted arms in horror, little whimpering noises coming from his mouth. He looked down at Price, understanding, seeing what was to come. Then he looked at me, his expression a question, a plea. I shook my head. *Sorry.* I couldn't help him. There was a louder crack, a definite, uncompromising noise, and Coop howled, falling to the floor.

Katherine screamed and cursed.

Coop's legs were collapsing in on themselves, closing into hinges that hadn't existed on his body seconds ago. He was a writhing spider, too late to do anything to prevent the poison that bent his body into an incorrect shape.

McDouglas was on me. He had his gun out, and he pointed it in my face.

"I don't know how you're doing this," he shouted, *"but you need to stop it right now."* His hands shook, making the gun waver as he stared at me. Katherine screamed and I pushed her away from me. This seemed like the sort of thing she shouldn't be close to, not that anything around her was much better.

My eyes drifted to McDouglas' face, then to the barrel of the gun, then back to Coop writhing on the floor as his body broke apart. I said nothing. I raised my hands up at my side—*I'm unarmed. I surrender. Don't shoot*—but the action didn't have much enthusiasm behind it. I had a feeling that nothing I did from this point forward mattered very much at all. I remembered Jasper up in the closet, all folded in on himself like Price was currently, like Coop was working his way to being. I remembered the match in Jasper's hand, the one he never got to light. This house—Master Vale—had very particular opinions about the sorts of things that went on here, about people—me, specifically—leaving.

Don't. That was what the rule had been. What the rule seemed to be.

"Oh," I said, "it's too late for that." McDouglas was unlikely to know what I was talking about, but that was low on my list of concerns at the moment.

Coop was fighting, trying to keep his bones together. He was losing. He knew it.

"Make it stop," McDouglas shouted. *"Make it stop right now."* His eyes were wet. His face wasn't the face of a trained officer comfortable taking action in high-pressure situations, but rather of a terrified child seconds away from hiding under a bed.

Blood poured from Coop's mouth. His jaw wasn't straight anymore. Like with Angelica, one of his eyes was starting to lose its position and texture. Breathing didn't seem to be coming easily for him at the moment, likely due to the gaping hole that cracked across his chest as his body folded itself lengthwise. Something inside him made a popping noise and his blood splattered across the wall.

"I am going to count to three," McDouglas yelled, his red face only a couple of feet from mine. *"And then I am going to shoot you in the fucking head."*

"NO," Katherine screamed. She moved closer, which was probably ill-advised. *"Put the gun down."*

Coop's choked gurgles were quieting. His eyes rolled back in his head, pointing towards two different corners of the ceiling. It wouldn't be much longer for Coop now, which, at this point, was good news.

"One," McDouglas yelled. He stepped forward and pressed the barrel of the gun directly into my forehead. I felt the cool metal against my worry lines. The gun shook in his hand, but from this range he was unlikely to miss.

I raised my hands a little higher in the air. It was all I could do, really.

Coop was still and silent, a broken spider on the floor.

"*Two*," McDouglas yelled.

I looked at him past the barrel of his gun. "I can't do anything," I said. I wasn't sure what exactly he was expecting out of me. We'd broken the rules, all of us, and we were about to face the consequences, as unpleasant as they might be.

"*Put the fucking gun down*," Katherine screamed.

The last sputter of bloody air escaped from Coop's lungs—whether from his mouth or through the deep crevice in the center of his chest was unclear.

"Three," said McDouglas, his voice suddenly serious, a decision made. His finger tightened on the trigger.

Then his chest snapped in half.

Katherine shrieked.

Something wet hit my face. I had a feeling it was blood.

McDouglas dropped to his knees. The gun clattered to the floor.

Katherine sprang away from McDouglas' body, flattening herself against the wall. Her feet skittered and slipped in the blood, as if she could somehow escape through the wall if she only pushed hard enough. She shouted something at him, something that might have been his name.

He wasn't listening. He was already halfway to becoming a dead spider, shattered arms bending into his split ribs, legs twisting themselves into something unrecognizable. He flopped onto his back, howling, his chest opening and cracking, revealing to the room the inside parts of himself that no one ought to see. McDouglas seemed to go faster than Price and Coop, jerking and spasming on the floor, shouting and gurgling and snapping and cracking and twisting and eventually going still, his ripped skin sagging as his limbs relaxed into their contorted positions across his body. His eyes were on me when his face split, and then they weren't anymore, drifting in two different directions by necessity.

And then it was over. Three bodies bent and broken and lying in a pool of blood, some of it theirs, some of it the house's. I stared. I could do little else. It would seem I had once again lost the capacity to make any sort of noise—not a single sigh, whimper, or cry, let alone actual words. The best I could do was breathe—long, forceful exhalations out of my nose that tickled my mouth, which was seemingly glued shut forever.

The silence was back, so real that it was practically tangible, a monster that filled the room with its presence. If I hadn't known better, I would have sworn I could reach out and touch it, scratch it behind its ears. I would have sworn it could have bitten me.

The front door crashed open, and I nearly rediscovered my ability to scream. Jones raced in, gun drawn. Her clothes were tattered and she had scratches covering her face and hands, little trickles of blood leaking down the lines beneath her eyes, along her mouth. She had feathers sticking out of her frizzed hair. The birds had gotten her all right.

Jones skittered to a stop just a few feet into the house, and it looked as if her body stopped functioning. Her eyes went wide; her jaw slackened. The hand holding the gun dropped limply to her side. She gaped at the carnage of the house.

"What . . . ," she started, looking at the pools of blood, the dead-spider remains of her fellow officers. Her eyes landed on me. She looked as if she wanted to raise her gun but couldn't quite find the coordination. Her mouth moved. *You?*

I shook my head. Time for words. Time for a lot of words.

Explanations. Clarifications. Pleas for mercy. I wasn't capable of any of that, but it seemed in my best interest to try. I opened my mouth.

Jones' gaze shifted. It landed on something just behind me. Her mouth closed. Her eyes widened. The next breath that came from her was sharp, unsteady. Horrified. She took a step backwards.

Behind me, Katherine made a small noise. A sort of choked whimper. I turned, my pulse hammering in my ears.

Master Vale stood directly behind her.

I had never seen Master Vale in the light of day before, only in shadows. The sunlight streaming into the hallway made his skin look so pale as to be nearly transparent, the angry lesions screaming red across his body in stark comparison. I could see how his clothes, dirty and ragged, hung from his emaciated form, dangling loosely, as if his bones had shrunk to the slightest of twigs. He towered over Katherine, his twisted body looking as if it could be twice her size. He was the stillest I'd ever seen him, his gnarled limbs like those of a statue as they hovered just behind Katherine, not touching, not yet. He was smiling, his cracked lips pulled back to reveal an overjoyed row of rotted teeth. He was so, so happy.

I suddenly felt as if my legs had been taken from me, my guts sliced open. My chest didn't feel like it had exploded so much as it felt like a boat rapidly filling with water and descending into the depths faster than I could bail it out. I was sinking.

Katherine still had her purse clenched under her arm, her keys trapped in her fist. Tears streamed down her face and her mouth looked as if it were trying to form words with little success. She must have seen something in Jones' face, in my face, some look that communicated what words never could, because the color drained from her cheeks and her tears stopped as suddenly as a faucet shut off.

Master Vale's hand—all knotted knuckles and needle fingers—came to rest on her shoulder.

Katherine's arms dropped to her side. Her keys clattered to the floor. Her purse landed at her feet. She stopped blinking.

I was underwater. The world around me was black, the sky barely visible from my depths. I struggled, my limbs pushing and heaving as they pulled me towards the surface, seemingly miles away. But I was a strong swimmer, and I surfaced with a gasp.

"*NO,*" I shouted.

Master Vale's arms closed around Katherine like a bear trap. Katherine screamed, a sound that shook the house, and then he had her. He pulled her backwards, his long legs lunging towards the open mouth of the basement. Katherine kicked and struggled, feet off the ground, trying to run in midair. She writhed in his grip but he had her. He had her, and he was laughing.

"*Mom,*" Katherine screamed as she disappeared into the black of the basement.

The door slammed behind them.

TWENTY-SIX

I was no longer underwater.

I sprang to life, slipping on the blood and nearly tripping over what turned out to be McDouglas' leg as I sprinted towards the basement door.

"*Margaret, stop,*" Jones shouted, starting after me with her gun arm functional once more. I scarcely had time to consider her before her body was ripped from the ground, sailing into the air and slamming into the ceiling. Her gun clattered to the floor and she howled, pinned like a butterfly to corkboard. I barely heard her. I would have to worry about what sort of fate the house had in store for her later. My mind was a screaming cyclone, and I had much bigger problems at hand.

I yanked at the basement door. The thing wanted to fight me, wedging itself tightly in place, but I planted a leg against the door-jamb and heaved it open. There was nothing but blackness below, the basement a gaping maw of nothingness. I took the stairs two at a time.

"Theodore Vale," I shouted as my feet slammed against the dirt floor, *"get your goddamn hands off my daughter."*

The scent in the basement was monstrous. I couldn't believe I hadn't been smelling it this whole time. There was death down here all right. I could hear the hum of flies. They slapped across my face as I ran. I didn't even bother looking where I was going. I knew exactly where he had taken her. My shoulder smacked into a support beam, knocking me to the side. But I kept moving, heading straight for the little room in the back, the place where he had taken the children one by one.

The light from the stairs barely reached this part of the basement, but it didn't matter. The world was flickering again, starting to dance between the *now* and the *then*. I could hear screaming in dueling sets—Master Vale's laughter and Katherine's shrieks.

He had her there in the corner, just inside that little room. It was the same spot in which he had set up the table in the *then*, the place where he had done that thing to Angelica's head. Katherine was fighting but Master Vale's skinny limbs were stronger than they looked. He had her pinned down, his knees on her thighs, his hands on her shoulders. She was screaming and he was laughing, laughing, laughing. His lips were peeled back in a grin and his black teeth were bared, a pit viper ready to strike. I remembered what he had done to Angelica, sinking his teeth into the space where her skull had been, smiling with blood shining on his lips.

I didn't stop running even when I tackled him.

"NO," I screamed, tumbling in a heap with his body. The world was shifting around me and I felt his aching, felt his rage and his hunger, and I tasted something like metal, something tinny and wrong. Even still, I managed to keep screaming, shouting at him to stop, to leave Katherine alone, to listen to me immediately.

Master Vale roared beneath me. He was writhing and slippery, and I couldn't get a good grip on him, but I had him off Katherine. He was on the floor with me, and Katherine scampered backwards, pushing herself away from him as fast as she could. A crunch sounded as she hit something solid.

Hal's corpse, black and broken and dead like a spider, tilted against the wall. His limbs were wrong. His chest had been cracked open. His face was in pieces, the dried-grape shells of his eyeballs pointed in two directions. The match that had once been in his hands had fallen to the ground, broken in half and useless. And here I'd been thinking I'd never see him again.

Katherine let out a scream that launched my world back into the *now*.

Master Vale's head snapped up. His milky eyes locked onto Katherine.

My hand collided with his jaw and he made a snarling noise as he flopped to the side. I could barely see Katherine in the dim light, could only hear the shriek of her screams in between her panted breaths. She scrabbled away from her father's corpse, and I didn't need to see her to know that her face was contorted, terrified. Next to me, Master Vale snarled, his fingers scraping the floor.

"*Run,*" I shouted.

Katherine was still screaming, still pulling herself backwards on her wrists, heels digging into the dirt of the floor. I dragged myself onto my knees and stumbled towards her. "*Get out of here,*" I said. "*Go. Run.*"

Katherine clambered to her feet. Master Vale was behind me, pushing himself up. I got myself upright as fast as I could, head swimming and hands grabbing for Katherine. I dragged her forward, pushing her out of the little room and in the general direction of the stairs.

"Mom?" Katherine was saying, her voice high and wet.

"Go," I shouted, shoving her with all my strength. *"Get out of here this instant."*

Behind me, a growl. Master Vale was on his feet.

Katherine ran. Her shoes slapped across the dirt floor. I whirled around to face Master Vale. He went to chase after Katherine, but I stepped in front of him. I was patient. I was flexible. I could play by the rules all goddamn day, every rule you set for me. But there were limits to these things, and Master Vale was about to hear mine.

No one deserves to live like this, Hal had said.

No one deserves to live like this, Edie had said.

No one deserves to live like this, Katherine had said.

No one deserves to live like this, I thought. *Goddamnit.*

"NO," I shouted.

Master Vale's head snapped towards me. I had gotten his attention.

"Absolutely NOT."

Master Vale growled. He straightened, stretching his body back into that upright, too-tall position: his shoulders rolled back, his chest puffed out, his hands curled into fists at his side. He glowered down at me, his face bent in anger. He was a starving lion.

"You listen to me, you goddamn creature," I said. My voice boomed against the cold brick of the basement. All the water that had been drowning me had turned to fire. I could feel myself burning, glowing. I would set this whole house ablaze if I had to, so long as it meant I took Master Vale down with me.

Master Vale took a step towards me. He was a circling hawk.

"There are rules to these things," I snarled, *"and consequences for breaking them."*

Master Vale started making that noise again, the scream-laugh.

"I've let you live in this basement as a courtesy," I said, my voice sounding as if it were being projected from a megaphone; I was barely recognizable. "I let you do whatever you liked to me. I let you send your pranksters at me. I let you crush anyone who tried to take me from you." Master Vale took another step towards me but I didn't budge. He was going to listen, goddamnit. "But I am *through*. Do you hear me?"

Master Vale's lips curled back, baring his teeth. He was a pack of wolves.

"That is *my* daughter," I said. "This is *my* house, and I refuse to share it with a monster." It felt like my words were rattling the foundation. It would crumble beneath me, and I hoped it crushed Master Vale to death. *"You broke the rules, you son of a bitch."*

Master Vale was close now, very close. I had to crane my neck to look him in the eye, but I stood my ground. I wasn't a rabbit. I wasn't scared. I wasn't bending any further. And I wasn't going down without a fight.

I raised my arm, pointing towards the stairs. *"Now get the FUCK out of my house."*

His scream-laugh turned into a roar. His mouth stretched open, jaws nearly tearing at the edges, revealing a dead blackness inside. He roared and roared, but I could roar too.

I took a step forward. My lungs were a goddamn flamethrower. *"GET THE FUCK OUT OF MY HOUSE."*

I saw a video once of a jumping spider going after an insect. I remember how, when it attacked its prey, it leapt through the air, limbs bent at sharp, grasping angles, ready to land with precision and violence. Anyway, that was what Master Vale did, mouth open, screaming.

I darted away just in time, my legs propelling me backwards and out of the little room. Master Vale landed on all fours, squatting with his knobby knees near his ears. He growled and stretched himself back up onto his legs, hands curling into fists. The world flickered, *now* turning to *then*.

I didn't move. "Were you not listening?" I raised my arm again, pointing. *"Get out of my house."*

A fight was coming.

Master Vale roared again, and I wondered if he even knew any words at all. Perhaps he had forgotten them over the years. Or perhaps he had never found them useful in the first place, not when he had more forceful ways of getting what he wanted. He took another long stride forward, hands reaching out to me. I stepped back, dodging his needle fingers.

"Don't you understand?" I snapped. "You're not in charge anymore. *I* am. You do what *I* say now. Now *get out.*"

Master Vale took another step forward. He towered over me, an impossibly tall being built of lesions and rage. His mouth was almost foaming, dark spittle spewing between his teeth. He smiled, a low whine of a laugh sounding from his wide mouth as he closed in. I was nearing the wall, I knew. It wouldn't be long before the brick pressed against my back, trapping me. Master Vale's laughter increased.

"Get out," I shouted.

Master Vale leapt again, gnarled fingers outstretched. I darted back, but I wasn't fast enough this time. He caught me in the chest, knocking me backwards. My head collided with the wall, and I was down, the dirt floor beneath me and Master Vale above.

"Now," I shouted, but the world was spinning, flickering. I felt rage that wasn't mine, hate and aching and hunger that throbbed from Master Vale's limbs as he crawled on top of me, pinning me

down. His hand met my face with a slash—clawlike nails scratching across my cheek and twisting my head to the side. The world jolted again, and I felt something wet and warm on my face. Whether it was my blood or whatever it was that oozed between the sores on Master Vale's skin was anyone's guess. My breath puffed against the dirt of the floor. I turned to face him once more, blinking eyes forcing me back to the *now*.

"Get out," I said. His face was close, milky eyes boring into mine. I didn't have to shout. He could hear me. But he didn't listen.

His fingers wrapped around my throat.

I tried to choke out another command, but his hands tightened and I couldn't breathe, my throat closing in on itself. The world flickered back to the *then* and I could see everything. I saw the hate in his family's eyes whenever they looked at him. I saw George Vale's paddle come down on Master Vale again and again and again. I saw how the whole of his family had died like sick apples dropping from a tree. I felt a hateful happiness, the kind that comes from burning an ant to death with a magnifying glass. But with the happiness came a hunger—a hunger that crawled through his body and into mine as his fingers twisted around my neck.

I saw how he had found them, the children. I saw how he had brought them to the house, one by one, when the hunger surged up in him. I saw how he'd crushed Angelica's skull and ripped out Julian's intestines and sunk sharp blades into Charles and Constance and sawed the legs off James (his name was James) and chopped off Henry's arm (I was wrong—his name was Henry) with some kind of cleaver and sunk his teeth into their flesh afterwards, every last one of them. That might have been a problem, because eventually Master Vale died, shaking violently in the basement, alone and starved despite the unending supply of meat.

I saw how it didn't end there, how it all came around. I saw how he did something to Elias' mother (Hattie—her name was Hattie) that made Elias the way he was and later made Hattie die and slowly, slowly made Elias die too, full of hate, alone in the room that would later be Hal's office.

I saw Master Vale whisper to Jasper night after night until Jasper did what he did to Fredricka and Blythe and, when he finally came to his senses, tried to light the whole house on fire but failed, failed.

I saw Master Vale suck the joy out of Edie's soul and smile down at her as she slipped into breathless sleep.

I saw him hovering over Hal in his office, whispering, whispering, whispering, until Hal bought the cans of gasoline and Master Vale crushed him like a spider in the basement.

I saw the blackness and the blood and the screaming and the hate, hate, hate that stood in the place where Master Vale's soul ought to have been. And then I wasn't seeing very much anymore because there was nothing but red behind my eyes and fire instead of air in my lungs and Master Vale's drool dripping into my mouth, and I wasn't breathing, not anymore. I saw the whole cycle of it, the violence that started and ended everything, the moon and the sun coming around and around, but I kept fighting because I would be goddamned if I was going to be a part of it for one second longer. I'd been moving in wretched little circles for as long as I could remember—longer—and I was not about to have it all end like this, snuffed out in the basement only to flicker back, likely in September. I would twist my life into a line that pointed towards something worthwhile for myself, for Katherine, even if it killed me. Which, at the moment, it seemed intent on doing.

There was a crack—a sharp, wet sound—and Master Vale was wrenched off me and tumbled to the side. I gasped and choked, sucking in air through what felt like knives. The red faded from my eyes and my brain was shuffling back into the *now* slowly and steadily.

Katherine stood above me, her wide eyes shining through the dim light. Hovering high in her hands was the wooden paddle, "Master of the House" emblazoned on the side. She must have found it on the basement floor, still lying where I had dropped it as Hal and I fled Master Vale last year.

I blinked back the *then* and struggled to my feet. Beside me, Master Vale groaned and shifted onto all fours, preparing to spring.

The paddle crunched into Master Vale's temple. *"Back the fuck away from her, you bastard,"* Katherine screamed.

Master Vale fell to the ground, his jaw twisted. He pushed himself up, angry eyes on Katherine. Katherine swung the paddle again.

"I don't know who you are—"

The paddle connected with Master Vale's forehead. He roared.

"—or where you came from—"

The paddle struck his jaw. A spray of brown fluid splattered across the floor.

"—but if you touch my mother again, I will fucking kill you."

I was up on my shaking legs at Katherine's side. I touched her shoulder. "Katherine," I said. My voice was raspy.

Katherine raised the paddle high above her head and swung it down in a mighty arc.

Master Vale caught the paddle in his hand. The wood slapped against his pale skin but he held it there, firm and true. He smiled. His knotted fingers wrapped around the worn wood. Katherine tugged at it, shoulders heaving as she tried to wrest the paddle from his grip. His smile only widened. He ripped the paddle from Katherine's hands.

Katherine took a step back. Her empty hands shook. I followed, still grabbing at her shoulder.

Master Vale shifted himself onto a knee. He raised the paddle high in both hands, a mad grin nearly cracking his face in two. He brought the paddle down over his slim thigh. It snapped in half, splinters spraying across the room. The pieces clattered to the side as he stood, towering over us once more. He was laughing again. All of this was so tremendously funny.

"Fuck," Katherine whispered.

Before I could even figure out what to do next, Master Vale was in front of us, his arms wide at his sides, blocking us in. He seemed to be daring us to try to come at him, just begging for an excuse to dig his sharp fingers into our flesh. Katherine flinched, then backed up. He laughed and it was a scream again, so loud that my ears buzzed.

Master Vale took a step forward.

We took a step back.

"Go away," I said, but my throat was too sore for me to sound menacing. "Leave us alone."

Master Vale only laughed harder.

The wall would appear behind me again, I knew. We would be right back where I'd started, pressed against the brick with Master Vale ready to pounce, not leaving, not following the rules, even now. He moved closer, closer, closer. I could see dents in his head, angry welts where Katherine had gotten him with the paddle. He could be hurt, it seemed, but not enough to stop him. He was laughing so hard.

"Mom?" Katherine asked, but there didn't seem to be any specific question she had in mind. The wall came up behind us, unforgiving.

I grabbed at Katherine's hand. "It's all right," I said, although it certainly wasn't. The world was flickering again, and Master Vale was so close I could smell him, could see the crisp borders of each lesion on his skin, could hear how his laughter changed as he wound up, got himself ready to pounce. I shifted, moving in front of Katherine. Master Vale would certainly be able to go through me, but at least Katherine might be able to escape while he was doing so.

Master Vale roared. He sprang forward, arms outstretched.

His arms were knocked to the side and a figure stepped in front of us.

Fredricka.

I could just make her out in the dim light. Her face—the part of it that was left, anyway—was that of a statue, and a menacing one. In the years I had known her, witnessed her pliant and calm responses to everything that happened in this house, I had never seen her so thoroughly finished with something.

"I believe ma'am asked you to leave," she said, her voice stone.

For a moment, Master Vale looked almost taken aback. He considered Fredricka for the briefest of seconds before snapping at her like a rabid dog. He moved forward again, prepared to strike.

Another figure appeared at Fredricka's side: a short, stocky woman who appeared to be filled with barely contained maternal rage.

"You'd best listen to my friend," Edie said. Her voice was sharp. "She means business."

Master Vale snarled. He took a step back as he considered the women in front of him. I wondered if this was the first time in over a century that so many people had mustered up the strength to express their displeasure with his actions. For a moment, it was as if he wasn't sure how to respond. Then the hate fell back over his face and his sharp fingers swung at Edie.

A jet-engine noise sounded to my left. Elias. He stood next to me, his face a full nightmare as he howled at Master Vale. Master

Vale must have remembered him, because he jumped back, startled but still angry. Fredricka and Edie stepped aside and Elias lunged forward, leapt at Master Vale with gnashing teeth. Master Vale stumbled backwards, moving quickly to avoid Elias' propeller blade of a mouth. He snarled and spat but kept moving backwards as Elias advanced.

With Fredricka and Edie on either side of me and Elias wreaking havoc on Master Vale in front of me, I started to feel a twinge of hope. None of us, it seemed, was willing to put up with Master Vale's nonsense for a moment longer. I stepped forward, following Elias as he chased Master Vale backwards through the basement.

"Go away," I shouted. "Get the hell out of here."

Katherine was at my side, still clutching at my hand. *"Get out, you fucking monster."*

Elias' roars were finally overpowering Master Vale's screams. Master Vale tripped and landed in the dirt and Elias was on his legs, teeth tearing at the bits of flesh and fabric that clung to his body. Master Vale howled and kicked, dragging himself backwards, barely able to shake himself loose from Elias' unforgiving fangs.

"Get out," I shouted again, and this time Fredricka joined in, her voice louder than I'd ever heard it before.

The light grew brighter as we neared the stairs. Katherine and Edie joined me in shouting, Katherine's curses and Edie's admonishing cries nearly drowning out Elias' jet-engine noise. Master Vale's claws dug into the dirt as he dragged himself farther away. Elias' teeth were in Master Vale's ankle and something black was oozing from him, something that didn't quite look like blood. Master Vale swung an arm at Elias and knocked him off, but it didn't stop the boy's howling, didn't stop the swirling maw of his mouth.

Charles and Constance appeared from across the basement. They ran full tilt at Master Vale and set on him viciously, swiping at him with their fingers. Their sharp nails dug into his flesh, tearing him open across his arms, his chest, his legs. Master Vale's flesh split, fresh gashes standing out amid the lesions. He roared, swinging his arms at the two of them. He knocked Charles to the side but Constance held on. She grabbed at his mouth with her small hands and pried him open. With a slash of her finger, she ripped a line from the edge of his lip to nearly his ear, turning his face into a gaping smile. He howled. The house shook.

"*Get out,*" we shouted, Katherine and Fredricka and Edie and I.

Master Vale was retreating rapidly now, dragging himself towards the stairs as fast as his scrabbling arms could find purchase in the dirt. He was leaking that black ooze, which dripped down his skin and onto the dirt, leaving little smudges behind him. His screams had taken on a desperate tone. He grabbed at the stairs, frantically trying to pull himself upright. Just as he touched the wood, Julian leapt from the railing, landing square on Vale's chest.

Master Vale roared and writhed, but Julian roared louder. He raised his hand, pointed and precise, over his head and buried it deep inside Vale's sunken stomach. Master Vale screamed. Bucked. Julian held on. He gripped Vale's skin—leaking something thick between his fingers—and *pulled*. A spray of what might have been blood hit the wall, along with a fistful of entrails. Master Vale screamed and thrashed, finally shoving Julian off him. He dragged himself up the stairs, his guts trailing in his wake. Elias was right behind him, biting and snarling.

"*GET OUT,*" we shouted. We had to be loud to be heard over the roaring and the screaming and the jet-engine noise, and we were loud—quite loud indeed. The lot of us ran up the stairs, chasing after Master Vale and Elias. Charles and Constance darted around us, their fingers caked with Vale's blood. Julian climbed along the handrail. They joined us in our shouting, pointing towards the top of the stairs, towards the front door. *Get out get out get out*.

Master Vale reached the top of the stairs, hands grasping the doorframe to drag himself up. The boy with one arm—Henry—caught him by the wrist and hauled him through the door and into the hallway. We raced up the stairs behind him, still shouting (*Get out get out get out*). I slipped on a bit of Vale's blackened intestines. I paid it no mind.

The house was filled nearly to the brim with flies, their fat, buzzing bodies turning the air black. The source was immediately apparent—Jones was still pinned to the ceiling, eyes gaping, flies swarming from her open mouth. There was a bit of a gurgled scream in the air, but it was nowhere near as loud as Master Vale as he clawed down the hallway, pranksters still on him.

Henry was playing tug-of-war with Master Vale's arm. Master Vale snarled and shoved and kicked, making sweeping imprints in the pool of blood on the floor, but Henry held on remarkably well. Henry made a roar that rivaled Elias at his most vicious and, with a mighty heave, ripped Vale's arm off at the socket. There was a tearing noise, the sound of soft meat and brittle bone, and a spray of black ooze landed across the body of one of the broken police officers. Master Vale screamed, and Henry sank his teeth into the flesh of Vale's severed biceps, ripping fabric and flesh off in a chunk.

It was horrible, certainly, but I'd grown used to horrible things. It wasn't even the most horrible thing I'd seen today.

"GET OUT," we shouted.

Blythe was on the wall, her jaw unhinged. She shrieked and snapped and pounded on the plaster with blackened fists. She pointed at the door, shouting, *Get out*. Smoke poured from her eyes.

Master Vale dragged himself down the hallway with his re-maining arm. Black sludge oozed from the shoulder where his other arm used to be, tattered flesh hanging in its absence. He was leaving a trail behind him, intestines and sludge mixing with the blood that pooled on the floor. Charles and Constance rushed forward, grabbing at him with their sharp fingers. He kicked at them but they held him still. Julian leapt onto his chest, a foot landing in the hole ripped across Vale's stomach. Master Vale wailed.

On the ceiling, Jones choked and sputtered. The spewing of flies from her mouth had dwindled, and she could wave an arm now. She dug her fingers into her mouth, pulling out wings and legs. "Get out," she croaked. "Get out."

James dragged himself down the hallway, slipping between our legs and heading straight for Master Vale. He caught Vale by an ankle and crawled up Vale's body, fingers sinking into flesh, pulling and pulling. Master Vale flopped and kicked, but the other pranksters had him pinned down. Charles and Constance slashed at his thighs. Julian sent a fist into his hip. James wrapped his arms around Vale's leg and twisted his body. Something snapped, a sharp sound like twigs breaking. Master Vale howled. The black liquid leaked through what was left of his tattered pants. A sound like meat ripping echoed through the room and Vale flung the pranksters off him, one of his legs dangling not quite right from his body. The leg, caught in the sheath of his pants, trailed behind him as he dragged himself along the floor. James grabbed it by the knee and gave it a yank, ripping the fabric of Vale's pants. He sank his teeth into what used to be Master Vale's calf.

The pranksters pointed at the door and it flew open, wood nearly splintering as it slammed against the wall.

"*GET OUT*," we shouted, and Master Vale was listening. His nails left lines in the blood as he dragged himself towards the open door. He wasn't screaming anymore. His breath was ragged and wet, his broken chest heaving. Pools of black oozed from every part of his body. His leg was in the middle of the hallway. Henry was still gnawing on Vale's arm.

Just as Vale reached the door, Blythe dropped from the ceiling. She shrieked, the cracks in her charred skin glowing red. Smoke billowed from her mouth, her eyes, her gaping oval of a mouth. The ooze dripping from Vale's wounds began to bubble. His skin blistered and popped, boiling. Smoke poured from the holes the pranksters had torn in him. He screamed, and flames danced from his throat. He hurled himself backwards with his one remaining arm, kicking at the floor with his one remaining leg. He landed on the porch, leaving traces of himself on the doorjamb.

Even as Master Vale retreated, we were still shouting, GET OUT GET OUT GET OUT. Fredricka and Edie were at my side. Katherine was gripping my hand, her fingers clenching mine so tightly that I could feel tingling in my fingertips. Jones was above us, pounding on the ceiling with both arms now freed. Elias was spitting and snarling down the hallway, and—to my surprise—his mother, Hattie, had joined him. She put her hand, barely there, on his shoulder, his dirty shirt visible through her fingers. Her eyes burned and her lips cracked as she opened her mouth to shout along with us (*Get out get out get out*). James dragged himself through the blood with Henry following, traces of Vale's arm still on his face. Charles and Constance skipped down the hallway. Blythe clung to the wall with clenched fingers. We were all here— all present, all pointing, all screaming. All through. And my God—we were a motherfucking *army*.

Angelica stepped out from the living room, moving towards Master Vale with a calm grace. Her face was just as placid as it had been the day Hal and I saw what had happened to her head, her eyes tilted towards horror without a care in the world. She stepped through the front door and stood over Vale's broken body, staring down at him as if he were just the most interesting thing she had ever seen. She raised both her hands over her head, clenched them together, and brought them down upon Master Vale's skull with strength I didn't know her small frame possessed. When she raised her hands again, they were covered in black. She brought them down again. Again. Again. Choked, wet noises sounded from Master Vale. The screaming stopped. The house was silent.

The pranksters stepped aside, leaving a path for me. Katherine released my hand and I walked down the hall, stepping over Vale's severed leg, the bits of his arm that Henry had dropped. I walked to the front door. I stepped onto the porch.

Master Vale was a whimpering, quivering mess. He was bleeding his version of blood from what seemed like every inch of his body. Most of his guts had spilled out of the hole where his stomach had been and trailed behind him. Loose flesh dangled from where his arm should have been. I could see the remains of his femur poking through his pants. He was still gently on fire, his skin smoking through ruptured blisters. Something terrible had happened to his head and one of his eyes wasn't right anymore; it drooped from its socket in a red and yellow mess. He pulled himself backwards and tumbled down the steps, landing on the lawn with a splatter.

In the shining light of day, Theodore Vale looked small, fragile. He wasn't the strong one anymore, not in this house. He might have been the strong one in the past, the one with the violence and the vengeance and the never-ending cycles, but we—the things that lived in this house—we could overpower him. In the end, we were the strong ones. We were still here, and we had sent Vale away, broken and weeping. In the end, Vale was weak.

I stepped to the edge of the porch, stopping just at the top of the stairs. From this vantage, I towered over him, impossibly tall. I opened my mouth and he flinched.

"This is our house," I said. "And you are no longer welcome."

I heard a throat clear behind me and I turned. Fredricka stepped up to my side, large as the house itself, her face calm as a cloudless day. She had an axe. I wondered where she had found it—we didn't own one, to my knowledge—but she held the thing as if it had always belonged in her hands.

"Ma'am?" Fredricka said. She offered me the axe.

"Thank you," I said. I took the axe from her, feeling the cold wood of the handle in my hands. The thing was heavy, but I had a feeling I'd manage. I strode down the steps, coming to rest just before Vale. His head tilted up towards me, pleading with his one good eye, his ripped-open mouth forming words he could no longer speak. I raised the axe high over my head. It swung down as if it knew exactly where it was heading.

There was a crack, the sound of a watermelon splitting in two.

And Master Vale was no more.

The silence that followed felt like an exhalation. A calm settled over everything, like a leaf floating to the ground. The world paused, relaxed. There was a clatter from inside the house—Jones crashed down from the ceiling with a grunt. The carcass of a bird slid off the awning and plopped into the grass. All was still.

It felt as if the world blinked and shook its head, coming to after a mighty nightmare. The day was lovely, the nearly cloudless sky quiet and cheerful. Birds chirped nearby, giving the walls of the house a break for once. A soft breeze rustled at a nearby tree and a few yellowing leaves danced to the ground. Even the police cruisers in the driveway seemed peaceful, glittering in the sunlight. The remnants of Theodore Vale were the lone spot of darkness in all of it, disintegrating into a body-shaped pile of ooze in the yard. But even he couldn't besmirch the loveliness of the day. I pulled the axe out of what was left of him and set it next to the steps. The ooze-covered blade seemed almost to glisten in the brightness of the day.

Behind me, the pranksters drifted out of the house and down the steps of the front porch, out into the yard. They blinked in the sunlight, looking around as if they hadn't seen a blue sky in centuries. They were still a rough sight to look upon—pale and wrong in the Technicolor world—but they seemed to be on the mend. Angelica's eyes were both back where they were supposed to be. Constance's smile didn't gape so frightfully. James lifted himself up and hobbled around the yard on fresh legs. Henry stared at a bird in a nearby tree, wiping the remnants of Vale's blood off his mouth with a new hand. They seemed curious and confused, tilting their heads at the world like puppies hearing a strange new noise.

Jones emerged from the house. She was limping a bit and clutching at her arm, but none of her bones appeared broken, or at least not as broken as those of the other officers. Her hair was a wild tangle of feathers and she had fly entrails on her chin. Her eyes had a glassy look to them, and for a moment, she stared at the pranksters as they wandered about the lawn. She nodded as if they were exactly what she'd expected to see.

"So. Your house . . ." Jones swallowed. She gestured in a vague sort of way to the structure behind me. Cobalt blue with white trim, an envy-inspiring porch wrapped around the whole house, and a turret—an actual turret. "It's haunted?"

"A bit," I said.

Jones nodded. She nodded again. She looked down at the remains of Theodore Vale, slowly stirring in the light breeze, and nodded some more. She seemed incapable of doing anything else.

"I think we've fixed it, though," I said.

Jones let out a breath that was not particularly steady. She seemed to be focusing most of her efforts on not having a panic attack. She looked at the cruisers in the driveway, waiting for no one, and took a long, deep, unsteady breath. "I need to call somebody," she said, something she must not have found time for while she was being attacked by a flock of suicidal birds. She ran a shaking hand through her hair and pulled a feather from just behind her ear. She tossed the feather away from her as if it might cause her bodily harm. "I need to call everybody." She limped down the steps on legs that seemed moments away from giving out, carefully avoiding Vale's body as she moved towards the cruisers. "Homicide," she muttered to nobody in particular. "Ambulance. Fire department."

"There wasn't a fire," I reminded her.

She didn't seem to hear me. "And that psychic who helped us find that kid a few years back," she continued. "Probably the church. They'll want our statements. Photographs." She glanced at James as he skipped through the yard. "Lots of photographs."

I watched Jones make her way to her cruiser and get inside. I figured I wouldn't interrupt any further. She looked as if she needed a moment. She'd earned it. We all had.

Katherine stepped up to my side, looking a bit dazed. She was covered in blood—mostly other people's, I was happy to see—and she had splatters of Theodore Vale's ooze on her face. Her shirt was torn, and her hair, crusted and knotted, stuck up at odd angles. I had a feeling I was in a similar state. My clothes were likely ruined, every inch covered in some sort of fluid. I could feel blood drying along my face. I ran a hand through my hair and pulled out a tooth. I frowned at the thing. I wondered who it had belonged to.

"The police are going to have a lot of questions for us," Katherine said.

I slipped the tooth into my pocket, nodding. "They certainly will," I said. Hours upon hours of questions, likely. It would sound more than a little unbelievable, all that had occurred here, and the three broken bodies of police officers just inside the house wouldn't make anything better. Luckily, we had Jones on our side, and judging by the way Jones blinked in her cruiser, slowly picking feathers from her hair, she was not about to forget what she had seen today for quite a while.

The pranksters ambled farther and farther away from the house. I wasn't sure what exactly pranksters did once the joke was over, but they seemed to be filling their time nicely. Charles and Constance started down the driveway, followed by Julian, presumably off to reunite themselves with whichever of their ancestors were still living. James was occupying himself by attempting cartwheels in the yard, and Henry was doing his best to climb a tree. Blythe scampered up the side of the house and perched on the roof, her legs dangling off the awning. A bird landed on her shoulder. Angelica plopped herself in the yard, cross-legged, and started plucking blades of grass. Making herself some sort of crown, it seemed. Blythe and the bird started whistling a little tune together. Angelica joined in. It was nice, in its own sort of way.

"I think I'm supposed to fly out tomorrow," Katherine said. She blinked, her eyes narrowing. "I'm pretty sure its tomorrow, anyway."

I nodded. I understood. Time was funny around here, moving in stops and starts and circles. At least it used to, anyway. I had a feeling that things were about to get a tad more linear.

"If it's okay," she said, "I might reschedule my flight. Stick around for a while. At least until all this gets settled." She glanced at me hopefully. "If that's all right, that is."

"Of course," I said. "My home is your home."

Across the yard, I saw Elias and his mother walking hand in hand, heading towards the woods. Elias still had his dark mess of hair and his dirt-gray clothes but he seemed calmer somehow, slack shoulders suggesting he wasn't in the mood to bite passersby anymore. I couldn't see his face but I had a feeling that his eyes had lost their milky void and his teeth had rounded out at the edges—no longer the most intimidating thing in the house. Elias' mother—Hattie—seemed calmer as well, her skinny limbs no longer in danger of snapping. She looked like a woman taking a nice stroll in the woods with her son, not somebody heading back towards her own grave at all. Hattie held a garbage bag in her hand, the one that contained her bones.

"Sorry about that," I called after her. Hattie and Elias said nothing. They might not have heard me, or perhaps they didn't feel like starting a conversation about the number of times I had haphazardly dug up Hattie's bones just to get Elias to shut up for a week. Regardless, I was glad. After a moment, they disappeared into the woods.

Edie sidled up next to me. She heaved a heavy sigh and smiled. "My," she said, "that was quite the ordeal, now, wasn't it?"

I chuckled, considering the day. "Yes," I said, "I suppose it was."

"Touch and go there for a moment," she said, gesturing behind her at the basement. "But it all worked out in the end." She grinned towards Katherine. "Your mother is a force to be reckoned with, you know."

Katherine gave a little smile. "I know," she said.

Edie looked down at Vale's former body for a moment, her hands on her hips. She nodded at his remains as if looking down at a pie that had come out of the oven just perfect. A job well done. "Well," she said, a decisive tone to her voice, "I had better get out of your hair." With that, she hopped down the stairs and, carefully stepping over Vale's body, started down the driveway. I wasn't particularly sure where she was going.

"This is your house," I called after her, "remember?"

Edie waved a hand behind her. "You ought to sleep well tonight," she said. "Get some rest—you've earned it." Soon, she was a dot at the end of the driveway, following after Charles and Constance and Julian to God knew where.

I watched her leave, and stared out into the cheer of the day without fully understanding any of it. My brain was still struggling to catch up with all that had occurred, and it would much rather simply watch as the breeze made the grass dance and Angelica finished her crown and set it atop her head. It was far preferable to thinking about the bodies strewn about inside the house, or just how much time it was going to take to clean up all the dead birds in the yard. Jones still sat in her cruiser, staring out the window at nothing in particular. Her brain was struggling to catch up as well, it seemed.

Fredricka stepped into view at my side. She'd gathered the axe from the steps and rested it against the wood of the porch with a *thunk*. "If ma'am doesn't mind," she said, "I'm rather tired. I think I'll rest now, unless ma'am needs anything."

"No," I said, smiling up at her. "You've been wonderful, Fredricka."

"Good," Fredricka said. She lifted the axe and walked back into the house, then closed the door behind her.

Katherine and I were alone on the porch, as alone as we could be around here. Slowly, Katherine turned, then sank down into one of the rocking chairs just behind her, and I followed suit. The wood of the rocker creaked beneath me and I thought it might as well have been my back. I heaved out a sigh. *God*, it felt good to sit down. Edie was right—today had been an *ordeal*.

"So," Katherine said, "Dad's dead."

I sighed. "I suppose he is."

Katherine nodded. It might've been a shock for her, but given the events of her day, it was likely nowhere near the most shocking thing she'd experienced. She would deal with it in time; we both would. I started slowly rocking back and forth. It felt soothing, in a strange sort of way. Katherine joined in.

"I'm sorry I tried to have you institutionalized," she said.

"Oh, it's fine," I said. "I probably would've done the same thing if I were you." I motioned back towards the house. "Thanks for your help down there in the basement. You've got a mean swing."

"Of course," Katherine said. She pointed down at the smudge on the ground, all that was now left of Theodore Vale. "Thanks for kicking that fucker's ass."

"It was no bother," I said.

We rocked in silence for a moment, not particularly thinking about anything, or at least I wasn't. Blythe and Angelica and the bird carried on with their tune (*It all comes around with the moon and the sun*). James was cartwheeling himself down the driveway. All around us, the day went about its business, sending cheerful sunlight and a calm breeze down upon the carnage. There was a sweet smell to the air, and the light seemed to glisten, a little wink in our direction to prove that no matter how terrible things could get—and things could get quite terrible indeed—all would be fine in the end. It could be a rule, perhaps, if any rules existed in this bright new world.

Fredricka opened the door again, poking her head through the crack. "I just wanted to bring it to ma'am's attention," she said, "that the house is in quite a bit of disarray. And there are a substantial number of flies."

"I know," I said. "Thank you, Fredricka."

Fredricka nodded, her duty done. "Would ma'am like me to prepare some tea for her before I rest?"

I glanced at Katherine. Katherine shrugged.

I smiled. "Tea sounds lovely."

ACKNOWLEDGMENTS

First and foremost, I would like to thank my family—my lovely spouse, Cameron, and my (also lovely) mother, Victoria—who provided both moral support and beta reading services for this novel. I can't express how much I appreciate your notes, feedback, and enthusiasm, as well as your willingness to read what ended up being multiple iterations of this novel's ending. I couldn't have done it without y'all. Many thanks, of course, to additional friends and family members who cheered me on during this process. You know who you are and how much you rock.

Seventeen million thank-yous must be extended to Katherine Odom-Tomchin and Sharon Bowers at Folio Literary Management for their unwavering enthusiasm for this novel and commitment to finding it the perfect home. You two are the best people to have in my corner, and I thank my lucky stars on a daily basis that you took a chance on me and my little story.

I also owe endless thanks to my editor, Jessica Wade at Berkley, for believing in this book and supplying her infinite editorial

ACKNOWLEDGMENTS

genius. You helped make this book exponentially better not only through your thoughtful theme- and character-focused notes, but also with your sharp eye for the dumb continuity errors and nonsensical elements my brain managed to completely overlook. I bow down in wonder! Huge thanks to everyone at Berkley in general for all the hard work done to get this book off the ground and into the world. It is the very definition of a team effort.

Finally, I would like to thank my cat, Ash (the Mighty), who taught me the very important skill of writing with my body twisted at a forty-five-degree angle so that my lap would be unimpeded by the presence of a computer and, thus, of greatest use to sleepy kitties. It could be argued that this is the most vital literary skill of them all.